Stone Dreaming Woman

by

Lael R. Neill

This is a work of fiction. Names, characters, places, and incidents are either the product of the author's imagination or are used fictitiously, and any resemblance to actual persons living or dead, business establishments, events, or locales, is entirely coincidental.

Stone Dreaming Woman

Cover Art by *Debbie Taylor*

The Wild Rose Press, Inc.
PO Box 708
Adams Basin, NY 14410-0708
Visit us at www.thewildrosepress.com

Publishing History
First Vintage Rose Edition, 2013
Print ISBN 978-1-61217-649-9
Digital ISBN 978-1-61217-650-5

Published in the United States of America

Lightning had already started to flicker when she became aware of hoofbeats behind her. She turned and saw Sergeant Adair coming toward her, posting precisely to a high trot. She spent a moment envying him his elegant mount; it did not escape her that his posture was equally elegant. He drew up beside the buckboard.

"Miss Weston? It looks as if we're in for a storm. Would you like me to drive for you?" Jenny, already fed up with years of being patronized by men, saw red.

"It might surprise you. Sergeant Adair, but in spite of the fact that I am a woman I do many things quite well for myself. Driving is one of them."

"At least let me escort you home."

"Thank you, no," she said decisively.

"Forgive me for offering where nothing was necessary…"

"Or welcome," Jenny snapped.

"Good day, Miss Weston." Totally aloof now, Shane touched the brim of his hat and heeled his horse into a high trot again. His use of her name came out somewhere between cool and disdainful. What was worse, for the third time she found herself saying "good day" to his retreating back. Furious, she slapped the old mares with the reins. They tried to come to a choppy trot, but they could not decide which one would be first to change gait.

Just then the sky opened, and immediately on the heels of a violent lightning flash came the ripping crack of a very close strike. Both mares reared, screaming, and in an instant Jenny found herself fighting for control.

Praise for Lael R. Neill

"*STONE DREAMING WOMAN* charms, delights and warms the reader's heart. I fell in love with Jenny and Shane and didn't want the book to end. Hope to see a lot more from this new author."

~Fleeta Cunningham, author of the Santa Rita Series

~*~

"A captivating read from page one!"

~Tiffany Green, author of Innocence Lost

Dedication

To the Rainbow Goddesses,
who hung in there with me every step of the way
and never let me lose faith.
You know who you are!

Chapter One

The creaky old train approached the small station with a bump, a sigh, and a great exhalation of steam. Before it came to a brake-squealing stop, Jenny spotted her uncle on the platform and waved to him through the window. Though muffled to the ears, he seemed glad to see her, giving her a hearty wave in return. She rose, gathered her things, and made her way back to the door where the conductor waited for her. The young constable in the Red Serge of the Royal Northwest Mounted Police with whom she had been chatting during the trip from River Bend preceded her down the stairs and held his hand out to help her down.

"*Mam'selle*," he murmured with a polite nod. She thanked him in French and scarcely heard his reply. The conductor also held out his hand to her, but she ignored him and flew into her uncle's arms.

"Uncle Richard!"

"Jen, you look beautiful!"

"It's so good to see you!"

Their words came out simultaneously. She hugged him and kissed his cheek as he swung her around, laughing. Since her childhood, her uncle had always smelled of the same shaving soap and his one and only brand of pipe tobacco. The scent instantly took her back twenty years.

He bore an amazing resemblance to her father.

They looked enough alike to be twins, but the similarities stopped at the surface. Her father, John Weston, a fiery and uncompromising scientist, a physician and surgeon, fought tooth and nail for his patients. He could be hard and unbending when he felt himself in the right, which, she reflected, seemed like virtually all the time. Richard, however, had left a career as a history professor to become an author. He had written a comprehensive analysis of the Third Crusade, now mandatory reading for serious historians everywhere. A retiring, gentle, and sympathetic soul, he poured so much feeling into his work that his first novel, *By the Grace of God*, chronicling the life of Eleanor of Aquitaine, enjoyed such resounding success that if he never wrote another word he could live comfortably the rest of his days. After a year of burdensome celebrity in New York, he fled to the woods of Ontario, where he bought a small ranch and settled down in peaceful obscurity to write to his heart's content.

"I swear you don't weigh any more than a bag full of thistledown, and you look more like your mama every day. How's my girl?"

"I'm fine, and the trip wasn't bad at all. I'm not even tired. I'm all ready for the grand tour of Elk Gap."

"Elk Gap is not very grand, so the tour won't be much of a tour. Here you see it all." He gestured down the street. Where the sparse snow had been driven down, the unpaved Main Street looked like a morass of icy ruts. Board sidewalks flanked it. A few businesses and some whitewashed clapboard houses with postage-stamp yards took up the near side of the street, while the far side boasted establishments like Mrs.

Hammill's, which, he informed her, functioned as a hotel, boarding house, and the town's only restaurant. In a line with it stood a general store, a bank, a feed store, a livery stable, a smithy, and a barbershop where a friend of the proprietor could also slip into the back room for a discreet sip of moonshine or a couple hands of poker of an evening. An impressive three-story building reared itself just across the side street from the train station. A sign next to the door proclaimed *Angus A. MacBride, M.D.* Around the corner to the right she saw the post office, Calvary Presbyterian Church, and a block of houses, after which the street came to an abrupt end. True, there was not much to Elk Gap, but the local countryside, its high, rolling hills beautiful beyond belief, more than made up for the unprepossessing little town. The rustic setting instantly absorbed her. While she gazed around, her uncle directed the porters to place her three trunks in his old-fashioned spring-seated buckboard. A moment later he broke into her thoughts.

"I realize it might be a little early for supper yet, but why don't we go into Mrs. Hammill's? A little break might be relaxing for you after such a long trip."

"That sounds like a good idea. We can have a nice, private chat. Do you realize I haven't really talked to you since you came back from doing research in Europe? The last time you were in Virginia only four days, and I was still in medical school. We didn't have a chance to visit at all." She thrust a leather-gloved hand through his arm, and he patted it affectionately.

"We can talk to our hearts' content now. There'll be a lot of long, quiet evenings in the next few months."

"I just need a peaceful place where I can regroup

right now. It's been…it's been difficult for me lately."

"Well, you're where you can relax and do exactly as you please. The quiet here in Elk Gap saved my sanity."

"I could use a little bit of that," she sighed.

"I know. I read between the lines in all your letters. You know, it looks like the weather is going to turn bad before nightfall. It's been unseasonably warm this winter, but here that could change in an eyeblink. We'll need to get going. I'll treat you to dinner first, though. And Jenny, you're all steel inside, just like John. He inherited all the drive and determination in the family and passed it on to you."

"I know. It's a shame I wasn't born a boy."

"Don't ever say that. You're much too pretty to wish away your good looks." He patted her wind-pink cheek. "Now let's go have supper. It's a good three-quarters of an hour drive home, and it can get pretty chilly without some fuel in the furnace." He escorted her across the rutted street, carefully choosing the smoothest path.

"I can see I need proper winter boots. Perhaps I should come to town and do a little shopping."

"Of course. Any day you want. If I'm not busy, I can have my hired man drive us, or you can come by yourself. Elk Gap is a quiet town. You can drive unescorted without a worry in the world."

"It's not considered in bad form?"

"Not here, Jen. This is the frontier. Ladies are more independent than they are in New York. That should suit you nicely."

He opened the door of Mrs. Hammill's boarding house and she found herself directly in the large, plain dining room with whitewashed shiplap walls. In the warmth she detected the delicious odors of frying steak, onions, and apple pie. Suddenly she felt ravenous.

"I'm going to take you up on that dinner. I'm hungry. I know I eat more than is ladylike, but I burn it off. Father says it's because I have such an active brain."

"When John makes an observation like that I'd believe him. If I said it, on the other hand, you could call it an old wives' tale and you'd probably be right," he said with a smile. He helped Jenny with her Russian sable coat and hung it on a nearby hall tree. She left her matching hat and muff on a shelf, and Richard hung his red-and-black chopper jacket and black stocking cap next to hers. He escorted her to a table not far from the staircase that led to the upper floors.

"Did I see a sign next to the door that said Royal Northwest Mounted Police?" she asked.

"Yes. Two officers are assigned here in Elk Gap, and a third comes up from River Bend now and then if they need him. They live upstairs, and they use the room back there as their constabulary." Richard gestured to a door at the rear of the dining room. It bore a twin to the sign on the outside of the building.

"Goodness, does anything actually happen here?"

"I gather that a few years back Elk Gap was a wide-open, rough town. There were moonshiners and ladies of ill repute, and there was a running war among the loggers, miners, trappers, and farmers. Now it's so quiet I can't imagine anyone so much as locking a door."

A moment later a dark-haired, moon-faced teenage girl in a white bib apron came to their table.

"Hello, Mr. Weston."

"Hello, Maddie."

"We have roast chicken with bread dressing or sirloin steak and mashed potatoes. They both come with a dinner roll and your choice of corn or green beans. What will it be?"

"Jenny?" Richard inquired politely.

"I'll have steak, medium rare, please. With green beans."

"Make that two, Maddie."

"And tea?"

"Of course."

"No coffee?" Jenny asked.

"No, ma'am. I'm sorry. We only make coffee if we know ahead. We can make it for you, but it will take a while to brew."

"This is Canada, after all," Richard reminded her gently.

"Tea will be satisfactory. I just arrived on the train from New York, and for a while I forgot where I am."

"Well, welcome to Elk Gap. I'll take your order back to the cook. It won't be long." Maddie did everything but curtsey as she took her leave.

"So, Jenny?" Richard prompted. She knew exactly what he meant.

"I've written to every hospital on the East Coast. I've had plenty of completely insulting offers of nursing positions, and one hospital would hire me providing I limited my practice to obstetrics, gynecology, and pediatrics. And don't even mention finding a practice I can buy into. I'm a surgeon, Uncle Richard. A surgeon and an internist. I want to practice general medicine, and so far nobody seems willing to let me."

"And for that you spent all that time in pre-med and medical school," he sighed.

"And of course there's Father. You know he will have his way, come what may. He took it in very bad grace when he lost the battle against my going to medical school. Now he has it in his head that I should marry the son of a friend of his, and nothing else will do."

"Phillip Hildebrand, right?"

"Yes. Phillip makes my skin crawl. His father operates his investment company just a hair this side of the law, and Phillip wants to go into politics. That's the dirtiest business on the face of this earth. I've had all I can take of men who think they can push me around and patronize me just because I'm a woman. Truth be known, I'm probably smarter than ninety-nine percent of them."

"You get no argument from me on that score, Jen."

"I know." She heaved a sigh. "You were always on my side in all this mess. I don't think I'd have been able to stand up to Father and go away to school if you hadn't backed me." She looked up at her gentle uncle. Rimless bifocals fenced in his mild blue eyes and only the lightest dusting of grey touched his thinning, sandy hair. But he had yet to see his fortieth birthday; he was a full twelve years younger than his brother John.

Jenny and her uncle carried obvious family connections. Both were petite. Jenny, perhaps five feet three, at the outside weighed a hundred ten pounds. They had the same oval face and tawny Weston hair, but she tamed her heavy, curling leonine mane only by braiding it or winding it into a knot. Her mother, a Virginia Brisbane related to the historical Custis family, had given her melting, dark eyes. The rest of her was delicately pretty. A big, horsy, pushy woman might have fared better in a male-dominated field like medicine, but a mind as keen as her father's lay concealed under femininity reinforced by years of training in genteel New York manners. When her Weston intellect emerged, it often shocked people.

Richard reached out and took her hand. "Sweetheart, while you're here I don't want you to worry about anything. Write all the letters you want and see if you can't find a position acceptable to you. I'll help in any way I can."

She gave him a wistful smile. "Thank you, from the bottom of my heart. I know you're risking your relationship with Father…"

"No, I'm not. You forget I'm the Old General's son too. I know how to handle John's bluff and bluster." Jenny found herself agreeing with her uncle's assessment. Under Richard's quiet exterior, the proverbial velvet glove concealed the iron hand. She'd realized early on that he had developed a deceptively unassuming demeanor as his defense against a father who raged and cursed and intimidated in order to get his way.

Maddie arrived with their meal. It looked wonderful, and when Jenny cut into her steak she found it perfectly done. The cornstarch gravy with chopped wild mushrooms and onions gave the meal a surprisingly sophisticated touch. She cleaned her plate with gusto.

"Didn't you have anything to eat on the train?" Richard asked.

"Mrs. Dean sent me off with a hamper, but that

didn't last forever. My breakfast this morning was an apple and a glass of milk between trains."

"No wonder you're hungry. Now about dessert…"

"I smelled pie when we came in."

"I think I did too. Mrs. Hammill's deep-dish apple pie is the stuff of legends. She serves it hot with cream."

"You know, I think I still have a few cracks to fill, and apple pie is my favorite dessert."

"Apple pie it is." At that moment the front door opened and a tall young man in the uniform of the Royal Northwest Mounted Police came in. He paused at the doorway to remove his hat and parka. His fair complexion looked pale despite the cold outside. He put his hat aside, rubbed at his very black, wavy hair with a gloved hand, and started toward the stairway.

"Shane," Richard called. The young man paused.

"*Bonjour*, Richard." Even Richard's broad smile did not alleviate the seriousness of the officer's face.

"Jenny, may I present my friend, Staff Sergeant Shane Adair, Royal Northwest Mounted Police. Shane, my niece, Miss Jennifer Weston."

"*Mam'selle* Weston. *C'est mon plaisir. Pardonnez moi…* Ah, excuse me. I mean, my pleasure, Miss Weston." He nodded politely to her, but his face looked anything but pleased. His tone seemed as stiffly formal as his appearance, and for no good reason Jenny felt her hackles raise.

"*Je suis enchantée,* Sergeant." *There. That'll show you I'm no ignoramus*, she thought smugly. In spite of her feelings, she favored him with her best Southern Belle smile. Not even the merest flicker across his granite face acknowledged her perfectly precise French.

She took in his regular features, strongly square chin, lips rounded in a typically French way, and surprising agate-grey eyes. Heavy cheekbones gave his face a masculine angularity. *He's not unpleasant looking, if he would only smile.*

"How are you now, Shane?" Richard asked. From the stress her uncle laid on the question, she felt it was much more than social politeness.

"I'm quite well. And you?" The reply was brief to the point of terseness.

"Couldn't be better, now that my favorite niece is here for a visit."

Almost reluctantly his gaze went from Richard to Jenny. "Well, Miss Weston, I hope you enjoy your stay in Elk Gap. If I may be of any service to you, you've only to let me know." He turned slightly as though he were going to take his leave, and when Jenny took a second, careful look at him, he seemed pale and tired.

"Won't you join us for dessert? Apple pie will be my treat," Richard offered.

"Thank you, no. Perhaps another time? I've been up to North Village. I had to investigate a shooting, and I need to write my report and get it countersigned in time to post it on the evening train to River Bend. With all my other paperwork, that may be a tight squeeze."

"Definitely another time. You know you're welcome at my house, day or night."

"Thank you. But I really must be on my way. It was nice to make your acquaintance, Miss Weston. Good day." He nodded toward Jenny by way of acknowledgment but did not wait for a reply.

"Good day, Sergeant," she said to his retreating back. She watched briefly as he climbed the stairs. It was instant distaste on Jenny's part. He seemed like the kind of sourpuss who did not even like himself. But she decided not to voice her opinions to her uncle, who obviously thought a great deal of the dour young man.

"Have you known Sergeant Adair long?" It was a purely polite inquiry, and she could not have cared less about the answer.

"Ever since my first day here. He's been an incredibly good friend to me. When I came here I had no idea under the sun where I was. He helped me find my house and also my housekeeper. He's actually a barrister. He could practice law anywhere in Canada, but he'd rather do police work. He single-handedly settled all the fuss the Indians, the loggers, the farmers, the trappers, and the railroad men had for years. There's not a man jack hereabouts who doesn't think the world of him."

"You included, it seems."

"Of course. He's gone far out of his way to help me." It was on the tip of her tongue to say that boorish behavior was no recommendation of a man's character, but in deference to her uncle, she held her peace.

Less than half an hour later they were on their way home. Richard's ancient team, which he fatuously called "The Girls," were hard-pressed to achieve a wheezy trot. It took them nearly an hour to arrive at Richard's small ranch. Knowing the proximity of their barn, with its feed and comfortable, warm stalls, they turned a fraction before he drew up the left rein and commanded them *haw*. Jenny looked about with awe. They moved down a lane curving around an orchard, toward a snug two-story log house that looked to have been reinvented and added to over generations. One single chimney, flanked by two dormer windows, rose from the center of the roof, and a capacious farmer's porch ran the entire length of the front.

"Well, this is home," Richard announced. "It's probably going to seem plain to you. I don't have electricity. There are, however, running water, indoor plumbing, and a telephone. I added the telephone and the plumbing. I can stand kerosene lamps, but a backhouse and a pump were just too primitive."

Just then a man in work overalls and a black-and-green chopper jacket came from the barn. Richard beckoned to him. "That's my hired man, Toby. He's slow and he's deaf, but he's a top stockman and he keeps a good garden." Richard pointed to Jenny's trunks and pantomimed taking them inside. Toby nodded. But to Jenny's clinical eye he did not look mentally impaired. *I'll bet money he's only deaf. If he could be taught to read and write he's probably as smart as the rest of us. If I'm here long enough, I might try.*

Richard and Toby took a handle each on the first trunk and Richard pushed the front door back, pausing politely to let Jenny enter first. The door opened into an old-fashioned assembly room, with a scrubbed heart-pine floor covered with a bright, braided rug.

A relic of the house's earlier days, a huge natural stone fireplace with an ancient "reckon" to hold cooking pots formed a large part of the center wall. A relatively new wood-burning cook stove stood at right angles to it, and an odd set of bunks ran along the front wall between the window and the outside corner, obviously a holdover from the early days when the farmhouse had its origins as a one-room cabin. A pleasantly solid woman with silvering dark hair and huge dimples stood before the stove, stirring a pot.

"Well, Mr. Weston, I think you've just made it home in time. It's going to rain any minute."

"Jenny, Mavis Conner, my housekeeper. Mavis, this is the favorite niece you've heard so much about."

"Mrs. Conner," Jenny said with a polite nod.

"Mavis, please," she corrected with gentle firmness. "And welcome to Canada. It's grand to meet you, after everything Mr. Weston has told me."

"Come up and see your room, Jen. Mavis devoted a lot of time to making it livable. Before, I had just been using it for storage." With Toby following, he took up the handle of the trunk again and led her to the right, through an archway into the front parlor. The room exuded comfort in the form of a large oriental carpet, two oxblood leather wing chairs flanking the double fireplace, a cameo-backed settee in scarlet velvet, and several occasional tables that held elaborate crystal-bowled lamps. At first she had thought to head through the door at the back of the living room, but a peek inside revealed Mavis's bedroom on the right, then a hallway through the pantry, leading past the rear kitchen door to the bathroom at the back. Instead she followed the men up the stairs to the traditional children's dormitories. Richard had long ago claimed the larger room on the left, but when she saw her own bedroom, it reached out and welcomed her. At first glance it appeared simple, a far cry from her chamber in New York with its jacquard satin draperies and marble-topped walnut suite imported from Germany; however, that room had held nothing but turmoil. Though small, this promised peace. The furnishings consisted of a washstand, an armoire, a bonnet box highboy, a cheval glass, a single brass bed, and a delicately carved rosewood lady's writing desk with cabriole legs that Jenny remembered well. It had belonged to her late Aunt Alix.

"Oh, Uncle Richard! Aunt Alix's desk!" she exclaimed, her throat tightening with emotion at the memory of her beloved aunt, dead tragically young during her first childbirth.

"It's yours now. Call it a late Christmas or an early birthday gift. I figured you might need somewhere comfortable to read and write in private." She came to him and his arms went softly around her. For a moment she was afraid she might cry.

"You're way too good to me, you know," she murmured against his shoulder.

"You're worth it, sweetheart. I want you to be happy while you're here."

"I'd be happy in a barn, but this room is lovely. Who made the curtains? Mrs. Conner?" Their glazed chintz, delicately flowered in an abstract swirly blue with mauve roses and green leaves here and there, matched the bedspread, the dust ruffle, and also the skirt around the washstand.

"Of course she made them. She loves to sew. I gave her a sewing machine last Christmas, and she has made herself an entire new wardrobe over the year."

"Perhaps I could coax her into helping me make a divided riding skirt. I detest riding sidesaddle. You do have a saddle horse, don't you?"

"As a matter of fact, I haven't. However, it would be a small matter to get you a good mount. There's a man around here who trains horses. He's an absolute genius. An Iroquois Indian named Thomas Wise Hand. Of course I'll have to ask Shane to be our go-between, because he speaks Iroquois."

"Well... Let's just see, shall we?" she demurred. She wanted nothing to do with the sour-faced young police officer.

Less than an hour later she had unpacked her belongings and managed to strew them all over the small room. Her medical textbooks fit nicely into the shelves below the dormer windows, and she had hung her clothes in the armoire and placed her lingerie and nightclothes in the highboy. Mavis had certainly gone the extra mile. All the drawers were freshly lined with butcher paper, and she had put a handmade lavender stick in each one. Jenny picked up one stick and rubbed it gently between her palms, held her hands to her face, and inhaled the newly released fragrance.

Her hands still smelled of the lavender when she lifted a leather box from the bottom of her trunk. She started to put it in the bottom drawer of the highboy, but instead she sat down on the bed and opened the case. It contained her important papers, including diplomas, grade reports, internship and residence evaluations, and a list of all the hospitals she had written to and their answers. They read like a roster of every heartbreak she had ever known. She leafed through the stack of replies until she came to the one that had been more important to her than all the rest of them put together. It bore the return address of Northtown Surgical Clinic, the internationally famous and preeminent experimental and teaching hospital in New York City. Her father had been on the staff there since before her birth, and as soon as she was old enough to decide she wanted to be a doctor, too, her one and only goal had been to join its staff along with him. Every insult and slight she had borne from her male professors and colleagues, every night she had gone without sleep in order to study, every smutty innuendo she had pointedly ignored, every friendship she had passed up, every sacrifice she had made, had been directed toward the one hope that a single-page letter shattered. She knew its contents by heart: *At this time there are no vacancies on our staff; nor, for the foreseeable future, are there any plans to hire women as staff physicians*. She put the envelope back in the stack with a sigh.

I gave seven years of my life for that letter, she thought bitterly. *I sacrificed my relationship with Father just so I could get a rejection letter from Northtown. And I'll bet my bottom dollar he had something to do with it. Academic credentials don't come any better than mine, yet here I am after all that work, an outcast in a man's world. Well, I still have some fight left in me. There has to be some place in medicine for a woman doctor. I swear I'll find it, and then I can thumb my nose at all those insufferable stuffed shirts. I'll have my revenge, and it will be so sweet.*

She forced herself to put the letters aside and pigeonhole the anger that surged up inside her. There was nothing she could do at the moment, so she stuffed all the ire, all the hurt, and all the disappointment into a far corner of her mind, put the box of letters in a drawer, and continued unpacking.

When she finished putting her things away, she decided to take her uncle's advice and rest. She did not feel particularly tired; nevertheless, she stripped to her shift and snuggled into the featherbed with her heavy human anatomy text. Soon the warmth that enveloped her made her realize the trip had left her wearier than she had wanted to admit. The tome became more and more ponderous, closing altogether across her hand as she fell asleep.

Chapter Two

The next morning Richard immersed himself in his work, leaving Jenny at loose ends. She acquainted herself with her uncle's quiet house and the housekeeper. In contravention of Jenny's strict New York propriety, which dictated the cook should always receive the honorific "Mrs.," Mavis she was and Mavis she would remain. By contrast to the formidable Mrs. Hall, who ruled the kitchen of the sumptuous Weston mansion with an iron fist, Mavis had a much more informal style, making Richard Weston's comfortable assembly room home to all. Life in the house focused about the round dining table, whether for a leisurely breakfast or a session of potato peeling, mending, and small talk. Jenny sat herself down with the wool plaid shirt that needed to have the cuffs and collar turned. She unpicked the stitches and applied herself to practical sewing while Mavis peeled potatoes for dinner. It was during a period of companionable silence when Mavis suggested that Jenny take the plunge into Elk Gap society.

"By the way, the church is having a box social tomorrow night. I hope you want to attend," she said.

"Box social?" Jenny echoed. "You know, I've never been to one, and I'm not certain I really want to start now."

"Heavens, child, you've led a deprived life," Mavis

responded with her dimpled smile. "Of course you want to go. It'll be your chance to meet the whole town."

"I don't want to give anyone the impression I'm looking for a beau. That's the farthest thing in the world from my mind," she protested.

"I realize that. I just think you should go and get acquainted. Of course, you'll be eating dinner with whoever buys your basket, but that's not really as important as getting to know people. Besides, Mr. Weston said he plans to attend, and I'm also going. Everyone not bringing or buying a box is bringing pot luck."

"Well, perhaps you're right. I have to get acquainted sometime," Jenny sighed, picking up her small, stork-bill scissors to clip a ragged edge. "Uncle Richard is certainly hard on cuffs, with as much writing as he does, and he won't wear sleeve protectors because he says they're not comfortable. Next time around, these sleeves will have to be cut off."

"There's a quilting party Sunday evening at Millie Tillman's house, too. Millie's husband runs the general store in town?" Mavis's voice went up questioningly, and she waited for Jenny's nod of recognition. "Millie is a sweet woman. A bit of a busybody, but she means well. Anyone you don't meet tomorrow night you'll be introduced to then. I understand the people around here are perhaps simpler than you're used to, but you'll come to like Elk Gap eventually."

"From what little I've seen, I like it well enough already," Jenny protested. "The only thing about a box social, aren't you supposed to pack the picnic supper yourself?"

"Naturally. Why?"

"Because I've never learned to cook. Tea is about my limit."

"Never learned to cook?" Mavis echoed, incredulous.

"No. At Parkfield, Father always had a household staff of at least eight, plus a fulltime cook with a helper. In fact, he has employed the same cook since before I was born, and no one who values their life would go into Mrs. Hall's kitchen without her express permission."

"She sounds like quite a forbidding lady."

"She's on the stern side, but she's very devoted to what she does, and one of the best cooks in New York," Jenny said with a small, nostalgic smile. She had realized early on that Mrs. Hall's gruffness was the only way she expressed the vast amount of love stored within her.

"Well, since you sew well enough, I think it's high time you learned to cook. I'll teach you, if you want me to."

Jenny felt a ripple of amusement at Mavis's observation. *I should be able to sew. I'm a surgeon, after all.* "Why not learn to cook? I'll have a lot of free time while I'm here."

"Good. I'll help you with the box social, since there's scarcely time for you to learn what you're doing before tomorrow, but after that you'll be on your own."

"Fair enough," Jenny responded as Mavis gathered up her potatoes to rinse them in the sink. She dumped the peelings into a clean bucket, which Toby would eventually take to the barn for the pig.

"Have you ever been to a quilting bee?" Mavis asked at length.

"Oh, yes. We had those in New York. I do like to embroider, but I'm afraid sewing is the only homely skill I've acquired."

"Mr. Weston did mention you'd been away at school. Was it finishing school?" Jenny cringed, then decided to sidestep the question for the present.

"No, I attended the University of Virginia. I studied French, German, Latin, and Greek, plus a lot of other things like natural sciences."

"How impressive! And French will stand you in good stead here. A lot of people hereabouts speak it, because the voyageurs were the first white people who settled this area." Mavis dunked the potatoes vigorously in a pan of water in the sink, then set them to boil. Jenny was mentally asking forgiveness for the social fib when Richard came into the room. But Mavis's comment stuck with her, and she connected it with Sergeant Adair's accidental use of French when they met.

"My, you two certainly look busy," he said, adjusting his spectacles.

"We have been. Your shirt's mended now, but when you wear the cuffs through again, I'm afraid it's the end."

"That old shirt doesn't owe me anything. I've had it since before I went to the Continent. Anyway, thanks for fixing it." He leaned down to bestow an appreciative peck on her forehead.

"You're welcome. How's your work going today?"

"Very well, but I do need a break." He sat down in his accustomed place, and Mavis wordlessly handed him a mug of tea.

"Mrs. Conner...I mean, Mavis...has talked me into

going to the box social at the church tomorrow. I'm glad you're going with us."

"I'm a little ahead of schedule. I can afford the time. I don't want to be a complete hermit, after all."

"Good. I'll be glad for a familiar face." Richard smiled at her, and she looked at her uncle, seeing a thousand small details at once. Though he so resembled her father, a world of difference resided behind the unlined face and lively blue eyes. All the men in the Weston family tended to go bald; Richard's hairline had started to recede, but his hair, like Jenny's, was still a tawny, darkish blond. She did not think he looked thirty-eight, although her father showed every day of his extra years. *Fiery people like Father seem to age faster*, she thought.

"How big is the congregation at Calvary?" she asked at length.

"Oh, a couple hundred, I'd guess. Everybody in town, except those who attend Our Lady of the Angels. We have very few Roman Catholics, though. Father Andre's parishioners are mostly Indian."

"That sounds so small after Park Avenue Methodist," Jenny remarked. "We had more people at early Sunday service than you have in all of Elk Gap."

"Well, tomorrow you'll meet most of them."

"Good. I'm looking forward to it." She fudged a bit on that statement, too. At that point she could not have cared much less about anything social, especially if it involved men. But by the next afternoon she managed to work herself into an acceptable state of anticipation. She dressed carefully, selecting a navy wool skirt and vest and a white blouse to complement her outfit. When she had done her hair, she opened her jewelry case and deliberated.

Most of her very real jewelry had come down to her through two families. As the only girl on the Weston side, it comprised quite a legacy. She passed over an elegantly simple black cameo ringed with pearls, touched her grandmother's wonderful diamond-and-pearl necklace, then picked up a topaz-and-diamond bar pin in platinum filigree that her late Grandmother Weston had given her for her sixteenth birthday. She tilted it in the light, watching the diamonds wink back at her around the hexagonal center stone. When she held it against the high collar of her blouse, she decided the effect pleased her very much. Carefully she fastened the pin at the bottom of her collar and turned once before the cheval glass to check her general appearance. With satisfaction she decided she looked nice enough to attend anything in New York.

Mavis, too, wore her Sunday best and had just finished winding an old-fashioned knitted fascinator around her head when Jenny came downstairs.

"Well, Jen, we're ready. Toby's bringing the team around. You'd best wear your furs. It's cold outside," Richard advised.

"You've done so well with Toby, Mr. Weston. Perhaps he's not as slow as everyone thinks," Mavis remarked, picking up her coat. "You know, he wasn't born deaf. He was as right as rain, going to school and everything, until the scarlet fever when he was ten years old. He nearly died, and when he got over it he couldn't hear any longer."

"Really?" Jenny said. "Well, that just reinforces what I thought when I first saw him. He may not actually be retarded at all."

"That's a possibility," Richard allowed. "He does well enough when I can make him understand what I want."

The physician in Jenny lit up like a lantern as it had when she first saw Toby. "I had an idea about him a while ago. Would you object if I try to teach him to read? He may have the foundations for it already. If he could just communicate, it might open up a whole new world for him."

"That's a splendid idea," Richard said, opening the door for them. He took her wicker picnic basket and gave her a hand up into the seat of the buckboard. He could afford a much nicer buggy. Heaven only knew why he drove an old rattletrap of a farmer's wagon. But Richard had become an anomaly in the Weston family: an artistic and unrealistic daydreamer whom the details of day-to-day life touched only lightly.

"Uncle Richard, why do you drive this thing?" she asked. "It's awfully open to be running around with during the winter."

"It was in the barn when I bought the place," he replied with a shrug. "The weather's not that bad, if you dress for it. If it's too raw outside, I stay home." He helped Mavis up, then came around to take the driver's seat. He settled himself, clucked to The Girls, shook the reins, and they were off.

At that latitude in January, full dark fell by five o'clock. Fortunately a decent moon rode part way up the clear, dark sky, illuminating the road with long, sharp shadows. He whistled tunelessly as the horses trotted along, while Jenny let her mind go blank and merely enjoyed the crisp night.

A collection of idle conveyances already surrounded the church when they arrived. Richard quickly tethered and blanketed The Girls before ushering Jenny and Mavis inside. The solid and surprisingly large brick building boasted a big fellowship hall in the basement. They hung their wraps in the outer hallway, and Mavis showed Jenny where to put her basket. About twenty baskets lined two long tables; she placed hers on the end. Soon they would go to young men who would then claim the donors as their partners for the evening. In theory, no one knew which basket belonged to whom, but in practice, most of the swains had been well coached beforehand.

Jenny went through so many introductions that her head swam by the time the pastor moved to start the proceedings. She sat between Mavis and Richard at a long table near the right side of the hall, and just as Reverend Aubrey came to the front of the room, three figures in red tunics slipped in. The first, quite tall and slim, had crisp, light blond hair. She recognized the second as the French-speaking constable from the train. The third one drew a smile from Richard. Jenny looked the other way.

"Do you know that shorter officer in the middle?" Mavis asked Richard.

"That's Constable Laurence Bernard. He comes up from River Bend sometimes, usually when there's an emergency here. He seems a very personable young man, although I've only spoken with him on two or three occasions," Richard said. "And, Jenny, the tall, blond fellow is Shane's partner—actually his subordinate officer—Corporal Paul Weller. I'll introduce you when the opportunity presents itself."

"I think I told you Constable Bernard was on the train with me. We had rather a nice conversation, all in French, of course," Jenny responded.

"Well, ladies and gentlemen, welcome to our box social," Reverend Aubrey began. The tall young man had such a rich, resonant voice that Jenny wondered if he could sing. "Shall we stand for a word of prayer?" he said with formality. The room filled with the sounds of scraping chairs and shuffling feet, then all went quiet. Jenny bowed her head but cut her eyes sideways at the three police officers who stood in identical reverent parade-rest poses against the far wall.

A minute or so later the auction started. Some baskets drew frantic competition; others went quietly to the first and only bidder. To Jenny's astonishment, Richard paid an entire dollar for the basket that turned out to belong to Ruth Grayson, the postmistress. As Richard came forward to claim his basket, Jenny saw Shane and Paul trade a pointed look, and surprise on other faces in the crowd, too, with a few gasps, and not inconsiderable murmuring. *There must be a story here*, Jenny concluded.

Richard escorted Ruth back to their table. "Jenny, this is Miss Ruth Grayson, our postmistress. Ruth, may I present my niece, Miss Jenny Weston," he said as he seated Ruth. She seemed quiet, graceful, and perhaps a year or two older than Jenny herself. She wore her sleek walnut-red hair drawn back into an elegant figure-eight chignon and her dove grey dress with delicate ruching about the collar flattered both her graceful figure and her hazel eyes.

"Miss Grayson. How do you do?"

"Pleased to meet you, Miss Weston. I understand

you're here for an extended visit?"

"Yes I am. I just completed graduate school, and I need time to breathe," Jenny replied.

"Did you bring a basket?"

"As a matter of fact, I did. Mrs. Conner insisted. But it looks like it'll be the last one sold. And since I don't know anyone here, it's immaterial who buys it." Jenny was being less than cordial on purpose. She did not care to make friends in Elk Gap. The fewer people who knew her, the fewer who could intrude on the very big grudge she had against a world that would not accept women in medicine. At the moment, that grudge sat very heavily upon her shoulders.

As Reverend Aubrey moved down the table, it became obvious that Jenny's basket would indeed be the last one up for bids. And while Paul and Laurence entered successful bids and partnered with properly modest and nicely turned out young ladies in the course of things, Shane had yet to open his mouth. Reverend Aubrey held up Jenny's basket.

"Bids, anyone?" he asked, peeking inside. "I can't tell you what's in it. That wouldn't be fair. But I can tell you that it smells wonderful." An uncomfortable silence settled over the room.

"Fifty cents," Shane said. Jenny's heart slammed through the floor.

"Sergeant Adair has bid fifty cents. Going once, going twice… Sergeant Adair, you are about to share a real feast. Will the lady who brought this basket please stand up?" Jenny could not miss the surprised gasp and delayed polite applause when she rose. Shane took the basket and came to the table.

"Good evening," she said coolly. Right now the

only man exempt from her grudge was her uncle. Consequently, Sergeant Adair collided squarely with the arctic blast that swirled inside Jenny's heart.

"Miss Weston. Such a surprise. I thought I was going to save Julia Tillman from being a wallflower."

Her hostile eyes transfixed him with a withering glance that, to her chagrin, seemed to have no effect. "I've never been a wallflower in my life. I'm not about to start now." She took a cue from Ruth, who had begun quietly unpacking her basket.

"This looks like Mavis's doing," he remarked.

"It is. I've never learned to cook."

"I wouldn't miss her fried chicken for the world."

He allowed her to serve him, then thanked her perfunctorily.

"I'm surprised to see you here, Shane," Ruth remarked.

"Why, Ruth?" He fixed her with a level look that could have gone completely through her. She looked down with a confused expression.

"Well…no reason, really. Just…surprised, that's all." Jenny caught Richard's eye. His expression warned her away from the subject. Shane fell silent, all his attention purposefully fixed on his food.

Conversation at the table inevitably drifted to the political situation in Europe. Will Tillman, sitting next to Ruth, gestured with a crisp drumstick; his wife had also contributed fried chicken to the potluck.

"It seems to me there's always trouble in the Balkans," he opined. "Everybody wants a piece of those countries. Germany wants Austria and half of France, and the Good Lord only knows what the French want. Truth be known, I doubt *they* even know. You've been in Europe recently, Richard. What's your opinion?"

"I went to research the High Middle Ages, not to study current events. But you're right. The Balkans have always been the best route between Europe and Asia. Whoever controls them controls commerce. And I agree. There's so much unrest in Serbia. It's going to erupt and take the rest of Europe with it."

"Why do you want to dwell on the past? It's over and done with," Andy protested.

"Those who do not remember history are condemned to repeat it, after all," Richard said.

"Attributed to Voltaire," Jenny interjected.

"Thank God we won't be involved," Ruth said.

"Oh, we will. The minute Britain gets dragged in, we'll go." It was the only word out of Shane so far.

And I hope you're the first to enlist, Jenny thought sourly.

"At least we won't have to serve unless we want to." The source was Paul Weller, who had bought Mary Ann Tillman's box. He sat two places down from Jenny. Richard stopped the conversation for further introductions, then picked up the topic again.

"Oh? How so? You'll be needed for security here at home?"

"Just so. Police officers are exempt from conscription."

Jenny looked at the chevrons on Paul's right sleeve, then at the insignia on Shane's and decided on a different tack to let the unforgivably dense sergeant know what she thought of him. She would pretend he was not there for a while. "Corporal Weller, I don't understand what your ranks are. Could you explain it to me, please?" Paul looked surprised that she had asked him, which was just what she was after.

"Well, Miss Weston, everyone starts out as Constable. That's Laurence Bernard. He was only recruited about six months ago. Non-officers begin with Corporal. Then it goes to Sergeant, Staff Sergeant, and Staff Sergeant Major, and Sergeant Major. There is such a thing as Corps Sergeant Major, but there's only one of them, and it's an honorary thing. Actually, any non-officer rank above Staff Sergeant is uncommon. They're usually relegated to administration, recordkeeping, and the like, and most of them are at Headquarters in Regina. Officers start as Inspector, Superintendent, Chief Superintendent, Deputy Commissioner, and Commissioner. These other badges are sharpshooter ranks. They begin with cross pistols and cross rifles. The crown cross pistols and crown cross rifles Sergeant Adair and I both have are the higher grade. And this one that looks like a star is a five-year service badge." He pointed to Shane's left sleeve.

"I hope you're not offended. After all, one is simply expected to know military ranks and badges and the like."

"Oh, no. I'm not offended. Not in the least. After all, you've only been in God's country a few days. One must begin somewhere." He responded loftily, picking up on her flirtatious overture. She decided she liked his wit, his open countenance, and the easy smile that lit his blue eyes. Shane, however, sat expressionless. Tired circles smudged the light skin beneath his eyes, and at one point he rubbed the front of his left shoulder moodily. It aroused Jenny's clinical suspicions, but she said nothing.

The strained evening died a merciful death, and Richard reclaimed The Girls. Politely Shane escorted Jenny to the wagon.

"Thank you for the supper, Miss Weston," he said after she had accepted Richard's hand up to the buckboard.

"You're welcome, Sergeant. But you should thank Mavis, not me. And I thank you for rescuing me. I was about to sully my perfect record and become a wallflower for the first and only time in my life." Her tone was as icy as she could make it.

"I sincerely apologize. It was gauche of me to imply that, and I wish I could take back my words. Well, then, good evening." She watched as he strode off down the street, catching up with Laurence and Paul in the next block. Richard swung the team out toward North Village Road.

"Well, now, wasn't that a completely unmitigated disaster?" Jenny sighed.

"Yes. In more ways than one," Richard agreed.

"I gather Shane is no longer seeing Ruth Grayson. But then, it was never serious between them," Mavis remarked. "It was more like they were the only two of an age for each other, so it was natural that they keep company. Ruth is too gentle a soul to accept that Shane's occupation can be dangerous. It preyed on her mind, I think," Mavis observed. Jenny began adding the sum in her head. *That could explain a lot. He's been jilted and he's as fed up with women as I am with men.*

Chapter Three

The next few days at the quiet ranch slid past quickly. Jenny helped Mavis with the housework, which was not onerous since Richard contracted their laundry out to a sturdy German woman and her equally big-armed, slow-witted son, and everything beyond the front flowerbeds belonged to Toby. For Jenny's energetic nature the idyll ebbed, and she knew she had to do something or she would wind up with cabin fever. Besides, Mavis had been delighted when she asked for help with a riding skirt, and she wanted to go to town to see what Tillman's General Store had in the way of suitable fabric. So on Friday morning, Toby hitched The Girls to the buckboard, and Jenny meandered her way into town with an extensive shopping list in her jacket pocket. She hummed as the mismatched old horses sauntered down the road at a very low trot. The day was calm and unseasonably warm, making the spotty snow seem aged and decaying, and overhead the sky hung leaden with low, rounded clouds.

Eventually Elk Gap came into view down the tree-lined road. She made her first stop at Barnes and Sons, the livery stable and also the local feed-and-seed store. The proprietor, a youngish, burly man named Josh, loaded two fifty-pound sacks of grain for The Girls into the buckboard as though they weighed nothing, and welcomed Jenny to town. She perused the half-dozen horses he had for sale, ruling out four out of hand. He puffed up with offended pride and presented another two—a small, skittish young mare that seemed barely green broke, and a gelding that looked all right standing but paddled badly above a walk. In the end she declined them all and found it difficult to break away from Josh, who insisted that she did not know the first thing about horses and had no idea what a great bargain she was passing up. Finally she bade him good day with some firmness and returned to her buckboard. Then she tied the team to the hitching rail in front of Tillman's and went inside. The proprietor, in his indefinite fifties, his thinning, dark hair parted down the center and relentlessly plastered down, came from behind the counter.

"Well, Miss Weston, good morning. I'm Will Tillman. I remember you from the box social. What can I do for you?"

"Yes, I certainly remember you, too. It was a rather…memorable night."

"I hope your visit is proving pleasant."

"It is indeed. I needed the same peace and quiet Uncle Richard has found here. Besides, I just graduated from school, and I haven't seen my uncle in three years. He's always been my favorite relative."

"Mr. Weston is a very pleasant gentleman," Will agreed.

"I'll doubtless have the pleasure of seeing you and your family in church again. I have a grocery list here from Mrs. Conner, and I also need to look at your yard goods."

"Give me the list and I'll have Andy fill it. And our dry goods are through that doorway." He pointed off to his right where, at some time in the past, two buildings had been joined by an archway cut through the brickwork between them. "If you don't find what you need, let me know. I can always order anything you'd like."

"Thank you. I won't be long."

"Oh, take all the time you want, and please call me if you need help finding anything," he said amicably, picking up the list she had laid on the thick glass counter.

Mr. Tillman, she had to admit, ran a large and varied dry goods inventory. There had to be at least fifty bolts of cloth on the tables, plus notions, knitting needles, yarn, crochet hooks, and thread, needlework supplies, hat forms, and a few printed patterns. She found what she needed almost immediately: a bolt of dark blue denim. But she wandered around, looking at the cloth, until a striped cotton broadcloth caught her eye. The delicate pattern, several shades of blue on a white background with a red thread running through it, simply shouted Mavis. She picked up the bolt, and also selected a brown-and-blue madras that would coordinate well with her denim. She dawdled for another few minutes, picked up two spools of thread, some blue buttons, and a simple woman's shirtwaist pattern, then carried everything back to the counter. But by that time Millie, a tallish, neat woman, was behind it. She wore a primly starched, high-collared blouse with a cameo at her throat, and a practical black serge skirt.

"Miss Weston, so good to see you again."

"My pleasure entirely, Mrs. Tillman."

"Did you find everything you need?"

"Yes, I did. I'd like three yards of each, please. No, on second thought, five yards of the blue stripe, if you would?"

"Of course." Millie measured out the denim and cut it precisely. "You're going to sew?" she asked rhetorically.

"Mrs. Conner has agreed to help me make a riding skirt. I'm going to make a shirt to complement it. And the blue stripe is for Mrs. Conner by way of thank-you."

"Oh, Mavis will love this. Truth be known, she's been casting covetous eyes at that bolt of cloth ever since we received it."

"Do you think five yards is enough?"

"Oh, that depends," Millie answered, wrinkling her brows thoughtfully. "Now, if you bought six yards, she could make anything she wanted to."

"Very well. Six yards. I know very little about clothing construction, but I'm about to learn. By the way, could you total the cloth and the notions separately? I don't want to spend Uncle Richard's money for it. I'd rather pay for it myself."

"Well, let me see..." She jotted the figures down on a receipt form. "It's twenty-five, and thirty...forty... Two dollars and eighty-six cents." Jenny reached into her pocket and drew out three Canadian dollar bills; she'd had enough foresight to change her American currency at the bank next door. Millie counted out four pennies and a dime, and then Jenny paid another four dollars and eleven cents for the groceries. She pocketed her dime and turned the pennies into a large bag of lemon drops. Millie thanked her before instructing her teenage son Andrew to carry the boxes of groceries out to the buckboard. He covered them carefully with the ubiquitous tarp that everyone kept in an open wagon, and Jenny decided on the spot that she liked Andrew, a polite, pleasant lad with a quick smile, freckles, and huge hazel eyes. He gave her a half-shy hand up into the buckboard before wishing her good afternoon.

The last stop before returning home was the Post Office. She tethered The Girls one last time and climbed down, using the wheel hub as a step. When she opened the front door, a bell on a spring tinkled brightly.

"Coming," a feminine voice called from the back of the building.

"Hello, Miss Grayson. Does Uncle Richard have any mail today?" Jenny asked.

"Miss Weston, good afternoon. How nice to see you again. Ummm…let me see. Yes, he does. Two letters." She took them from a bank of pigeonholes behind her and handed them across the white-painted wooden counter.

"Thank you, Miss Grayson."

"Ruth, please," she responded, her voice softly sweet. "And I do look forward to seeing you at church Sunday." In spite of being reminded of the disastrous box social, Jenny was touched by Ruth's sincerity. She took her leave, tucked the two letters into her skirt pocket, untied The Girls' reins, and climbed back up into the driver's seat. She flicked the reins against the rumps of the ancient mares and clucked them up into their lumbering trot.

January was an odd time for a thunderstorm. However, as Richard had observed when she arrived in Elk Gap, the weather had been unseasonably warm.

When she cast a critical eye aloft, the freshening wind and the boiling mammatus clouds overhead disturbed her. She clucked again to the old mares, trying to speed them up, but when their gait did not change she resigned herself to a soaking.

Lightning had already started to flicker when she became aware of hoofbeats behind her. She turned and saw Sergeant Adair coming toward her, posting precisely to a high trot. He rode a handsome jet-black warmblood gelding with tall white socks and a blaze face. She spent a moment envying him his elegant mount; it did not escape her that his posture was equally elegant. He drew up beside the buckboard.

"Miss Weston? It looks as if we're in for a storm. Would you like me to drive for you?" Jenny, already fed up with years of being patronized by men, saw red.

"It might surprise you, Sergeant Adair, but in spite of the fact that I am a woman I do many things quite well for myself. Driving is one of them."

"At least let me escort you home."

"Thank you, no," she said decisively.

"Forgive me for offering where nothing was necessary…"

"Or welcome," Jenny snapped.

"Good day, Miss Weston." Totally aloof now, Shane touched the brim of his hat and heeled his horse into a high trot again. His use of her name came out somewhere between cool and disdainful. What was worse, for the third time she found herself saying "good day" to his retreating back. Furious, she slapped the old mares with the reins. They tried to come to a choppy trot, but they could not decide which one would be first to change gait.

Just then the sky opened, and immediately on the heels of a violent lightning flash came the ripping crack of a very close strike. Both mares reared, screaming, and in an instant Jenny found herself fighting for control. For all that they were ancient, the mares were still much stronger than she was. Shane whirled his horse, leaped down and grabbed for the team, and as the lightning flashed again, a half-grown black bear burst from the underbrush and galloped across the road, bawling in fright as it ran. The gelding went straight up, tearing his reins from Shane's left hand. As the mares settled, the black tucked his rump under and fled in sheer terror. Jenny looked on with horror as he headed straight for a barbed-wire fence. Then suddenly he went down on the grassy verge, his forelegs tangled in a loose loop of wire discarded by the farmer who had built the fence. She leaped from the buckboard and bolted toward the fallen horse.

Shane obviously had the same idea. The Girls were quiet old things. Even if they did not stay put, it would be a small matter to catch them later. He loosed a long-legged stride but could not match her head start. As the rain poured down, she threw her jacket over the gelding's head and held him down, quelling the thrashing that threatened to shred his forelegs.

"Easy, easy, big man," she murmured. "Whoa, now. Easy. Easy, boy. Easy, now. Yes, that's the way. Easy. Whoa, now. Shhh. Hush. Settle down. That's a good boy." Under the blindfold, with the gentle touch of her hands and the soothing sound of her voice, the gelding quieted. Shane came to his knees next to her.

"You're stronger than I am. Hold his head and keep him still," she commanded. She moved to the barbed wire around his legs, where the pouring rain sluiced the blood away. Gently she unwound the wire and freed his legs, ignoring the insults the barbs inflicted above her driving gloves. When she finished with the coil of wire, she tossed it out of the way, up against a fencepost. She ran knowing hands down the gelding's forelegs, testing the tendons and flexing his knees. Then she looked up at Shane. "He appears to be all right. All of those cuts are small and shallow. I know it looks bad, but a little blood goes a very long way in the rain, especially on white. See if you can get him up." She removed her jacket from the horse's head.

"Come on, Midnight. Up. Up, up, come on, Midnight. Get up," Shane urged, lifting on the reins and prodding a wet shoulder with his boot. The horse rolled up onto his chest and levered himself upright. He stood spraddle-legged and shaking with fear, his eyes still rolling wildly. Shane quieted him, speaking a few words she could not understand and stroking his neck and head until the gelding calmed.

"Thank heaven he's back on his feet," Jenny breathed, ignoring the pouring rain. She went to the horse's head, stroking underneath his jaw and talking to him softly. "But you can't ride him yet. You're much too upset, aren't you, big man? But you're all right, Midnight. We'll get you in a nice, snug stall, and you can get over everything. That's okay. You're doing just fine now, aren't you?" Almost as an afterthought she turned to Shane. "Come to Uncle Richard's with me. We can put him up in the barn and see to those cuts." She shivered abruptly, realizing she was chilled to the bone. For all the good it would do, she pulled her sodden jacket back on. She gathered The Girls' reins and climbed up to the driver's seat while Shane tied Midnight to the back of the buckboard. He came around to her side.

"Now will you let me drive?" he asked.

"Do I have any choice in the matter?" she snapped. Mutely he walked to the shotgun position and took one long-legged step up, wrapped his rain poncho about himself and sat as far from her as he could manage. She roused the mares to their usual stiff trot.

"Thank you very much for saving Midnight," he said at length.

"Tell me that when we've had another good look at his legs," she responded through gritted teeth. The fright was still very much with her. When the lightning flashed and thunder roared again, The Girls decided their barn was the best place to be and picked up their pace.

By the time they made it to the barn, she was wet to the skin, although her wool jacket was still reasonably warm. Shane stepped down and swung the barn doors open, and The Girls gratefully pulled the buckboard inside. Jenny secured the reins to the brake lever and scrambled down before he could offer to help her. He looked at her, shrugged when she ignored him, turned Midnight into a vacant loose box, and closed the barn doors as Toby came out of his room.

Toby turned his attention to the team while Shane unsaddled Midnight. Jenny went into the tack room, snooped through the contents of several shelves, and came up with a bottle labeled "Universal Livestock Disinfectant" that advertised itself to be a sovereign remedy for wounds, saddle sores, ulcers, umbilical cords, and virtually anything else since the beginning of time. She uncapped the bottle and tipped a drop or two onto her fingers and sniffed it. It appeared to be alcohol seasoned with iodine. She dug into her jacket pocket for her handkerchief.

"Here, Sergeant," she said as she let herself into the loose box. "I'll need to clean those cuts. This should do the trick." He looked at the bottle. "I'm glad you haven't taken his bridle off yet. You'll need to hold him. He may go through the roof. This stuff is almost pure alcohol." She soaked her handkerchief and knelt next to Midnight's forelegs. Gently she sponged at one or two of the smaller punctures to see how the horse would react, then worked her way up to the largest cut behind his left fetlock. The gelding shivered and started to lift his hoof; otherwise he tolerated it while she adorned his white socks with patches of brown goo. She could hear Shane murmuring to him, but she could not understand what he was saying. At length she realized she did not even recognize the language he was using. It was full of unfamiliar long vowels, choppy consonants, and sibilants like wind in grass.

Her task finished, she stood up. "There. We're done. Fortunately it's all superficial and he should heal uneventfully. None of those cuts is deep enough to require sutures. However, if it's possible, you probably shouldn't ride him until tomorrow, so you'll have a chance to see if he's going to come up lame."

"Thank you very much," Shane responded stiffly, looking into the indefinite space over her head. Nevertheless, he ran his hands down the gelding's legs, avoiding the patches of cattle medicine, then made him lift his hooves and flexed his knees and shoulders. Finally he looked directly at Jenny. "I truly owe you a debt of gratitude." Jenny did not reply, but stood watching as he removed Midnight's bridle and paused to rub the gelding's poll. The horse relaxed under his master's touch, his ears flopping comically.

Toby, finished with the two mares, let himself into the loose box. He pointed to himself and then to Midnight. Shane nodded and moved aside as Toby began rubbing the gelding down with an old towel.

"Well, I guess you'll have to come in, won't you?" She heard the hard edge in her voice and did not like it, but then, she did not like Sergeant Adair much either. For all that he was a handsome man, he had all the endearing charm of a dill pickle. She began to feel sympathetic toward Ruth Grayson.

"I assure you I will stay out of your way." His tone had an arctic blizzard behind it. She went to return the bottle to the tack room and pulled the door shut behind her. In the dim, storm-filtered light she scooted her left sleeve up. A ragged wound on the inside of her left wrist looked worse than anything Midnight had; not all the blood on the white stockings had been his. She held her breath and sloshed the viscous disinfectant into the cut, gasping at the sting that brought tears to her eyes. Then she looked up to see Sergeant Adair in the doorway, an expression of genuine concern on his face.

"Miss Weston, are you…"

"I'm all right," she interrupted, dropping her sleeve and standing as tall as she could. She replaced the bottle and brushed past him, leaving him to close the tack room door.

Rain still poured from the dark sky. She decided to leave her purchases in the buckboard until it abated. Shane sprinted to the house, running only far enough ahead to open the front door for her. Mavis turned from the kitchen counter with surprise on her face.

"Jenny! Shane! Whatever happened? Jenny, you're soaked!" she exclaimed. Richard put his week-old newspaper aside and came into the assembly room.

"If you will excuse me, I need to go upstairs and change. As you noticed, I'm wet to the skin," she said, looking at her uncle and pointedly ignoring Shane.

Once in her room, she removed the two wet letters from her pocket and set them on the still warm railroad stove to dry before she took off all her clothes, more or less in a wad, and dumped them in the drawer at the base of the armoire. Everything would need to go to the laundress except her wool jacket. Hopefully that would dry. She hung it over the foot of her bed where the air could get to it. Shivering, she donned fresh underthings, then reached beneath the bed for the medical bag she had yet to use. She sat at Aunt Alix's desk and cleaned her hands with alcohol, gritting her teeth for a second pass at the cut on her wrist. *Here I am,* she thought, *first in my class at med school, brilliantly successful internship and residence years behind me, and my first patient is a horse.* She wound gauze around her wrist and made a clumsy knot, tightening it with her teeth. Then she rubbed a dab of Honey Almond Cream into her hands and spent a moment working it into her cuticles.

Downstairs, Shane ritualistically hung his hat, rain poncho, and gun belt on the pegs by the doorway, pausing to tuck the free end of the pistol lanyard into the front of his tunic. In his oilskin rain poncho he had fared better than Jenny; his tunic was dry and his breeches only minimally damp about the knees. He accepted his customary Blue Willow mug and stirred the usual one-third of a teaspoon of sugar into the steaming tea. He was ready to take his place at the round dining table, but Richard led him into the parlor. They sat in the two leather wing chairs that flanked the fireplace.

"So, what happened out there today?" Richard prompted at length.

"There was a slight…incident with Midnight," Shane said carefully. He recounted to Richard what had happened. "Fortunately he seems all right, but I definitely can't ride back to Elk Gap tonight."

"Of course you must stay here. You know you're always welcome."

"I appreciate your hospitality."

"And if Midnight does come up lame, I'll drive you to town tomorrow." After a moment, Richard changed the subject. "But as soon as you're up to it, I do need a favor."

"Anything I can do. You know you needn't ask."

"Can you go to Thomas Wise Hand and find a saddle horse for Jenny? She told me she was going to go to Josh Barnes, and I certainly don't want that. There's also a nice, light saddle in the barn. Hopefully it'll fit. Otherwise the livery stable will have something appropriate. I don't care what I have to pay. Just get a dependable, well-broke horse. And keep in mind that Jenny is an expert horsewoman. She's even ridden in dressage and hunt seat competition, so don't insult her with a broken-down old nag."

"I wouldn't recommend Josh Barnes to my worst enemy. He'd cheat his own mother. If Midnight is all right, I'm going out to North Village tomorrow. I'll see what I can do. And yes, I could tell Miss Weston knows her way around horses. She…doesn't know about what happened to me, does she?"

"No. I don't carry tales out of school. It might go a long way to mend fences if you were to tell her why you haven't exactly been in top form the last two weeks."

"I'm fully prepared to apologize to her for Monday. And for today, too, for all that. But I'm not at liberty to discuss what happened to me. It's still an open case."

"I'll smooth things over with her for now. Then perhaps you two can at least tolerate each other." He left Shane staring into the fire, pondering his idea of Jenny Weston. At first he had thought her only another shallow professional beauty like all the society girls who had spurned him at Royal Dominion University. But there was something about her—call it an air of level-headed competence—that he could not quite put his finger on. Society debutante she might be, but there was more to her than that. She was a mystery, and the police officer in Shane lived to unravel mysteries.

****

Jenny stood before the mirror on the highboy, pulling the last of the tangles out of her wet hair, when Richard knocked on her door.

"Jen, can I have a word with you, please?" he asked.

"Come in, Uncle Richard. I'm decent." Not only was she decent, she had dressed to kill in a café-au-lait silk blouse trimmed heavily down the front with ecru Alençon lace, and had chosen to adorn the base of the high collar with a diamond-heavy gold filigree bar brooch. Her brown moiré godet skirt had a wide, pointed antebellum waistband that emphasized her tiny waist. She tucked a gold-trimmed tortoiseshell comb into the left side of her hair and another behind her right ear.

"I'm afraid you'll have to excuse my loose hair. It's too wet to do anything else with."

"I'll excuse that, and gladly." He sat down on her bed, motioning her to the chair that went with Alix's desk. "But you look like you're dressed for Sunday dinner at John's mansion."

"I have very few casual clothes," she replied coolly. "I left my hospital things at home."

"Well, perhaps Mavis will help you remedy that. However, I actually came here to talk to you about Sergeant Adair."

"What about him?"

"He's my friend. He will be my guest from time to time, and I know I do not need to remind you that this is my home and you owe it to me to be polite to any guest I choose to entertain. And rest assured I just had a similar conversation with him."

"What brought this on? Did he say something?"

"No, only that he was puzzled as to why offering to drive your team offended you. He's prepared to apologize."

"No. I want no apology. We...had words. It's true. He did offer to drive for me, and I did decline, somewhat...decisively. I'd prefer that he say as little to me as possible. But your point is well taken, Uncle Richard. This is your home, and out of respect I do owe you the duty to be civil to your guests."

"Arrogance always invites retaliation, you know,"

Richard said softly.

"Do you think I was…"

"I do. I think you still are. Look how you're dressed. You're flaunting wealth to the point of snobbery. You're obviously out to make him feel like an impoverished backwoods hick. You're angry with your father, with the medical profession, with men in general, and you want to take it out on Shane. I'm here to tell you he doesn't deserve it." She bit her lip. Her uncle was right on the money.

"I'm sorry, Uncle Richard." She felt like a chastened ten-year-old.

"And I am only going to say this once. You're wrong about Shane. He's a gracious gentleman, as educated as you are. He's had some trouble lately, and we need to give him the benefit of the doubt. Well, come down soon. Dinner is ready." He rose and exited the room, leaving it up to her whether she would comply with his request.

Within a few minutes she glided down the stairs. She had changed into a more simple forest green wool skirt and a plain cream pongee self-tied blouse adorned only with her gold pendant watch, and had gathered her damp hair into an elaborate chignon at the back of her head. She kept her eyes demurely down and pointedly ignored Shane; nevertheless, he looked awestruck as he rose from his chair. He made as if to set his empty tea mug on the piecrust table next to the wing chair, but missed and dropped it on his toe. Momentarily ignored, it rolled off onto the carpet. She could not restrain a giggle as he bent to retrieve it.

"Ready for supper?" Richard asked, standing back to let her precede him into the assembly room. She took the Blue Willow mug from Shane's hand as she passed him.

"Here. Let me wash that for you," she said unctuously, her dark eyes flashing. Shane's cheeks flushed.

"*Merci beaucoup, Mam'selle,*" he said stiffly, his Johnny-come-lately English having deserted him in his hour of need.

"*De rien*, Sergeant," she responded, her cultured Parisian French obvious against his rough Québécois. Richard cut his eyes at Shane, too, and he reddened even more. Pointedly she washed the cup and dried it, then leaned over to place it above his plate.

Richard said grace, seated Jenny, and Mavis served their food. Jenny sat primly across from Richard, as remote as the Snow Queen, ignoring Shane and paying attention to her meal.

"So, Richard, about the Balkan situation? Do you really think it means war? And if so, how soon?" Shane asked. It might have been inappropriate table conversation in some polite homes, but at table in the Weston household any topic was fair game, including very frank medical discussions. It did set them off and lasted nicely until their meal was finished, although Jenny spoke only when she was directly addressed, and for his part, Shane ignored her.

"Shane, you're staying the night?" Mavis asked.

"I have to. I can't ride Midnight just yet."

"Well, the bunks are made up fresh. I'll get you an extra blanket, too. It's going to turn cold tonight."

"Thank you."

"If I may be excused, the night's young, and I can get in a good hour or two of work before bedtime,"

Richard said.

"Of course. And I can always stand study time." Jenny rose a fraction after he did.

"Good night, Richard. Miss Weston," Shane said. Finally she looked directly at him.

"Good night, Sergeant." She gave him a remote nod worthy of her self-imposed role as Snow Queen and followed Richard upstairs.

The letters still lay on the cooling railroad stove. She picked them up and examined the first one. It bore the return address of the family home in New York. Richard's name was on the front in the elaborately curlicued cursive she recognized as belonging to her Aunt Eleanor. She set it aside, turned the other over, and her heart stopped at the sight of a Northtown imprimatur. Resisting the temptation to savage the envelope then and there, she sat down at her desk, took out the delicate filigreed letter opener that had belonged to her late Aunt Alix, and slit the flap. With shaking hands she drew out the single sheet of stationery within. Unlike her other letter from Northtown, this one was handwritten, and when her eyes skipped down to the signature, it read simply, "Stuart." Her mind conjured up an image of her father's superior, the Chief of Surgery, a tall, stocky man with greying dishwater-blond hair, sprightly blue eyes, and one of the keenest minds she had ever known. She had always been fond of Stuart Hoffman. He had been one of the few men who had never patronized her or treated her like a simpleton just because she happened to be female. Her eyes skipped back to the top.

Dear Jenny, I wanted to give you time to make it to Canada and get settled before writing to you. I know that the rejection of your application to Northtown was arbitrary and abrupt, and I apologize. However, it was something over which I had no control. I only hope you did not take it badly.

I wanted to tell you that I fought for you. I waged the greatest battle I have dared since I was appointed to the Board of Directors, and I was not successful in budging those old fuddy-duddies from their viewpoint. But I did wring a concession or two from them. One is that if you will find an active practice to join, then reapply in a year with references from any physicians with whom you are associated, the Board will reconsider your application. I think (optimist that I am) that at that point I can prevail. Your credentials are absolutely the best I have ever seen, and I know that you would be a great asset to Northtown's staff. Keep up the faith, Jenny. Do your best and I will do mine. In the meantime, write to me and let me know how you are doing. Sincerely, Stuart.

Her heart surged up into her throat and nearly choked her. So all along she'd had a very influential champion without realizing it. She had been close to giving up, but now that a door opened to her, if only a crack, she vowed she would make the best of it. If she had to write to every single doctor in the whole United States, she would find a place for herself, do her best, and hang onto her dream.

Considerably cheered, she took her favorite *Modern Obstetrical Procedures* to bed with her. She opened it at random and absorbed herself in the section dealing with manual podality. She read until her eyes grew irresistibly heavy, then blew out the hurricane lamp.

She immediately sank into such a deep sleep that when she next opened her eyes she was unaware that any time had passed. Enough moonlight shone in through her window that she could read her watch. It was nearly six o'clock, and not a sound disturbed the old farmhouse. She lay in the luxurious soft warmth of the bed until she woke completely, then she rose, stoked the little railroad stove, and dived back into the warmth of her bed. Not until the room warmed up did she rise and dress, taking her time, watching false dawn light the sky. When she heard her uncle stirring in the next room, she knocked softly on his door.

"Uncle Richard?"

"You're up, I take it?"

"I have been for almost an hour. Do you think it's safe to go downstairs?"

"Mavis is probably up already, but do you want me to go make sure the coast is clear?"

"I'd appreciate it. I don't want to intrude on your guest's privacy."

"Tell you what. Just come downstairs with me, and if there are no lights on you can go back up until I wake everyone." She trailed Richard down the stairs but need not have worried. Shane sat at the table with a mug of tea, and Mavis had already started breakfast.

"...to make your bed," she was saying. "I'd just have to unmake it later to send the sheets to the laundress. Oh, good morning, Mr. Weston. Jenny."

"Good morning, Mavis," Richard replied.

"I'll set the table," Jenny volunteered, mostly so she would not have to acknowledge Shane.

"Did your work go well last night, Richard?" Shane asked.

"Very well. I squeezed in an extra hour before I went to bed. That explains the late morning. I apologize if I'm getting you off to a bad start."

"No. I'm just going up to North Village. In this weather that's only an hour from here, give or take. Now if I were getting started from town this late, it would be a different story."

Jenny, standing with her back to the telephone, nearly jumped out of her skin when it rang. She turned and picked up the earpiece. "Richard Weston's residence. Jenny Weston speaking," she said.

"Miss Weston, this is Corporal Paul Weller, Royal Northwest Mounted Police." His voice came through the crackling static on the line.

"Oh, yes, Corporal Weller. I remember you."

"By any chance is Sergeant Adair there?"

"Yes, he is."

"What a relief!"

"Would you like to speak with him?"

"If I may, please." Jenny turned to Shane.

"It's Corporal Weller," she said, holding the earpiece out to him.

"I knew I should have telephoned them. Thank you." He stepped to the phone and tipped the mouthpiece up.

"Hello, Paul… Yes, I'm all right. I'm fine. There was a little incident with Midnight yesterday afternoon, and I had to stay here at Richard Weston's place. If Midnight isn't lame, I'm going up to North Village, and then I'll come back to town." He listened a moment. "That's fine with me. I'd actually prefer that you and Laurence do the short patrol together so he learns the beat the way I set it up. I'll see you this evening, or if I can't make it back I'll let you know... No, Paul. Midnight didn't throw me, and we didn't fall. I was dismounted when he was frightened by a bear and ran away. He got tangled and fell, or he'd have run full gallop into a barbed-wire fence. He has a few little cuts, but nothing major... All right. I'll see you this evening, or I'll telephone you and have one of you bring me another horse." He said goodbye and rang off. "Poor Paul. I did give him a turn, I'm afraid. I was just so...absorbed with what was going on that it totally escaped me that he and Laurence would worry when I went missing without a word."

"Well, then, it's a good thing I have a telephone," Richard said, then pronounced the blessing and seated Jenny before taking his own chair. Mavis came to the table with a plate of bacon and eggs and another of pancakes.

"I'd have made oatmeal, because I know how much you like it, Shane, but it takes so long. There simply wasn't time this morning," she said.

"This is wonderful. Thank you." He let Mavis serve him, politely waiting for Jenny to begin before touching his own food. *Backwoods or not, at least he has some manners,* she allowed grudgingly.

Chapter Four

A few minutes later Shane was on his way. He reined in his racing mind and paid attention to the trail that went abruptly uphill through the mixed conifer and hardwood forest. However, he was so familiar with the path after riding it at least twice a week for the last six years that his mind was soon off on its own rabbit trail again. No matter how many times he drew himself back to the present, he could not push Jenny out of his thoughts.

His artist's eyes had seen and his memory copied down a thousand small details about her, including the stubborn whorls of dark blonde hair at the nape of her neck and the little dimple below the right corner of her mouth. He wanted more than anything to loosen that hair, twine his hands into it, and kiss that tiny dimple. He knew her skin, innocent of powder or paint, would be soft, with the slight tackiness of finely woven silk, and he could immerse himself in the dark, sweet fragrance that clung about her. It intrigued him; he had never encountered it before and could not place it. He also knew how warm and yielding her body would feel against him and how her lips would meet his with only a slight hesitance as she returned his kiss. Perhaps she would be brave enough to touch his cheek or slide a hand behind his neck, and perhaps he would catch and kiss those same scented fingertips... And suddenly, in spite of the cool day, he found himself needing to take off his clothes and roll naked in the nearest snowbank.

A lot of girls have affected you that way, and you know what came of all of it, he told himself. *The moment they find out you're a half-breed, you are instantly lower than the dirt beneath their feet.* Then, as they tended to do in moments like this, his thoughts went back to his university days, the six torturous years he spent in Ottawa. He had gone to college not knowing what to expect, but talent and intelligence could take him only so far. His popularity with his professors did not extend to popularity with his peers. Even though he had tried to keep his background a secret, his Irish name, his backwoods manners and provincial French, and his Indian-black hair eventually gave him away. After that he heard it all: Métis, dirty Indian, half-breed, Mick, filthy shanty bastard...and the list went on. All that kept him at Royal Dominion had been his promise to Angus MacBride to complete the education Angus financed. That is, until he discovered hockey. His athletic skill was his ticket into acceptable society and a fraternity, and after that life at Royal Dominion at least became marginally bearable.

Then there was Claudine. Beautiful Claudine, dark and mysterious. At the time they met, his naiveté kept him from realizing her real nature. By the time he had figured out that he gave up almost ten years to her while she lived the life of a *demi-mondaine* and a kept woman for every one of those years, he had been so in love—or so in rut, he corrected himself—that he could barely see straight. She had originally contracted with him to paint her portrait. At first she had desired a simple study, sitting, clothed in sumptuous forest green velvet, but gradually she changed her mind until the portrait became a study of her posed as an odalisque, reclining nude on a pillowed chaise longue. From there to her bed turned out to be a very short distance. When she found his style of lovemaking, a product of his Iroquois upbringing, to be superb, unique, and fulfilling even to one of her jaded tastes, she took it upon herself to make a gentleman of her little diamond in the rough.

Their affair dragged on for a full three years. Pleased with one portrait after another, she kept him well. He had money and clothes, and under her tutelage he acquired a polish of sophisticated manners. Then, abruptly, she told him it was over, for she had found a lover who wanted to marry her and keep her in the style to which she had aspired all her life. When he protested and declared his undying love, she laughed at his youth, mocked his poverty, and sent him away, bruised, heartsore, and very much the wiser for the experience.

I wasn't even good enough to be dirt under the feet of an old whore, he said to himself. *What on God's green earth am I doing raising my eyes to a genuine lady like Jenny Weston? I do know what I'm doing. I'm riding for another fall, only the latest of many. And Claudine, wherever you are, I know you're laughing at me. Still.*

So why do you keep trying to deny what you are, Shane Patrick Adair? Own up to the fact that your grandfather was an ignorant squaw-man, your father was an illiterate, impoverished shanty Irish immigrant who followed the railroad, and you're related to half of North Village in one way or another and probably a bastard to boot. Not only are you not good enough for a real lady like Jenny, you could also damage her reputation past mending. Everything about her says stay away, keep your distance. Get a horse for her because Richard asked you to, bring it to him at the ranch, and then get the hell away from Jenny Weston and stay there.

His mental soliloquy proved oddly cathartic and left him with at least some sort of peace, as though he had faced the worst in himself and managed to live through it. He let the soothing rhythm of Midnight's powerful gait lull him, and by the time he could see the clearing around North Village, he was in harmony with himself again.

To his relief, everything was quiet in the settlement. When he had satisfied himself that all was well, he mounted, drew up the right rein, and touched his heel against the gelding's flank.

"All right, big man. At least that's what I heard her call you. We have an important errand," he said aloud. Midnight twitched a polite ear backward and stepped out.

Thomas Wise Hand's horse ranch lay somewhat east of North Village, down a well-defined trail that Shane had traveled often. He always stopped there when he rode territorial rounds. *Thomas is a genius where horses are concerned, as though he can read their minds,* Shane thought.

He emerged from the woods and skirted the mossy split rail fence that bounded Thomas's snow-pocked pastureland. He turned down a lane toward the rude log house where Thomas, his wife, and their two youngest children lived. His thirteen-year-old daughter, Esther, poked her head shyly out the door, giving Shane a tentative smile.

"I would speak with my uncle," he said. She gestured to the rough barn as she came to open the gate for him. He guided Midnight through, then glanced up and saw Thomas on a big red gelding, flying around the edge of the pasture fence. He bolted up to Shane and brought the gelding to a plowing stop despite the fact he was riding bareback.

"Ho, Grey Eyes," he said by way of greeting.

"Uncle," Shane replied respectfully.

"I would ride against you, but this one is no match." Tactfully he gestured to his gelding. Shane knew Thomas was letting him off because of his shoulder.

"You told me Midnight was fast, when you chose him for me." The older man grinned at the oblique compliment, his eyes almost disappearing in the weathered folds of his skin.

"He is the issue of the Grandfather of Horses, after all. He has carried you well. But what happened?" He gestured to the marks on Midnight's forelegs.

"He was frightened by a bear and stepped into barbed wire. It's not bad."

"No. He is a brave horse. A horse for a warrior, Grey Eyes." Obliquely he referred to the fact that Shane had not yet requested induction into the Warrior Society even though he was eligible.

"You chose well. And one I know needs a horse. Would you choose again?" He'd waited until there was a polite way to work his business into the conversation. It was the Iroquois way. Coming directly to the point would have been rude.

"Maybe I will choose. If I have the right horse."

"A woman. A woman very wise and very skilled

with horses."

"A Stone Dreamer," Thomas said. "A healing shaman." It was on the tip of Shane's tongue to tell Thomas he was wrong, but he had known the old man all his life. Thomas lived half in and half out of the spirit world, and there were times when he simply knew things that were beyond everyone else's ken. Yet again, Shane himself had observed an air of self-assurance and competence about Jenny that clashed with her society background. He remembered her cleaning Midnight's cuts and entertained the possibility his great-uncle might be right.

"A Stone Dreamer," he agreed. Thomas nodded. The men rode slowly in silence for some time.

"Did she help you?"

"She helped Midnight."

"Mmmm." Thomas touched his chin thoughtfully. "She will need a horse of power, a horse as wise as she is. One that will take her anywhere, in winter as well as in summer."

"Yes."

"You wait here," he commanded. Shane halted Midnight. The gelding dipped his head and rubbed his nose on his knee, shook his head until his bridle rattled, then sighed, rested a hind hoof, and stood patiently, eyes half closed. Thomas disappeared over the crest of a rolling hill while Shane looked around, taking in the beauty of the wild back country. This was his world. He loved the area, the secretive woods and the clear river he followed on his rounds. The smooth, orderly wheeling of the sky and the turning of the seasons resonated peace inside his soul. He was just considering all the Elk Gap area meant to him when Thomas came back over the hill. He still rode the red gelding, but this time he led a gold mare by a rope war bridle. She was almost as tall as Midnight, but she had a very Arab look about her. Shane had heard some people refer to these Arab-looking mustangs as Mountain Lilies. Her color was deep burnished gold, her face marked by a straight blaze, and she had a delicately tapered muzzle. A generous blanket of white spots covering her rump trailed over her hips to drip down her hocks, and she had four white socks. Her short mane and tail made streaks of white cloud against the gold of her coat. She had the classic Appaloosa striped hooves and white sclerae that gave her eyes a bright alertness.

"Your Medicine Horse!" Shane exclaimed aloud as Thomas pulled both animals to a stop.

"You know this one. She is very wise, very fearless. In the old days she would have been a warrior's first mount."

"Has she a name?"

"New life, new name. Let the Stone Dreamer call her as she will. She will learn. Would you ride her?"

"Of course I trust you, Uncle, but yes. I will ride her." Shane dismounted and took a bridle from his saddlebags. He had taken it from Richard's barn. It matched the light saddle the former owner of the ranch had left there. He wanted to make sure Thomas had trained the mare to rein; when he acquired Midnight, he had been trained only to the war bridle. Thomas took Midnight's reins while Shane dropped the loop off the mare's muzzle. He warmed the light snaffle bit in his palms for a moment, then pressed it gently against her lips. She took it politely, licking at it and settling it behind her front teeth. It took a bit of adjustment before he could drop the headstall over her ears and buckle the throatlatch. The last animal the bridle had been fitted to had evidently been smaller. He swung up, waited for a moment to ascertain that she would stand to be mounted, and touched her flanks. The mare moved out with liquid smoothness. He ran her through all her gaits, making her change leads at the canter, turning her repeatedly, and pulling her up short. She performed flawlessly, and to his surprise, she was even newly shod. He returned to Thomas.

"You have done well with this one. How much?" Up to this point, their conversation had been in Iroquois.

"Ten dollars," he replied in English. Shane was stunned. That was fully twice as much as he ever demanded for a horse.

"Done. I will bring it to you. I normally don't carry that much cash."

"You will return, Walker Between Water and Sky. You are a man of honor." He dropped back into Iroquois. "Goodbye."

"Goodbye, Uncle." It did not get past Shane that Thomas had addressed him by his ceremonial name, rather than his childhood name, Grey Eyes. He gave Thomas back his rope, took the mare's bridle, mounted Midnight, and started back down the trail toward North Village.

Chapter Five

The clicking of Mavis's Singer Sphinx filled the farmhouse. It had taken only an hour to rough out the riding skirt, although Mavis had yet to decide what to do with her striped broadcloth. She considered a skirt and a shirtwaist but had changed her mind five or six times.

"Jenny, would you mind stirring the chicken?" she asked, looking up from the sewing machine. "It should be almost ready to bone by now."

"If it is, I'm sure I can handle it. How difficult can it be, after all?" *And even if I can't cook I know bones,* she added to herself. She went into the kitchen, tied a flour sack towel around herself by way of an apron, and picked up the big slotted spoon Mavis had left on the far edge of the stove. She fished up a drumstick and the meat fell off in two pieces. It took a little delicate fiddling to lift out the splinter bone. Jenny wondered if veterinarians called it a fibula or if it was something else. Humming, she took out a bowl and started dipping the chicken out and picking off the meat with a fork. It was hot; she had to go very carefully.

"How's the chicken coming?" Mavis called from her bedroom behind the living room.

"It's done, but it's so hot yet that boning is slow work."

"I'll help you." The sewing machine stopped, and

Mavis came into the assembly room. "Well, well, I think you're about to have a visitor."

"Me?"

"Yes. Come to the window and look." Jenny came to stand next to Mavis, stretched up and peered out the window above the sink, to see Shane riding down the lane, posting to an easy trot. He led a golden vision of a mare that moved with such ethereal grace her hooves scarcely seemed to touched the ground.

"What on earth…"

"Wash up. I'll take over the chicken. I know Shane isn't coming to see me." Jenny did as she was told and was drying her hands on her towel apron as he tethered both horses to the rail and stepped up onto the porch. He started to knock, but she beat him to it and opened the door.

"Come in, Sergeant."

"Miss Weston," he acknowledged, politely removing his hat. "Yesterday Richard asked me to go to our local horse breaker, Thomas Wise Hand, and get a saddle horse for you. There's one outside for your approval, if you'd like to try her." Instead of going all the way up to her room for a wrap, she took Richard's black-and-red chopper jacket from its peg and thrust her arms into the sleeves. Shane opened the door for her, but she had eyes only for the palomino Appaloosa mare tethered next to Midnight. She walked around the horse, talking to her and touching her shoulder. The animal turned her head and regarded Jenny, blinking thoughtfully.

"Oh, she's beautiful! She… Look at that Arab head, and that round rump and deep chest. She'd have stamina to keep going all day. She's…she's incredible.

I haven't words! What's her name?"

"Thomas wouldn't tell me. He said 'new life, new name.' You have to name her. I've heard these Arab-looking mustangs referred to as Mountain Lilies, but she's technically only part mustang. She and Midnight both have the same sire—a Kentucky thoroughbred." Jenny was overwhelmed and, for the moment, speechless.

"I could call her *Ma Petite Fleur de Lis des Montaignes*. My Little Mountain Lily. Do you know your name?" At the sound of the words, the mare looked around and her fathomless gaze met Jenny's.

"I think she understands it already."

"Do you, Fleur? Do you know your name already? Huh, sweetheart?" Jenny held out her hand and Fleur lipped it gently, taking in Jenny's scent. Then Jenny cupped the mare's nose in her palms and exhaled into the soft, gold-rimmed nostrils. In response, Fleur blew hay-scented horse breath across Jenny's face. Shane had seen that done before; it was the way horses greeted each other. Fleur had just accepted Jenny into her herd.

"There's a saddle in the barn. If it fits her, would you like to ride with me a while? I'll take you up to the top of the ridge north of here; there's an exceptional view. Or if you'd prefer to try her alone, that's fine with me, but please stay on the North Village Road. It's easy to get lost around here until you know the area." Shane's invitation was shyly given, as if he expected a smart rejection.

"I do need a guide, except…" She gestured to her skirt. "You wouldn't mind if I wear jodhpurs?"

"What's the matter with jodhpurs? I'm wearing them myself."

"My jodhpurs are the kind meant to go with Pinks. However, my Pinks were fitted to me when I was fifteen and the jacket is too short now, so I didn't bother to bring it."

"Miss Weston, I couldn't care any less what you wear," he said, perhaps a little too abruptly. "We probably won't see anyone else. I'll check the saddle fit." She left him to it and returned to the house. Upstairs in her room, she dug around until she found her black jodhpurs. When she put them on, they felt a bit snug—and a bit daring, which suited her just fine, thank you. She tucked the tail of her plain white shirtwaist down into the waistband and sucked in her stomach to do up the last button. Then she dropped a black cardigan over the blouse and took up her tweed jacket. On the way out she snagged Richard's black watch cap from the pegs by the front door. Knowing that the outfit made her look like a tomboyish gamine, she plastered a satisfied grin on her face and closed the front door behind her.

Shane led Fleur out of the barn just as Jenny came skipping down the steps. "I'm ready. And thank you for responding to Uncle Richard's request so quickly. Now I can go into town without having to use that awful buckboard and those poor tired old mares."

"I'm glad to be of service," he responded stiffly, obviously wary of her.

Toby crouched to give her a leg up. She settled into the saddle and sat the mare easily, even though Fleur was perhaps a little larger than was ideal for her. When she was comfortable, she kicked her feet back out of the stirrups so Toby could correct the length of the leathers. Shane mounted a moment later. He heeled Midnight and turned him down the lane toward the road.

By the time they were at the end of the lane, she could tell her demonstration of horsemanship had left him more than a little impressed. She took extra pains to move properly with the horse, keeping her posture correct in every line. She knew she had good hands, and by the time they turned left onto the North Village Road, she read Fleur with precision.

"You really do know how to ride," he ventured at length. She felt a rush of smug satisfaction, having wrung even grudging praise from the aloof Mountie.

"Thank you. Maybe all those years of dressage lessons with Aunt Eleanor actually paid off." He asked Midnight for a trot and Fleur matched it, with Jenny posting with unconscious grace.

"I'm taking you up past the trailhead to North Village. It's maybe half an hour up to a view point where we can see way out across the valley. You'll be able to look down and see Richard's farm. Want to canter? That mare is as smooth as silk." Though it was proper to demand a canter from either a walk or a trot, Jenny had been taught that it was more formal to slow the horse first. She twitched the reins and Fleur dropped to a walk, then a mere brush of her heels brought the mare into a canter that was as fluid as the surface of a summer lake. She stubbornly set the pace for both of them. Though Fleur stood perhaps a scant half-hand shorter than Midnight, the strength of an intact mare might easily give a gelding a run for his money. After a reasonable time Shane reined Midnight in, and he dropped reluctantly to a walk.

"That's enough for now. Midnight seems to be going well, but I don't want to press him."

"That's wise. After all, you still have to ride back to town. But then, if he does show any lameness we can trade horses and Midnight can rest up in Uncle Richard's barn for a few days. Fleur is a big horse, and I'm certain she's more than strong enough to carry you." Jenny did not know whether the few exchanges that passed between them were getting less strained or more uncomfortable.

Then Shane guided them off on a side trail. She watched as he leaned down to make sure his powerful rifle was clear in its scabbard. It was a huge Model 1895 .303 Winchester Center Fire, similar to Teddy Roosevelt's favorite "Big Medicine." To Jenny it looked as huge as a field artillery piece.

"Do you always ride around armed like you're expecting war to break out at any moment?" she asked.

"What? This?" He gestured to the rifle.

"Yes. That and the huge revolver, both."

"The revolver is part of the uniform. It's fine for sobering up rowdy drunks and stopping fights, but you always carry a rifle in the woods. You never know when you're going to encounter one of Mother Nature's less friendly critters, and personally if I do I'd much rather have that rifle on my side. It's much more powerful and accurate than a pistol. Bears don't hibernate continuously, as you found out yesterday. They get up now and then, and they're always out of sorts when they do. And though it's not the season for it right now, we've all shot mad wolves from time to time." Her idea of wolves came from the Brothers Grimm, and the mere mention of rabies gave her chills. It was the only communicable disease known to man that was one hundred percent fatal.

They came to a place where the trail had washed out down to exposed rocks. Fleur lowered her head and picked her way through, scarcely slowing. Thomas Wise Hand must have spent years training her to render her such a good hill horse.

After a long climb they broke out onto the top of a ridge. For a while they had to ride single file, and then they came to a bare peak. The whole valley back toward Elk Gap was spread out before them like a snowy cloak, and on the other side, a whitewater river tumbled down a canyon. To the north, the horizon was hemmed in by high hills. Jenny had never seen anything like that panorama before.

"Oh, my," she breathed. "And you're right. I can see Uncle Richard's house, and there's the barn."

"Impressive, isn't it?"

"I've never seen anything like this. Is that the Elk River?"

"No. It's a tributary called the White Fork. It empties into the Elk River down by the railroad bridge." She tore her eyes from the incredible scenery to look at him. She had never seen hair so black on a Caucasian before. Black European hair was always some shade of very dark brown, but his was Oriental black, the highlights glassy and colorless as obsidian. She also noted that his beard was spare and fine and his sideburns ended of their own accord without the clear delineation of a razor. It all pointed to Indian blood. Mixed-blood people were often handsome in the extreme, she knew; the observation certainly fit him. His face seemed a study in contrasts: square-jawed, heavy cheekbones that lent a slight concavity to his cheeks, and a very straight and vaguely Irish nose; yet it was saved from harshness by large eyes, slightly full lips, and the long, doubly thick lashes of a child. She turned her gaze back to the panorama before he realized she was staring.

It was not long before the cold wind on the ridge forced them to start back. He led down the narrow part until they could double up along the trail.

"I think Fleur passed the test," he said at length.

"Test?"

"I was watching how she acted during the rough parts of that trail. I didn't want you on a horse that could panic and strand you way out in the back woods. I know you're an excellent horsewoman, but out here in this rough country you need a mount that will take care of you as well as Midnight takes care of me."

"I only intend to ride her around Elk Gap."

He shrugged. "One never knows," he said remotely.

They had another brief canter on the way back, and then he rode with her to the barn. Toby turned to them, ready to take their horses.

"Well, did you find the mare satisfactory?" Shane asked.

"Quite satisfactory. Thank you very much."

"Then I'll take my leave. *Au'voir*, Miss Weston." He touched his hat brim and turned Midnight back down the lane. This was the fourth or fifth time she had been subjected to his abrupt leave-taking and had been forced to say some sort of goodbye to his back. This time she did not bother. Instead, as soon as he was past the first curve in the road back to Elk Gap, she heeled Fleur and went for a joyous canter in the opposite direction.

Chapter Six

By Tuesday the respite in the weather ended decisively in a blustery arctic cold front. Shane, who had postponed his visit to North Village as long as he could, started out Wednesday morning in the tail end of a storm that had dumped more than two feet of new snow over Elk Gap and dropped the temperature at least twenty degrees. Fortunately someone with a wagon and a team had driven through around dawn, so Midnight did not have a struggle until they started up the North Village trail. With equanimity he stepped into the unbroken drifts under the winter-bare trees, picking up his hooves as they climbed. Shane's stomach tightened as he approached the first ford that crossed the creek, doubly treacherous now that the trail was obscured. But he knew he would never look at that crossing the same way again if he lived to be a hundred, because only a short while ago in that selfsame spot he had come perilously close to dying. He stopped Midnight at the bank and scanned the trees for danger, real or imaginary, then touched the horse's flanks again and let him pick his own way between the stones that lined the creek bed.

The next stretch of trail was the worst. The creek went through a series of riffles that narrowed into a steep-banked waterfall, so for perhaps a quarter mile the path veered eastward onto smoother terrain. It picked up the creek upslope, crossed one more ford, and eventually culminated at North Village. They had almost made it back to the creek when Midnight's ears flicked as though he heard something that did not belong to the familiar woods. Reflexively Shane reached for his rifle and had it half way out of the scabbard when an overpowering weight abruptly slammed into him from behind. A choking arm snaked around his neck and he saw the flash of a huge Bowie knife. He kicked his feet from his stirrups and threw himself backward against his assailant. Then Midnight, who did not like carrying double under the best of circumstances, rebelled against the burden. He reared straight up, and the weight of two large, struggling men on his back, as he stood on the layer of ice under the new snow, pulled him over backward. Shane twisted as they fell, driving his elbow into his adversary's gut. The horse's weight landed across his left leg as the combined force knocked the wind out of his assailant. Midnight rolled away and leaped to his feet. Shane only had time to turn over and face the knife wielder before he gathered himself and slashed at Shane's face, missing only as the latter ducked backward.

"Bart Hankins!" he exclaimed, trying to put enough distance between them to fish his pistol out from beneath his bear parka. He knew instinctively that in his present weakened condition he did not have the stamina to go one on one with a powerful, rugged woodsman like Bart. He had to stop this quickly or it would not end well for him.

"You dirty injun bastard! I'm going to kill you, just like you killed my brother!" Bart hissed. "You gut-shot him, and he screamed for a week before he died!" He made it to his knees and lunged forward. Shane dug up a handful of snow and flung it at Bart's eyes. It blinded him for only an instant, but it was time enough for Shane to roll onto his back and lash out at Bart's chest with both heels. He connected soundly and felt the shock up to his hips as he threw Bart backward. At the same time he found his pistol lanyard, gave it a yank, and the big Colt slid into his hand. As Bart shook off the vicious kick and flung himself forward again, Shane cocked the hammer of his revolver and pulled the trigger. He did not bother to aim. Not only did he not have time, but at such a point-blank distance he could not miss. The report resounded through the trees with an echo like thunder, the recoil slammed the pistol grip into his hand and the side of Bart's head exploded in a cloud of blood and brain matter. Shane rolled out of the way of the convulsing body that fell toward him and slumped backward in the snow, his heart trying to claw its way out of his chest. His half-healed shoulder throbbed with liquid agony, and he realized that the cushion of snow was all that had saved his left knee.

It was Midnight that finally brought Shane back to the present. He was not used to seeing his master lying on the ground. His equine curiosity took over, and he reached down and nosed at Shane's cheek, inhaled deeply, and huffed out a steamy cloud of warm breath. Shaking in the aftermath of adrenaline overload, Shane pushed ineffectually at the gelding's nose and levered himself up into a sitting position. Then, after several minutes, he was able to grab a stirrup and haul himself to his feet.

He finally dared a look at his enemy. Bart lay perhaps a foot from the creek, his blood soaking into the snow. As Shane stood above the body, his breathing slowed and he was able to make sense of Bart's words. They took him back to the ambush he'd survived three weeks ago. After he was shot, he had emptied his revolver in the general direction of the sniper, not knowing whether he had hit anything. Bart's brother Red had retreated through the trees, giving Shane only enough of a glimpse to recognize him. After that he had no energy to waste on pursuing his assailant. The situation degenerated into a tooth-and-nail fight to stay mounted and make it back to Elk Gap without losing consciousness.

He was not sure he was in much better shape now than he had been that terrible afternoon. Weak and aching, he gathered his reins. It took him three tries to make it into the saddle. Numbly he turned the horse back the way they had come and prepared for another endurance ordeal that would test his determination for the second time in a month.

By the time he made it to the North Village road, he was chilled to the bone and shaking inside his furs. On the way into Elk Gap, he rode past the entrance to Richard's lane and found himself sorely tempted to stop, but doggedly he kept on, from one breath to the next, until he passed the outskirts of the town.

The sight of a blanketed Brandy tethered outside Mrs. Hammill's told Shane that Paul had finished short patrol around town and gone inside. He said a prayer of thanks in every language he knew as he reined Midnight to a stop next to the mare. He set himself to dismount, but pain tore through his shoulder, and he barely managed to get his left foot out of the stirrup before falling backward against Brandy. She could be cranky when she chose, but this time she sidestepped into him and kept him on his feet. Then out of nowhere Paul materialized next to him and put an aiding arm around his partner's shoulders.

"Shane, what on earth happened to you?" he asked.

"Up on the trail. I was attacked. Bart Hankins had a knife. I shot him. You'll have to ride up and get the body. I couldn't... Midnight fell with us..."

"Let's get you inside. You can tell me the rest then," Paul interrupted, guiding him up the steps and into the warmth of the small room they used as their constabulary. He let Paul help him out of his furs and press a mug of tea into his chilled hands. He gasped out the rest of the story while the welcome warmth suffused back through his bones. This time he managed to make sense.

"I knew you shouldn't have tried that ride in this cold. You've been pushing yourself much too hard over the last couple weeks. You should have let me go. I know enough French to get by with those people," Paul said impatiently. "But I guess it doesn't matter now. Are you all right?"

"I...I think so. My shoulder hurts, and Midnight fell on my leg, but I can tell nothing's broken. It just has to wear off."

"All right, Shane. You haul your backside upstairs and get yourself into bed. I'll go up there and investigate things and write it up. Let me have Midnight so I can bring the body back."

"Go ahead. But...it's bad, Paul. I shot him point blank in the head."

"I'll take a tarp with me. Don't worry. I'm a big boy. You get up to your room, or do I need to haul you up there by the seat of your pants?"

"I'll go. I promise." He put his empty cup down on the desk and left the room, feeling at least a hundred years old. Suddenly the stairs to the third floor looked as tall as the Matterhorn. He managed them one step at a time, and when he arrived in his room he shucked out of his tunic, pried his boots off, and lay down heavily on the bed. He pulled the top blanket around himself and fell asleep in a heartbeat.

When he awoke, dark had fallen and he had missed supper. Even though he had not eaten since breakfast, he was not hungry. Moodily he consulted his pocket watch. At barely six-thirty, it was too early to go to bed, especially after his long nap, and for once he had completed all his paperwork. He stood up, flexed his shoulder, and found it much less sore than he had feared. Listlessly he went to the table where his portable easel held the study of three wolves he had started a month ago. Picking up a pencil, he made a few strokes, grew bored, and took a fresh piece of paper and started to doodle. As he sat thinking, his mind drifted back to the previous Friday when he had been stranded at Richard's farmhouse, and he realized he was trying to sketch Jenny's face. But his artist's eye was not satisfied with his memory. While he knew he had reproduced her features with reasonable accuracy, the crackling, vibrant intensity of her personality had escaped him. With a sigh he rose, took his hockey skates out of his foot locker, snagged his heavily beaded white wolf parka from the armoire, took up his hat and cavalry gauntlets, and left the room for the short walk to the church.

The Calvary Presbyterian Church choir always

rehearsed on Wednesday night. Those who did not sing gathered next door at the old millpond to skate. Once an early sawmill had occupied the site, but it had burned down years ago. The smoke-blackened stone foundations remained as the only evidence the mill had ever existed. The pond eventually became the main recreation site for the Elk Gap children: a swimming hole in summer and a safe place to skate in winter.

Though he had walked slowly, he found himself one of the first to arrive. He sat down on a log next to Will Tillman and let his skates slump to the ground. That night he felt ambivalent about skating, and doubly so if the local boys started their usual sandlot hockey game.

He and Will traded pleasantries, and then the conversation lay momentarily dormant while Will filled his pipe. Shane took the opportunity to look around. A few more people had arrived, among them Ruth Grayson. He still could not think of her without a twinge of regret. He knew now that he actually had not loved her. However, the abrupt way she had broken off their relationship had left a raw spot. He understood her reasons, though. Too soft and sensitive to deal with the dangers of his work, she worried herself to distraction the moment he left her sight. The incident with Red Hankins had proved that, fortunately sooner rather than too late. In the end he had assured her they would remain friends, but his November-born personality, tending to see things in black and white rather than shades of grey, decided then and there that he would not go out of his way where she was concerned.

Ruth started toward the frozen pond, then apparently changed her mind and came up to the bonfire. Tactfully Will excused himself, though Shane wished he had not.

"Hello, Shane," she began. He had never liked the hesitant timidity in her tone.

"Hello, Ruth." He heard his own voice flat, the only remnant of his Iroquois accent. It came back in times of emotional stress.

"May I sit down?" By way of reply he slid over, pulling his skates after him. She gave him an intense look, her eyes yielding when his did not. "I just want to say that I'm...I'm very sorry..."

"Don't apologize. If whatever was between us was wrong for either of us it was wrong for both. It's best aired at the outset. You couldn't live with my occupation and I can't live without it. It's as simple as that." She had been looking at her hands. Finally she lifted soft eyes to his.

"I tried, believe me. I tried very hard."

"I know you did. I shall always be grateful to you for that. Still in all, how do you think it made me feel to know that I made you unhappy?"

"It's not that at all. It was never your fault. I'm sorry for the way things turned out between us, but it was inevitable. I only regret telling you when and how I did. I should have waited until you were better. I was just...overwhelmed by what had happened."

"It was no extra hardship, not really. I'm grateful for your honesty. It's one of those situations where getting the truth out into the open was better done sooner than later."

"I thought you'd feel that way. You're that sort. How is your shoulder?"

"Healing well. It's a little sore yet, though I'm

drawing again. I'm not up to rounds or hockey, but it's only a matter of time."

"I'm glad. Well…" She sighed and looked away.

"Yes?" he prompted.

"I really do wish you all the best. I'm very fond of you, you know. I suspect I always shall be."

For an instant he felt a familiar rush of affection. Ruth was a dear person. "I know you'll find happiness," he said. In the dancing light of the bonfire he saw the sparkle of incipient tears in her eyes.

"Thank you," she whispered, then she fairly ran from him, stopping at one of the logs around the pond to put her skates on. He looked past her and happened to see Richard's wagon pulling up in the snowy field next to the pond. The figure next to him did not look tall enough to be Mavis. It had to be Jenny. *Wonderful,* he thought wryly. *I looked forward to not seeing her for at least another month.* However, his mind sized her up against Ruth. In contrast to Ruth's softness, Jenny had courage enough for an army. It showed in the way she had run after Midnight with a total disregard for her own safety. And he had to admit he respected her horsemanship and her quick mind. Curiously, he found she held some mysterious attraction for him, but whether it would prove to be simply the fascination of a puzzle or something deeper he did not yet know. He watched Richard give her a hand down from the wagon. Remarkably graceful and delicate in all she did, she managed to look slender despite her heavy clothing and the bulky fur coat. Her hand was still through Richard's arm when they came to the edge of the pond.

Shane watched as they laced their skates and chatted with several of the new arrivals. Practically everyone at Calvary had arrived by now. The Tillman tribe had already taken to the ice, along with the equally numerous Redfields. Jenny and Richard glided sedately side by side, and as Jenny limbered up she did a fluid turn, skated backward in front of him for a while, then resumed her position at his side. It appeared she skated as well as she rode. Shane sat moodily on the log, bundled in his silver-white wolf parka bright with bands of brilliantly colored beadwork, and watched the skaters. Warren Redfield flew up to the edge of the pond and executed a violent spray stop that came within half an inch of the bank.

"Sergeant Adair, come on! You're missing a good game," he called.

"Sorry. My shoulder's not up to hockey yet," he replied with a halfhearted wave.

"Well, next week, then." The boy dug his skates in and flew back to the game that was heating up at the far end of the pond.

Shane was not the type to sit on his hands. He quickly had enough of being the Little Match Girl watching everyone else have fun. He was good enough on skates that he would not fall unless he was showing off, and at any rate, Angus would not be there to give him a public bawling out. He stood up slowly, keeping the pain off his face only with effort. Why he had come skating after such a horrendous day was beyond him. There was always next week, after all. Deep inside he knew, against all logic and despite his mixed feelings, that it had to do with the possibility of seeing Jenny Weston again.

He picked up his skates and went to one of the logs at the edge of the pond. He levered off his Strathcona boots, familiarly called "high browns," pulled on his skates, and then tied them carefully before stepping onto the ice.

Like the rest of the local boys, he had skated since he could walk. However, he rarely skated simply for its own sake. In his mind, skating and hockey were inseparable. In college he had thrown himself into the sport, since it bridged the great cultural gap between him and the rest of the students at Royal Dominion. He played Right Forward and captained his team for two years, the last of which ended in an undefeated season. At times he missed the excitement, but, he reflected, he would not trade places with anyone. He loved his home and his work, and he had a wide circle of friends. What more could a person want? But hard on the heels of that thought the answer welled up inside his heart: acceptance for what he was, and more importantly, love.

He was deep in reflection, his feet moving automatically, when he joined the procession of people skating counterclockwise around the pond. Little Alice Redfield, still wearing two-bladed training skates, waddled around against the traffic, bumped into his leg, and abruptly sat down, giggling. Alice, an angel child, barely four, blue-eyed, golden-haired, apple-cheeked, and still baby plump, had long ago wormed her way into his heart. He went down on his unbruised knee and set her back on her feet.

"Alice, you're going the wrong way. You have to skate the same direction everyone else does. See your sister over there?" He pointed to Belinda and her inseparable friend Julia Tillman.

"Yes," Alice said, favoring him with a pixie grin.

"Well, go skate with her. That way you won't run into people. Now give me a hug, then go on." Alice threw her arms around his neck.

"Your coat tickles," she giggled, giving him a squeeze. "Can I skate with you?" Skating "with" someone, by Alice's definition, consisted of hanging on for dear life and being pulled around the ice at a frantic pace. He indulged her as often as he could, but his shoulder felt so painful that he did not want to bend down.

"Maybe later, Alice. I'll tell you what. I'll take you to Belinda. How's that?" Fortunately she stood tall enough that he did not have to stoop to reach her. Holding his fingers in a red-mittened hand, she duck-paddled along beside him, then finally gave up and let him tow her. He turned around in front of her and she gleefully grabbed his thumb with her opposite hand. Then she pulled his gauntlet off and plunked down on her backside again. He had sunk half way into a brown study, but Alice proved irresistible. Her laughter went to the center of his heart like summer sunshine. This time he picked her up, settling her carefully on his right forearm.

Shane liked children, and it was reciprocated. They flocked around him wherever he went. Even though he had no living siblings, he had long ago become very used to babies. By Iroquois custom, North Village children were raised Indian fashion: all adults parented all children, the older children watched the younger ones, and the children themselves formed one big group of brothers and sisters.

Still carrying Alice, he took a shortcut across the center of the pond and arrived in front of Belinda and

Julia.

"Good evening, ladies. I have a delivery for you," he said, relinquishing Alice to her older sister.

"Thank you very much, Sergeant Adair," Belinda said, corralling Alice, who still wanted to follow him.

Soon the notes of Ben Redfield's harmonica floated over the lake, carrying well in the cold, still air. He was playing *Shenandoah*, a tune that even Shane, with his completely tin ear, could feel.

"Dance with me, Uncle Richard?" he heard Jenny ask as he carefully skated past them.

"Why, Miss Weston, I'd be honored," Richard replied loftily, bowing over her hand. She glided into his arms, and they began a sedate circuit of the pond. Easily following his long, slow turns, Jenny appeared to be thoroughly enjoying herself.

Ben stopped playing and shook the condensation out of his harmonica at the same moment Shane coasted up. He executed a quick but decidedly inelegant turn and came to a spray stop. Jenny stepped out, keeping hold of Richard's hand.

"Good evening, Miss Weston. Richard." He solemnly touched the brim of his Stetson.

"Good evening, Sergeant," she responded primly. However Richard seemed determined to make something of their chance meeting.

"Hello. I'm surprised to see you here, since you're usually on rounds the last two weeks of the month."

"Paul will be taking rounds for me this month. We're going to swap off from now on. I can't say I'm sorry. He won't have it easy. The trail to North Village is barely passable right now. I know because I tried to get up there this morning."

"I'm glad Superintendent Shepherd found someone to do that for you. You deserve a respite, however brief."

Shane made a wry face. "It'll be brief. I'll have to do Paul's report, and both his handwriting and his spelling are abominable." Ben began to play again, this time a Strauss waltz. Shane made a great effort to appear casual in Jenny's presence. "Miss Weston, may I have this dance—with your permission, of course, Richard?" he asked, extending his hand. He saw her surprised look. Then her eyes went quickly to her uncle's face as though pleading for rescue.

"Naturally you have my permission. As charming and delightful as my niece's company is, I'll not monopolize it."

As he swept Jenny into his arms, he wondered what imp had made him say what he had. Her hand came to rest across the top of his shoulder. Since her hand was cushioned by her sable muff and the thick fur of his parka, he barely felt her light touch. Ditto for the small, gloved right hand that lay ethereally in his. But it still quickened his heartbeat and brought blood to his cheeks in a way that Ruth had never managed to do.

Jenny had perfect manners to go with her expensive appearance. Her eyes sought his face as he pushed off, letting her skate forward for the moment. Then he guided her into a gentle turn, which she executed as easily as he did.

"I was watching you dancing with Richard earlier. You're quite good," he remarked after they had both picked up the rhythm of Ben's waltz.

She gave him a debutante's staged smile that looked no more than skin deep. "Thank you. But from your hockey skates I'd expect you to be involved in that game over there."

"Normally I would, but I've had a demanding day. I tried to go up to North Village, but the last half mile is impassable right now. It was a difficult slog back to the road. Besides, I like to dance. You must, too."

"As a matter of fact, I do." Politely looking up at him, she followed his lead. During his college years in Ottawa he had learned to dance and actually enjoyed it. From there it was a small transition to ice. Two gentle turns made him realize she was even more proficient than he had given her credit for. She followed easily, as light as a feather against him. Richard's somewhat indifferent skating skills had not presented Jenny at her best. *There's way more depth to her than I realized,* he thought. *I wonder what else she is going to do that will surprise me.*

Then a violin joined Ben. "Who's playing now?" she asked.

"That's Jacques Delacroix."

"Oh, yes, the barber here in town. I've heard his name, but we've never met."

"That's not surprising. He keeps to himself. He's a good musician, though. Somewhere along the line he's had formal training. He's not the common run of hoedown fiddler you usually find out here in the back country."

"Yes, I can tell he's no rank amateur." As Jacques warmed up to his music, Shane became a little more daring, and soon he and Jenny were dancing in wide, sweeping turns as though they were in a ballroom instead of on the ice. As Jacques dragged Ben through "Tales of the Vienna Woods," Shane became so absorbed in what he was doing he did not realize almost everyone else had withdrawn from the ice to watch them dance. Then, after once through "The Beautiful Blue Danube," Jacques paused to retune, and Shane came to.

"Well, it looks as though we collected quite an audience," he remarked. "Thank you very much for the dance."

"It was my pleasure entirely." She set a toe pick into the ice and dipped the smallest curtsey, and he had the feeling that the onlookers would have applauded had they not been muffled in gloves and mittens. He gave her his arm to escort her back to Richard.

"You skate so well. Have you taken lessons?"

"Years of them. And you?"

For the first time he smiled just a little. "I'm afraid I'm just a rusty old college hockey player," he said self-deprecatingly. "May I have another waltz later, or is your program full?"

"I believe there may be a space or two left."

"Then consider them filled."

"You flatter me, sir."

"Believe me, Miss Weston, that is indeed my intention." This was the same kind of courtly flirtation he engaged in with Belinda and Julia. He did not expect it to penetrate Jenny's hard veneer.

She returned to Richard's side, skated with a few other people, including Reverend Aubrey, and Shane retreated to sit by the bonfire for a while. But after escorting Belinda around the pond and then Julia, followed by the slightly older Mary Ann Tillman, he found his way back to Jenny. He checked by dragging his left skate behind him and gave her a shallow bow, extending his hand.

"Miss Weston, I believe this is my dance," he said.

"Why, Sergeant Adair, I do believe you're right! This *is* your dance, sir."

He drew her toward him only with difficulty. His arm had turned stiff, and when he held his hand out for hers, there was a flash of pain.

"What did you do to your shoulder?" she asked. His eyes flared wide for an instant. He had thought he covered it well.

"Midnight fell with me today," he said. It was the truth, but not the whole truth. Mentally he crossed his fingers and asked forgiveness for the white lie. "You know he's a good hill horse. I've had him for five years, and we've been through some dicey places together. Until today he's only fallen with me once, and that was more my fault than his. But today, coming down from North Village, we encountered some ice under the snow, and before either of us realized what was going on, he went down."

Her forehead puckered. "You didn't land with your arm extended, did you?"

"No. I had sense enough to tuck my elbow in, but I did land on it. It's really nothing. I'm all right and so is Midnight, but both of us will ache for a day or two."

"If you're sure it's nothing…" She was cutting a little close to the bone, and he could not help shutting the door on the subject.

"I assure you, there's nothing wrong. I'm a bit sore here and there, but it's nothing to bother Doctor MacBride with." His tone suddenly became as cold as the winter evening. He went into full guarded mode, unwilling to risk another cold rejection.

"I'm sorry, Sergeant. I didn't mean to pry, really." She looked down as though properly chastened. Then she turned her eyes to his face and gave him a melting smile. "It's only that I'm concerned for you." The latter was obviously designed to disarm his hostility. It worked beautifully. His face and his heart both softened immediately.

"Please excuse me. I didn't mean to be brusque. I...I'm not exactly at my best right now."

"Then why don't we sit out this dance? I could use a few minutes next to the fire."

To turn beside her he pivoted on the tip of his left skate, the quick, ungraceful move of an ingrained hockey player.

"I'd be glad to accompany you, but why are you smiling like that?"

"Your hockey turn just now. It wasn't pretty, not at all like the way you were skating when we danced."

He smiled crookedly. "When you're chasing the puck down through a line of defenders who'd just as soon rip your head off as look at you, pretty is the last thing you think about." He gave her his arm, and she let him escort her off the pond. They both paused, politely allowing one another a balancing arm as they put on blade guards. Then they made a cautious way to one of the logs, long ago roughed into benches, about the bonfire. She sat down, and he sat only close enough to her to be polite.

"So you played hockey at university?"

"Royal Dominion in Ottawa. Right Forward. I was captain for two years. Our last season went undefeated."

"My, what an achievement! Do you ever miss it?"

"Sometimes. But I like my work, and I have a lot of friends here." The arrival of Nora Redfield with a chilled and tired Alice forced Shane to move a little closer to Jenny. The silver fur of his flashy parka brushed her sleeve. She slipped her right hand out of her glove and touched it.

"What is your parka made of? It's absolutely beautiful, especially the beadwork."

"It's wolf, lined with lynx, and the hood trim is wolverine fur because it doesn't frost over with the moisture from your breath. The beadwork is a modern thing. They used to use dyed feather quills pounded flat, but the dyes bleed when they get wet, and beads are both more sturdy and more colorful." His parka had bright geometrically patterned bands, perhaps two inches wide, down the center of the back, around the neck, and down both sides of the front storm closure, where it turned in an arc and went around a few inches above the bottom hem. An identical band ran over the top of each shoulder and down the outsides of the sleeves, meeting the strips around the neck and cuffs. The corners had been rounded out with big, curving swirls of bright primary colors.

"It's spectacular."

"Thank you. Someone up in North Village made it for me. It's actually warmer than my bear furs, but the beadwork is somewhat delicate, so I don't wear it in the woods."

"Would you show me the lynx fur?" Obligingly he turned the bottom of the storm closure back, revealing the soft, stipply tan lining. She touched it with the backs of her fingers. "It's so soft."

"It is. Rabbit is actually softer and warmer, but it

sheds. I had a parka lined with rabbit once. I gave it away because whenever I wore it my Red Serge came out grey, and it would take me half a day with a wet cloth to get the hair off."

"I understand why you got rid of it."

"The breeches are forgiving, but anything you get on a Red Serge shows." Hoping to deflect her attention, he changed the subject. "How is Fleur? Have you ridden her?" he asked. Jenny smiled with delight.

"Every single day. That mare is a miracle. She will do literally anything I want her to. I think I'll start training her in dressage. She's almost there already."

"I'm glad she meets with your approval. I had some misgivings."

"Why ever?"

"Richard told me about your background and the blood horses your family owns."

"Appaloosa is a recognized breed."

"I've seen some downright ugly Appaloosas."

"She certainly isn't one of them."

He looked down. "No. She isn't. Then if you're warmed up enough, may I have that dance?"

"I'm quite comfortable now. I'd be pleased." At the water's edge she rested her hand on his forearm while she slipped off her blade guards, then allowed him to balance against her shoulder while he did the same.

This time they did not dance but merely skated side by side, hands joined right to right and left to left. He was grateful for her understanding; his shoulder was aching, he was tired, and the only reason he had not already started for home—indeed, the reason he had come in the first place—was the sable-wrapped, chin-high enigma skating next to him. He knew he would do it again, given the chance.

And to his surprise, he was already planning to see her again.

Chapter Seven

The cold front ran into a raging blizzard that isolated Richard's farmhouse for an entire week. Finally it blew itself into exhaustion, and Elk Gap dug out. Jenny had busied herself with sewing and learning to cook, and had even been pressed into a final proofreading of *Milestones.* It gratified her to no end that she discovered three typesetting errors.

The morning routine of the Weston household varied little. After she heard Richard stirring in his room, Mavis started the fire and made tea, and she and Jenny often enjoyed a chat before he showed his face downstairs. As a result, ten o'clock came before dishes were done and the day's chores began. Since Toby cared for the animals, even to gathering eggs and milking the cows, and the laundress came weekly, wintertime brought a tangible paucity of work. Jenny helped Mavis out of a desire to keep busy rather than any necessity, and, on the morning that would prove to be the biggest turning point in her entire life, she had just returned the last of the tea mugs to the shelf when Mavis parted the curtains above the sink.

"It appears we have a visitor who's in quite a rush," she said.

"Oh?"

"Yes. Look. It's Shane, riding at a dead gallop." Jenny stood on tiptoe to peer over Mavis's shoulder.

Through the winter-bare orchard she glimpsed the big, white-stockinged gelding flying down the lane. Shane was riding like an Indian, up and forward in the saddle with his legs plastered against Midnight's sides and the hood of his wolf parka blown back. He did not check his speed until he was up to the porch, where he bounced down before the horse stopped. The cold had reddened his face, and his hair lay every which way in wind-ruffled confusion. He flipped the reins around the porch rail and took one long-legged step over all three stairs. Jenny pulled the door open before he had a chance to knock and closed it behind him.

"I need to…use the telephone," he gasped. "I have to…to call Angus MacBride. There's been an accident at North Village." He caught his breath forcibly.

"What happened?" Jenny's calm question caught him off balance.

"A thirteen-year-old boy stepped in a leg-hold trap. It almost took his foot off, and when he realized he couldn't get out and he'd lie there until he froze to death, he took out his hunting knife and finished the job, then tied his belt around his leg and crawled home. I've controlled the bleeding, but without medical attention in the next few hours he'll die. I have to call Angus right away and pray he can make it all the way up there." Jenny's mind smoothly shifted gears.

"Take me with you. I'm a medical doctor. I'm fit to make the trip, and I'm an hour closer." *Now I've done it,* she thought. *The cat is out of the bag and all of Elk Gap will think they have a two-headed sideshow freak on their hands. But I had to own up. A life is at stake.*

"You're a what?" She watched his light eyes go wide with shock and surprise as he sat abruptly on the nearest kitchen chair.

"Medical Doctor. University of Virginia, Class of 1907. Internship at Atlantic Memorial, Arlington, Virginia, and Surgical Residence at Mount Hope General Hospital, New York City."

"You are telling me the truth, aren't you? If so, you're a godsend!" The relief and gratitude in his eyes erased the misgivings she'd had only a moment before and loosed a return rush of gratitude in Jenny. Possibly Sergeant Adair could prove himself the exception to the jealous hostility she had experienced from every other man who knew of her academic and scientific achievements.

"I'll show you my credentials, if you'd like," she offered, extending professional courtesy.

"That's not necessary. You couldn't have me on about something that serious. Can you really help Jimmy? Do you have everything you need, then, or do we need to go to town and get supplies from Angus?"

"No, there's nothing I need. It's all upstairs."

"Oh, Miss Weston, that explains so much!" She had no idea what he meant by that remark. "Would you come with me, then? Jimmy Richardson may not have much time."

"I'll go change clothes."

He finally found his feet. "Wear whatever you have that's warm. It's cold out there," he called as she flew up the stairs. "Mavis, I need to get Fleur saddled. If she comes down in the next minute or two, I'm in the barn." This time it was Mavis who said goodbye to his retreating back.

Jenny took the stairs two at a time, and on her way to dress she stopped momentarily to stick her head into her uncle's room.

"There's a medical emergency at North Village. I'm going with Sergeant Adair."

"So you told him?"

"Yes. I wouldn't have, but it's a traumatic amputation. That means there's not a moment to spare. I have to leave immediately." Without waiting for his reply, she ducked into her room, yanked off her skirt and petticoat, then pulled on two pairs of skating socks and her divided riding skirt. Two sweaters followed, and she reached beneath her bed for her black alligator medical bag. She rejected her wonderfully warm sable coat because she could not ride in it. That left only her somewhat unsatisfactory brown tweed jacket. It would have to do. At that moment Mavis came up the stairs with her own hip-length black fox coat in her hands.

"Here, Jenny. I know it's too big, but put on another sweater. You'll freeze otherwise."

"Thank you, Mavis. I promise I won't wear it out."

"So you're a medical doctor. I swear, I never! Well, then, good luck and Godspeed."

"I only hope I can treat this case successfully. That's how it's done, Mavis. One case, one patient, one procedure at a time." She put mittens on over her rabbit-lined gloves and let Mavis tuck her own heavy, knitted fascinator down the front of the jacket. By the time she was back downstairs, both Toby and Shane were outside with the horses. Shane took her bag and secured it in his saddlebag while Toby gave her a hand up. She gathered Fleur's reins and followed Shane's breakneck gallop down the lane and out onto the North Village Road.

Even at the pace he set, she paid attention to where

she was going. In the fortnight she had been riding Fleur, she had seen the trailhead to North Village, but mindful of his warning to stick to the road until she knew her way around, she had not done much but explore the first quarter-mile. She had turned back when the going became rough.

As soon as the trail started up the hill, he slowed to a walk. It climbed precipitously, full of switchbacks and rough places, and would obviously be dangerous at a faster pace. Twice it crossed a creek, where the footing became precariously icy. She wondered if Midnight's fall had been in one of these treacherous spots. She gave Fleur her head and let the mare choose her own path. Fleur put her nose down and picked her way deliberately until the trail smoothed out, then relaxed and pulled up the hill with all the legendary Appaloosa strength and stamina and the quiet confidence of consummate training.

The farther they went up the ridge, the deeper and darker the woods became. Then they dropped over the top and onto a relatively flat area or, Jenny thought, an area at least less steep. She saw smoke ahead, and a thinning in the trees that might be called a clearing. That had to be North Village. When the trail widened. she drew Fleur abreast of Midnight.

"Is that where we're going?" she asked, pointing vaguely to their left.

"Yes. It's not far now. But we're still not moving above a walk. Come summer, when the snow is off, you'll see just how rough this is." She took his warning to heart and dropped back, letting him break trail.

The sun was climbing toward noon as they arrived in North Village. "Village" seemed a dignified name for the varied structures laid out circle-fashion, like an Indian encampment. She counted only three substantial log buildings. Her heart twisted when she took in the rest, a strange and ramshackle combination of wattle and daub, hides, salvage lumber, and brush. *Don't tell me people actually live in those,* she thought, a chill going through her. *They're just asking for an epidemic here.*

"This is North Village," he said, with one all-inclusive gesture of his left hand. He paused to indicate a white clapboard structure a hundred yards or so to the west. "That's the schoolhouse and also Father André's church."

He rode through the center of the circle, past a depression in the snow that looked like a very large fire pit. She tried not to stare as dark eyes peered from doorways and childish faces peeked out from behind corners. It seemed routine to Shane, for he did no more than glance around as he led her to the largest house in the village, a good-sized shotgun log cabin with a cedar shake roof and a porch set well off the ground on sturdy piers.

Shane dismounted and tied his reins around the porch railing, then turned to help her down. This time, however, Jenny did not wait for him but tethered the mare herself while he untied her medical bag.

They were met at the door by a tall, graying woman of indefinite age. Her eyes, so black they lacked clear delineation between iris and pupil, regarded Jenny without expression. She wore a belted buckskin dress with a blaze of bright beadwork across the shoulders, and she had drawn her hair back into a single, wrist-thick braid. Shane said something to her in his language of soft sibilants, and Jenny realized she had heard the same Iroquois when he had quieted Midnight while she cleaned his wire cuts. The older woman nodded, ushering them into the warm cabin.

Jenny took it all in with one brief glance. To her right, a huge fireplace of river-worn granite stones dominated the whole wall; a fire leaped brightly on the hearth. One rocking chair stood close to it, draped with a bear robe; an ancient Sharps buffalo rifle dominated the mantelpiece; and a collection of traps, snowshoes, parflèches, and bright, dried corn hung suspended from the rafters. Then the world narrowed to her patient.

She had expected to find him in the bedroom, but instead he lay beneath a three-point Hudson's Bay blanket on the long table at the far end of the room. His slim body made only a small, pathetic shape beneath the cover, his face ashen and his eyes filled with terror. Shane spoke to the woman who hovered beside him, evidently his mother, and she and a slightly younger boy stood aside.

"His name is Jimmy Richardson," Shane volunteered. "These people are his mother and his brother, and the other woman is his aunt. Incidentally, this is her house. They want to know what you need." Jenny peeled her coat, gloves, and scarf off in one motion, dropping them on a bench.

"Hot water to wash, and I need to boil my instruments. Then the fire must be put out completely."

Shane gave her a questioning look. "You want them to put the fire out?"

"Ether is flammable."

"Oh. Of course."

Jenny turned to the boy. She stroked the sweaty

hair from his forehead and took his hand reassuringly. "Jimmy, everything will be all right. I'm a doctor and I'm here to help you. Don't be afraid. Do you understand?" He nodded, drawing meaning from her tone even though he might not have understood everything she said. His pulse was racing from shock and fear, but it was strong. At least she had that much to go on.

Shane had evidently forewarned them, for a large kettle of water just below a rolling boil hung over the fire. She set her medical bag on the bench next to the fireplace, sorted out the instruments she would need, set them in a rack, and lowered it into the scalding water. Then she dipped some out into a graniteware basin, rolled her sleeves back, tied an apron over her clothes, washed her hands, and rinsed them with alcohol.

"Sergeant, I'll need your help in a minute, but all I'm going to do now is examine him." She turned the blanket back, and Jimmy whimpered in terror. Shane laid his hands gently on the boy's shoulders, speaking to him softly in Iroquois. She lifted the makeshift bandage away from his lower leg—Shane had only folded something like a towel around it—and swallowed hard at the abomination she saw. The trap had all but severed his leg just above the ankle. Its jaws had shattered and degloved the tibia and fibula, and she could see where he had severed the last remaining strip of skin. *You brave, brave child*, she thought, near tears. She replaced the makeshift dressing.

"I'll perform a proper amputation and give him a stump he can walk on," she said quietly. Shane nodded. "Tell him I think he's very brave, and tell him he'll walk again. Also, tell him I won't touch him until he's completely asleep, and he won't feel a thing. You can handle the ether for me, but if you're the least bit squeamish, don't stay. If you start to feel lightheaded or sick, get out immediately. Understand?" He looked startled as she took charge, but she kept her gaze level, asking for his acquiescence to her authority.

"I understand."

"Good. And ask him when he last had anything to eat or drink." She took a new ether mask from her bag, filled the reservoir, and set the mask aside while Shane talked to the boy.

"He said he ate supper last night but all he's had today was water early this morning."

"Good. That's probably going to save him a lot of misery. Tell him that in a few minutes he'll go to sleep, and when he wakes up he'll feel better, his leg will be fixed, and everything will be all right." She completed the final preparations for surgery. She took the rack with her instruments from the boiling water and wrapped a sterile towel around it, then brought it to the table and set it down out of Jimmy's line of vision.

"Now, please have them put the fire out." After a little discussion, the boy's aunt went outside, and a moment later two men with metal buckets took care of the fire by the simple expedient of shoveling everything from the hearth and taking it outside. Jenny adjusted the ether mask, and Jimmy did not wince when she pressed it over his face and secured it behind his head. His eyes searched hers, then drifted oddly and closed. She waited the proper interval, then tested his corneal reflexes and adjusted the ether drip again.

"All right, Sergeant. Just watch this, please. I think there's plenty of ether. If not, here's more." She set the bottle at his elbow. "I may ask you for more or less ether. If I do, here's the adjustment knob. This way for lighter, that way for heavier. Only a quarter turn at a time unless I tell you otherwise." She tied on a surgical mask, then pulled the blanket up to the boy's waist. Fortunately someone had removed his pants or she would have had to cut them off. She reset the tourniquet high on the boy's thigh. Then she rinsed her hands with alcohol again, took a pair of sterile gloves from her bag, broke the seal, and slipped the gloves on. She carefully cleaned the leg with alcohol, draped it in sterile towels, and prepared to get down to serious work. She made two semicircular incisions in the skin, the one over the shin concave and the back one like a long shirttail. However, when she came to the nitty-gritty business of dissecting the muscles away from the tibia, tying off arteries, and severing the fibula very high, Shane looked away. Eventually she reached up into the incision with a bone saw.

"I may have to ask you to steady his leg. Just let me see how I do here." It was the first thing she had said since she started. "No, stay where you are," she amended. "I'm managing fine by myself. He's so young and small that his bones aren't heavy." She sawed through the tibia and rasped the raw bone smooth, working very carefully. This was where it counted. Irregularities in the bone tended to become spurs later. After a time she concluded by bringing the muscles down to pad the end of the tibia, then approximated the flaps of skin and stitched them with precise, interrupted silk sutures. She loosened the tourniquet, then waited as the stump pinked up with returning blood. As she expected, the wound oozed slightly here and there, but there was no overt bleeding. She cleaned it once more, then applied a heavy, soft dressing and taped it down.

"All right, Sergeant, that's it," she said with a sigh. He turned off the ether drip and set the mask aside. The rank, clinging odor filled the room, along with the cloying, urine-like stench of blood. But Jenny scarcely noticed, filled with the elation of a successful surgical procedure, a life saved. This was medicine, the very purpose for which she had been put on earth. She placed her instruments carefully in the same basin she had used to wash and gave them a rough cleaning, rinsing her gloves at the same time and folding everything in a towel. Not until she removed her mask did she realize she had been working in a state of concentration that approached a trance. Now she felt limp with the aftermath of her own adrenalin. She dried her instruments and returned them to their case, promising a more thorough scrub when she had the time. Finally she asked for clean water, carefully washed her hands, and paused to rub a dab of Honey Almond Cream into them against the drying effect of alcohol.

"As soon as this place airs out they can light the fire again," she said. "I'd like to get him into a bed before the ether wears off. Is that possible?"

"I think so," Shane replied. He turned to speak to the older woman. She nodded gravely, gesturing to the back room Indian-fashion by pointing with her chin. Jenny understood instantly.

"Can you carry him?" she asked. "I'd really like to get him settled and comfortable before he wakes up." Shane slipped his arms beneath the unconscious boy. Jenny unbuttoned Jimmy's clean though faded shirt and maneuvered it off, then turned the bedclothes back over his sleeping form, taking extra pains to make sure they were tented over the bandage.

For the first time since they arrived, she took a close look at Shane. His face looked drawn and parchment pale, and he clenched his left fist against the outside of his leg in an effort to steady it.

"Sergeant, you're as white as a ghost. I think you'd better go outside and get some fresh air. I can see to everything for now."

"Won't you need an interpreter?"

"Not right away. He'll sleep for another hour or so at least. Generally speaking, the total time a patient was anesthetized is also how long they take to wake up. Go on. Outside. You look terrible. Go." She made a shooing gesture, and he capitulated without argument, pulling the bedroom door nearly closed behind him. She returned to her patient, pressing a stethoscope to his chest and listening with satisfaction to a strong, young heart and clear lungs.

In the front room, Shane confronted two anxious women. His stomach churned and his head swam from the odor of ether, and he did not want to talk to either of them at that moment. "He will be well and he will walk again," he said, slipping easily back into Iroquois.

"She is certain?" the older woman asked.

"Grandmère, I have to go outside and see to the horses. I'll be back." He took up his parka and made as quick an exit as he could without being obvious. He shrugged the parka onto his shoulders and drew in a grateful draught of chill, winter air. It cleared his head, and his stomach calmed to a bearable level as he descended the steps, patted Midnight's rump, and talked softly to both horses until Fleur acknowledged his presence with a glance and the flick of an ear. He loosened their cinches and tossed ponchos over the saddles. A few more breaths of the pristine, cold air sufficed; now he could return to the house. As he climbed the porch steps, the older woman came out to meet him, wrapped in the bear robe from the rocking chair.

"My grandson, I realize it is not completely proper that I should speak to you so openly, but I must. This woman...is she the measure of the old healer?"

"Yes, she is. She may exceed him in many ways. Her education is better than his. There are circumstances in which she knows more than he does. And why should a tribal elder apologize for addressing a warrior, even when that warrior is the son of her daughter?"

"Yes, Grey Eyes. You are right. I am within the bounds of propriety to speak to you as I may not have been three moons gone. And I hope you are right about this woman." He turned to her, looking down from his six feet plus.

"She saved his life. Since she has said he will walk again, he will."

The older woman averted her eyes. "She did well," his grandmother agreed, and he realized that, as she had often done in the past, she quizzed him only to get his opinion. Then Jimmy's mother and younger brother came out onto the porch. The boy waited until Shane acknowledged him with a nod.

"Mother would know when she can go to Jimmy," he said, a little uncomfortable because his mother, an old-fashioned woman, still observed tribal taboos about speaking directly to adult male relatives.

"When the healer leaves, she may sit at Jimmy's bedside." In the past he had often chided his aunt for observing the old ways, but not now. It was simply not worth the effort.

He went back inside, left his parka on the bench, and pushed the bedroom door open. Jimmy looked up at him, glassy-eyed. He could tell the boy was making a valiant effort to control his terror in front of Jenny.

"I'm glad you came right back. He woke up much sooner than I thought he would. He's a very strong young man. I've given him an injection of morphine. He'll sleep now, and he'll be fine. But please explain to him that as soon as the stump heals enough to bear his weight—about a month—I'll see that he's fitted with a good prosthesis. He'll walk as well as you or I. Modern prosthetics aren't crude like they used to be. We've come a long way from the days of pirates with peg legs." The boy's eyes followed Jenny's face. Though she still doubted how much English he understood, he seemed reassured by her soft voice. Shane translated for him, patiently answering his few questions. Eventually he answered in groggy monosyllables, then his eyes drifted closed. She pulled the covers higher around his shoulders and gave his thin cheek a pat. Her hands stroked his eyelids closed and, understanding her meaning, he smiled faintly. Jenny led Shane from the bedroom, then turned to him.

"Tell them that he'll be fine. He can only have fluids until tomorrow morning. He can sit up if he wants, but he should stay quiet. Tell them not to bother the dressing. I'll come back tomorrow to change it. Here is medicine for him if he's in pain. Two tablets every four hours. Can they understand that?"

"I'll explain so they can." He turned to the two women, and Jenny noted with some curiosity that the younger would not look directly at him. She wished she could understand the strange language they used. The women spoke briefly to each other, and then the younger looked directly at Jenny for a long moment and murmured a soft, shy sentence before disappearing into the bedroom. The boy left, closing the heavy front door with effort, and Shane, Jenny, and the buckskin-clad older woman were alone in the room.

"What did Mrs. Richardson say to me?" Jenny asked.

"She thanked you for the life of her son. Do you want me to take you back now, or do you need to stay longer?"

"There's not a lot I can do now. Jimmy will probably sleep the rest of the night. We can leave if you want to, but I'd appreciate it if you'd bring me back tomorrow. I've another favor to ask of you between now and then. Oh, I so wish I could talk to these people!"

"I'll bring you back, and I'll handle whatever else you need. Just let me know when you're ready to leave. We're only going to have another hour or two of good moonlight, and then it's going to get very dark very quickly. I'd really like to be back down on the road before then. Midnight and I know the trail well enough to negotiate it safely, but you and Fleur don't yet."

"Fine. Here's medicine for Jimmy. Explain it to them, and then we can leave." She went to her bag and doled out ten pills into an ancient stoneware cup that Shane remembered from his childhood. Then she retrieved Mavis's jacket from the time-polished rude bench while Shane spoke with the older Indian woman. She was tall and square-shouldered, with long, slender hands, and Jenny was struck by a marked similarity in their facial bone structure. The woman broke away from Shane and studied Jenny intently for some moments before touching Jenny's shoulders lightly and speaking a few involved words. Jenny looked questioningly at Shane.

"She has given you a ceremonial name. It translates as Stone Dreaming Woman. I'll explain the significance on the way home."

"I'm honored, then, considering how it was meant." Jenny bowed her head respectfully. The woman was still watching her closely.

"You are not married?" she asked, switching to oddly accented French. Jenny was surprised, but contained it.

"*Non, Madame.*"

"*Et votre mère?*"

"*Ma mère est mort, Madame.*" The woman nodded gravely, her face expressionless.

Shane put his gun belt on, fastened the lanyard to the ring on the butt of his pistol, and reached for his parka.

"You are leaving now?" the older woman asked. Jenny had to listen closely to follow her unusual pronunciation.

"Yes, Madame. My horse and I do not know the trail yet, and it will be dark soon."

"Go with God," she responded. Jenny picked up her bag, and Shane took it from her, escorting her to the door. The woman's somber eyes followed them until the door closed.

Silently he tightened both cinches and retied her medical bag behind Midnight's saddle. She mounted. It was a long step up, and his eyes reproached her momentarily for not waiting for his aid. He turned Midnight out of the icy cul-de-sac.

"You did so well today," she ventured. "Thank you for helping me. It would have been very difficult without you." He stared straight ahead for a moment, then turned to look at her.

"That ether came very close to making me ill. You breezed through it like it was a Sunday picnic."

"That's what I've been trained for. I've seen and done a lot of surgery. I was uneasy too, at first. Besides, you were tossed in the deep end. Amputations are almost as messy as childbirth."

"I've seen babies born and I'm used to blood. But I've known that boy a long time, and that made it hard."

"He'll be all right. I know a doctor in Arlington who does nothing but leg prostheses. He's the best, and one letter will be all it'll take."

"These people can't pay."

"Do you think I don't know that? Granted, I was born at night, but it certainly wasn't last night! Believe me, it won't be a problem."

"Well, if you say so. You're certain he'll walk?"

"Of course he will. The important thing is that the trauma was low enough that it left his knee intact, with a reasonably long stump below it. Are you sure you want to come back with me? I think Madame LaPorte and I have enough French to communicate, and today seemed to be difficult for you."

"It's only because.. because I was shot in my left

shoulder not long ago, and Angus used ether when he removed the slug. I've never been so miserably sick in my entire life. Excuse me, it's crude, but, well, after a whole day, my belly hurt as bad as my shoulder did."

"Both ether and morphine can cause vomiting. You probably had a double dose, especially if it wasn't on an empty stomach. When did this happen, then?"

"The Thursday before you came to Elk Gap. And then the day we met at the skating pond, when I told you Midnight had fallen with me? Well, that wasn't the entire truth. The brother of the man who shot me took another try, out of revenge. I'd come up here to North Village, and he jumped down from a tree and tried to stab me. Midnight threw us both and went down in the process. I managed to unholster my pistol. We were wrestling around on the ground, and I killed him. I can't say anything more because my actions are still before a Board of Inquiry. I left his body where it was, came back to Elk Gap, turned the whole mess over to Paul to investigate and write up, and went to bed. I still don't know why I went skating that night. I think it was just to see if you would be there."

"But that's only been three weeks ago! You should have told me!"

"Why? You needed help, and I was the only one who understood what needed to be done."

"Well...because... How bad was your shoulder?"

"Not too bad. It missed everything important. Once I quit throwing up I was all right."

"But that can be such a dangerous injury. The subclavian artery is huge. People bleed to death very quickly if it's severed. And there is a very big nerve right next to it, too, called the brachial plexus. Damage it, and your arm will be paralyzed. I'll show you my human anatomy text. It'll scare your socks off. But if I'd known about all of this, you wouldn't have been within a mile of that operation."

"Well, I'm glad you didn't know, then. Besides, I doubt I'll be sick again. I think it was mostly in my head." She rose a little in the stirrups, absorbing the jolts with her knees as Fleur started to descend.

"It's the kind of reaction that goes away over time," she agreed. "Hopefully this is the only time you get tangled up in a mess like this, though. I don't even know if it's legal for me to practice medicine in Canada."

"It is. There's reciprocity for most licensed professionals. You can practice here any time you want to. However, if you stay, you'll eventually have to sit for the board exams here in Ontario and apply for a work visa. If you want, I'll take you to Ottawa myself..." He broke off, biting his lip.

"I just heard a very big 'if' at the end of that sentence."

"If the Board of Inquiry clears me and I'm still with the Northwest Mounted." Now it was Jenny's turn to bite her lip.

He drew a tentative breath and went on. "You see, Paul never found Hankins' knife. Since there were no marks on me, he couldn't prove Bart was armed when he attacked me. *Prima facie*, it looks as though I killed an unarmed man."

"Oh, no! But what will happen to you?"

He shrugged as well as he could under his heavy parka. "If I'm cleared, nothing. I'll just go back to work. If not, I'll be discharged. I could even be indicted on criminal charges. If the Board finds against me, I will almost certainly lose my bar license even absent a formal indictment. So you see, a good portion of my life is on the line. But there's no use worrying. It's out of my hands, and I'm going to do what I can until they call me to River Bend."

"So you're on duty now?"

"Yes. Angus just cleared me to go back to full duty last Monday."

"I wish I had known all this before. Initially I had a very adverse opinion of you, and I'm sorry. And about the day we met? If I had known you'd been shot only four days earlier, I'd have frog-marched you upstairs and put you to bed myself."

The beginnings of a smile tugged at his cheeks. "The top floor is for Mrs. Hammill's gentlemen boarders. No ladies are allowed."

"I'm not a lady, Sergeant. I'm a medical doctor." He looked down, and she sensed he was trying not to laugh.

"Would you mind explaining something to me?" he asked at length.

"What's that?"

"Why did you hide the fact that you're a physician? That would have gone a long way toward changing the bad first opinion I also formed of you."

She sighed. "That's a long story. My father is Chief of Neurosurgery at Northtown Surgical Clinic in New York. You've probably never heard of it, but believe me, there's not a physician on this continent who hasn't. Northtown is one of the foremost research clinics in the country. I hope to practice there someday. It's been my only goal in life since I was ten years old.

The only problem is Father. He has been blocking the Board's approval of my application. You see, he's a strict, old-fashioned, unbending man. He tolerated my earning a Bachelor of Science degree, but then he wanted me to come home, marry the man he'd chosen for me, and become the proper New York society matron. Needless to say, I refused, and what's more, I entered medical school against his express orders. We haven't spoken save in passing for five years. And after all that work I still couldn't find either a hospital that would hire me as a staff physician or a practice to buy into. I asked Uncle Richard to keep my secret because I didn't want everyone here looking at me like I'm some sort of sideshow freak."

"Sideshow freak?" he echoed. "No, I don't agree with that at all. People here can't afford to hold prejudices. There are simply no choices to be had. There are doctors aplenty in big cities, but out here? Well, see for yourself. Angus is the only doctor between here and the Quebec border. Granted, there are a couple doctors in River Bend, but west of town the only other one I know of is clear up at the north end of my territory in Castlereigh, and I suspect he's running from some sort of trouble. I leave him alone because he's needed so badly. People out here die for lack of simple medical care. Just two months back a teenage boy severed an artery in his leg with an axe. Angus was out on a call somewhere and nobody knew what to do. I tried to help him, but...but I was too late. Last summer a farmer named Charles Gunther died of blood poisoning from a broken arm. We regularly lose women in childbirth, too, and I know that doesn't have to happen. There's a place for you here, probably a very big one. Please give it careful consideration. At least talk to Angus and see what he has to say. You're truly needed, and if I may make a purely personal observation, you're the strong, levelheaded type who does well on a frontier."

"Thank you for your confidence. You argue your case effectively, barrister that you are. I really hadn't considered staying here, but it's a pleasant place so far. And as far as talking to Doctor MacBride goes, I have to. I'm out of surgical dressings. I'll have to beg some supplies and also find out where he orders his."

"I'll take you there in the morning and introduce you, then." She looked out over the landscape, brilliant in the slanting moonlight. It was so quiet that all she could hear was the creak of tack and the susurration of the horses moving through the dry snow.

The moon was just dropping below the horizon when they arrived at Richard's little ranch. Shane turned down the lane with her.

"Mavis said she would leave food for us. Please come in with me? I know you had to have missed supper," Jenny said as they approached the house.

"Mrs. Hammill will feed me. She doesn't mind, as long as I don't make a practice of it."

"Please? It's so cold out. I know you could stand to warm up. And even though you might not welcome the reminder, right now it won't do to let yourself get chilled."

"All right. Just for a while, though. It's getting late, and it'll be an early morning for both of us." With something that amounted to telepathy, Toby came out to take the horses. It surprised her. Usually by this time he was sound asleep. Shane took the medical bag, and they came into the assembly room, still redolent of supper. She divested herself of four layers of clothing, then went to the stove and peeked into a pot that had been left on the back to stay warm.

"Ham and beans. And the other one is corn bread. How perfect for such a cold night!" She put two more sections of split alder into the firebox and pulled the pan over it, then placed the teakettle right behind it. "This won't take fifteen minutes, I promise." She measured tea into the warmed ironstone teapot, and he gave in and set the table while she tended the stove. Very soon the beans were hot. She put the corn bread on a plate and brought the whole to the table. Then she ladled beans into his bowl and hers and poured tea for them both. He rose and bowed his head while she said the blessing, and then they both sat down.

"Do you remember what that Indian woman called me today? Stone Dreaming Woman? You said you'd explain it on the way down, and we both forgot," she began after they had assuaged their initial hunger pangs. His hands paused on the corn bread he was buttering.

"You're right. It slipped my mind entirely. Well, when a boy like Jimmy is fourteen or fifteen, he undergoes a manhood ceremony. It consists of certain ritual preparations, and then he goes into the woods and fasts and prays until he has a vision. It is interpreted by the shamans and elders, and it determines the course of his future. At that time he is given a man name and a ceremonial name. Boys who dream about weapons and game are warriors and hunters. Future shamans dream of birds and flying and are often called Dream Flyers. Chiefs and leaders have visions of bears, but those whose visions are of mountains and hills—things made of rock—are called Stone Dreamers. They become healing shamans. However, women don't undergo the vision quest. Except under unusual circumstances they do not have ceremonial names. It was an honor for Madame LaPorte to give you one. She is a tribal elder, so she speaks for everyone. And when she asked if you were married and your mother was alive? When you said no, that severed your connection to your people. You see, their families are matrilineal. And since you are single and obviously have no children, you are without any tribal ties. In effect, you are eligible for adoption. So, in giving you a ceremonial name, she made you Iroquois. Now you may be adopted into a family if you choose."

"Interesting. But you speak their language so well, and aboriginal languages are always very complex. They're difficult to learn unless you do it as a child." He could have ignored the unspoken question, but he decided to sidestep it instead.

"As I said, my grandparents raised me after my family died in a smallpox epidemic. Since he was an old-fashioned voyageur, we lived way out in the woods. All my playmates were Iroquois children. I even went to Father André's mission school until I was eleven, when I had gone as far as the mission school could take me and I transferred to the school in town. I had to live with Mavis and Ira Conner during school term then. Mavis civilized me. Ask her, and she'll probably tell you it's the hardest thing she ever did."

"You're fortunate. It'd be hard to work with those people as closely as you do without speaking their language well. I wished this afternoon I could communicate with them a little better."

"As you saw with Madame LaPorte, most of them have enough French to get by. But if you ever decide to learn Iroquois, I'll teach you."

"You're certainly working on me to stay here, aren't you?"

"How did you ever guess?" There was a mischievous sparkle in his eyes.

"As I said earlier, I was born at night, but it wasn't last night." She buttered a morsel of corn bread and felt it literally dissolving in her mouth. Mavis's corn bread was another of her miracles.

"All jesting aside, you are a very shrewd and open-minded person. Knowing what I do about your background, I was wondering if you'd object to coming to the Indian village with me. After all, it's a far cry from—what was it? North...what?"

"Northtown Surgical Clinic. Sergeant, my oath precludes racial prejudice. Indians have the same blood as everyone else, and need is no respecter of skin color. Also, I grew up in a remarkably frank household, and I've escaped a good many of the current biases. My mother passed away when I was ten, and although I was basically raised by two aunts, they confined themselves to teaching me things like etiquette and embroidery, and they left the issues of moral guidance to Father. Since he is a physician, he was very frank with my questions. Even though we're not close now, he was attentive to me when I was younger."

"You're fortunate."

The mantel clock softly chiming eleven interrupted their conversation.

"Goodness! I hadn't realized it was so late. Please,

stay here tonight. If you don't, you face that long ride into town only to have to get up early and come all the way back here and ride to town again. And I can tell you're tired." He drew breath to demur, but she interrupted him. "Don't you dare say no. You still need your rest. And if you do insist on leaving, I won't hear of your coming for me tomorrow. I'm perfectly capable of finding my way to Elk Gap unescorted."

"I didn't realize the railroad tracks ran through Richard's house. But they must. I've just been flattened by a freight train!"

She giggled and filled his bowl again, giving him a full blast of Southern debutante cane-syrup charm. "Good. You're staying. I'm so glad."

"I can't do much else."

They finished their food, and he helped her clear the table. She discovered they made as good a team doing something as mundane as picking up dishes as they did saving a life. She rinsed the bean pot and the bowls, then put all the dishes in the pot and covered them with water. Then she dried her hands on the flour sack towel and anointed them with her favorite Honey Almond Cream.

"There. That's good enough. We'll do them with the breakfast dishes in the morning," she said. He had moved behind her to return the butter to the cooler, and when she turned she bumped into him.

"Sergeant! Excuse me!" A toucher, she laid her palms above the breast pockets of his tunic by way of apology. Impulsively he covered her hands with his.

"Miss Weston, I can't thank you enough for what you did today, for being kind enough to come to North Village with me, and for saving Jimmy's life. He'd

have been in dire trouble without you, Miss Weston..."
He paused awkwardly, stumbling over her name. "No,
I... Doctor Weston? I'm not certain how I should
address you now. After today, 'Miss Weston' sounds so
frivolous..."

" 'Jenny' will do quite nicely, Sergeant."

His gaze leveled on her, and he gave her a deeply
searching look that was all grey eyes and hugely long
lashes. "I have a first name too, you know," he said
softly.

"Touché. Shane." She smiled and felt her cheeks
flush. "Then have a good night."

"You too." Her hands lay trapped against his Red
Serge. She turned them beneath his and held them palm
to palm for a moment.

"Until tomorrow, then...Shane," she said, her
composure disturbed by his nearness.

"I look forward to it." Then he reluctantly let her
hands go, drawing a deep, nervous breath.

"Jenny? May I call on you, then? With Richard's
permission, of course."

"It would be my honor entirely."

His hands went slowly to the points of her
shoulders, and he drew her to him. She closed her eyes
and tipped her head back. All her senses were full of
him, from his warmth to the masculine scent of soap,
sunshine, and the wool of his Red Serge. She let her
hands travel to his muscular shoulders, and as he
gathered her into his arms, her left hand slipped over
the standing collar of his tunic to the slightly long hair
at the nape of his neck. It felt soft, satiny, and much
finer than her own. Then his lips met hers, gently and
tenderly, the stimulating touch of warm velvet. As she

flowed up against him, the night turned to fireworks.

The kiss was exactly what she would have expected from Shane: undemanding, powerful, and thoroughly exciting. Then he held her close and pressed his cheek against her hair and she let her arms encircle his back. He was a big armful for her. His lips traveled across her cheek and he nuzzled into her hair.

"Oh, Jenny," he whispered, sending a shiver from her heels to the top of her head. Then they kissed again. This time his red-clad arms engulfed her and she was lost in the incredible power that was Shane Adair. She went weak all over and plastered herself against his chest. She wanted to blurt out that she loved him madly, but that was a frightening idea. She laid her hand against his cheek and backed up a few inches. His face held high color and he was breathing hard through flushed, slightly parted lips.

"Do I owe you an apology now?" he whispered. Her arms tightened about him. Then she raised her head just enough to look up into his eyes.

"No. That was just as much my idea as yours. Don't apologize to me unless it was just a one-time impulse and you intend never to repeat yourself."

He proved to her that he was up to her one-line stingers. "Chèrie, I'll kiss you goodnight every night for the next eighty years if you'll have it," he said softly.

"In eighty years I'll be a hundred and five! Who in their right mind would want to kiss a hundred-and-five-year-old woman?" The grey eyes tilted again.

"A totally smitten one-hundred-eight-year-old man," he whispered, holding her hands against his chest. She laughed softly.

"I swear, one of your ancestors had to have kissed

the Blarney Stone!"

"Just wait eighty years and you'll know that I've never meant anything more."

"I'll check again tomorrow, thank you."

"Tomorrow, gladly." He raised her hands to his lips.

"Then good night, Shane."

"Good night, Jenny." He leaned down and bestowed a chaste peck on her forehead.

"Sleep well."

"I don't think I'll sleep at all, after this," he sighed.

"I'll see you in the morning." She backed away from him, letting her hands run softly through his. Then she was gone, leaving behind an aura of Honey Almond Cream.

When she came up the stairs, she saw a thin slice of light under her uncle's closed door.

"Uncle Richard?" she called softly, rapping one knuckle against the center panel.

"Come in, Jen." His voice was quiet too, lest they wake Mavis. Jenny let herself in. Richard was at his desk, two books open and papers spread around him.

"I just wanted you to know that Sergeant Adair is here. We've just come down from North Village, and since we have to go back tomorrow, he's staying the night."

"Mavis told me what went on. How's the boy?"

Concern flitted over her features. "I revised the stump until it will bear weight. He'll walk again."

"Quite a baptism by fire, wasn't it."

"Not really. My first patient was actually Sergeant Adair's horse."

Richard choked back laughter. "Oh, Jen! But out

here physicians do occasionally treat animals."

"I've nothing against that. They have the same feelings we do. Just don't ask me to perform large animal obstetrics. I'm not that strong. Well, I'm exhausted. I'm going to bed. I just wanted to let you know what's going on under your own roof."

"Thanks, sweetheart. I'm going to stay up for a bit. It's going well tonight."

"Genius burns the midnight oil," Jenny said with a laugh. She bent down and kissed the top of his head. "Good night. Sleep tight." They had exchanged those words since she was just a child.

She floated into her room, still high on the champagne bubbles in her blood. She crawled into bed, pulled down the snuff lever on her bedside lamp, and snuggled beneath the covers, her senses still full of Shane's touch and the daring kisses.

Chapter Eight

When she awoke, it took only a moment for her mind to take up where it had left off the night before, with Shane in the lamp-lit kitchen. And when she thought of the numerous eligible men who had endeavored to court her, he was so far ahead of the pack he eclipsed everyone else.

She rose and dressed quickly in the cold of first light, putting on her new madras blouse and her riding skirt, two pairs of socks, and throwing on a navy cardigan. She came downstairs, riding boots in hand, as quietly as she could manage, noting as she passed the marble-cased Newhaven on the mantel that it was nearly six-thirty. No one had risen yet, and the silence of the old house wrapped around her, calm and comforting. She tiptoed into the kitchen. In the dim glow of dawn she could see the outline of Shane's body muffled in blankets on the lower bunk. He stirred as he heard her come in and poked his head from beneath the covers. His face looked warm and flushed with sleep, and rumpled hair spilled over his forehead, giving him a boyish appeal that belied his age. Then he yawned, and one hand emerged. He scrubbed it over his face, removing the last traces of sleep, and raked his hair back.

"Good morning, Sleeping Beauty," she said, smiling. "I hope I didn't wake you."

"No. I was awake—mostly awake, anyway. I just didn't want to make noise and disturb anyone else." Since the fire had not totally gone out overnight, she stoked the stove and pulled the teakettle over the burner atop the firebox, then fed the fireplace to warm the room. He watched her from the shelter of his cocoon.

"Did you sleep well, then?" she asked.

"I didn't just sleep. I died."

"Me too." She came around the table and sat in the chair he usually occupied at meals. "Go ahead and stay there until the kitchen warms up."

"If you're going to sit next to me, don't pussyfoot around." He stuck his hand out from the side of the bed and patted the bunk next to his legs, but it was cold in the room; his hand immediately disappeared beneath the covers again.

"That's something doctors don't do…" she protested.

"I'm not your patient." Reluctantly she capitulated. Presently his hand reemerged and reached toward her. She took it shyly in both hers, but not before solicitously making sure his shoulders and arm were covered. She looked down at the hand she held. It was strong and vitally warm and the fingers long and tapered, the sensitive hand of an artist. Suddenly she wanted that hand to caress her again as it had last night.

"A penny for your thoughts," he prompted at length.

"Do you realize what Aunt Martha would say if she could see me now?"

"You told me last night you're not a lady—you're a medical doctor."

"And you just told me you're not my patient."

"Could I have a convenient relapse?"

"Not unless somebody comes along and shoots you again, God forbid!"

"No. Once was way more than enough," he agreed with a sigh.

"Well, it's a foregone conclusion that your occupation is dangerous. How many times have you been involved in a firefight, then?"

"Only four times, counting that one. Two you know about. Then once a couple moonshiners took a potshot at Paul and me. They're in prison in Ottawa now, serving hefty sentences for attempted murder. Another time was last August. It was a little more frightening. Three men escaped from prison and took off into the woods. They were real desperados. We cornered them in a mine, and they only surrendered after we threatened to dynamite the adit and leave them there to starve. But that's over the course of six years. I've fired my pistol a few times to break up fights and quiet noisy drunks, but that really doesn't count. And now everybody around here knows we won't stand for anyone disturbing the peace regardless of how mean they think they are, so by and large Elk Gap is quiet."

"Yes. I heard how it was before you came."

His wry smile said a volume. "True, I had my hands full for about a year. But gradually the troublemakers decided it wasn't worth tangling with Mounties and either settled down or moved on."

"But I know your territory isn't just Elk Gap. How far does it go?"

"To the Quebec border, then clear on up to Castlereigh in the north. That's a good eighty miles. When I ride rounds it takes me two weeks, and that's if

I can keep moving at a pretty good pace. If I stop at all the Indian villages, it takes longer."

"Knowing you, you probably do."

Again the wry smile. "I do, but they're not quite the same Iroquois as the people I'm used to. In North Village they have some very different customs, and a lot of their mythology is more like the American Plains Indians. Their speech is a little different, too. In fact, the Iroquois farther north call them Stray Dogs because they don't appear to belong anywhere except to themselves. Don't ask me how that ever happened. The first time I rode into the village outside of Five Mile and said something, one of the elders said, 'Stray Dog' and everybody laughed. I patted Midnight and asked him if he had let that huge fart I had just heard. Everybody laughed again, including the elder who had made the comment. To this day he calls me Stray Dog and I call him Horse Fart."

"Stray Dog and Horse Fart!" Jenny repeated, suppressing laughter. "Oh, Shane! That's the funniest thing I've heard in years!"

"I'd like you to meet them someday. They're good people."

"I think I'd like that very much. Well, it's getting warmer in here now. I'll leave and let you get dressed."

He sighed melodramatically. "I was just getting to enjoy this." Pointedly his hand tightened on hers.

"You can hold my hand later. Mavis will catch us. Besides, the teakettle's boiling."

"Well, all right, then. If you must." His tone, full of euphuistic disappointment, sent a warm rush of amusement through her. She went to the stove and measured tea into the ironstone pot, poured boiling water on top of the loose tea, and then disappeared through the back kitchen door, which led to a small part-hallway, part-pantry and the recently added bathroom. When she emerged into the parlor, Mavis was just coming out of her own room.

"Good morning, Mavis. I started tea."

"Thank you. I was awake, but I didn't want to leave my room until I heard Mr. Weston moving around upstairs. Sometimes he's a late riser. Often I reserve that time for whatever hand sewing I need to do."

"I understand. When his writing is going well, I've known him to stay up all night. Oh, by the way, Sergeant Adair is here. He is taking me back to North Village, and it was so late when we got back last night that it didn't make sense for him to go all the way home only to turn around and come back here this morning."

"And the Indian boy?"

"I gave him a stump that will bear his weight. I know where I can get a prosthesis for him. Eventually he'll walk again."

Mavis shook her head. "You a doctor. My, my. I would never have guessed in a million years."

"Women doctors aren't that common, after all."

"All right, ladies. I can hear you talking in there. It's safe. I'm decent," Shane called. Jenny and Mavis came around the corner from the living room. He was dressed, washed, and his wild hair tamed. He had made his bed neatly.

"My, don't you look like Merry Sunshine this morning," Mavis observed. Jenny took the tea mugs from the cupboard and filled all but Richard's, which she left on the top of the warming oven. Mavis took her own, and Jenny brought Shane's to the table. She watched him put sugar in his tea.

"It was a late night last night. I'm afraid Jenny got chucked into deep water." Mavis turned to Jenny and cocked a maternal eyebrow at his use of her first name.

" 'Doctor Weston' sounds so pretentious and stuffy, doesn't it?" Jenny interjected.

"Well, yes. I'll give you that." Mavis rattled pans and banged the cooler door as she retrieved a bowl of eggs. Jenny heard Richard on the stairs and hurried to fill his tea mug and take it to him. Another day was beginning.

Less than an hour later they were on their way to town. Jenny once again felt dowdy, bundled into Mavis's oversized fox jacket. *Shane is so exotically handsome in that magnificent silver wolf parka with all that bright beadwork, like some romantic hero straight out of one of Cousin Elizabeth's penny dreadfuls. I wonder what Aunt Eleanor would say,* she thought. *She always did have an eye for a good-looking man.*

"What are you looking at?" he asked eventually. The question caught her by surprise.

"I was looking at that beautiful beadwork on your parka, trying to figure out if it's right on the leather or if it's appliquéd."

"What's that?"

"Done on another piece and then sewed on."

"It's appliquéd, then. Those strips aren't totally decorative. They cover the seams between the sections of hide, so wind can't blow in."

"But won't it wear out?"

"If it does, I'll get it fixed, or have another made. All I have to do is furnish the pelts, and that's not hard. And as I told you, I never wear it when I'm going to be in the woods for any length of time. I have a bear parka and leggings for rough work, but because it isn't lined it's not as warm as this."

For the millionth time she marveled at the twist of fate that had brought her here. *But I've heard it said that nothing ever happens by accident. Perhaps this is meant to be.*

They moved at a trot through the broken snow. Fleur matched her stride to Midnight's, and they fell into rhythm like a well-trained draft team.

Jenny was enjoying the ride in spite of the cold. All too soon they arrived at the outskirts of Elk Gap, where they slowed to a walk even though the street was still deserted. The only sign of life was Paul coming out of the livery stable. He kicked his chestnut mare into a canter to catch up to them.

"Hello, Paul," Shane called across the street.

"Good morning, Miss Weston," he said, politely touching gloved fingers to the brim of his Stetson. "Shane, I had a notion where you were. This time I didn't worry."

"There was a medical emergency at North Village. Jimmy Richardson stepped in a leg-hold trap and severed his foot. I came down to Richard's to telephone Angus, but when I got there I got the surprise of my life."

"Oh?" Paul prompted, falling in next to Jenny. Shane looked down at her, his eyebrows raised expectantly.

"I'm actually a medical doctor."

"Oh, my goodness!" Paul exclaimed on the end of a long sigh. "That would be the surprise of my life, too. But what are you doing way out here?"

"That was my question," Shane said.

"I worked myself half to death in school, and I couldn't find a practice to buy into or a hospital that would hire me in anything but a nursing capacity. It was so frustrating I decided to come out here and visit Uncle Richard for a while and forget the world. But it seems it caught up with me."

"I suggested she go talk to Angus. You know how hard it's getting for him to make house calls. In fact, that's where we're going now."

"That's a good idea, Miss…ah, Doctor Weston."

Shane laughed. "I made the same mistake," he said.

"You may call me Jenny if you'd like."

"That's gracious of you, if you don't think it's too familiar."

"No. You're Shane's partner, after all. I'm probably going to be in contact with you from time to time."

"You're riding short patrol?" Shane asked after a minute or so.

"Yes. I wanted to get it out of the way. Afternoon is when we're going to get calls."

"Good idea. And I may not be home very soon. After we've talked to Angus, we have to go back to North Village. It'll be late this afternoon before I get back."

"Well, I'll ride with you as far as the clinic, then." After about half a block Paul turned off with a salute as Jenny and Shane stopped in front of Angus's office.

Before either one thought of it, Shane boosted her down from the tall mare. She caught a tiny tightness around his eyes.

"Shane, you shouldn't do that yet," she said in an

undertone, her hand lingering against his left shoulder.

"I'm all right, honest. It's just a little sore deep down, that's all."

"Well, then, since you're not my patient, I'll let Doctor MacBride get after you."

"Oh, believe me, he certainly would," he replied grimly. He opened the clinic door and ushered her into the waiting room. The small foyer had six or eight mismatched kitchen chairs around the institutionally white walls and an enormous hall tree next to the door. The whole room was permeated with the medicinal odors of alcohol and Lysol. To Jenny, that must be how heaven smelled.

A hallway led to the left, obviously toward the examination rooms. Almost directly ahead of them a stairway led to the second floor. The hallway continued to the right, into indefinite obscurity.

Another of the ubiquitous little railroad stoves kept the anteroom warm. Shane helped her take off Mavis's fox jacket and hung it on the hall tree. She folded the fascinator and laid it on the seat, along with two of the three sweaters. As he was unbuttoning his own parka, they heard Angus MacBride's voice down the hall.

"I'll be there directly," he called.

"It's me. This is a social call," Shane responded.

"Well, then, you can indulge an old man and come back to my study. So why have you so graciously condescended to come calling on such a fine day?" The gravelly, disembodied voice carried a rough undertone of sarcasm.

"Careful, Angus. There's a lady with me." He directed Jenny past the stairs and down the short right-hand hallway that led to the doctor's study.

At first she was almost afraid to raise her eyes. The big room looked like the den of a mad scientist straight from the pages of Mary Shelly. To the right stood a fireplace flanked by two windows. Solid bookcases covered the rest of the walls. In one corner the doctor had placed a round table with a binocular microscope and a globe of the world on it; in the other hung a fully articulated human skeleton. The small pelvis and the large nuchal crest marked it male. Finally she looked at the good doctor himself. He stood behind a large walnut desk full of papers, books, and other oddments.

"Well, Miss Weston! Welcome to my lair. To what do I owe the honor of your visit?" She gave him her best cane-syrup Brisbane smile. From church she remembered the large, broad-shouldered man with thinning white hair and blue eyes that regarded the world levelly. Right now they calmly studied her over a pair of Ben Franklin reading glasses. Mutely she handed over a small leather case roughly the size of a wallet. He raised his eyebrows.

"Go ahead. Look at what's inside," she prompted. It contained miniatures of both her diplomas and her licenses to practice medicine in Virginia and New York.

"Sit down, won't you please?" he offered, ignoring the case for the moment. Shane seated her in a large maroon leather wing chair and took another for himself. Angus's face remained neutral as he perused each document in turn. "My, my, my! Summa cum laude, too! What an achievement, Doctor Weston. You've every right to be proud of yourself. I won't say it doesn't surprise me, though, since Richard never said a word about it."

"Thank you, Doctor MacBride. And I asked my uncle not to tell anyone. I didn't want to come here and be regarded as some sort of sideshow freak."

"So, before I ring for Madame Dubois to bring tea for us, may I inquire as to the purpose of your visit?"

"My immediate purpose? Yesterday I answered an emergency up at North Village. Traumatic amputation. A boy stepped in a leg-hold trap. I gave him a stump that will bear his weight as soon as he has a good prosthesis, but I'm out of supplies. I need to borrow some dressing and bandage material and a bottle of isopropyl alcohol, and I need to know what supply house you order from."

"Easily done." Angus summoned his housekeeper and asked her to bring them tea. She whisked off into the kitchen and returned a moment later with a tray. Graciously Angus poured for them. Jenny declined sugar and took her cup delicately, while the ornate Vienna Regulator on the wall rained a painful shower of seconds on the room.

"Thank you for the tea. It's certainly welcome on such a cold morning."

"You're more than welcome. But it looks like there's something more behind your visit today."

"In a way, perhaps. You see, I've been looking for a post for quite a while, but no hospital wants a woman doctor, and I couldn't find a practice to buy into. That's why I came to visit Uncle Richard—to rest and regroup, if you will."

"Had you thought of practicing here?"

"Not really, until last night, that is. Shane has told me you're spread rather thin. Have you ever given a thought to an associate?"

"Many times, Doctor Weston. I'm sixty-eight and I have osteoarthritis in both hips. I can't ride anymore, and there are places where a buggy simply won't go. North Village is one of them. And I'll have to admit I've seldom seen credentials as stellar as yours." He paused to sip his tea; his ancient moustache cup amused Jenny to no end. She tensed, knowing what was coming.

"And the fact that I'm a woman?" She nearly held her breath in anticipation of his answer. She felt like a turtle that had stuck its neck out a very long way.

"So what? You're probably more intelligent than I am. I only graduated in the middle of my class. Although I daresay I probably devoted rather more time to perfecting the fine art of ale consumption than you did." He paused for the expected chuckle, but she only smiled politely. "So, are you truly interested in frontier medicine? It's rough hereabouts, both the country and some of the people."

"It doesn't come much rougher than yesterday," Shane interjected. "She breezed through it like it was a Sunday picnic, while I'll admit I almost got sick."

Jenny went to his rescue. "Admittedly, it was rather ugly. A couple inches of the tibia and fibula were degloved, but Sergeant Adair had controlled the bleeding well. After that, it was a textbook transtibial amputation. It's medicine, with a capital M, Doctor MacBride. It's what I was meant for."

He nodded. "I know just how you feel, lass. And let's be on a first-name basis or we'll be doctoring each other to death." His white moustache stirred as he smiled. "Would you like to try practicing with me for a few months and you can see how you like it? I'll warn you, you get all the house calls outside of Elk Gap, especially North Village, because I can't make that trip any longer. But can you handle the language problem with those Indians?"

"I speak French, Doctor...ah...Angus. I can get by even if Shane can't be there to translate for me."

"And either Paul or I will escort her until she's familiar with the country," Shane volunteered.

"But will your patients accept me?"

Angus gave a snort. "They'll have no choice. Oh, there may be a few holdouts at first, but I'll sort them out in short order." She felt like hanging onto her breastbone to keep her heart in place. She was actually going to practice medicine, the very thing she had longed for since she was old enough to understand what medicine meant to her father. She would be able to help people, to alleviate pain and cure illness, to see babies born, to ease passing, to dedicate her life to life itself! She wanted to jump up, run out in the street, and shout it to the rooftops. At the very least she wanted to hug someone. However, behind his huge desk Angus MacBride was not a candidate, and even as unconventional as she could sometimes be, she did not want to hug Shane in front of anyone else just yet. Instead she sat there, holding her teacup in shaking hands, smiling until her face hurt.

"I told her I'd help her with a work visa and with the boards here. I think she has a year or until the expiration of the later of her United States licenses, but I'd have to check," Shane informed them.

"Well, then, Jenny, welcome to my practice." Doctor MacBride stood up, leaned over, and held out his hand. She met it firmly, a whole galaxy of stars materializing in her eyes. "Now come back to the clinic and let's get you some supplies. The first of my patients is due in a few minutes." As if on cue, the front door opened, and when they came past the waiting room, a very pregnant thirtyish woman was taking off her wrap.

"Ah! Mrs. Mattson! You're just in time to meet my new associate. Doctor Weston, this is Mrs. Edith Mattson. Mrs. Mattson, Doctor Jennifer Weston. She is going to join my practice for a while and see if Elk Gap agrees with her."

"Pleased to meet you, Mrs. Mattson," Jenny said very properly.

"My pleasure entirely, Doctor Weston. Welcome to Elk Gap. I do hope you decide to stay."

"Thank you. So far it seems like a cordial place."

"Well, Mrs. Mattson, if you want to go to the first examination room on the right, Doctor Weston and I have a little business, and then I'll be right in." Angus took them to the supply pantry at the end of the hall. As he was doling out the supplies Jenny needed, he kept up a running medical history of the patient. "Edith and her husband Roy have a farm northwest of town. In fact, their land almost abuts your uncle's place. There's only one other farm in between. They do pretty well, cattle and the like. She's due about the first of May. I make it a girl by the fetal heart rate, but you know how often you can go wrong on that score. Twenty-eight years old, gravida four, para three. Two boys and a girl, all surviving. All her pregnancies have been uneventful and the deliveries unremarkable. I don't anticipate anything else this time, except she's probably going to deliver very quickly. It may even be precipitous, so if you get a call, don't dawdle. Last time it was less than three hours from the onset of labor. The Good Lord put that lady on earth to be a mother. There. That's everything you ought to need. Come back if it's not enough. And don't bother with ordering supplies yourself. I'm sending off tomorrow, and I'll include a little extra of everything I routinely use. Then we can discuss it later. But is there anything specific you'd like me to order for you?"

"No. Not really. I may run low on suture silk, but I'm not there yet."

"All right, then. Shall I see you Monday morning?"

"Bright and early!" she agreed with a sunny smile.

As Shane stowed her supplies in his saddlebags, he looked as happy as she felt. She relieved him of guilt about not helping her to the saddle when she led Fleur around to a raised corner of the board sidewalk and used it as a mounting block. Then they rode side by side out of town. Shane was beaming.

"I swear, you're happier than I am," she observed.

He looked at her. "It means you're staying, at least for a while. And I intend to take every opportunity to persuade you to make it permanent." It was on the tip of her tongue to make some remark about flattery, but she realized he was completely sincere.

Chapter Nine

A few days later, a quiet snow was falling when Shane, looking like a ghost with the snow on his parka, came through the gloom. He handed Midnight off to Toby, then jumped up and down on the porch to shake the snow from his furs. Mavis opened the door before he had a chance to knock.

"Mail," he caroled, his voice chipper.

"Hello, Shane," Jenny replied, laying her dust rag aside and coming out of the parlor.

"I have Richard's mail. And I've brought you something. But wait a minute." He set a few letters and a package down, hung up his parka, hat, and gun belt, then stuffed his gauntlets down one sleeve of the parka.

"Tea?" Mavis asked, handing him the Blue Willow mug.

"Thank you, yes. I needn't say it's cold out there." He set the mug on the table and untied the string around the blanket-wrapped bundle. "All right, Jenny. Close your eyes." She obeyed, screwing up her face appealingly. He set the blanket aside and shook out a parka much like his own, save that the fur was a sleek silvery brown and the lining was white. Similar bands of beadwork decorated it, but instead of swirly geometric patterns Jenny's bore depictions of wild roses. "All right. You can look now."

Jenny's screech of surprise made him wince. "Oh,

Shane! That's beautiful! It's incredible!" Her voice dropped to a whisper with shock. She reached out and touched the sleek fur. "What's it made of?"

"River otter," he replied. "Better than mine, even. It's virtually waterproof. And the lining is winter-trapped marten fur. They turn brown in summer. Here. Try it on. I told them you and Helen Richardson are about the same size, so they measured it on her."

"Good. Now I can have my jacket back," Mavis said dryly. He held the parka out, and Jenny slipped it on. It came properly a fraction below her hips and the sleeves were just the right length.

"Oh, look! It couldn't fit better. I have to go look in the mirror!" She flew upstairs, with Shane close behind her. He showed her how to fasten the double-buttoned storm closure, and she stood before the cheval glass, admiring the beautiful parka. She examined the beadwork, stroked the satiny fur of the left sleeve, and even went so far as to take up her hand mirror and pirouette carefully to look at the back. Then she turned to him.

"Shane, thank you so much. This is a...a work of art. It's almost too beautiful to wear."

"Don't thank me. The North Village women made it for you, to thank you for saving Jimmy Richardson's life." She turned slowly before the mirror. Then reluctantly she took off the parka and hung it in her armoire.

"But I do need to thank you. You did help me, after all. And I love the parka."

"I'm glad. Even though it's snowing a little, it's not all that bad outside if you're dressed for it. Perhaps you'd like to ride with me and try it out?"

"I was beginning to think you'd never ask. Go downstairs and drink your tea while I change my clothes." Gently she shooed him out of her bedroom and reached into the armoire for her riding skirt. Then, mischievously, she put it back and took out her daringly snug jodhpurs, which she much preferred.

After Shane escorted her home, she examined her mail. One letter bore the return address of her cousin Elizabeth in Arlington. The second came from the prosthetist detailing the measurements he needed and instructions on how to make a cast of Jimmy's stump. She took the reply upstairs and slid it into her medical bag, then decided to answer Elizabeth's letter while she had time. As she was sitting at the kitchen table with pen and paper, the telephone rang. It was such an uncommon occurrence that she flinched and scribbled on the page. With a disgusted sigh she capped her fountain pen and set it down, then rose to pick up the earpiece of the telephone.

"Richard Weston's residence. Jenny Weston speaking."

"Jenny?"

"Shane! What…"

"When I came in, there was a message for me from Superintendent Shepherd. They want me in River Bend tomorrow, so I'll be leaving on the 5:30 train. You know what that means." She could hear the worry in his voice. However, long ago she had learned that the telephone was not always completely private. She had to speak in code.

"Yes, I do. You'll let me know the outcome, won't you?"

"As soon as I know."

"You're in my prayers, you know that."

"Thank you. That's reassuring. And if…well, just say I'll always be grateful to you for helping Jimmy Richardson."

"That was no more than my Hippocratic Oath."

"Be that as it may, I'm still grateful. Well, I need to get ready. Good night, then."

"Good night, Shane. Godspeed." She hung up the telephone after he rang off. The house was quiet except for Mavis's sewing machine—she had finally decided what to do with the lovely striped cotton—and the rippling crackle of the fire in the fireplace. If Richard had heard the telephone ring, he'd ignored it.

Jenny's heart was no longer in her letter. Instead, she picked up *The Iliad,* went to the rocking chair, and sat staring into the fire with thoughts of Shane. *The Board of Inquiry can't find against him just because Paul couldn't locate a hunting knife in three feet of snow after it was all trampled to death. They have to clear him. Don't they?* She had no idea whom she asked; whoever it was did not answer.

The next morning she tried to sleep in as long as she could because she knew she would chew her nails to the elbows before afternoon. She managed to finish her letter to Elizabeth, explaining where the scribble had come from, and volunteered to do the handwork on Mavis's blouse so she could put the skirt together. Mavis had admired her handworked buttonholes in a way that made it seem a supreme compliment. Afternoon came and lengthened, and she began to feel like a cheap pocket watch wound much too tightly. Richard came down for tea precisely at four o'clock, as was his habit. Dinner was nearly ready, and it was time for a break. As they sat together at the round table, she could hear the Newhaven on the mantelpiece. It seemed to be ticking slower and slower the longer she listened to it.

"...so I believe I'll have the final chapter proofed and corrected by the end of the week!" Richard concluded triumphantly. She hauled herself to the present.

"That's grand, Uncle Richard. You've worked on this for three years that I know of."

"Then it's time to finish *Through a Glass...*" The telephone interrupted him, and she swallowed hard, lest her heart leap out of her throat. Since she always sat closest to the telephone, it was her job to answer it. She took the earpiece from its cradle.

"Weston Residence. Jenny Weston speaking."

"Doctor Weston?" She recognized Millie Tillman's voice.

"Yes, this is she."

"I have a person-to-person call for you from River Bend. Go ahead, River Bend. Your party is on the line." Jenny heard static and a few indefinite clicks as connections were made and dropped.

"Jenny?" The voice was unmistakable.

"Yes?" Mindful of two pairs of eyes on her, she did not say, "Shane."

"Well, it's over, and I can stop getting gray hairs. So can you, for that matter." *Damn you, Shane Adair, for keeping me on pins and needles!*

"Is everything all right, then, I hope?" There was a maddening pause at the other end of the line. Finally he answered.

"Yes. Everything worked out well. In fact, It's

even better than I'd dared dream. I'll tell you about it when we can talk more freely. Since I missed the one o'clock train, I'm staying with the Shepherds, and they're taking me to dinner. A sort of celebration, if you will. I wish you were here with us. We'd paint the town red. I'll be on the train tomorrow. I'll tell you then, if you can see your way clear to meet me at the station."

"I have to go to town tomorrow anyway. I have a letter to post."

"Good. I'll see you then?"

"Of course. Where are you calling from, if I may ask?"

"Headquarters. I have to leave. Bob is ready to go home. I'll see you tomorrow."

"I'll be there. Good night, and enjoy your evening."

"I will. But I'd enjoy it more if you were with me. Good night, Jenny." She replaced the earpiece and rang off, and turned to find Richard's and Mavis's eyes on her.

"What was that all about, Jen?" Richard asked.

"Sergeant Adair. Without his permission I'm not really at liberty to give you the details, but he had a larger problem than you realized, Uncle Richard. He'll probably tell you about it in his own good time. He called me to tell me that it was resolved satisfactorily. He also said he had more news. The telephone being what it is, he couldn't tell me exactly, just that it's cause for celebration. I'll find out tomorrow. I'm meeting his train, since I have to post Elizabeth's letter in town."

"I won't say Millie Tillman listens in on telephone conversations, but she always did have a nose for gossip." Mavis sniffed.

"Well, then, when you see him tomorrow, tell him if it's really cause for celebration, he's invited to dinner to celebrate. We'll do something special, won't we, Mavis?" Richard said with a broad smile on his face.

"Of course, Mr. Weston."

Jenny turned her face aside to hide a sudden blush.

The next day she felt uncharacteristically restless. She saddled Fleur and took a long and gentle, if cold, walk down to the river, arriving in Elk Gap a full hour ahead of the train. It took a little badgering to convince Josh Barnes to saddle Midnight for her, but as she led the gelding down the street amid a sulky, chill snowfall, her pendant watch read 2:45. Elk Gap was deserted. The wet, cold snow had driven everyone else inside, but she could not have cared less. She was dressed for the weather, and she found the privacy of the storm welcome. She tethered both horses to the rail reserved for draft wagons, then tossed rain ponchos over the saddles and ducked into the shelter of the train terminal. She gazed through the snow, listening rather than watching. Finally the train whistled for the Elk River crossing, and she felt her heart hit her chin. It did not quite resume its proper position until the train pulled up.

Shane was the only passenger to debark. He stood on the platform for a moment, looking around for her.

"I'm here, Shane," she said softly, stepping from the shelter of a doorway. She took three small steps and ran into his arms. It was the first time he had encountered the fact that her mother's Southern roots had made her an impulsive hugger. He returned her embrace.

"I'm so glad the Board of Inquiry cleared you," she said.

"That's only the lesser half of it. Look." He slid his parka down and turned his right arm toward her. The four chevrons of a Staff Sergeant were gone and in their place was a crown.

"Oh, my! You've been promoted! You're an officer now! Inspector, isn't it? I'm so happy for you! You've worked so hard. I know this is well deserved."

"The promotion came way early, too, just like my last one did. But it's partly that I'm a barrister, and I'm probably going to go into administration eventually. You see, the Northwest Mounted will someday have jurisdiction over all of Canada, and I hope I can rise in the ranks as it does." She looked up at his face, noticing that his cheeks were pink with excitement.

"You'll do it if you want to. I know you'll be successful. You're intelligent and educated, and you're too good a police officer not to."

He squeezed her shoulder. "Now it's my turn to say thank you for your faith in me."

"It's not mere blind faith. I know you well enough by now."

"Within the year they'll assign two more officers to Elk Gap. I'll be glad to have them here. I won't have so many reports to do, so I'll have more time to spend with you."

"As I said before, one of your ancestors must have kissed the Blarney Stone," she teased.

"Does it work on you?"

She reddened furiously, but she was determined not to let him have the last word. "That remains to be seen. Keep trying."

"You're such a flirt," he accused softly, releasing her shoulders. He led her down from the station platform and untied the horses' reins. "I'm surprised you brought Midnight."

"I had trouble getting Josh to let me have him. I'm beginning to understand why you're not fond of that man."

"Well, there's more to it than the fact that he can be unpleasant. He's dishonest. Don't ever buy anything from him. That's why Richard asked me to go to Thomas to get you a saddle horse." Jenny mounted, and Shane followed her a fraction of a second later.

"Shane, Uncle Richard has invited you to dinner. He wanted to have a quiet celebration to congratulate you on your good news."

"I'd be honored," he replied, pressing Midnight's reins. It was beginning to seem natural to ride toward home next to him.

"Tonight's not much of a party, just a special dinner, but we're so happy for you. And it was such a surprise to hear from you yesterday. Whatever possessed you to telephone me?"

"I promised to let you know about the Board of Inquiry as soon as I knew anything. I certainly took some teasing from Bob about it, too. And of course he had to tell Marie, and then I was in for a real interrogation. She thinks it's terribly sad that I'm still single, especially since I get on so well with their girls."

"How many children do they have, then?"

"Elise is eleven, Frances is eight, and Jacqueline is just five now, I think. I try to keep track of birthdays, but it's difficult. I've known them since I started here, when Elise was quite young and Frances hardly more than a baby."

"You're fond of them, aren't you?"

Shane smiled quietly. "Truth be known, any of the three can wind me around her little finger. Elise is quite the little lady, Jacqueline is the born sympathizer, and Frances is the tomboy of the bunch. I don't know how many times I've climbed trees after her, and this morning she was on the roof of the porte cochère. She's a redhead, too."

"Oh, dear! Redhead temperament! My, they sound absolutely precious. I'd love to meet them sometime."

"You will. I'll take you to River Bend, perhaps the next time there's something good at the Opera House."

"I'll hold you to that," she replied, smiling. "I'm not certain I'd know how to act in the big city, though."

"You? You grew up in the upper crust of New York society! I'm the one who's strictly a hick. To me, River Bend is the big time!"

Chapter Ten

The days drifted easily into one another. Jenny saw patients, delivered two babies, including Edith Mattson's strong, hungry daughter, whom they named Laura Anne, and basked in the heaven of an actual medical practice. She worked with Toby, who had proven surprisingly easy to teach, since he still had the rudiments of reading from his early schooling. They were both delighted when the door to the rest of the world suddenly opened for him.

Another delight was that Jimmy Richardson had adjusted beautifully to his prosthesis, and on Saturdays, when she accompanied Shane to North Village, he was walking and running with only a trace of a limp. He was terribly proud of the caulk boots she had managed to find in his size. While most of the young people of North Village went about in old-fashioned moccasins, he wore logging boots, the mark of a man.

Those idyllic days were to be short-lived, however. One windy morning when she was turning out of Richard's lane on her way to town, a slight figure on a scrubby bay horse galloped full tilt down the road and pulled to a stop next to her. She turned around and recognized Jimmy.

"Stone Dreaming Woman!" he began excitedly. Jenny held up her hand.

"Slowly, Jimmy. In English. *Ou en Français.* I

speak no Iroquois," she said. He took a breath and bit his lower lip, groping for words.

"My brother, much fever. You come?" It was plain that Jimmy had not applied himself to the English lessons he received in the mission school.

"I will come. *Mais, venez-vous avec moi un moment, s'il vous plaît,*" she said in very slow French, hoping he would have less trouble with that. She beckoned to him, then turned and cantered back down the lane. She led them up to the back porch and dismounted. Jimmy followed, clearly terrified.

"*Un moment,*" she repeated, gesturing to him to sit on the steps. Suspicious of Indians, Toby put down his hoe and came across the yard, his hands outspread, questioning. She took the notepaper and pencil he carried in the breast pocket of his shirt.

"His brother is ill. I am going to North Village," she printed. Ball-and-stick letters were still easier for Toby than her idiosyncratic handwriting, though he had no trouble with Richard's clearer copperplate script. Toby nodded and touched his temple to show he understood. Then she went into the house, where she ran up the stairs two at a time and grabbed her medical bag from beneath her bed. The contents received a cursory inspection before she crossed the small landing and tapped on her uncle's door.

"Yes?" he called from within. She poked her head inside.

"Jimmy Richardson came from North Village. He says his brother is ill with a fever. I'm going up there. Can you do me a favor and telephone Angus and tell him where I've gone? I don't really feel I can take the time."

"All right. Be sure and tell Mavis."

"Mavis went out to the garden, and I'm really in a hurry. But you can tell Shane where I am if he comes out here or calls. I really don't want him up there, though, until I figure out if there's something serious going around."

"All right. Be careful."

"I will, Uncle Richard, but don't wait up for me. I could be a while." She pulled the door closed, careful to make no noise. Richard had a great aversion to slamming doors.

Her arms loaded, she skipped down the stairs. She tied her medical bag and her jacket behind the cantle of the saddle. Jimmy was already mounted, and as soon as she had tucked her toes into the stirrups, he lashed the poor bay into a gallop. She had no choice but to follow.

Their breakneck pace did not slacken until the horses began to climb. Clearly he was anxious, because he kept glancing back at her to make certain she followed.

When they reached the clearing around which North Village clustered, she felt the usual pang of shame and regret that people had to live in such a fashion. Winter had left the ramshackle houses that much sadder and wearier. Porches leaned farther, walls stood a little more crooked, and more and more tarpaper had been added everywhere. Jimmy bounced down, and she noticed with satisfaction that he took as much of the shock on his stump as on his good leg. *Exceptional healing*, she thought, giving herself a mental pat on the back. Then hard on its heels came the thought that the young heal well given half the chance. She paused to tether Fleur to a hitching rail and unfasten her medical bag, and Jimmy led her into his own house.

Unlike Madame LaPorte's log cabin, this was a box-framed board-and-batten shack with a leaning porch. Two children, a boy of about eight years and a girl somewhat younger, retreated to a corner when Jimmy opened the door. Jenny smiled at them as Jimmy said something in Iroquois. The girl looked at Jenny for an instant, but the boy, his eyes fixed on his older brother, gestured toward a door in the back wall.

This house, too, was a two-room shotgun, somewhat better than the run of shacks in North Village in which an entire family lived in one featureless room. She heard voices in the back, and then the door opened and Jimmy's parents exited, followed by the thin, wizened priest she remembered as Father André from Our Lady of the Angels. The priest looked at her as though seeing an apparition.

"What are you doing here?" he asked in his very Parisian French.

"I am a doctor, Father André. If you remember, I treated Jimmy when he injured his leg in the trap. He came for me, saying that his brother is ill."

"A doctor?" the priest echoed. Jenny felt herself becoming impatient and took a deep breath.

"Yes. I've been practicing with Dr. MacBride for the last few months." Father André looked hard at her for a moment, then shook his head slowly.

"The Good Lord never ceases to surprise us, does He? I doubt there is much you can do for Johnny. He received a valid Last Sacrament, but..." He broke off with a sigh and a helpless gesture of spread hands and shook his head again. "I'll come with you as interpreter if you'd like me to."

"Thank you, Father. I'm learning Iroquois, but I haven't come too far yet."

He gave her a sad smile full of wrinkles and weariness, ushered her into the miniscule back room, and turned away, leaving her with her patient.

She swallowed against a lump in her throat when she saw the boy, a thin, slightly taller version of Jimmy, lying unconscious and hyperpyrexic on a pallet of hides and worn blankets. His dark face was flushed hotly save that there was a pale margin around his lips, and as she watched, she noted his erratic breathing. She shook her head. Why had these people waited so long to call her? With a nod to Madame LaPorte, who sat on her knees a few feet away, she opened her medical bag, produced a thermometer, and tucked it into the boy's armpit. But the bright red, sandpapery rash across his chest sounded a more grave alarm within her. Scarlet fever—deadly, and very contagious. And in the next room, three innocent children were defenseless against it. She said a silent prayer that the killer would go no further than this room, but in all probability the streptococcus already had done its ugly work. She plucked the thermometer from Johnny's armpit and read it: 105.8. And the axillary temperature usually ran at least a degree lower than the actual body core temperature. The hideous fire had already wrought irreparable harm, and even as she read the strip of mercury, Johnny's breathing failed for several seconds and resumed with a lurching gasp. Cheyne-Stokes Respiration. It indicated irreversible and terminal neurological damage to the respiratory center in the brain. At that moment Father André entered again, as quietly as a cat. His faded blue eyes questioned her.

"Father, I'm sorry. He's too far gone. It's a matter of time now, probably within the hour. All we can do is wait out the end. Madame, I'm very sorry." Renee LaPorte translated for Helen Richardson, whose face registered no change of expression. Jenny listened with her stethoscope as Johnny's heart stopped. Then she drew the blanket over his face and tried her best not to cry. Once outside the shotgun shack, she turned on Father André.

"Why did they wait? He must have been ill for days!"

"He was, but Doctor MacBride is old and frail, and these people have their own ways of treating things."

"Ways that lead to this!" Jenny retorted, softly but nonetheless vehemently. "If I'd been summoned earlier, he might have had a chance!"

"All is as God wills it, my child," Father André murmured, and she wanted nothing more than the luxury of flying at him. However, she knew the futility of arguing. She had been caught out by this attitude before.

"Be that as it may, we can help keep the disease from spreading. It's scarlet fever. The early symptoms are sore throat, headache, rash, fever, chills. The schoolhouse will be ideal for an isolation ward. Please go among the people and have any who have experienced these symptoms, especially children, come to me there. If we can isolate the sick ones, it'll minimize the risk of contagion, and scarlet fever is one of the worst for spreading. Can you get them to cooperate, Father? And I'll need a few people to help me, but be certain they know they've had the disease. One episode of infection confers lifetime immunity."

He continued to look down at her with timeless patience.

"Every adult here has had the disease. It'll strike only children, like all diseases do in North Village."

"Then can you get the parents to help? I'll check the children for sore throats, but it's imperative that all who have any symptoms whatsoever be isolated. And get some of the men to barricade the trail so that no one will accidentally come up here." Father André nodded, and it struck her that she did not have to give him directions. He had doubtless seen enough epidemics that he would know exactly what had to be done. After a long, sorrowful look toward the mean little house of mourning, he left, and she was alone in the muddy village square. She turned toward Madame LaPorte, who had followed her out of the Richardsons' shack.

"I will help you," the Indian woman murmured in very provincial French.

"*Merci, Madame*," Jenny responded.

By afternoon Jenny had five children in the schoolhouse infirmary. The North Village children reminded her of little squirrels, all dark eyes and furtiveness. Raised in the woods, they were silent, woodsy little things themselves, and it took a lot of cozening on her part to overcome their fear of a white woman. She dispensed aspirin for fever and sprayed throats, though she did not know how much good it would do. Once the disease took hold, it could only be allowed to run its course, and the most she could do was provide good supportive care. The ones who were actually ill were isolated and bundled onto pallets on the floor, attended by five Indian women, among them Madame LaPorte and her sister, who held her deep, maternal grief behind expressionless black eyes.

Just before dusk Jenny checked into the progress in barricading the trail. Four men had dragged a large log across the path just below the village, and after some digging in the schoolhouse, she found a sheet of paper and a charcoal crayon, printed a large sign reading QUARANTINE—SCARLET FEVER, and affixed it to the log. She had no more than finished her task when a voice called up to them and she stepped over the log to see Shane riding up the trail. She moved out to warn him off.

"Don't come any closer. There's scarlet fever here. We've had six cases and one death already." She backed up a step as he pulled Midnight to a stop a little closer than she would have liked.

"Jenny…" he began, but she silenced him with a shake of her head. "No," he insisted. "I'm in this now, so I may as well stay. You're going to need help."

"I have all the help I need. The only thing I need from you is a burial permit. Johnny Richardson died about four hours ago. They'd waited so long to call me that he was comatose when I got here, and there was nothing to be done by then."

His eyes flickered downward. "That's too bad. I've known Johnny a long time. He was a good boy. But how about the other children? We have to work with the ones we can save."

"Not *we*. *Me*. Don't come in." She moved as though to block his path, but he heeled Midnight over the log and she was forced to step out of the way of the big warmblood. "Why did you do that?" she demanded as he swung down from Midnight's back.

"As I said before, you'll need help."

"There's plenty of help here. Father André is with us, and Madame LaPorte. We have enough French to communicate nicely. You have had scarlet fever, I hope?" He nodded, his face tense.

"A long time ago. I don't specifically remember, but I must have had it. I had everything else. There's an outbreak around here every few years."

"Well, as long as you're here, please make out a permit so the body can be buried as soon as possible. That's one small thing we can do to help prevent contagion."

"As soon as I put Midnight up. Jenny, this is a brave thing you're doing."

"I'm a doctor; it's no more than my duty. Would you have told Doctor MacBride he was doing a brave thing?"

"Perhaps I take Angus too much for granted," he replied cryptically.

Later, as she went from child to child in the schoolhouse, changing cool compresses and administering aspirin, she had to admit to herself that Shane's presence was comforting. She had never known anyone so strong and so quietly competent. She could not imagine a situation he could not handle. Then she realized she had begun to feel a deep fondness for him, and in her life that was very much an unknown quantity.

In the half-dark of the schoolhouse she meditated on that for a few minutes. She had never had a regular beau, though her father was staunchly in favor of Phillip Hildebrand. However, she and Phillip, thrown together by parental agreement, had never developed any sort of attraction for each other, and deep inside

Jenny suspected the Hildebrands' motives. After all, the Westons had a great deal of money, and she could reasonably be expected to inherit it all. Idly she wondered if it would matter to Shane whether she inherited money or not. Her first impulse was to doubt it absolutely.

She did not have time to speculate long, though. The worsening condition of ten-year-old Marie Ansiaux claimed her entire attention. Marie's fever climbed to equal Johnny's, and in spite of endless fever baths and cold packs she died shortly before dawn. As though untouched by the death, Madame LaPorte washed and readied the small, fever-ravaged body, and Jenny, who had thrown so much of her energy into keeping the girl alive, felt compelled to question the older woman.

"Madame, was she related to you?" she asked.

"The granddaughter of my late sister," she responded, undoing a braid and brushing out the baby-fine, dusky hair. "Her mother is lucky. She has four others, and this is the first she has lost."

"Lucky?" Jenny prodded. "It's tragic to lose any child so young."

"Tragic for a white woman, perhaps. Here we have two babies to keep one. Some have two families, or even three."

"And you, Madame? How many children did you have?"

"Five. I kept none." There was deep sorrow in the black eyes then, and Jenny had the distinct feeling she had probed too far. But to her the mere concept of bearing two children so that one would grow up was repugnant. She wanted to rage at the poverty around her, at the dirt and the ignorance, at the lack of proper medical attention, and ultimately at God for letting it all happen. But the helpless whimper of the youngest victim, a sturdy-legged boy of two, brought her back to reality. If the Chinese proverb were true and the journey of ten thousand miles begins with a single step, there were several steps she could take right here in North Village within the next few days.

She went to his pallet and picked him up, balancing him against her left shoulder. He whimpered again, a high, drawn-out moan rather than a cry, and made a halfhearted effort to thrust a finger into his mouth. She spent the next half hour coaxing him to drink, and considered it a victory when she managed to spoon half a cup of water into him. With adequate fluids he had a chance, as he seemed much less sick than the others.

The next morning Father André and the men from the village carried their sad, small burden up the hill to be buried. Jenny, though, stayed behind, tending the four remaining children and catching an hour's nap when she could. Later she watched the group come back, Shane's bright tunic conspicuous against the more somberly dressed Indians. He walked in the middle of the party, with Father André on one side and Jimmy Richardson on the other. As usual, she observed with satisfaction that Jimmy had lost all but a hint of his limp. She breathed on the streaked windowpane and rubbed it with her cuff to see better. Her heart constricted as Jimmy stumbled heavily against Shane. Then she saw that it was more than a stumble as Shane caught Jimmy's inert form and lifted the boy in his arms. The look of alarm on Father André's face did not escape her either. Her heart constricted into a cold knot. It was probable that another one of the Richardson children would contract the disease, but did it have to be Jimmy? He had been through so much already. She ran from the schoolhouse as Shane turned down the path.

"Is it...?" she called softly. He looked at her, his face grave.

"I'm afraid so," he responded, glancing at Jimmy, unconscious in his arms. When she reached them, she could diagnose it without even touching her patient. His face was flushed save for the characteristic pale ring about the lips, and his breathing was stertorous. Through the half-open collar she could see the classic rash at the base of his throat. Sadly she shook her head.

"Bring him inside," she murmured.

She had the gut feeling that she could do little for Jimmy. It was a diagnostic sixth sense she possessed in equal measure to her father's. This time it made her strive all the harder. As much as she wanted to deny it, she had developed an attachment to the boy. Shane, too, seemed to catch her determination, spending hours sitting by Jimmy's pallet, speaking quietly to him when he awoke, and sponging his body endlessly until his own hands became waterlogged. She marveled at his patience and his physical ability to sit cross-legged for so long at a time. Long since she would have become as stiff as a board. But in spite of aggressive doses of fluids, endless fever baths, and Jimmy's own heroic strength, twenty-six hours later the fever won.

Helen Richardson, who had now lost two sons, sang an odd, breathy song as she prepared the body for burial. She had cut her hair in mourning the first time; now it was even shorter. Jenny signed her third death certificate, Shane provided the appropriate burial permit, and, as evening fell, another sad procession trekked up the hill to the burial ground. This time she followed the pine coffin, and before they were halfway up the hill, Shane fell in step beside her, looking pale and tired and seeming as numb as she herself felt. *If anything, he's worked harder than I have*, she thought, finding a new measure of respect for him.

It seemed forever until they reached the top of the hill, but just at sunset Jimmy's coffin was lowered into a freshly dug grave, and Father André's Latin drifted around her like the sulky, cool wind that blew damp clouds before it. Unable to understand Father André's accented Latin as well as Shane apparently did, she was left alone with her thoughts. She was not a crier; she tried in vain to remember the last true tears she had ever shed. However, it was a struggle against her tight throat and stinging eyes every time she thought of the thin, fever-worn boy whose life had been cut short so pathetically soon. He had been buried in his new boots, the scarcely used prosthesis in place.

Dear God, why? her mind screamed. *Why? That death should never have happened! It was useless and it was senseless! These people are so crowded together here, their housing and sanitation is so bad, and they're too poor and too uneducated to know the difference. That's the real reason behind all this tragedy, this preposterous acceptance of the notion that you must bear two children to keep one.* Standing beside Shane, her short nails digging into her palms, she made a vow. The blood of the Old General that ran in her veins saw the enemy. It was ignorance. Well, if these people couldn't lick ignorance alone, they could with her help.

The battle was joined. She said farewell to New

York and to her dream of a surgical practice at Northtown, knowing now that Elk Gap had a grip on her heartstrings. It no longer mattered that she and her father would remain estranged. Her life was now here, among these people who so desperately needed her, and perhaps with a certain tall man in a red tunic. She came to as Father André said something that had the ring of finality to it. The service must be over, she concluded, as Shane had replaced his hat and two men were filling in the grave. The villagers filed off, one by one, while Helen Richardson and her elder sister, Renee LaPorte, remained by the grave a moment longer. She said farewell to Jimmy, vowing that his death would not be in vain. Shane, so observant that she found it eerie, noticed as she looked back over her shoulder.

"That was hard for you, wasn't it?" he asked.

She turned her eyes up to him, surprised at his directness. "Well, a little bit. From a professional standpoint, I let myself grow fonder of Jimmy than I should have." That admission came hard. He nodded, the serious lines of his face unrelieved.

"I understand. I saw it happening to you. It just means you have a heart, that's all," he said, giving her a sad half-smile, which seemed to be all he could manage at the moment.

When they reached the schoolhouse, two of the women who had not gone to the funeral had brought supper. Silently one of them gave Jenny and Shane bowls of some sort of fragrant stew that had large chunks of meat, carrots, and potatoes in it and handed them each a piece of fried bread. She sat at one of the benches, while Shane folded his long legs beneath him to sit next to her. For some time they ate in silence, both too tired for words. He looked especially worn, she thought. Even though he had been out in the cool air, his face looked pale, and the usual Irish ruddiness across the tops of his cheekbones had faded. With clinical eyes she watched him as he ate. He was one of those clear-skinned people who would not show a rash easily, but he seemed to have no difficulty swallowing. She set her concern aside. After all, he had told her he was immune to scarlet fever, and she had no reason to doubt him.

"Is there something wrong?" he asked.

Guiltily she flinched. It must have been obvious that she was watching him. "No, not really. I was just noticing that you look a little tired. What's in this stew, anyway? It's very good." She could not have cared less about the stew. The comment was merely to deflect his attention.

He grinned wryly. "It's bear meat," he responded.

"Bear meat?" she echoed, staring at her spoon with suspicion.

"You haven't eaten bear before?"

"No, but I guess it won't hurt me," she muttered, taking another bite and chewing deliberately.

"It's good for you. I've eaten a lot of it in my life. The only thing is that it has to be cooked thoroughly."

"Oh? Bears can carry trichinosis?"

"Of course they can. They're omnivores, after all," he replied with a shrug.

"Well, that's logical," she agreed, wondering why that fact had been left out of her medical training. Probably nobody in Arlington would ever see a medical practice where people ate bear meat. Finding it amusing, she smiled. "I'm really out on the frontier now. When I took parasitology, nobody ever mentioned bears."

"Your education geared you to a civilized medical practice. How do you feel about the wild frontier now?" He emptied his bowl, wiping up the last of the gravy with his bread.

"These people need a lot of help they're not getting now." She felt the intensity of his eyes on her.

"Does that mean you're staying?"

"For the present, yes." Even his obvious bone-tiredness did not keep the broad smile off his face.

"I think Angus wants you to stay, too. His arthritis gets worse every winter, and you know how hard it is for him to answer calls in the outlying countryside."

"I've no trouble with that, now that I'm learning my way around. Soon I won't need a guide." The front door interrupted their conversation. Renee LaPorte, her bear robe about her shoulders against the night chill, let herself in silently and crossed the room to sit beside the pallets of the three remaining children. Her soft moccasins made no noise on the plank floor, and she sank down cross-legged with the ease of a lifetime of practice. Jenny could not help but see beauty in her dignity and simple grace, and despite her age beginning to show, she was a handsome woman.

"Shane, didn't you tell me she's one of the village elders or something like that?" Jenny asked.

"She sits on the tribal council, yes. Why do you ask?"

"Everyone seems to defer to her judgment. She's a natural leader. Is it unusual for a woman to be on the tribal council?"

"Among the Iroquois it's actually quite common.

The Council's not hereditary or patriarchal or anything like that. People who have a reputation for intelligence and wisdom are just nominated by consensus of opinion."

"Well, Madame LaPorte certainly fills that bill. I'd love to get to know her better. She's fascinating."

He rose somewhat abruptly. "I'm going to get more stew. Can I bring you some?"

"No, thank you. I'm fine. I should go check the rest of my patients before we turn the lights out."

He paused, his long legs straddling the bench. "Do you think the epidemic may be running its course?"

"Well, perhaps. Aside from Jimmy, we haven't had a new case in four days, and I suspect he was sick for a while and didn't tell anyone. The incubation period is two weeks. Once we've gone that long with no new cases, the quarantine can be lifted." He nodded, seeming a little pleased at her optimism.

Of her three patients, only one was still acutely ill. The other two had passed the crisis and would recover. One of them, a six-year-old girl, worried her. The youngest boy had bounced back, but though the girl's fever had fallen, she remained lethargic and unresponsive. Brain damage was a definite possibility. Jenny had noted in the records that this case bore monitoring for some time. The girl's dark eyes followed as Jenny tried to coax her to respond, but she acted as if she did not care what went on around her. Perhaps she was simply too weak to react yet, Jenny hoped, but her mind dredged up a catalog of possible aftereffects, including idiocy and deafness. At this point all she could do was wait and see. The third child, a slightly older girl, was at the height of her fever. Jenny would watch with her tonight, even though she had only managed an hour or so of sleep in the last twenty-four, and she would pray that this case would be the last.

Thick candles provided the only illumination in the schoolhouse. She had no quarrel with the kerosene lamps in Elk Gap, but these smelly deer tallow candles were a shade too primitive. They made it difficult to read her thermometer, but as she tilted it this way and that, the feeble light finally caught the ribbon of mercury. Good. Alice's fever was down half a degree. She had thought the girl would throw off the worst of the illness tonight, and she was not disappointed. She checked once more to make certain all three children were snugly covered, then looked at her watch. It was nearly one o'clock, and the interior of the schoolhouse had become frankly cold. Doing up the top button of her cardigan, she opened the isinglass door of the old stove, laying five sections of alder into it as quietly as she could. She made a mental note to tell Shane they would need more wood by afternoon. After gazing into the fire for a while she closed the door, raising it carefully so the catch would not clatter.

After a minute or so, she concluded that her nocturnal perambulations had not disturbed Madame LaPorte, who dozed upright in a corner next to the children's pallets, or Shane, who had picked the coldest and most remote corner of the whole room to spread out a blanket. Taking up her candle, she tiptoed across the room to where he lay, one blanket doubled beneath him and another tossed haphazardly over his body. He had taken off his Red Serge and folded it for a pillow, though he was still wearing the rumpled white shirt that went beneath it. He lay curled tightly on his right side, and as she watched he drew up his legs a little more. *He needs another blanket or two. It's cold in here*, she thought, but she was hesitant to risk waking him. He needed his rest. This was the first night he had slept more than two hours since the beginning of the epidemic.

She watched for a few minutes more as the uncertain candlelight picked out the slight concavity beneath his cheekbone and shadowed his eyes. He looked as self-possessed in sleep as he did awake. When she had first met him, that unshakeable composure had irritated her past bearing, but long since she had moved past her desire to assail it. Watching him with Jimmy Richardson had shown her that he had a very sensitive heart indeed.

Even her heavy cardigan was inadequate in this end of the schoolhouse. She was certain he would soon awaken of his own accord unless he had more covers. Setting her candle holder on the nearest table, she took up two clean blankets from a stack on one of the tables, shook them out together, and draped them over him, settling them gently around his shoulders As she was fighting an irrational urge to smooth the jet black hair that hung awry over his forehead, he opened his eyes languidly and turned just a little to look up at her. She gave in to her impulse and gently stroked his tumbled hair back. He smiled.

"Thank you for the blankets. I was getting cold. How's everything?" he asked in an undertone.

"Fine. Go back to sleep. I'll come for you if I need you." She laid a gentle palm on his shoulder, and his right hand emerged from the blankets to cover her fingers briefly. The print of his warm fingers remained on the back of her hand even after he settled himself back beneath the blankets. She noted again that his hands were always warm, even after he had been outside in the cold.

"Good night, Jenny," he murmured.

"Good night, Shane." Her hand lingered against his shoulder for a second more. She would have kissed him had they been alone; instead, she combed his unruly hair back from his forehead again, then stood and wandered back to the warmth haloing the potbellied stove.

She managed to nap off and on for the next few hours, awakening fully at dawn when a dog barked outside the schoolhouse. She sat up, stretching, and the first thing she noticed was that Shane was already gone, leaving his blankets folded neatly where he had slept. Madame LaPorte still sat cross-legged next to Alice; she looked up at Jenny and nodded. Helen Richardson, beside her, waited to acknowledge Jenny until her older sister had done so.

"All is well with her," she said. Jenny was finding it easier to understand her oddly accented French. "The fever is nearly gone."

"*Bien*," Jenny replied, kneeling on the other side of the pallet. She did look better, and when Jenny pressed her palm against the girl's smooth forehead, she felt the normal warmth of a sleeping child.

"Is the sickness over?" Madame LaPorte asked, turning her dark eyes to Jenny.

"Perhaps. We must wait to see. If there are no new cases in fourteen days, it will have run its course."

"Until the next time," the older woman added.

"God willing, there won't be a next time. There are

medicines, called vaccines, that can be given to children so they will not become ill, and there are other ways to prevent the diseases that kill so many of your babies. Madame, perhaps at one time it was necessary to have two children so that one would grow up, but that is no longer true. With your cooperation, I can teach your people how to keep their children healthy." The Indian woman's gaze was intense with an odd mixture of hope and disbelief. "I am telling you the truth, Madame. If I can only work with everyone here, to show them how to eat well and to keep clean, how to keep their drinking water pure, and if I can inoculate the young children…" Jenny broke off; from Madame LaPorte's expression it was plain the last term had lost her completely. "I mean, give them medicine that will keep them from becoming ill. If I can do that, not nearly as many will die. But I need your help, Madame." Jenny was overtly pleading now, and the more she spoke, the darker the other woman's expression became.

"The old white healer has not done this, and he has many years and is very wise," she replied at length. Jenny saw a door slam behind the black eyes.

In this situation it would not do to challenge Angus MacBride's competence. It would only antagonize the older woman, who evidently respected him a great deal. "Prevention of disease with medicines is possible, Madame. Doctor MacBride is too old and too frail to come to North Village anymore. He cannot bring you these medicines. I can. Please believe me, they can help. They can save children like Marie Ansiaux and Johnny and Jimmy Richardson." Jenny's voice trailed off as the woman slowly shook her head.

"Such words from one so young. No. We have our

own ways of living and dying, Stone Dreaming Woman. Live with us for a while and you too will understand." Jenny's excitement gave way to the Old General's temper, and she wanted to grab Madame LaPorte by the shoulders and shake her into submission.

"Is it your way of life to suffer unnecessarily? To allow your children to die before their time? Those deaths did not have to happen. They could have been prevented. I can prevent more like that in the future. Just let me have the chance!" The Iroquois elder gave her a look of timeless pity, then rose in one fluid motion, uncrossed her ankles, and left the room. Jenny wanted to run after her and scream that she simply had to listen, had to cooperate, had to give her people a chance; but on a deeper level she knew it would do no good. Then she became aware of Helen Richardson's eyes on her. Though she had understood little, if any, of their conversation, Jenny had no doubt that the silent woman knew exactly what had transpired. Raging inwardly at injustice, ignorance, and stupidity, she felt that she had to get out of the confines of the schoolhouse or go mad. She pointed from Helen to the three children, then from herself to the door, and Helen, understanding, nodded. Jenny threw on the grey cardigan and strode outside, into the equally grey day that had been sullied by intermittent showers. Still boiling inside, she started briskly up the hill. She did not mean to go to the cemetery, but since the path led that way, she followed it without thinking.

The steep path stretched perhaps half a mile, and by the time she reached the end, her anger had in large part subsided. She walked around the perimeter of the cemetery, noting a few of the names on the markers. Then she came to the Richardson plot with its two new graves. She stood for some time gazing down at Jimmy's final resting place. Lost in prayer, she did not realize when Shane came to stand beside her. When she became aware of him, he stood quietly next to her, holding the brim of his Stetson in both hands. They looked at each other.

"I know. It's hard, isn't it?" His question was more of a statement.

"It is. And those deaths were so unnecessary. I talked to Madame LaPorte about vaccinating the North Village children, and she walked out of the room. And did you know there are vaccines against smallpox, diphtheria, and tetanus now? I expect one for pertussis—whooping cough—will probably come any day."

"And scarlet fever?" Shane asked.

"No. It's a different breed of cat. It's bacterial. You really can't vaccinate against bacteria. The others are caused by extremely tiny things termed viruses. We don't exactly understand viruses yet, or why vaccines can be developed for viral diseases. There is a lot of exciting research going on. But someday we'll have medicines that can fight bacteria. One is being researched right now. It's called, well, sulpha, for short. It was only just discovered, but it will kill bacterial infection when it is applied topically to wounds. It won't be long until we find a way to administer it orally. It's going to open the door to a whole new field."

Shane shook his head. "Do you really think the vaccines work?"

"I know they do. The pertussis—whooping cough—vaccine is still experimental, but if I can only have a chance, I know I can enroll these children in a scientific study and vaccinate them so they won't get it anymore. But Madame LaPorte seemed to think since Doctor MacBride hadn't already done it, it isn't worth doing. I didn't impugn him in any way. I only told her that it's not physically possible for him to come up here anymore, so in effect they're stuck with me, but she couldn't accept that as a final answer."

"Even though I'm an outsider I do carry some weight in Council. Jenny, I'd go way out on a limb for these people. If you really want to vaccinate the children, I'll see that you have the chance."

"And can you get them to either move their backhouses or dig a new well and fill the old one in? Uphill from the school would be an ideal location. It's not so far that hauling water would be difficult, but it's far enough away that there won't be any contamination from the backhouses. Clean water will eliminate things like typhoid, cholera, dysentery, and meningitis—all the water-borne diseases. And get them to promise to send for me the minute anyone is ill? I'll come immediately, no matter what else is going on. The delay is likely what killed those three children."

"Oh, Jenny, when you get the bit between your teeth you really run, don't you?" he asked rhetorically. He walked a few paces, and she fell in beside him.

"That's the only way to accomplish anything."

"When I was only two years old, the smallpox epidemic that killed my family started here and eventually spread down to Elk Gap. Angus told me I also had it, but of course I was much too young to remember. He didn't call mine smallpox, though. He called it something else. Some kind of rash. Very…something."

"Varioloid rash?" His eyebrows raised.

"That's it."

"Well, you were fortunate. It's the least severe form. It's not disfiguring and it doesn't even make people that sick. However, you'll be immune from now on. On the other hand, I've been vaccinated. And if I can vaccinate these people, there will no longer be smallpox outbreaks here."

He nodded. "For the sake of my family I'll help you, Jenny. Any way I can. As I said, I'm the long arm of the law. I do have some influence with the tribal elders. I'll speak for you at the Council fire."

"I have a suspicion that Madame LaPorte may be the key."

"She probably is. In that case… Well, just say I have an advantage. She listens to me."

"I do hope so. Well, at any rate, I've left the schoolhouse too long. As much as I'd like to stay here with you, I really have to get back. Would you do me a favor and tell the men we need wood this morning?" He nodded in reply, and she started down the trail, leaving him standing alone at the cemetery.

Oh, Shane Patrick Adair, you liar, he said to himself. *You're no outsider. There are the graves of your whole family: Grandpère, Maman, your sister Louise… Only your father is missing, and nobody ever seemed to know where he went. When are you going to tell her you're Walker between Water and Sky, a half-breed who actually went on a manhood vision quest and joined the Warrior Society? When are you going to confess your grandmother is a full-blooded Iroquois? When are you going to come clean that you don't know if your parents were ever married, and that when you needed a birth certificate to matriculate at Royal Dominion, Angus falsified his records to say he had attended your birth? Will you ever be ready for her to denounce and revile you as the filthy Métis bastard you are? You've led her on too long. She'll come to love you, and you'll break her heart the same way you broke Ruth's, just by being who and what you are. Dante must have had some special place in his Inferno for men like you.* Then hard on the heels of that thought came another: *He did. You're living in it.*

Silently he moved between the graves until he stood above his grandfather's resting place. *It hasn't been that long. Grandpère, you've only been dead, what? Five years now? Going on six? At least I was back from Ottawa before you passed away. You never really saw me in uniform, because you were blind by then, but you knew. You knew and you were proud of me. You wouldn't be so proud of what I'm doing now, though, by being dishonest with Jenny. But I love her so much it's painful to consider. I love her more than my own life, and she's as far above me as the moon. I know her family is rich and aristocratic, and then there's me. I can't even really hold my head up in either world, white or Iroquois. Truth be known, I'm the real Stray Dog, not these people. I belong nowhere, to no one.*

With sorrow and desolation choking him, he dropped to one knee next to his grandfather's grave, took off his gauntlets, and pressed his hand into the soil, as though he could connect physically with the man who had been the pole star of his life since he could remember, the man who taught him to draw and to be a woodsman, the man who laughed, sang, and loved life, as simple as it was. But if life had been simple for Jean-Louis LaPorte, his grandson carried the burden of two worlds upon his shoulders. At the moment he felt crushed by it.

"Oh, Grandpère, if your campfire is among the stars, look down at me. Tell me what I must do. I can't walk the white man's path any longer. It's too painful, too long, too lonely. I'm not welcome in that world. But I'm not really of The People either. You saw to it that I would move beyond their simple ways, but right now it's so hard. Please help me." His words came out in an agonized whisper, and he did not even realize he was speaking Iroquois until he heard his own last sentence. Shane, who had never wept at the loss of his grandfather, finally gave vent to his long-held grief with short-lived, silent tears. He remained on his knees, looking down at the still grave through blurred eyes, while around him the chill, unheeding rain fell.

Eventually he knew what he had to do. He had to face his dilemma like a man and clear his conscience. When a plan of action became apparent to him, he came back to the present and felt the rain soaking his shoulders and back through the wool of his tunic. He said a mental farewell to his grandfather's grave and started down the path toward the schoolhouse. After a brief stop at the pump to clean the knees of his breeches and rinse the mud from his hands and the tears from his face, he walked slowly up the steps. Feeling the weight of the world still crushing down on his shoulders, he let himself in. Jenny was there, sitting at one of the long tables, completing her daily records. She looked up at him and smiled. The sweet trust on her face made him wince. When she took in his wet hair and his wet coat, a frown of concern puckered the clear skin between her brows. She capped her pen and stood up, coming over to him.

"Oh, look at you. You're soaked. You have to be cold, and right now that won't do. Come over by the stove and take off that jacket." In a gesture that seemed impulsive to him she took his hand and led him to the far corner of the room, where the fire still warmed the big, potbellied stove despite the lack of wood.

"It's not that cold out," he protested. "I'm fine. I'm accustomed to this sort of thing. It happens all the time. Besides, wool is as warm wet as dry."

She caught both his hands, and a welter of conflicting emotions boiled up inside him. "Well, perhaps you're right. Your hands are warm."

"They're always warm. If they ever get cold, I'm cold all over." She kept hold of his hands, an even more unsettling gesture.

"Shane, I want to thank you for staying here even after I told you not to. I don't know how I'd have managed without you. You're so good with these people." She looked up at him earnestly, and he would gladly have drowned himself in the dark pools of her eyes. He could not maintain contact with them. Instead he looked down at their intertwined hands.

"I knew what you were up against. You're a fine physician but you're still out of your element here in North Village. I had to make it easier for you, if I could."

She moved a step closer. "I've learned a few things about you over the last few days. You're a very concerned, caring person. I admire that." She was near to him, so very near. He felt his heart hammering in his chest. It had to be now. He had to tell her, to come clean and unburden his conscience, or he would never have the gumption for it again.

"But there's something I need to tell you…" He broke off, frozen between languages and half immobilized with fear. *If I tell her now, it's over. I can't. I just can't.*

"What, Shane?" She cocked her head a little, her voice softly concerned.

"Um, I have to go back outside. With the funeral this morning, I forgot to feed the horses. I also have to tell the men about the wood." Abruptly he dropped her hands and almost fled from the room. In his head, the derisive little voice that had called him *Métis* now added *coward.*

Once outside, the cool air and the rain calmed his racing mind. He went to the small corral where Midnight and Fleur stood under the shelter of a makeshift half-enclosed loafing shed. It had a small loft to store a limited amount of hay against the times when he stayed in the village. He climbed the ladder to the loft and forked down fodder enough for both horses, then checked their water. Midnight came up to him, wanting attention, and lipped at the front of his tunic when it was not immediately forthcoming. Shane scratched his poll and down the top of his neck, stroking his mane. He vowed to give the gelding a good grooming as soon as the rain stopped and he dried out. After talking to the horse for several minutes, he felt his anxiety ratchet down several notches.

The routine tasks gave him focus to the point at

which he could consider the very big question of Jenny more objectively. If he could not tell her about himself and his background now, the right time would come. Or perhaps it would not. The situation might just resolve itself. For the present he would simply wait, let things ride, and see what happened. Much more composed now, he gave Midnight a final pat and went back toward the schoolhouse.

The last four days of the quarantine went quietly. The remaining three children recovered unremarkably and went back to their families, although Jenny resolved aloud to give the oldest girl a hearing test as soon as she had time to regain her strength. Then, on a day that hinted at the first blush of summer, they rode down the steep trail from North Village, Jenny eager to reclaim her life and Shane, still dodging the question he had asked his grandfather, not at all eager to reclaim his heart.

Chapter Eleven

It had become Shane's habit to go to North Village early so he had a reason to stop by Richard Weston's house on the way back. The gentle late June morning, so quickly warming after the ending of fickle Canadian spring, was soft with the promise of summer. When he arrived at Richard's ranch, he put Midnight in the barn, hopped over the three steps up to the porch, and knocked on the door, which Jenny opened immediately.

"Well, you look like the cat that swallowed the canary. Come in!"

"Hello, Jenny. Mavis." He waved at Toby, who was sitting at the table, obviously in the midst of a reading lesson. Toby smiled and waved back, then made a tactful retreat to the barn. "I do have good news, Jenny. I spoke to the North Village Council again last night. You can vaccinate everybody, and they agreed to move the well—in fact, the digging is supposed to start today. I know it took a while. There were some holdouts that needed convincing."

"Oh, how wonderful! You're a real miracle worker!" She wanted to hug him but, mindful of Mavis, restrained herself.

"And I have something more."

"Oh? What's that?"

"In all that mountain of paperwork I had to take care of while Paul was on holiday, there's an invitation to a formal ball. It seems Adrian Beaufort is giving a reception for the Governor. It's Saturday after next. Would you like to go with me?" The invitation came at her like a high fly to left field.

"I don't know..."

"Please? I have to go. His big shindigs are obligatory for us. There's no easy way for me to get out of it. So please, become a New York debutante for me for an evening and go as my guest?"

"A formal ball? The only gown I brought with me is a winter one."

Mavis cocked an eyebrow at her. "Winter gown? Phooey. Nobody in River Bend will know the difference. Go and have a grand time."

Jenny knew the advantage of giving in gracefully. "Very well. I'd love to go with you."

He broke into a wide smile that could have lit the room. "Thank you so much. Now I won't have to spend a long, boring evening being gracious to all the widows and wallflowers in River Bend. Instead I'll have the privilege of being gallant to you." He paused long enough for her to smile back at him. "As I said, it's Saturday after next. I'll come for you early in the morning, weather permitting. It's about a three-hour ride to Bob and Marie Shepherd's home. It'll be much more interesting than taking the train. We'll stay there overnight and come back Sunday, with your permission, and of course, Richard's."

The next week and a half passed with all the stately speed of a homesick snail. Jenny had never immersed herself in anticipation of a social occasion before, but now, even despite her medical practice, she found herself counting the days. And when Saturday eventually did arrive, it was hard for her to believe it came no faster or slower than any other Saturday since the beginning of time.

True to his word, Shane rode up to the house just in time to share breakfast. In spite of herself, Jenny was so excited she could scarcely eat. Everything she needed had been packed in her saddlebags, ripped out, packed, repacked, and packed again. Finally they were ready to leave.

"Have a lovely time," Richard said, accepting Jenny's farewell kiss. "I'll see you tomorrow afternoon."

"Thank you. I know we'll enjoy ourselves."

"Take care of my girl, Shane."

"Don't worry about Jenny. She's in the capable hands of the law," he replied, smiling wryly.

Richard waved as they set off down the lane.

"How much do you remember about your train ride in?" Shane asked after they had turned off the main road.

"Just trees and snow. Constable Bernard and I were talking, and since our conversation was in French, I had to pay attention."

He chuckled. "Laurence is somewhat provincial, isn't he? He still insists on speaking French with me. Well, the trail along the right of way isn't much. The way we're going is quicker, and it'll be steep until we pick up the railroad tracks."

"Were Laurence's people voyageurs too?"

"No. Huguenots. It seems France is good at running people out, doesn't it?"

"No worse than England, although my family didn't have to emigrate. The Westons came to the

Carolinas on a royal land grant in the late 1600s. My Brisbane ancestor, though, was a British officer who came during the Revolution. He was wounded too badly to serve any longer or to make it home on his own, so he stayed. The family tradition says he lost a leg. Eventually he recovered, went to work as a clerk at an import house, and married the boss's daughter. Supposedly they lived happily ever after—at least they had eleven surviving children, and they did become very rich."

"So you're English, then?"

"Basically, yes. But both halves of my family have been here so long we could be anything." She relaxed and went with Fleur's steady gait, raising up in the stirrups and leaning forward to help the mare climb. Suddenly Shane's hand came out in a hushing gesture and he pointed upslope to their left. A shy whitetail buck, antlers only velvet knobs, peered out from the brush. Since he was upwind, he could not decide what they were. He flinched and jumped as he tried to catch their scent. Finally Midnight stamped an impatient forehoof and tossed his head, and the buck broke upslope in huge leaps.

"He's beautiful!" she breathed. "We see does all the time, but rarely bucks."

"You'll see more, come fall, when they're in rut. And in all probability we'll run across more before tomorrow." He touched his heels to Midnight's flanks, and the tall gelding resumed his implacable, steady climb. She enjoyed the green, earthy scent as sunshine penetrated to the forest floor.

"This forest is so wonderful," she remarked at length.

"That's one of the reasons I like my job. I get to be outside on days like this. Then, on the other hand, I have to be out on nasty days like the one when The Girls tried to run away and Midnight got tangled up in the wire." The trail dipped momentarily into a clearing. A few minutes later the trees thinned out and they headed up what looked like a game trail.

"We're going to take a side trip here," he informed her. "We're about three miles from the top now. I think you'll like the view. You can see all the way down the Elk River." They climbed up a rocky, sparse hillside, then broke out onto a glacier-scarred promontory. She involuntarily caught her breath. To the north and west were more forested, rolling hills. To the east, though, a green-carpeted valley spread below them, containing at its depth a river like a ribbon of molten silver that had melted its way down.

"This is called Overlook Point. See that line cabin over there? Sometimes I stay there when I ride rounds." Her gaze followed his finger. A tiny shack was just visible through the trees. Then a piercing cry made her look up. Two eagles were riding the air currents. "They mate for life. I've seen that pair before, but I haven't found their aerie yet."

"They're magnificent," she whispered, unwilling to disturb the sound of the wind. "This is such a beautiful place. How did you ever discover it?"

"Oh, just exploring, a long time ago. Remember, I've lived around here all my life. Sometimes I stop here just to think." She looked from Shane to the eagles again. They were circling in a thermal, seeming to defy gravity by climbing without moving their wings. Only the attitude of a few primary feathers determined their direction.

"How free they are, not stuck to the earth with petty daily pursuits like us."

"Oh, they have their petty daily pursuits too. Somewhere they have a couple of hungry children to feed, and that's serious business, whether you're an eagle or a human. Maybe they don't have to go to receptions for the Governor, but they still have their worries."

"Is this a duty visit for you, then?"

"No, not completely. I wanted to take you to something really grand—at least grand by our standards. Besides, Angus said nobody would notice me for looking at you."

"You don't believe all of Angus's blarney, do you?"

"That wasn't blarney. You just wait. You'll be the belle of the ball."

"I've never been that in my life. I think too much, and I say what I think far too often."

"Be prepared to say it in French, then. The Governor is Québécois. But we'd best be on our way. It's close to noon, and you and Marie will need some primping time once we're there." He turned Midnight back down the trail toward the railroad right of way.

"How close are we, then?"

"We've come within a mile of half way. But the last part isn't nearly as interesting. All it does is follow the railroad tracks, and for the most part it's straight."

"But it's still an adventure for me. I've never been any closer to the woods than Central Park…" She was cut off by a gesture from Shane. He pointed to a creek bank downstream to their right, where a small brown creature was drinking.

"Mink," he whispered. Suddenly there was a bright splash, and the mink dashed off with a struggling trout in its jaws.

"There's supper," Jenny whispered with a silent laugh.

"He has his table to set, too."

"You make all these animals seem so human!"

"Well, basically we all have the same worries. It's just that animals are so much more direct. If Midnight felt like kicking someone, he'd do it. On the other hand, if I felt like kicking someone, I'd probably just make a nasty remark."

"I swear, you have the whole world figured out."

He gave her a slight smile. "Not you, Jenny. Not ever. There are a lot of things about you I'll never understand, but that's why women are interesting."

Their conversation drifted on like the creek they followed. The way became much easier after they intersected the railroad tracks. A wagon road ran parallel to the roadbed, and in its width they were able to ride side by side. Before she knew it, they were in River Bend. She remembered the railroad station that reminded her of a pagoda, and the long row of warehouses directly opposite. But now that she rode through the streets, she realized the city was larger than it looked from the train.

"This really is a good-sized town. I hadn't realized that before," she remarked.

"Almost fifteen thousand people. By train you only see the northwest corner." It seemed the entire town was draped in red-and-white bunting, and flags flew everywhere. He let Midnight walk unguided beside

Fleur while he took his holster off his crossover belt and dropped the revolver into his saddlebag. At Richard's he automatically hung the gun, belt and all, on the coat rack by the door before he did anything else.

"I have to do this before I get to Bob's house," he explained. "His girls all want to hug me the minute I dismount, even though they've been told time and again never to touch anyone wearing a sidearm. Of course Bob indulges them, but I don't blame him. They're real charmers."

"I think you probably indulge them a bit, too, don't you?"

"Well, I tell them stories and draw pictures for them sometimes, and now and then I let them ride Midnight."

"No wonder they're fond of you."

"Bob has been my boss for better than six years now, and I'm at his house every few weeks. I've seen the younger two, Frances and Jacqueline, grow up. Elise was already quite the little lady when I first met Bob."

"You said she's eleven?"

"I think so. I try to keep track, but I really can't remember whose birthday is which." He turned through a maze of streets into what appeared to be an older, gracious section of River Bend. They climbed a slight rise, and he indicated a white-columned brick house with a dignified porte cochère. Rose beds flanked the wide drive, with a profusion of riotously colored pansies at the foot of each bush. They stopped by the coach door and, just as Shane helped Jenny down, three little girls streamed from the house. They all laughed and chattered at once, at least one in French at any given time. Shane squatted down, while they instantly smothered him in hugs and damp kisses.

"Shane!"

"Maman! Shane is here! He has a pretty lady with him!"

"Will you tell us a story?"

"Can we ride Midnight later?"

"Draw us a picture, please?"

"Are you staying with us, then?"

"Girls! Girls! Let the poor man catch his breath!" The source of the voice was an auburn-haired woman in a brown dress. Shane rose with Jacqueline on one arm, Frances on the other, and Elise with an arm about his waist. "*Vraiment*, Shane, you spoil them so!"

"Hello, Marie. I see the girls are in grand form. How are you and Bob?" As the girls settled down, Jenny realized, to her amusement, that Marie and Bob had managed to produce a blonde, a brunette, and a redhead.

"Bob and I couldn't be better. Then this must be your young lady."

"Forgive me for not introducing you sooner, but I've been a bit occupied. Marie, may I present Doctor Jennifer Weston. Jenny, this is Mrs. Marie Shepherd."

"How do you do, Doctor Weston. It's such a pleasure to meet you finally! Come here, Jacqueline, before you muss Shane's coat. He has told us so much about you. Frances, take your thumb out of your mouth. You're no longer a baby." Any response would have been lost in the deluge of little girls and the simultaneous deluge of words. Murmuring a polite reply, Jenny shooed Jacqueline into the house ahead of her as they followed Marie. Elise's reward for decorous behavior was Shane's arm about her shoulders as they went inside.

"I trust you had a pleasant journey from Elk Gap, Doctor Weston?"

"Yes, quite, thank you."

"It is so lovely this time of year, *non*? Sunny, but neither too warm nor too cool. And you must wish to refresh yourself. I will have Juliette show you to your room." A thin, middle-aged woman in a white apron over a black dress stepped from nowhere. "Juliette, please have Doctor Weston's things brought in, and please show her to her room now. I know she needs to rest after such a long ride, poor child."

"*Oui, Madame*," Juliette replied. "This way, Doctor Weston."

Jenny smiled at Shane, still mired in little girls, and followed the maid upstairs. A younger maid, carrying the bundle from Fleur's saddlebags, followed a few yards behind them. Juliette opened the door to a lovely, well-appointed corner room with marble-topped furniture and rose-garlanded wallpaper similar to Jenny's room back home in Parkfield. She felt the cloak of New York manners fall back upon her as she looked at her reflection in the triptych mirror above the vanity table and undid her scarf.

"Juliette, could you please have someone touch up my gown? It's bound to be wrinkled after I carried it in my saddlebag for so long." She indicated the bundle on the bed. Juliette untied it and unfolded Jenny's favorite ball gown: forest green silk damask, with an empire waist and a graceful, narrow skirt with a back placket. The neckline had been cut to echo the shape of her grandmother's pearl-and-diamond necklace, and the top was heavily embroidered along the floral pattern of the damask with deep green silk, crystals, and seed pearls. The edges of the cap sleeves had been cut to follow the roses in the damask and a band of pearl-crusted lace below the bustline hinted at an empire waist. From beneath it hung a divided overskirt with a gathered train. The overskirt consisted of three panels of sheer, diaphanous, pearlescent silk in teal, embroidered around the Moorish-scalloped edges with deep green that matched the dress. Two panels on either side fell straight, perhaps two inches shy of the hem of the skirt, divided down the front and back, while the third had been gathered only across the back and formed the pointed, ornate court train. Though the train had been constructed to be detachable, a button-on wrist loop caught it up for dancing.

Jenny had not thought to need a ball gown in Elk Gap. The sole reason this one had gone into her trunk was that she did not want to risk leaving such a horrifyingly expensive designer original in Arlington. Early this morning she had packed it carefully, interspersing her nightclothes and extra underthings in the folds. Juliette picked up the dress and expertly shook it out.

"It is not too mussed, *Mam'selle*, but I will have it pressed. Ah! How lovely! Silk, is it not?" Her English was even more heavily accented than Marie's.

"Yes, it is. It's my favorite ball gown. It's from the House of Genesse in Paris. They have a New York branch now, you know."

"I will caution Adrienne to take extra care and use only a lightly warm iron. Do you require anything else, then, *Mam'selle*?"

"Not now, thank you. I'd like to wash up and rest for a while." Juliette left, assuring Jenny that if she wanted anything, she need only ring. Jenny poured tepid water from the ewer into the basin on the washstand. It was pleasantly perfumed and slipped soothingly over her skin, and the linen towel smelled of fresh air and sunshine. She patted her face and arms dry, then undressed and sponged herself all over. It felt refreshing, even though the ride had not been overly warm. When she put on her matching teal silk underclothes and went over to look in the mirror again, she noticed the sun had colored her cheeks a delicate pink. As long as her nose was not red she would not worry, although Aunt Eleanor would certainly have scolded her severely for risking her complexion.

Adjusting the triptych mirror, she touched her hair. She had done it up before leaving, and she had carefully coiled the back into several large barrel curls and pinned them into place. All she would need to do would be to unpin them and touch them up later. Then, thinking of Shane and the coming evening, she reclined atop the bedspread. Perhaps she should only close her eyes, just for a moment.

The next thing she knew, her hostess herself was knocking at the door.

"*Entrez*," Jenny responded. Marie bustled in. Now that she was not wearing her apron, Jenny detected telltale fullness in her bust and roundness in her belly. Coupling that with the high color of her cheeks and the way the sides of her hair lay, Jenny could draw only one obvious conclusion. She smiled at the thought of another little girl to climb on Shane.

"Forgive me for waking you, but it is nearly time to

dress. Juliette is bringing your gown up now. May I stay and chat with you a while? I do so want to become acquainted with the young lady who has so thoroughly captured our dear Shane's heart." *Oh, brother, not another one,* Jenny thought. But it was evident that Shane and his superior officer were close, and Marie seemed to be only a harmless, if somewhat gushy, Frenchwoman. Doubtless she meant well. Jenny rose and rubbed the sleep from her eyes.

"Please, Madame. Stay and talk with me. I welcome the company." Her full skirt buoyed up by what looked like a hundred petticoats, Marie sailed across the room to perch on a chair in a corner. Jenny meanwhile splashed water on her face, then proceeded to put on the rest of her underclothing, including the hated corset that Marie indulgently laced up for her.

"You scarcely need that, you are so slender," Marie observed, patting her own plump bosom by way of comparison. "And your French is superb. Did you learn it on the Continent?"

"No. Actually I've never been abroad. Right now there is too much unrest in Europe. I had a Parisian professor in college. I learned my accent from him. You sound Parisienne yourself."

"I am. My family emigrated when I was twelve. Business was poor in Paris, so Papa brought us to Montreal. But Shane has told us you are from New York. How did you come to be all the way up here?"

"I'm visiting my uncle. He's my dearest relative, and since he's been on the Continent doing research and I've been away at school, I hadn't seen him in three years."

"Then when will you return to New York?"

"I'm not certain I'll return. I may stay here," Jenny replied, bending down to unroll her hose and slip the right stocking on. It was of deep green silk to match the gown. Marie clapped her hands in delight.

"I do hope we can make a Canadienne of you, then!"

Jenny smiled, bringing a dimple to the corner of her mouth. "Perhaps," she replied.

"Shane seems so happy when he speaks of you. "

Oh, here comes the fishing trip, Jenny thought.

"Believe me, Madame, it wasn't always that way. When we met, we roundly disliked each other."

Marie laughed, covering her mouth coyly. "I disdained Bob at first, too. He is, after all, not French."

"That couldn't have lasted too long."

"No. Elise was born when I was but eighteen."

"When is this baby due, then?" Jenny asked, steering the conversation away from Shane.

"The middle of January. Bob so wants a boy this time. I only hope it's well and healthy as my others have been. I am so fortunate to have three and lose none, *non*?"

"You and your husband are indeed fortunate. Your girls are lovely. I understand why Shane indulges them."

"They do adore him. He always brings them surprises and tells them the most charming stories. And when he lets them ride his horse they talk of nothing else for days." Jenny was listening with only half an ear as Marie rambled on, waiting for the inevitable cautious probing about her feelings toward Shane. A rebuff would not do this time; she had to be tactful but noncommittal. While Marie talked, Jenny pulled the pins from her hair and brushed out the cluster of curls in the back until they cascaded over her right shoulder.

"As many parties and receptions as Shane has attended with us here in River Bend, this is the first time he has ever brought a guest. I believe you have taken his heart." There it was, and not even a question, Jenny thought, only a statement that requested elaboration. She stuffed several hairpins into her mouth to avoid answering immediately and tried valiantly to dredge up a carefully ambiguous reply. But she was rescued in the nick of time. Juliette returned with her gown, then was dismissed by her mistress.

"Shane and I have been seeing each other, it's true. But it's as much a professional as a personal relationship. You see, I have been practicing medicine in Elk Gap, and it's so rural that I don't yet know my way around the countryside. He frequently comes for me and helps me attend emergencies. If I continue sharing Doctor MacBride's medical practice, I will probably stay in Elk Gap. But you understand I do have a professional career, so I have given very little thought to…personal relationships."

"I see." *Marie is trying much too hard not to sound too disappointed*, Jenny thought. *She probably wanted me to say I was panting for Shane to propose so I could make a cozy little nest and start raising my own brood like hers. Well, life does have its disappointments.* Jenny gave a twist here and there to the stray strands of curling hair that framed her face.

"There. I'm finished," she announced, reaching for her dress. She carefully lowered it to the floor and stepped into it so as not to muss her hair.

"I will help you with the buttons and the train.

There is no need to call Juliette. She is busy with the girls." Marie did up the line of crystal buttons fastening the back of the gown, and Jenny settled the shoulders and the skirt properly. Then she shook a velvet pouch from one shoe. It contained the best items of her heirloom jewelry: her grandmother's breathtaking diamond-and-pearl necklace, with matching earrings, bracelet, comb, and ring. The necklace consisted of three strands of matching graduated pearls caught up in scallops by platinum-and-diamond bars. It draped gracefully around a huge central teardrop pearl with a diamond cap. Smaller identical teardrops formed the earrings, and a slightly larger one depended from the diamond-and-platinum bar across the top of the tortoiseshell comb. Marie gasped involuntarily.

"How exquisite!" she exclaimed, helping Jenny with the clasp. "Are they family heirlooms, then?"

"Of a sort. My grandfather Weston's wedding gift to my grandmother. Since Grandfather passed away when I was a still a little child, she gave them to me to wear to my coming-out party."

"How lovely of her, to give you something so dear to her."

Jenny's bittersweet thought was otherwise. Her grandparents had been so terribly ill matched that her grandmother had found solace only in her children and her one and only grandchild. She had been all too glad to give up everything that brought her late husband to mind.

"I loved my grandmother very much. She was a lady to the bone, always poised, always polite, always socially proper, always tactful and charming." Jenny removed her simple, ivy-patterned, gold-loop earrings, leaving them in a little trinket dish on the vanity table, then tucked the comb into the left side of her hair, where the pearl teardrop peeked from between deep waves.

"Do you resemble her, then?" Marie asked.

Jenny shook her head. "No. I look like my mother's people, except that the Westons all seem to have this sandy, darkish-blond hair. Now I'm ready, but you?"

"I have only to put my dress on. Juliette did my hair long ago. And a matron like me cannot be too concerned about looking young and lovely anymore. You will be the one who will turn heads." Marie gave an embarrassed laugh.

"Oh, no, Madame Shepherd! Don't say that! You look quite beautiful. I've noticed before that some women glow when they are expecting a child."

"Marie, please. There must be no formality between us. And yes, you may flatter me any day you wish. Come, then. I will change into my gown, and we will sweep down the stairs in all our glory and overwhelm our men." Jenny picked up her green, pearl-decorated evening bag, her gloves, and the light wrap, somewhere between a tippet and a shrug, made out of the same diaphanous teal silk as the overskirt of her gown. She thrust her arm through Marie's, and they glided down the hall in an apparent comradeship Jenny did not feel. She helped Marie with her voluminous pink lawn gown with its mountain of frothy lace around the neck. She thought for an amusing moment that it made Marie look like an enormous birthday cake. Marie, too, took up gloves, reticule, and a wrap, then gave her hair a pat and ushered Jenny out of the room.

At the top of the stairs, Jenny paused to let Marie precede her. She well knew the dramatic impact of being the coup de grâce. Marie glided into the parlor like a ship under full sail, and both Shane and Bob rose. Then Jenny floated in, a graceful sloop in the wake of a freighter. Shane's eyes grew round in surprise.

"Jenny!" he whispered. His tone left no doubt he was awestruck. She watched him with no small amusement as he proceeded to ignore whatever Bob was saying.

"Well, Shane, don't you think we should be going?" Bob prompted after a pause. Shane's eyes flickered from Jenny to his superior officer, then back to the vision in the green dress as though drawn by a lodestone.

"What...? Oh. Yes. It must be time. Should we walk? It's close enough."

"That's what I just suggested." Bob replied, with a grin that made Shane's cheeks flush. He settled Jenny's wrap over her shoulders and offered her his arm. She took it with a smile, and felt her fingers pressing his forearm.

"Jenny, you look so beautiful," he said quietly.

"Thank you," she murmured, the corner of her mouth dimpling. "However, had I a choice of ball gowns, I'd not have picked green. You and I look like Merry Christmas together."

"I've never seen anything like that gown. And your necklace..."

"Well, Shane, you are looking at a gown designed specially for me by the House of Genesse, and also Grandmother Weston's pearls. They were her wedding present from Grandfather."

"And you're with a little backwoods boy like me," he said with a disbelieving sigh. She gathered her train over her forearm and smiled up at him again, thinking that if she lived to be a hundred she could never be happier than she was at that moment.

Their destination was the one real mansion in River Bend. Shane had told her it belonged to a twice-over millionaire timber broker named Adrian Beaufort, and it was as elegant as anything she had ever seen, up to and including Parkfield. Liveried servants took the ladies' token wraps and escorted everyone into the banquet room. As they were seated, Jenny took a quick head count and came up with about sixty couples. She was also very aware that everybody knew everybody else, and everybody surmised who the Governor and his wife were, while nobody knew her. That would lead to a lot of speculation, and Jenny felt impish enough to play it to the hilt.

Somewhere in the background a small orchestra was playing softly. Ignoring the silly rule that young ladies must only pick at their food, she ate with relish, though she made sure her table manners were precise and correct to the last detail. She carried on a limited conversation with the white-haired gentleman next to her, discovering that he was the Barton of Underwood and Barton, Solicitors, and that he had read and thoroughly enjoyed *By the Grace of God*, although she did not divulge her connection to the book's author. And Shane, whose main interest in law school had been criminal law and penology, entangled himself in a debate with the Underwood of Underwood and Barton concerning the death penalty and mandatory sentencing. What Jenny heard impressed her, but after all, Shane had both a law degree and a good mind, and she knew he stayed as up to date in his field as she did in her own. Finally the servers cleared away the last of the meal, and the crowd adjourned to the ballroom. Jenny drew her gloves back on as they walked down the long hall.

"Shane, I noticed several other Northwest Mounted uniforms. And I did see Paul and Laurence. Are the others from River Bend, then?"

"Most of them, yes. Some are from the Academy, and some are active duty officers. Like I said, by and large they're bachelors and they're here to keep the widows and wallflowers happy. By the time the night's over you'll meet them all." When she had settled her long gloves, he gave her his arm.

"Remember when you called me a wallflower?" she asked as they walked down the hall.

He flinched. "That box social is one night I don't even like to think about. If looks could kill, I wouldn't even be a bad memory right now."

"If I'd known what had happened to you over the previous week, it would have been another thing entirely."

"At the time I had no idea you'd even care."

"Well, see what you get for underestimating me?" She dimpled at him again. Then she fell silent as they found their place in the Governor's receiving line. A stream of chatter flowed about them, above which she heard Marie talking to Bob a few places ahead. Jenny first met the large contingent of River Bend officials, then the mayor himself, who in turn introduced her to the Governor and his wife. She favored them both with a brilliant smile and a proper curtsey and watched him fall for her debutante charm. When they were through the line, Shane leaned over to whisper to her.

"I'll bet a month's salary he asks you to dance within the first five dances." She did not reply, but she looked back at the Governor, a stocky, florid man of about sixty, and his serious, purse-mouthed wife, and was inclined to agree. Governor Georges Marot looked like a man who truly appreciated the ladies.

They had been rather near the end of the receiving line, so the ball began soon. The Governor and his wife led the first dance, and then, after a polite interval, other couples joined.

"May I have the pleasure of this dance, *Mam'selle?*" Shane asked in his abominable Voyageur French. He extended his hand with exaggerated pomp.

"Certainly, Inspector Adair. I'd be most delighted." She slipped her right hand through the loop to hold her train out of the way, took his hand, and glided into his arms. Due to her heels, her hand on his shoulder tab was comfortably below her eye level. Hearing Aunt Eleanor's instruction that a lady always looks at the gentleman with whom she is dancing, she gazed up at him. To her amusement his cheeks held high color, and happiness had painted a pink patch across his forehead. "Then where did you learn to dance so well, clear out in a place like Elk Gap?" she asked after a moment.

"It wasn't in Elk Gap. It was at Royal Dominion. I had, ah, a cicerone who guided me through the mazes of polite society. A mentor, if you will, who made a gentleman of me."

Jenny grinned wryly. "Oh. That figures, doesn't it?" She understood all too completely. It did not take a genius to deduce what he meant, especially since he'd once told her his initial intention at college was to become a portrait artist.

"How about you?" he asked, declining to comment further.

"Me? I'm an old hand at balls like this. The private girls' school I went to made certain we were all proper little debutantes before we could even spell the word." *But,* Jenny appended silently, *I could attend another two or three thousand balls and none of them would be so exciting. I've never been escorted by anyone half so handsome as Shane in his incredible dress uniform. With that black hair and fair skin, he wears red so dramatically.* She felt invigorated and tingly inside from the touch of his hand, even through two pairs of white gloves. She smiled up at him, and for the moment nothing existed except the music, Shane, and the dancing.

Bob claimed the next dance, and then Shane's prediction came true. The Governor himself strode up and bowed sharply. His French was as Québécois as Shane's.

"*Mademoiselle* Weston, before your program is full, would you do me the honor of granting me a dance?" Jenny curtseyed back as he took her hand and led her officiously to the center of the dance floor. There he proceeded to drag her around dramatically, with all the finesse of a draft horse.

"So, Mademoiselle, your last name is not French, yet you speak like a native. How is that?"

"I'm from New York, Your Excellency. I studied French all my life, lately under a former Sorbonne professor at the University of Virginia."

"Ah, I understand. It is surprising to find an

obvious socialite like you in this remote village."

She decided to answer the implied question. "I am visiting my uncle for the summer," she replied, favoring him with a devastating smile.

"So that is how the rose has been transplanted into this wilderness, eh? I knew when I saw you at dinner that you were no product of River Bend, or even Ontario, for that matter. Such a lovely gown, Mademoiselle. My compliments to your couturier." He was trying to dance dynamically, fairly hauling her around, in contrast to Shane, whose quiet strength enabled him to float over the dance floor in the same easy way he skated. She smiled up at the older man.

"Even though I'm American, the gown is Parisian, Your Excellency. It's a custom design from the House of Genesse." That was intended to impress, and it evidently did. The man's graying eyebrows raised for the merest moment.

"My wife will be most interested. She has wanted a Genesse for years."

"Every woman should have at least one, sir." They chatted politely until he knew an acceptable amount about her background. The music came to a quick finale, and he stepped back and bowed over her hand.

"I thank you, Mademoiselle. And if I may, your program, please?"

"Certainly." She slipped the tasseled cord from her wrist and handed him the program. Every second dance was signed "Adair," with Shane's distinctive outsized. pointed capital A. (*Every dance*, Shane had said, to which Bob replied, *Every other dance; don't be a hog*.) There were a few other names, including Bob, Paul and Laurence, and five blank spaces. The Governor added

"Marot" to three of them and handed it back to her with a flourish.

"Inspector Adair must be your beau for the summer, *non*?"

"I'd scarcely call him that, sir. He's a friend of my uncle's."

"Inspector Adair's reputation precedes him. I have heard of him even in Ottawa. It is stellar officers such as he who will eventually give the Royal Northwest Mounted Police jurisdiction over all of Canada. You choose wisely, Mademoiselle," he said as he escorted her back to Shane. "Farewell for now, Mademoiselle. I look forward to the pleasure of dancing with you later." He gave her another courtly bow, released her hand, and retired, all dignity and pomp. Shane raised his eyebrows questioningly.

"It seems *Monsieur* Marot is most taken with you, Mademoiselle," he observed.

"Overcome with curiosity is more like it," she replied.

"Then I believe this is my dance?"

"Why, Inspector Adair, you're right! It is indeed your dance!" She smiled and gave him her hand. The orchestra's next piece was the "Emperor Waltz." She could not recall having enjoyed any one dance as much as she reveled in the quick, swinging pace of the familiar melody. She felt as light as a feather in Shane's arms as they whirled around the floor, and neither one realized, until the orchestra was through and the spell broken, that all the rest of the dancers, led by the Governor himself, had cleared the floor to watch them.

As she came to, there was a smattering of gloved applause, and it surprised them both to find themselves the center of so much attention. That spectacular dance, to the chagrin of many ambitious mothers and sighing girls, established Jenny as the acknowledged queen of the ball.

When the orchestra came to the end of the program and started playing extra pieces, she found herself mobbed by every eligible gentleman in the place. She danced twice more with Governor Marot, once with Bob, once with Paul, and once with the Mayor of River Bend, while managing to save every other dance for Shane. She noticed, too, that he had succeeded in coaxing a smile from Madame Marot while they danced, and when they returned from the floor she looked almost animated for a moment or so. Then the last dance was announced, and when she looked around for Shane, he was directly behind her. Music wrapped itself gently around them, and she allowed herself to dance quite close to him. At one point she felt his cheek brush her temple.

"Shane, I don't want tonight to end," she murmured. His hand crept a fraction farther around her back.

"I don't want this dance to end," he replied. "It makes me want to do an oil study so I can keep it forever." But it ended all too soon, and there were rounds of good nights and farewells to be said. Governor Marot expressed regret that he would not be able to attend any balls in New York so he could have the pleasure of dancing with her again, and the Beauforts cordially invited both her and Shane to call on them any time they were in River Bend. Then they were outside in the pleasantly balmy night. It was past one o'clock, and though Jenny's spirits were soaring, she was not a night person, and she was deathly tired. She clung to Shane's arm with both hands, her train gathered over the crook of her elbow.

"It was a lovely evening. I don't think I've ever enjoyed a ball quite so much. Thank you for inviting me," she said at length as they walked. Tactfully Bob and Marie had gone on ahead, allowing Jenny and Shane their privacy.

"I'm glad you accepted my invitation. Didn't I say you'd be the belle of the ball? You must have left quite a string of broken hearts behind you tonight."

"I only care about one." She patted the center of his chest. He covered her hand with his.

"That one's in fine shape. After all, I'm seeing you home." They walked in contented silence, while she luxuriated in the feel of her hand about his forearm. They were nearly at Bob and Marie's home when she stopped abruptly.

"Oh, bother. I have a rock in my shoe."

He swept her up into his arms and carried her toward the smooth river stone wall along the side of Bob's driveway. She let her arms encircle his neck and rested her head on his shoulder. He made a slow way from the sidewalk and sat down on the wall. She pulled the overskirt of her dress away so she would not risk marring the delicate fabric and slipped from his lap to sit beside him. It took her only a moment to shake the pebble loose. Then she replaced the offending footwear and looked up.

"Thank you for the loveliest evening of my life. I'll never forget it."

"I'm the one who should thank you," he replied. "Now I know how the frog felt."

"Frog?" she echoed.

"When he turned into a prince."

She turned slightly to face him. "I haven't kissed you yet."

"High time, then," he whispered, his lips very close to hers. Once again, echoing the night in Richard's assembly room, he lowered his face to hers and their lips touched. At first it was only tentative, only exploring, and she let herself go into the gentle strength that was Shane. His gloved hand ran across her cheek, down over her shoulder, and closed around her upper arm, bringing her closer to him. At the same time she let her hand stray to the back of his head, intensifying the kiss that was already drowning her in a tidal wave of warm pleasure. She parted her lips slightly and let the tip of her tongue touch the margin of his upper lip. In return he scooped her into his arms, overwhelmed with the sudden passion that threatened to sweep them away. Finally he broke the moment, leaning away from her. She felt his breath slip over her cheek and her arms closed around him, desperately wanting to prolong the exquisite moment.

"Jenny…"

"Hush, silly. Kiss me again."

"I can't. I'll forget I'm a gentleman."

"Remember? I'm not a lady." Her wit ratcheted down the intensity of the moment.

"All right, then." Her arms were still around him and he was holding her gently, as if she could disappear at any moment. The next quiet and deeply satisfying kiss brought a fitting end to their perfect evening. After the initial scalding, excited heat had subsided, she was tingling all over. He held her a moment longer, pressing

202

his face into her hair. She read the contour of his face as she drew her hand across his cheek and over his throat in a prolonged caress. It was something she would never forget. They kissed again, just as slowly and just as tenderly. Then he leaned back and looked at her, his eyes colorless in the moonlight.

She looked past him, into the moon-dappled shadows of the rose bed behind them, taking stock of herself. One thing was certain. She knew she loved Shane Adair as she would never—could never, she amended—love another. She took a long, slow breath to calm herself. Even after something as serious as the stolen, contraband kisses, his undemanding presence lay lightly upon her soul, and that made him all the more dear.

"I think we'd better go in," he said softly. She felt his breath stir her hair. "Marie and Bob will wonder what became of us." He rose and offered her his arm again, and when she interwove her fingers around the crook of his elbow, he covered her hands with his opposite palm. She wondered if her feet would ever touch the ground again.

Chapter Twelve

The next morning she woke when Juliette opened the velvet drapes and let the crystalline morning light spill across the bed. She burrowed out from under the covers, and the pink mist of the previous evening dissolved, leaving her wrapped in the warmth of Shane's last kiss. As she rubbed the sleep from her eyes she remembered the "Emperor Waltz."

"I trust Mademoiselle spent a good night?" Juliette asked politely.

"Yes, Juliette. I slept very well, thank you," Jenny replied, yawning and stretching away the last of her sleep.

"Madame instructed me to tell you that breakfast will be served shortly. Is there anything else you need now, Mademoiselle?"

"No, thank you, Juliette. You may go. Thank Madame for me, and tell her I'll be down right away."

"*Oui, Mademoiselle,*" Juliette replied, bobbing half a curtsey from the doorway. Jenny climbed into her riding clothes and washed her face, then pulled the pins from her hair. Because she had gone directly to bed without braiding it, it was full of what her mother called "mouse nests" and other snarls and tangles. She was in the midst of conquering the mess when she heard various shrieks, growls, snarls, giggles, and thumps in the hall. She pulled her door open to see Shane lying on his back in the middle of the Wilton hall runner. Frances was sitting on his chest and Jacqueline on his ankles. Elise was on her knees next to them, and she looked up as Jenny came out.

"My, what have we here?" she asked.

"We catched a bear," Frances said with a cheesy grin.

"Caught," Elise corrected with big-sister superiority.

"They catched me, all right," Shane said, shedding little girls as he picked himself up. "Come on, everybody. Go down to the table. We'll be right along." Elise took the two smaller girls by a hand apiece and led them down the stairs.

"You certainly were catched," Jenny giggled.

"Oh, they do that to me all the time. They think it's high fun to hide behind a door and ambush me."

"And of course you let them."

"Wouldn't you? They have such a grand time at it."

"Oh, yes, I imagine I would," she responded, giving her hair a parting flick with the brush.

"Are you ready, then, Mademoiselle?" he asked, extending his arm gallantly. Ignoring her loose hair, she flipped the brush onto the bed and accepted the proffered escort.

Breakfast was as hectic an affair as the rest of the day-to-day life of the Shepherds. Jacqueline upset her milk in her lap, and Frances amused herself by dangling her braids in the syrup. Through it all, Marie and Bob remained implacably calm. Finally, with Jacqueline packed off for a change of clothing and most of the syrup washed from Frances, they bade their guests farewell. Shane was again in the midst of a heap of little girls scrambling to hug and kiss him goodbye. As usual, they all chattered at once in two languages. Jenny took Fleur's reins from the stable boy, and as he was preparing to give her a hand up to the saddle, Frances's voice rang out above the general clamor.

"Shane, are you going to marry Miss Weston?"

"If she'll have me, sweetheart," he replied, and Jenny felt her face grow hot.

"Then you can't marry Jacqueline, and she *loves* you!" Frances wailed.

"I know all of you love me, but I'm much too old for any of you, even Elise. Now give me a hug. I have to leave." He gathered all three into his arms. Jenny received the second round of little-girl hugs before the stable attendant boosted her to the saddle. Lunch was duly tucked into Shane's saddlebags. However, Jenny's saddle was unencumbered because Marie had volunteered to ship her clothes home on the Monday morning train. Only the fantastic jewelry was going back with her, the velvet bag wrapped in a scarf and tucked into a safe corner of her saddlebags. Fleur and Midnight received their share of pats, while Marie and Bob assured both Jenny and Shane they were welcome any time they wanted to come to River Bend. Waving back over his shoulder, Shane led the way down the driveway and out into the street.

"Poor Jacqueline," Jenny mused. "I had my first episode of puppy love when I was about her age."

"Oh? Who was the lucky gentleman?"

"He was my second cousin, Arthur Brisbane. He was in his mid-twenties at the time. He completely shattered me by spending a summer on the continent, marrying a British girl, and never coming home."

"Insensitive lout, wasn't he?"

"Oh, terribly." She giggled.

"His loss was my gain." His grey eyes sparkled at her. He turned out onto the main street that led to the railroad station. As soon as they were out of town, he pulled the black gelding to a halt.

"I have to get rid of this tunic. It's just too warm. I itched all the way down yesterday," he grumbled. He stripped off his lanyard and belt, and the tunic followed. He folded it carefully and tied it behind the cantle of his saddle. She loosened her reins and allowed Fleur to crop a few mouthfuls of the sparse grass along the edge of the right-of-way while she waited. He took the holstered pistol from his right saddlebag and carefully slipped it onto his belt, then buckled it around his waist.

"There. I feel a lot more like myself now," he announced.

"You put your pistol back on," she observed.

"I always carry it in the woods. I haven't needed it very often, but..." His voice trailed off as he made certain his rifle was accessible.

"But you've been glad for it when you did?" she concluded tentatively.

"Oh, perhaps. As I said, there's only once I've ever had to shoot at a person when I haven't seen it coming first. I'm more afraid of animals. This is the beginning of rabies season, and wolves get that all the time. But that's not a job for a pistol." He patted the stock of the immense Model 1895. Jenny shivered. Though she was not the flighty type, the thought of rabies, with its universal fatality rate, never failed to send a chill down her spine. She was silent for quite a while as they rode side by side. Then she realized she did not know where she was.

"This isn't the way we came, so I'm lost already," she commented after a few minutes on the trail.

"No. Remember we're going home over the high trail? What would you do if you were really lost?"

"Follow the river?" Jenny guessed.

"That's good. If you follow a stream you'll eventually get to civilization somewhere. But how about when there's no stream close by?"

"I don't know."

"The best thing would be to give Fleur her head and let her take you home. I don't think horses ever get lost."

"You must not get lost easily either," she commented. The trail had led them into the woods, rank with the deep smell of moss and summer-warm duff.

"No. Grandpère taught me well. He'd been in the woods all his life. He'd forgotten more about trapping and tracking than most people will ever know. He was even better than the Indians. Even now I can generally pick up a trail that none of the North Village men can find."

"He sounds like a remarkable person."

"He was, in more ways than one. He was artistic, kind, and gentle, with an unbelievable wit. Heaven only knows where he came by it, living all his life isolated out in the woods, but he was as full of yarns as a sea captain. He taught me to draw when I was very young, and he was so patient with my mistakes. He always regretted never learning to read, and when I went to mission school he made me read to him nearly every night. I tried to teach him, but by then his eyes were getting bad." He was gazing up into the trees, lost in reminiscence. Jenny loved to start him talking about himself.

"I think you must take after him. You can certainly tell tales. The night you told Uncle Richard and me the story about the Wendigo and drew it, I had nightmares!"

He smiled gently. "I was fortunate to have the family I had. I wouldn't trade my childhood with anyone. I didn't even realize we were poor." He came abruptly back to the present. "Remember I said I'd show you a beaver pond? We're close to one now. It's really huge, and there's an old man beaver there that must weigh sixty pounds. He's too wily for traps. I've seen him shove a branch into a trap and spring it deliberately."

"Now that's what I call smart."

"I hope nobody ever gets him. He deserves to live a long life. We're going that way." He pointed to a trail branching off to the right, up a small creek that merged with the White Fork. Fleur turned obediently, content for Midnight to lead up the narrow trail. It was little more than a deer track, and branches kept tangling in Jenny's loose hair. Once she lost her scarf and grabbed at it as it landed on Fleur's rump. Impatiently she knotted her reins and let Fleur follow while she worked her hair up into a crude braid. Finally, when she thought she would have to protest if the going became any rougher, the trail leveled out and came into a clearing. Motioning her to be quiet, he dismounted. They tied the horses, and, moving as silently as she could manage, she followed him up to the edge of the trees. The beaver pond spread deep and dark before her. It was a very old pond, because a wide apron of meadow bordered it and the effluent end had silted nearly level with the dam. He crouched behind a big nurse log from which several small trees sprouted. She knelt beside him, and he pointed to the far end of the dam, where a huge beaver sat on a half-submerged log, grooming his coat.

"That's him," Shane whispered. She peeked over the log. The magnificent old animal had a pelt that glowed like satin in the sunlight, and he was meticulously preening every inch of it with the special combing claws on his hind feet. She watched him, fascinated, until Shane touched her shoulder and pointed upstream. She looked along his hand and saw a younger beaver swimming toward them at a leisurely pace, trailing a leafy branch behind him. They watched as the younger animal approached the dam, then dived abruptly, hauling the branch with him.

"Watch. I'll show you what they do when there's danger," Shane said. Abruptly he jumped up with a whoop, raised his arms, and ran toward the pond. The big male hit the water and his tail came down on the surface with a resounding crack that reverberated like a gunshot. The ripples in the water died, and the pond was deserted. "They'll be down for hours now. Come on. I'll show you the dam and their lodges." He extended his hand to her and helped her over the log but did not relinquish her hand as he led her down to the pond.

"Here's a doe with twins," he said, pointing to cloven hoof marks at the edge of the water. "Older does often drop more than one fawn. I've even seen quads once or twice. Those are this morning's tracks. They probably came to drink at dawn. And see what looks like a pile of brush over near the opposite bank? That's the beaver lodge. The entrance is under the water, and there's a breathing hole at the top. The beavers seal them up with mud so well that even a wolverine can't get in before the beavers have had time to escape. They have pathways under the water where they always swim. In some ponds you can actually see their trackways through the weeds."

"Do they really eat wood? There's not much nutrition in it."

"Not really. They eat the bark off young shoots. You remember the branch that one was carrying? That's winter food. They jam them in the mud and whenever they get hungry, they just pop out of the lodge and haul a few back. During the winter they won't ever come out from under the ice. They're less wasteful about their garbage than we are, too. All the leavings from their meals go into the dam." He interwove his fingers with hers as they strolled down to the dam. It was huge—perhaps seventy feet long and five feet across the top.

"That dam has probably been here a hundred years or so. It's been this big ever since I can remember. When they start a dam, they usually pick a wide place and fell some large trees in a horseshoe pattern, then fill it in with branches. And if the dam is ever breached, they all work on it, even the littlest kits." He bent and picked up a branch from which the bark had been precisely sheared. "See the marks from their incisors? Their teeth never stop growing. They have to keep them worn down by constant gnawing, or the teeth will actually grow clear around in a big curve and into the skull. In the extreme, it could eventually kill the animal."

"How long do they live, then?"

"I think somewhere around fifteen years. I've been watching that old man for quite a while. He was there before I went to Ottawa."

"He's magnificent. I've never seen anything like this before. You know, I've practically never been out of the city in my whole life."

"I can't imagine that," he responded.

"Really, I've learned so much today. It's been worth a couple weeks in school." She smiled up at him, warm inside. They strolled up the edge of the pond, and he pointed out the tracks of various creatures that lived around the pond—the general population of deer, raccoon, coyote, bear, elk—and one large track that Shane merely pointed to.

"You should be able to tell me what that is."

"Well, from the little points on that center pad it looks like a cat, but it's so big."

"Cougar. You wait until you hear one scream at night. It gives even me goose bumps. But I think we'd better go now. I want us to have time to enjoy lunch without hurrying. And I have a special place to show you." He helped her to the saddle, then set his foot in the stirrup and lifted himself easily to Midnight's back. They started down the steep trail, and she watched him as he rode. All wide shoulders and slim waist, he moved easily with the big horse, cushioning the occasional jostling with his knees.

The journey down seemed much shorter than going up had been, and soon they picked up the trail again. She always enjoyed riding through the woods. The wild beauty seemed to lift every worry from her shoulders, and she could not think of any better company than Shane and her brilliant gold mare.

"We'll be at the river in a few minutes," he said after a while. "If you listen, you can hear the rapids from here. They sound a little like far off wind." She thought she heard a faint rushing sound in the distance.

"Since you know so much about the animals, do you know all the trees and plants, too?"

"More or less. Some I know only by their Indian or French names, though." They chatted as the horses walked steadily, the sound of the rapids coming ever closer. From the position of the sun, she deduced it was already somewhat past noon. The trail had wound down to skirt the White Fork several times, taking off through the mixed hardwood and conifer forest when the river meandered into a big curve. This section had never been logged, and some of the ancient boles were as thick as she was tall. When she looked skyward, sometimes she could not see the tops lost among their huge neighbors.

"There's a big waterfall up here a few miles, too. I'll show you after we stop for lunch," he said, looking up toward the sun.

"I hope your place is close. In spite of that marvelous breakfast back at the Shepherds', I'm getting hungry."

"It's close enough. Don't worry. It's not more than two miles—just after the rapids. Want to see them? Grandpère called them Portage Rapids, and when the first cartographers and surveyors came, they adopted the name. The same with Singing Water Falls."

Jenny noticed the warmth that came to Shane's voice whenever he spoke of his grandfather. "Of course," she agreed. "Let's go."

As they rode, the roar of the rapids drew nearer and nearer. Shane again took a detour from the trail, this time drawing up beside a raging torrent of white water that crashed over huge boulders and boiled and frothed between them. Jenny felt the spray cold on her face in spite of the warm day.

"I'd hate to fall in there," she said, raising her voice to be heard above the din of the furious water.

"If you did, it would be the last thing you'd ever do. Nobody could get out of that alive. We've had half a dozen drownings here that I remember."

"I can believe it," she replied, looking at the raging river.

"Then you're really not going to believe how calm it is farther up. Come on." Heeling Midnight's flanks, he turned upriver, following a game trail that rejoined the main path as it started to climb. They went over a small rise, and the noise of the rapids faded into the distance. The horses' hooves sounded hollow on the deep duff beneath the trees. Then the trail descended back toward the river in a series of narrow switchbacks. The trees came to an abrupt line, and she found herself in a small, clear meadow where grass grew several inches high. Here the river ran in a deep, quiet pool the color of liquid emeralds, bounded by a clifflike rocky outcropping on the upstream side, a sharp defile on the opposite bank, and a gravel bar downstream. Ferns hung in clusters in the crevices of the outcropping, while swallows darted down the gorge to feed on flying insects. The shallow river bank was finely washed gravel, warmed by the sun, which was just now touching the depths of the gorge. She sat staring around in awe, but evidently he was accustomed to the place. He guided Midnight forward and loosened the reins to let him drink. Fleur crossed the gravel carefully, lowered her muzzle, and took a long, noisy slurp while Jenny dismounted.

"This is beautiful, Shane. I've never seen anything like this except in pictures."

"I'll see to the horses. If you're thirsty, go out on that rock and get a drink. The water's cold, even this time of year." He indicated a huge, glacier-scarred boulder next to the jutting cliff. The gravel crunched beneath her boots as she walked across the shingle and climbed out on the chunk of grey, polished granite. She flopped down on the warm rock, pulled off her scarf, and immersed her face in the emerald water. The cold was so sharp that it stabbed at her temples and eyelids. She shook her head quickly and wiped her face on her scarf, then leaned over to cup her hand for a drink. A flicker of motion deep in the water caught her attention. She sat up slowly, looking down into the clear water. The shadow was a fish that evidently lived beneath the overhanging rock. She watched as it swam lazily out, headed into the current, and hung suspended above the graveled bottom. She looked over her shoulder and beckoned to Shane, who left his saddlebags on the bank and climbed up onto the rock beside her.

"Look! There's a *huge* fish down there!" she said in a stage whisper.

"You don't have to whisper, you know. Fish can't hear." He dropped to the rock beside her.

"He's right there. See?" Shane went belly-down for a better look and followed her pointing finger.

"That's a big fish, all right. It looks like a Rainbow,

but I can't be certain that far down. It could be a Cutthroat or a Dolly. Whichever, it'd be nice in a frying pan."

"Do you ever fish here, then?"

"All the time. I'm going to have my eye on that one, too. I'll bet it weighs three pounds."

"Is that all?"

"Things look a fourth larger under water. Besides, three pounds is a big trout." The sun made a spiky Statue of Liberty halo behind her head as she leaned over to look into the green water again.

"Let's go have our lunch. I'm hungry," he said after the trout had taken refuge back under the rock. He gave her his hand as she stepped off the boulder, and they went back to the meadow, where they sat against a large log stranded on the bank by spring high water. He handed her a sandwich from his saddlebag. It was cold roast beef on freshly baked bread, sharp with the tang of Dijon mustard. She gazed out over the river and watched the swallows. Occasionally they belly-flopped in the clear water. He explained that was how they bathed. They were pert little birds with deep green backs and greyish underbellies, and she marveled at the agile way they flew, darting madly every which way and never colliding.

Their lunch ended with cheese and fruit, and as she picked at the remains of an apple, he flicked pebbles out into the water like a small boy. He seemed so at home in the woods that she could not imagine him spending the better part of six years in a large city like Ottawa.

"Shane? Was it hard for you to leave Elk Gap to go to college?" she asked idly. His face clouded.

"Terribly. I was very young and…and not exactly naïve, but so inexperienced. I was only sixteen, and homesickness literally made me ill. It would have made it easier for me if I had been able to correspond with my grandparents, but they were both illiterate. Angus was the only person I could write to. Things did get better after I was eligible to play hockey, but college life still had its rough moments. I'm glad I stuck it out, though. Without my law degree, I'd probably still be a constable."

They were on the trail again within half an hour. Fleur seemed rested and perky as they climbed back up the trail. She picked up her hooves smartly and was obviously asking for a good canter when they reached the main trail again.

"What did you feed that mare while my back was turned?" he asked. "She's all full of pep."

"I'd love to let her run. She acts like she needs it." She reached down and stroked the satiny shoulder.

"We'll have to wait until we get on the trail between Thomas's ranch and North Village. That's a couple hours, because we want to stop and see the falls, and we have to go home by the trail to the lake. I didn't tell you, but there's a good-sized lake upstream from the falls."

"Oh, my! I'm going to see all the great scenery. Will there be any left for later?"

He grinned. "All of my territory is this wonderful. Too bad I can't take you on rounds with me."

"You know, Shane, I'd love that. But it would be a little too daring, even for a medical doctor."

"Maybe. I'm riding rounds next month. For some reason strange things always happen in August. Paul and I have come to call it the August Curse. We've had escaped convicts, we've had to swim to an island in the middle of a lake to escape a forest fire, and the first time Paul went on August rounds with me his horse went over a cliff, fell on Paul, and broke his leg."

"It sounds like you could have used a doctor with you then."

"Well, his horse broke its back and I had to shoot it, and I had a dickens of a time getting Paul back to civilization. I wound up taking him to Thomas's place and bringing Angus up there, which of course he couldn't do now. But giving credit where it's due, Paul was brave about it. He never let out a peep."

"He seems to have healed well."

"Oh, he's fine now. It was just a grand scare all around."

"I'd never deny that police work is dangerous."

"I wouldn't either. You've seen that firsthand. And I'm glad it doesn't frighten you, Jenny."

She remembered the night of the box social and knew what he was talking about. "No. You wouldn't be who and what you are if you weren't a police officer, and I'd not change you by so much as a hair." He gave her a grateful smile.

Singing Water Falls was as much a surprise as the pool above the rapids had been. It was part of the same gorge, but the entire river dropped at least forty feet in a torrent that had gouged out a roily basin beneath it. Heavy shoulders of rock jutted, fern-hung, on either side of the tumbling water, where it fell into a plunge pool studded with huge, water-worn boulders. Without speaking, he pointed to the cliff across the river. Just at the edge stood a group of four does with fawns. She held her breath, lest the scene disappear before her eyes. It was so other-worldly that she half expected to see fairies or wood nymphs peeking out from behind the ferns.

"After how beautiful the river is farther on down... Shane, I just can't believe this. I just can't."

"There's a cave behind the falls, too. The North Village children play in it a lot. I wonder why nobody has ever drowned here. I think every little boy around has fallen in at least once. There's a saying, though, that the Lord looks after idiots and children."

"Did you ever fall in?"

He laughed merrily. "At least twice a month all summer! I must have been an idiot when I was a child. I got so daring that after a while when we played I'd fall in on purpose just to frighten everyone." She envisioned a clean-limbed, sun-browned little boy with glowing black hair and more than a spark of mischief in his eyes. Then she remembered her own girlhood and how her daring stunts had nearly driven her poor Aunt Martha to distraction.

"If I'd been there I'd have been right behind you. I was never the one to sit back and let the boys have all the fun. In fact, when I was nine, some older boys built a sled jump on a hill not far from our house. I was terribly angry when they wouldn't let me on it because I was a girl, so one night I waited until everyone went home and I went off the jump. I was so light it threw me over the landing, and I hit a tree and knocked myself out cold."

"Is that how you got that little scar under your chin?" Her hand automatically went to a tiny indentation under her chin, and she remembered Mavis telling her that Shane was nothing if not observant.

"No, that was from racing with my cousin on ice skates. I tripped over my toe pick and landed face first. Father had to sew up my chin. But I didn't think it showed that much."

"It doesn't. I never noticed it until I lifted you down from your sidesaddle at church."

"Well, I was quite a tomboy. I used to get mad when anybody said I couldn't do something because I was a girl. I even got in fights. You wouldn't have liked me at all if you'd known me then."

"I like you now, and you're still that way," he said with an impish grin.

"You keep that up, and you see if I ever go to another ball with you."

"We need to get back on the trail. We'll come here again, the first day we both have free."

"I'll take that for a promise, then. I'll even make lunch." She took one last long look at the falls, where the water sparkled and danced and made rainbows in the spray drifting up from the pool. Then she looked up at the cliff and saw the does disappear. Presently he touched Midnight's flanks.

"Do we have to leave already?" she sighed.

"I'm afraid so. I don't mind riding at night, and eventually I'll feel confident that you and Fleur can handle it, but not tonight. The moon won't be up until well after midnight, and it's going to be really dark." Reluctantly she reined Fleur around as he turned Midnight. He sensed it when her heart sank a little. "Don't worry. We'll come back soon when we can stay a while. I promised you, after all."

With a sigh, she directed Fleur in behind Midnight

and they climbed back toward the trees.

The sun had moved measurably in the sky when he steered off the trail again. She had noticed the trees ahead had thinned, but she thought little of it. Then she realized they must be near the lake he had told her about. *None too soon, either*, she thought. *I'm at the point of having to ask him to make a necessary stop for me.* Soon they broke out into a lush meadow surrounding a lake that was actually rather large, considering its location. High hills reared their heads to the northeast, but the lake itself was calm and glassy.

Shane halted Midnight and bounced down, then helped Jenny out of her saddle. He tied both horses to a convenient sapling and tactfully went one way into the brush, leaving her to go the other. She chose a suitably secluded spot to relieve herself, then she wandered down to the water's edge, trying to find a place deep enough to wash her hands without wading in. Finally she climbed out onto a fallen log and rinsed her hands and face. This time she dried her hands on her skirt and blotted her face with her sleeve. As she carefully picked her way back to the shore, a rustling sound in the bushes to her left distracted her. Curious, she followed it, finding a half-grown bear comically scratching its rump on another of the many fallen logs. She looked back for Shane and found him standing next to Midnight. Just as she started to call to him, a growl and a simultaneous crashing came from the undergrowth directly ahead of her. She stood rooted as a full-grown sow grizzly erupted perhaps thirty yards away. The horrific scene was playing out in slow motion. Grabbing his Winchester, Shane raced toward her.

"Jenny! Run! This way!" he screamed. Her trance

snapped and she flew toward him. He continued to shout at her, trying to distract the bear as it closed the distance between them. It was perhaps a scant fifteen feet away when he dived. His left elbow hit Jenny, knocking her backward. He rolled to his right, brought the rifle up in one motion, and, firing from the prone, he snapped off a shot just as the bear started up on its hind legs. The big Winchester roared, its muzzle flash shattering the day.

The bear collapsed, skidding on its chest before it somersaulted past him and landed a few feet shy of the waterline. Just as Jenny considered picking herself up from the gravel, he shouldered the rifle again. She decided to stay put. Then she saw the exit wound the .303 had left, directly on top of the shaggy neck behind the skull, and the odd angle the bear's head made with its body. There was no doubt in her mind the animal was dead. His perfect shot had shattered the first cervical vertebra.

The silence around Jenny was a palpable thing, a weight holding her down. She watched him as he lowered the rifle and climbed unsteadily to his feet. At the same time she picked herself up and ran to him, flattening herself to his chest. He laid the rifle down and wrapped his arms around her, steadying her as she trembled against him. For a moment she sobbed silently, tears forced from her by sheer terror. He wrapped his arms around her as far as they would go.

"It's all right now, Jenny. It's dead. You're safe. We're both safe," he said gently.

"Oh, Shane…"

"Shhh. *C'est fini*. Just hold me for a while, *non*? *Tout… C'est bon. C'est bon.*" His English slipped away in the face of the close brush with death. She gulped and got hold of herself by main force, willing the head-to-toe shaking to stop.

"You saved my life…"

His hand pressed her head to his shoulder to silence her, and she felt his face against her hair. Then her initial fright passed, and she relaxed against him.

"Are you all right?" he asked at length. "I hit you pretty hard."

"I'm fine. But are you? It looked like that thing fell right on top of you."

"It didn't touch me. But that was way too close for comfort." Thoroughly terrified, she clung to him, listening to his racing heart. He drew a shaky breath. "I see I'm going to have to give you a lesson about bears. Are you sure you're all right? Like I said, I knocked you down hard." She backed off to arm's length.

"Well, aside from being frightened out of ten years' growth…"

"You're not the only one! That's about the biggest grizzly I've seen in years. Do you know what she would have done to you? If she'd caught up with you, you wouldn't have lasted a minute. Jenny, if you ever see a bear cub, the mother is right there someplace, and they're as mean as piggy sows and a heck of a lot bigger. I know cubs can be cute, but stay away from them." She took his shaking hands in hers, recognizing the unsteadiness as the aftermath of adrenaline wearing away.

"I think we'd both better sit down a minute," she said with a sigh. He led her to the shoreline, and they sank down side by side. He stretched out on the sand, deliberately laying his head in her lap, and closed his eyes. She looked down at him, noticing that his face was still white with shock, and he had grass in his hair. Gently she brushed it away, toying idly with the mussed wave that slopped over the right side of his forehead. She had nearly coaxed it into place when he opened his eyes and smiled up at her. Guiltily she jerked her hand back.

"Don't quit," he murmured. She deliberated, hearing Aunt Martha tut-tutting in a compartment in her mind. Then she shut the door on her aunt and combed her fingers through his heavy, satiny hair.

"Shane, that bear could have killed you," she said at length.

"Either of us, or both." Reluctantly he sat up. "But there's no use worrying about that now. Everything turned out all right, so don't let it frighten you. But now do you see why I carry that rifle around? I'd hate to think what would have happened if all I had was this." He patted the blue .45 on his hip. "Come on. Let's take a look at what you were up against." He rose and gave her a hand.

The bear lay stretched out on the sandy beach, looking much larger than Jenny had thought. He bent down and picked up one forepaw, and the curving, scythelike claws nearly made her ill.

"Not only that, but they have teeth, too." He lifted a flew with his thumb, baring a huge, yellowed canine that looked as long as her little finger. Then he ran a hand over the gleaming fur. Jenny saw that what she had interpreted as grey was actually an overlay of silvery-white guard hairs over denser brown undercoat. "This is a prime pelt, too. Too bad we can't take it with us. The North Village people would appreciate it. This bear's in good condition."

"Why can't we take it with us?"

"It'd take me a good two or three hours to skin it out. We haven't that kind of time."

"If you have an extra knife I'll help you. Just show me what to do."

"I do carry a spare, but I don't want you to help me. Skinning's messy, smelly, and bloody, and this hide is probably full of ticks."

He looked surprised when she laughed. "Shane, I'm a surgeon! I know how to handle a knife! I've cleaned up a lot of really disgusting messes, autopsied a corpse that had been under water for two weeks in August, and blood doesn't bother me in the least!"

"The fact remains that if we stop and skin this bear out we'll be spending the night in the woods. Actually I do know what we can do. We can stop at Thomas Wise Hand's ranch, and I'll send him back here. He and his boys can take care of it. However, I do have to slit the throat so it'll bleed out. That keeps the meat from getting sour." He stopped to pick up his rifle, then went back to his saddlebags and produced a fearsome Bowie knife that looked to be razor sharp. It was no easy feat to lift the bear's huge head and get the knife into the proper spot to sever both pairs of jugular veins and arteries, but he knew what he was doing. A moment later a growing pool of dark, deoxygenated blood soaked into the fine gravel. Then he walked out on the same log Jenny had availed herself of earlier, washed the knife, and rinsed his hands. As he returned the knife to his saddlebag, he flinched and rubbed his shoulder. Jenny was on it in an instant. She came to him and cupped his elbow in a gentle palm.

"Are you all right, Shane?" she asked, her voice soft.

"I think so," he responded cautiously. "I think I do have a bruise, though. I landed on the point of my shoulder with most of my weight, after I pushed you out of the way."

"And you were moving fast. Let me look, please? You may have hurt yourself and don't realize it yet. You were pretty full of adrenaline for a while, and that keeps people from feeling pain." She saw the grass stain and a dirty scrape on his shirt where it lay over his shoulder. He was right about having hit hard.

"All right, Jenny. You're the doctor," he capitulated. She gave him her best warm smile and was gratified when he made a great effort to return it.

"Good. I'm sure you're fine, but I'm glad you're letting me reassure myself," she said, leading him back toward the beach. "Come over to that big log and sit down." Before he sat, she tugged his shirttail out of his breeches, then eased his shirt off, left arm first. When she saw his bare chest, her mind veered off in a totally unclinical direction. She had often observed that his waist seemed slender in proportion to the rest of him. Now she saw why. His upper chest and shoulders were bulky and strongly defined in a way that told her he exercised hard; every muscle was corded and cut. She was reminded of Michelangelo's exquisite David. Her trained eyes picked out the heavily developed pectorals and trapezii that obscured his clavicles, and, wrapped around his ribs, the small, highly defined serratus anterior and latissimus dorsi stood out in plain relief. She reluctantly left off recounting after the abdominal rectus and obliques. This was, after all, no anatomy quiz.

"My God, Shane, you look like a kinesiology text!" she exclaimed.

"I don't know if I've been insulted or complimented. What's kinesiology?"

"The study of muscles," she responded with a giggle. "And it's a high compliment. Do you work out with weights, then?"

"Yes, plus running and swimming and calisthenics. I had to get into shape to play hockey in college, and I just kept it up. When your worst enemy is the town blacksmith, you have to stay strong." His wry smile made her chuckle again. Then she came back to earth when she saw the darkening bruise on the point of his shoulder. She touched it, but he did not wince.

"Painful?" she asked.

"Not too much. I really don't think anything is wrong."

"Hopefully not. That's what we're going to find out." She looked him over, making sure his shoulders were symmetrical. She checked that from the back, too. And there she encountered more of the same exquisite musculature. The developed deltoids made wonderfully sharp indentations over his shoulder blades, and she could even pick out the tiny teres major and minor just below his armpits. She ached to caress that marvelous power; she did allow her fingertips to trace the tops of his shoulders, just to let him know she was indeed doing something besides ogling him. She swallowed heavily and walked around to his right side.

"All right. I'm going to check your collarbone. But I don't know how I'll find it under all those muscles. From now on, let me know if anything I do hurts, all right?" Her fingertips probed gently, finding the proximal end of the clavicle. She pushed on it, at first gently and then with some firmness, eventually palpitating its entire length, but he did not react. Then she turned to his shoulder joint. A blow to the point of the shoulder could result in separation or dislocation, but that caused the patient to carry the affected arm low and immobile. She had already ruled that out by the easy way he had been moving for the last half hour. But she could not rule out a fracture of the scapular fossa. She reached over his shoulder and palpitated the top of his shoulder blade. His fine, fair skin was sensual, and beneath it the muscles felt like marble. *Oh, Doctor Jennifer Catherine Weston, where is your professional detachment?* she asked herself. Then she took his arm and manipulated it through a full range of motion, encountering the bunched biceps brachii, and its fraternal twin, the triceps. She located the bursa down the front of the shoulder joint and squeezed with some firmness.

"Still no pain?" she asked as she eased his arm around in a big circle for the second time.

"Not really. It's just sore where I landed on it."

"Well, you're probably right. You're not really hurt except for that bruise. It's coloring up already, which is just what I'd expect for somebody with skin as fair as yours. If we were at Mount Hope I'd prescribe aspirin, an ice pack, rest for twenty-four hours, and then if you were experiencing stiffness or discomfort, moist heat. But the real curative would be Tincture of Time."

"Tincture of Time?"

"Yes. It's medical jargon for the fact that most patients eventually get better on their own no matter what you do for them."

"Then I'll live?" he asked mischievously.

"Well, when you do die, it won't be from this." She laid her hand over the point of his shoulder, feeling the heat of the coming bruise. "If you're stiff or sore tomorrow, try aspirin and a hot shower or a hot towel. Or just tough it out. But if it really bothers you, let me know, and I'll check you again."

"I have a sneaking feeling that it will. In fact, by tomorrow morning it may become excruciatingly painful." She cuffed the top of his head.

"You really are Irish, aren't you? Here. I'll help you with your shirt." She eased the sleeve over his right arm, then guided his left arm down the opposite sleeve. When she settled it over his shoulders, she saw the tiny, dark scar below his left collarbone, the remnant of the gunshot wound that had been responsible for their rocky beginnings.

"Does that ever bother you anymore?" she asked.

"No. For a while I woke up stiff in the morning, but that hasn't happened for a long time." She nodded approvingly, but her fingertips did not want to lose contact with the soft warmth of his skin. She knew she was pushing the situation. With a sigh she buttoned his collar, then worked down the front of his shirt. He caught her hands.

"Thank you, Jenny."

"For what? You're fine."

"For being gentle with me."

"Doctors are that way, Shane."

"I'm grateful for your concern. It's touching. But now we've been here about as long as I want to be. Let's get back on the trail." However, she stood her

229

ground, looking up at him, until he leaned forward and gently touched his lips to hers. She did reach around him then, her touch as ethereal as the summer breeze. One gentle, reassuring kiss was enough.

Moving tiredly in the aftermath of the crisis, he led her back to where the horses were tethered. He turned to give her a hand up.

"How far are we from Thomas Wise Hand's ranch, then?" she asked as she turned Fleur abreast of Midnight.

"Oh, half an hour, maybe. And when we get there, please do me a favor? Pretend you're a proper Iroquois maiden? It's best if you don't look too directly at Thomas, and don't speak to him. If you have anything to say to him, say it to me and I'll relay it. And if I signal you to stay behind, just stop and stay where you are until I either beckon to you or come back. All right?"

"Certainly. The last thing I ever want to do is give offense or embarrass you. But why can't I speak to him? Doesn't he understand French at all?"

"Not really. Moreover, the Iroquois would consider it immodest because you're a woman and a stranger. He's a shaman and he's old-fashioned and reclusive, even for an Iroquois."

The trail narrowed and forced her behind him. She watched him riding ahead, noticing that he had started to look tired. Her clinical mind told her it was the aftermath of the huge adrenaline rush, while the young woman in love wanted to take him in her arms and console him.

Eventually they broke out of the woods and into a big meadow that had been logged perhaps twenty years ago. The land there lay relatively flat and, she noticed, most of it had been recently fenced. They rode along a wagon track that paralleled the fence line. She guessed this was Thomas Wise Hand's ranch. Eventually she saw a cabin in the distance, with a big barn behind it and a few horses in the pasture. Shane was uncharacteristically silent as they approached the house. In Indian fashion he stopped outside and simply waited to be noticed. Presently a young boy of perhaps ten years emerged from the doorway and spoke to him in Iroquois. There was a lengthy exchange, and then the boy opened the pasture gate. Jenny, uncertain what she should do, hung back until Shane motioned her to follow him. Then across a rise in the pasture she saw a man riding a red horse at a breakneck gallop, controlling the animal with a single-reined rope bridle. Shane's palm-down gesture told her to stay where she was. When he kicked Midnight into a hard gallop, Fleur, recognizing her former home and her old herd, begged to follow, but Jenny halted her. For a minute or two the men raced, until Midnight began to pull away from the red gelding. Thomas capitulated and reined his mount in, and Jenny saw the two talking earnestly as they trotted back toward her. When they were close enough to hear, she realized they were speaking Iroquois.

As Thomas approached, his green-broke mount fidgeted. Jenny tightened her reins, touched Fleur's flanks, and urged her back. The mare moved off several obedient steps until she was a respectful distance away from Shane and Thomas, while Jenny watched Shane and heard more of the baffling language. Whatever Thomas said caused Shane to blush furiously before the older man slapped him on the shoulder so hard it shoved him forward over Midnight's neck. A moment later Thomas heeled his sorrel gelding, sweeping off in a thunder of beating hooves.

The boy who had initially greeted them was waiting at the gate. He gave Jenny a shy smile. Still in character, she broke eye contact and demurely looked away. Shane led out and she followed until she caught up and pulled abreast of him down the lane next to the fence. Far away in the pasture, Thomas was still galloping the half-broken gelding, ostensibly to tire him so he would be in a mood for training.

"What did he say to you, Shane?" Jenny asked at length.

"That he'd send his boys after the bear. He thanked me and said they would eat well tonight."

"No. I mean when he slapped your shoulder." To her vast amusement, Shane reddened again.

"You don't want to know."

"Well, I can guess. You look embarrassed half to death."

"He was impressed when you backed Fleur to give his horse room. He complimented you. He said you are modest. In the eyes of the Iroquois, modesty is a great virtue."

"Then I'm glad. I don't want to be a discredit to you."

They took a trail that skirted the eastern edge of North Village, obviating the necessity of stopping to visit. Then they picked up the steep, serpentine descent toward the Elk Gap Road. At the first ford of a small creek, Midnight asked for a drink, and Shane stopped to let him indulge himself. Fleur fell in beside him a moment later, gulping and swallowing noisily.

"Shane?" Jenny asked.

"Hmm?"

"How close are we to where that man with the knife attacked you last January?"

"It was right here, as a matter of fact. Why?"

"Look down there in the water and tell me if you see what I do." She pointed at an object glinting in the declining afternoon sunlight. It was edge up between a stone and a tree root, hard to see unless one happened to be at just the right angle. He dismounted, handed her his reins, and pushed his sleeve up to just above his elbow at the beginning swell of a bulky biceps. Then he knelt and fished around in the cool water. A moment later he came up with a dripping knife even larger than the one he had used on the bear. The wicked, curving point made her stomach tighten.

"Well, I'll be damned," he murmured.

"I hope not."

"Huh?"

Her reply was a giggle. "Nothing. Is that his knife, then?"

"It has to be. How on earth did you spot it?"

"The light was reflecting off the blade. I was in just the right place to pick it out."

"No wonder Paul couldn't find it. It went into the creek, and at the time it was mostly covered up with snow and half frozen over. Well, I'll have to write an addendum to Paul's report and give this to Bob Shepherd. Even though the Board of Inquiry cleared me, the Northwest Mounted doesn't like loose ends." He wiped the knife ineffectually on his wool breeches, then put it in his right saddlebag.

"What a day," she sighed.

"It has been pretty full, all right," he agreed. He lifted himself slowly to his saddle, taking his time to set his right toe into the stirrup.

"Well, we're close to home now."

"Home for you," he responded tiredly.

"Shane, you know you can stay with Uncle Richard any time you want to."

"I have plenty of time to make it back to town."

"If you stay with us tonight, we can ride into town together tomorrow morning." He looked across at her.

"You make that sound so tempting, Jenny. But I have to clean my rifle, and I need to write that report. It should go on the train tomorrow, and I can't do it in the morning. I have to ride patrol, and heaven only knows what else may crop up."

"Well, then, at least stay to supper. You'll never make it back home in time."

The instant he opened the door they were assaulted by the rich, spicy scent of apple pie. Mavis was standing at the sink rinsing dishes.

"My! It smells like you remembered you owe me a pie!" he exclaimed.

"For all the times you've brought Mr. Weston's mail, it's probably several pies," Mavis responded. "How was the grand affair, then?"

"Lovely!" Jenny said.

"Wonderful," Shane replied simultaneously.

"Oh, dear, how very sad. It doesn't sound as if you two enjoyed yourselves at all," she said with a tongue-in-cheek grin.

"Is Uncle Richard upstairs working, then?"

"Unless he sneaked out, yes."

"That reception must have been something," Mavis remarked, pouring tea for them.

"It was just an average overblown Beaufort party, but Jenny nearly caused a stampede. Even the Governor himself practically tripped over his boot laces to get her to dance with him," Shane replied. He and Jenny traded a poignant glance.

At dinner, Richard insisted on a complete chronicle of events. He seemed to enjoy it as much as they had. But, with his usual innate tact, he did not keep Shane long. It was not yet twilight when Jenny accompanied him to the barn.

"I'll walk to the end of the lane with you," she volunteered.

"I'd like that," he responded. She knew their goodbye would leave her full of longing. Leading Midnight, he walked slowly out of the light from the kitchen windows. As soon as they were in the balmy dusk again, her hand found its way into his.

"Thank you for not mentioning the bear in front of Uncle Richard," she said at length. "I'm afraid it would have upset him."

"It upset me plenty," he said grimly. "I don't even want to think about it ever again."

"Well, you saved my life. All I can do is say thank you, and that sounds so inadequate."

"There's a saying that all's well that ends well. I just hope you're not frightened of the woods now."

She shook her head. "No. That was probably a one-time thing."

"It was. I've been in the woods all my life, and that's the first time I've ever had to shoot anything bigger than a snake in self-defense. Oh, we've all shot mad wolves from time to time, but that's only humane. They would die in agony otherwise, and they do pose a danger of contagion. But I'm more adamant than ever that you learn to shoot. I think I'll get you a nice tame little Model '94 carbine. It's almost a smaller version of my rifle. I'd feel a lot better if you're armed when you start answering calls alone."

"Then let's just leave it at that. Thank you. And thank you for taking me to River Bend. These last two days have been a fairy tale for me."

"I said before that I'm the one who should thank you. I've come to realize that…that dreams do come true sometimes."

"I remember you telling me you dreamed we went to a ball. Did it live up to your dream, then?"

"That and then some," he replied. He stopped around the curve of the lane, just shy of where it met North Village Road. She looked up into his strong face, shadowed in the light of the westering sun. "I'll see you in town tomorrow, then, Jenny—although I don't want to say goodbye, even for that long." His voice sounded slightly hoarse.

"I know, Shane. I don't either. Saying good night to you means I have to come down off the pink cloud I've been floating around on for the last two days."

"Me too, though I daresay mine's a few miles higher than yours." He was so close, and she felt drawn to him by some power outside herself. She took a step nearer, into his arms, tacitly asking to be kissed. He held her close for a moment before they kissed, long and very tenderly. His lips touched her eyebrow, her temple, and her forehead.

"Oh, Jenny," he whispered.

"Shane…"

"Shh. It was a beautiful two days and you gave me a beautiful memory to keep." His finger softly against her lips silenced her.

"Good night, sweetheart," she whispered.

"*À demain*, then, *chèrie*." Sometimes he mixed languages when his emotions ran high; she found it totally endearing. He drew on his cavalry gauntlets, and she considerately held his reins while he mounted, though Midnight was so quiet he scarcely needed restraining. Her last glimpse of him was a wave as he trotted down North Village Road. She watched until she could no longer see him through the gathering dark, then floated back into the house, where Mavis had just finished the dishes. Illogically, she was afraid Mavis could read the last few minutes' events as though written on her forehead in India ink. For some time the housekeeper said nothing, but after a while she broke the silence.

"He's a good man," she said at length.

"Yes, I know," Jenny sighed. "Mavis, do you think I've been too…daring?"

"You've been walking around the bend in the lane and kissing him good night for months. No, that's not daring. I was your age once myself, child. Just remember, it's not a game anymore. Shane's a man, and you're playing for keeps."

Chapter Thirteen

Shane hoped to complete his paperwork before the somewhat airless office became unbearable. In the August heat he had bent the rules and spent the last half hour in his shirtsleeves, working on Paul's last day report. Long ago he had resigned himself to rewriting everything his partner submitted because of his atrocious spelling and indifferent punctuation. He was about halfway through when he heard the morning train whistle blow for the bridge over the Elk River. Reflexively he took out his watch and looked at it. The train, as always, was running on time. Soon it would pull up at the station. He picked up his tunic and began the long process of fastening all the buttons, buckling his crossover belt, and securing his pistol to the lanyard. Then he strolled outside to see if anyone would debark. As he stood beneath the shaded overhang of the sidewalk roof, he saw a tallish and somewhat heavy man walk around the edge of the platform. As the man paused to settle a Panama hat on his light brown hair, he was joined by a figure so familiar that it gave Shane pause.

If I didn't know Richard was in Cambridge, I'd swear... He remembered Jenny telling him how much her father and her uncle resembled each other. That had to be the answer. But what on earth would her father be doing here in Elk Gap?

He stood in the shade, watching the two men walk east along Main Street toward the livery stable. Their summer-weight linsey-woolsey suits stood out like beacon lights among the homespuns, bib overalls, work boots, and denims of the citizens of Elk Gap. He considered abandoning his paperwork, collecting Midnight, and making a quick run for Richard's farm, but then decided that would be tantamount to interference, especially since Richard had left town four days ago. He would discover the reason for their visit in due course. With a resigned sigh, he went back inside to resume his paperwork, but his police officer sense of something out of place was screaming at him like a hysterical banshee. He made a side trip to Mrs. Hammill's kitchen for a cup of tea to settle his nerves. He took it back to his desk, sat down, and stared into the cup as if he could read the future there. Then he gave himself a mental shake. *Finish your report,* he told himself; *then, if you want to, saddle up and ride out toward North Village. You can always make a stop at Richard's just to make sure everything is open and above board.*

Reluctantly he turned back to the report, but neither his heart nor his mind was in his work. He copied the word "certenty" as Paul had misspelled it. With a disgusted snort he reached for the bottle of ink remover, dispensed a measured amount on the page with the bulb-topped eyedropper in the cap, and when the ink dissolved he blotted it up with a piece of old sheet. He blew on the page until the spot dried, then deliberately wrote "certainty" before setting the pen aside and running frustrated fingers through his hair. He had almost decided to abandon his report and ride to

Richard's when he heard a discreet knock at the half-open office door.

"May I help you?" he called. The door swung open all the way, and he found himself looking at the two men from the train. Every hair on the back of his neck bristled, and he felt as edgy as a cat cornered in a room with a large dog of uncertain intent.

"Doctor John Weston, Inspector Adair." The man who looked like Richard held out his hand, and Shane grasped it across the desk. "As I can see you surmised, I am Richard's brother. There is more than a passing resemblance between us. And this is Mr. Phillip Hildebrand." Another handshake, pudgy and ineffectual. Shane remained standing, every word he had ever heard about John Weston coming to the forefront of his mind.

"Pleased to meet you both. Now, what may I do for you?"

"Inspector Adair, this is…ah…a matter of no small delicacy. You see, I understand from all my daughter's correspondence that you and she have been…keeping company, shall we say?"

"Yes. Jenny and I have been seeing each other, both professionally and socially. Why?"

"Because, well, Inspector, there appears to be some misunderstanding. You see, Jenny and Mr. Hildebrand are engaged to be married. They have been for some time. Perhaps I was more indulgent with Jenny than I should have been, but after she completed residency, she and I did come to an understanding. She wanted to visit Richard, since she had always been close to him and she had not seen him in some time. Our agreement was that she would return from Canada after six months and her engagement to Mr. Hildebrand would be formally announced so they can marry in the spring." Shane was momentarily paralyzed from the shock of John's oily words. He felt the blood drain from his face; however, iron discipline kept his expression neutral.

"I know of no such agreement," he replied stiffly.

"I had thought as much. She evidently did not tell Richard, either. I'm very sorry if this turn of events has shocked you. My daughter has always been the sort of person who sees the world in her own way. And you will realize that the six months was up some time ago. The plan was always that I would come and escort her home."

"Have you been in communication with her, then?"

"Always. I even telephoned her before we left New York. I'm surprised she didn't meet our train, but who knows what business she's attending to."

"I see."

"As I said, I'm sorry if the abrupt end of Jenny's summer romance has come as a surprise to you. But you must understand how impossible any relationship between the two of you was from the beginning. You of course appreciate how radically our social standing differs from your own, ah…mixed blood and dubious birth. You must agree you and my daughter must have no further contact with each other. It could do irreparable damage to her reputation. You wouldn't want to spoil her chance at the life that is really best for her, after all, would you? The life of wealth and privilege to which she was born?"

Shane heard only half of what John Weston was saying. Had the ground opened up and swallowed him he could not have been more surprised, and he probably would have been a great deal happier. Every childhood insult, all the times the college fraternity crowd had whispered slurs behind his back while making sure he knew they were doing it, every time he had trailed home to Mavis with a nosebleed from a playground fight came to the front of his mind. They were right, every one of them, and by implication he deserved all the deprecation and the snide remarks. He was Métis and probably a bastard to boot, and the stain would follow him to his grave. For an instant he remembered the day of Jimmy Richardson's funeral during the scarlet fever epidemic, and he wished more than anything before or since that he had found the fortitude to tell Jenny about his background. Now, however, it was at least a century too late.

John Weston stopped to draw breath. "Well, then, Inspector, if that is all, we need to…" At that moment Paul came across the dining room, halting when he saw the two men in the office.

"Excuse me, Inspector Adair. If you're busy, I'll…"

"No, Corporal Weller. These two gentlemen were just leaving. Weren't you?" He heard his voice sounding flat and very Iroquois.

"Yes, sir. I do believe our business here is concluded satisfactorily. Thank you very much for your aid—and for your understanding." Dr. Weston held out his hand again, but Shane ignored it. "Good afternoon, then, Inspector." He turned and led Phillip out past Paul, who came into the office and closed the door behind him.

"Good God, Shane, what happened? You look like you've seen a ghost!" he exclaimed.

"No, Paul. It was…nothing."

"That man looks so much like Richard!"

"That is Richard's older brother. I'm glad you're back. I really need to get going on rounds. I still have light enough to make it to the line shack at Overlook Point if I leave now."

"You weren't going until tomorrow," Paul protested.

"I know, but I've changed my mind. I have all my gear packed and ready. There's no reason for me not to leave now. Just put today's report in my in-basket, and I'll sign it when I get back."

"Sit down!" Paul commanded, pointing to the chair behind the desk. Surprised by the commanding firmness in his subordinate's voice, Shane obeyed. "Now tell me what really happened. I know Richard has only one brother—Jenny's father. So this has to concern Jenny. If it concerns her, it concerns you, and what concerns you concerns me. Now what was it? Out with it!"

Shane took a deep, uncertain breath before continuing. "Evidently Jenny was…not completely truthful with me. Of course no man ever wants to admit he has been taken for a fool, but evidently I've been a very large one. The man with Doctor Weston? Phillip Hildebrand? He and Jenny are engaged. All along she was planning to go back to New York. I was nothing more to her than a plaything for a summer."

Paul looked thunderstruck. "I can scarcely believe that! She's been so happy here with her medical practice, and I've seen a thousand times how she looks at you!"

"Well, it's over. Her father told me the agreement was that she would stay here for six months, then come home, marry Mr. Hildebrand, and assume her place in New York society. And there's more. I know I've never spoken of my family to you… I never told you this, but Madame LaPorte up in North Village is my grandmother. Her daughter took up with an Irish railroad worker. I don't know whether they were ever married or not. Besides being Métis I may well be a bastard, Paul. And somehow John Weston knew that."

"Shit," Paul whispered.

"Precisely."

"I wonder where he came by that information. It sounds like no more than a lucky guess to me. But wait a second! The buggy they were driving came from Josh's stable. Between Josh Barnes and the Camerons, they'd love nothing more than to see your name dragged through the mud."

Shane was still mired in the past, where up until a scant few minutes ago he thought he had won the fight to overcome the stigma of his origins. But he knew that one never accomplishes so impossible a task. Perhaps here in the safety of Elk Gap he had won the grudging respect of most of the locals, but the larger, crueler world had just reached out and sucker-punched him where he was most vulnerable. If he faced the bald truth, he was not worthy to tie Jenny's shoes, and moreover, any association with him, real or overblown, could indeed damage not only her reputation but her family's as well. He dared not risk that. He took a deep breath and watched his world implode.

"Be that as it may, John Weston is right. I'm not fit to aspire to Jenny. Phillip Hildebrand is. Everything about him says his family has old money. I can't compete with that. Now I really do need to leave for rounds. I need to clear my head."

"All right. I understand."

"I'll be back in a fortnight or so. Don't worry if I'm a few days late in. I'm going to take my time and stop at the villages. Until then, Elk Gap is yours." He stood up, and this time Paul did not protest. Instead, he held out his hand, and Shane took it. His left hand closed over Shane's forearm, the gesture reassuring.

"Be careful, please?" Shane nodded, his face expressionless and his eyes blank.

"Yes. Our August Curse. Thank you, Paul. Later, then." He brushed past his friend, picked up his hat, gauntlets, and big Winchester rifle, and disappeared out the door.

Chapter Fourteen

Jenny, taking an afternoon off after a late night childbirth, enjoyed the rare few hours alone while Mavis attended a meeting of the Presbyterian Ladies' Handwork Society. She set her book aside and came to answer the knocking at the front door, expecting Shane. So when she opened the door and saw her father and Phillip, her heart froze.

"What are you doing here?" she asked, her voice a shocked whisper.

"You're not going to ask us in, then, Jenny?" John Weston began.

"Of course, but..." Letting them into the house where there was no one to help her was the last thing she wanted to do, but she knew she had to give in. The situation was two against one.

"But what? Let's go into the parlor where we can talk." Her stomach twisted. Her father's definition of "talk" was that he propounded and his victim submitted. Reluctantly she led them into the parlor and deliberately sat out of the way on the sofa. Her father sat next to her, forcing her to the end, while Phillip was left standing. Then John Weston moved insolently to the other end of the sofa.

"What is it you want, Father?" she asked, keeping her voice steady only with effort.

"For you to come home with me and marry Phillip

the way you know you should."

"I'm sorry. I've found my life here. I'm practicing medicine, and I've decided to stay."

"Be that as it may, I will state this one last time and once only. Come home, marry Phillip, and do what you were born to do. Be the proper pillar of New York society whom everyone loves and respects."

"People love and respect me here. I even have a sweet little blonde namesake who is three months old now. I don't need New York."

"Oh, but you do, Jen. You do."

She shook her head. "I'm of age. You can't compel me any longer." She could not help but understand the pointed look that passed between Phillip and John.

"I've a proposition to make to you. Come home and join the staff of Northtown. I'll put in my recommendation for you. You've wanted to practice at Northtown for a very long time." She felt a distinct tug on her heartstrings. Joining the staff at Northtown had been her holy grail ever since the first time she had stepped across its threshold as a young child. Now here it was in front of her, an open invitation to the one thing she had ever really wanted.

"I'll even agree to let you practice medicine until our first child comes," Phillip appended, and received an immediate withering glare from his supposedly intended father-in-law. His words jerked her back to the present with a violence that was almost physical. It took her only a moment to recognize the ruse for what it was.

"How kind and condescending of you, Phillip. But I'm declining your gracious offer with my sincerest thanks. Now will the two of you please go back where you came from and let me live my life?"

"And let you live out here in this wilderness? Among these savages? Jenny, you should be thanking us for rescuing you from this…this abattoir! Have you taken leave of your…" Phillip's outburst was silenced by another glare.

"My, aren't you two brave to come in here, denigrate Elk Gap and Uncle Richard's home while he's away and unable to defend himself, and practically try to kidnap me?" Her father made an airy gesture that dismissed her concern as casually as though he were waving away a fly.

"I said you can practice at Northtown. You can be a surgeon. That's what you've wanted all along, isn't it?"

"Yes, but I wanted it freely, with no constraints."

"Freely, with no constraints, until your first child. And if you do not accept this offer, James Hildebrand will cease all donations to Northtown. He's hit the end of his not inconsiderable patience. You know that he practically funds Northtown's research singlehandedly. If you do not return with us, your selfishness is going to condemn a good many people to pointless suffering and early death when they are deprived of the medical advances Northtown is making practically every day. Why, only last week a little girl who was hit by a wagon was saved when I operated on her brain and removed a blood clot. I actually opened the child's skull, Jenny! I saw the human brain, living and functioning, right beneath my hands, so close I actually touched it! My patient is now home with her mother where she belongs, happy and active and completely normal. How many others like her does it take to convince you that Northtown's research is worth a small compromise on your part?"

Her chill escalated itself almost into nausea; Northtown had been a large part of her life even though she had not practiced there. She could never be instrumental in anything that could damage it. The tiny sounds she heard in the back of her mind were the screws in her coffin lid.

"Jenny, I promise I'll be a considerate husband," Phillip began. "I hold you in the highest regard, and I want you to marry me of your own free will. I'll never interfere in anything you decide to do. You'll have all the money you want, all the clothes, all the jewels. You will be free to see your friends as you choose, go to the theater, to soirees, and to any social functions you desire. I'll support your charities and I'll accompany you anywhere it would be seemly for me. You can practice medicine, as your father said, until we begin a family. All I ask is that you remain loyal to me and you behave as a proper wife should. And in turn I promise that I will be polite and considerate and treat you with respect at all times."

"My, Mr. Hildebrand, what a passionate declaration of undying love." Her voice dripped sarcasm. *But that was my last shot,* Jenny thought. *I'm out of ammunition. However, I will make you one promise right now. Even if you're successful in forcing me to marry you, there will be no children. I will never allow you to touch me. I'll force you into divorce if I have to.*

Her father sat back and crossed his arms arrogantly. "So, then, what will it be? Do you come back with us, or are you going to destroy Northtown all by yourself?"

"This is blackmail. You are selling me into prostitution."

"Eventually you will thank me. Both of you."

She stood up, dignified in defeat, and with the politeness beaten into him by the Old General, her father rose with her.

"Yes, I'll go back with you. I don't see that I have much choice in the matter. I'm doing this only for Northtown and how much I've always loved it. But as for thanking you, I'll tell you when I'll thank you. I will thank you when both of you are out of my life and I'm free."

"Sticks and stones, sticks and stones," her father mocked. "Go get ready. Leave your clothes and your books here. You won't need any of them again. Just bring the family jewelry I know you have with you, and enough clothes to keep you on the trip back. You and Eleanor can go shopping for a new wardrobe as soon as we reach New York. You'll have a great time doing that, I know." She shot him such a look of loathing that it would have made a lesser man quail. Then, with a defiant swish of her skirt she disappeared up the stairs, where she fell on her bed. But instead of weeping she pulled herself together and went to Alix's desk. She picked up her pen and drew out a sheet of her imprinted stationery.

Dear Uncle Richard, she wrote. *I have decided to return home with Father. Please do not worry for me. I will write to you as soon as I can. Rest assured I am doing this of my own free will. Father has made me see reason. I love you and I always will, and look forward to seeing you the next time you're in New York.* Then she signed her name. She changed from her casual brown gingham frock into a black skirt and a lawn summer shirtwaist, picked up her jewel case and dropped it into her hand valise, then packed fresh underthings and her Genesse ball gown, tucked toilet items down the side, and stopped to look in the cheval glass. She said farewell to her happiness, to one glorious summer, and to Shane. She would have to leave him without a word, because it was not beyond him to follow her. She came down the stairs with all the aloof dignity she could manage, trying to ignore her father, whose expression was neutral, and Phillip, who could not conceal a gloat. She made a side trip to the water closet, then settled her bonnet on her head and came out into the immaculate assembly room, where she left the note on the dining table.

"Good. You're ready, then. Come on. The sooner we're out of this disgusting place the better I'll like it," John Weston said.

"It's not disgusting. It's home to me, and even though you've won and I'm leaving, it will always be home."

"No. Jenny. I will make a splendid home for you," Phillip said, not ungently. She looked daggers at him.

"I may be compelled to live in your house, but it will never be my home, Mr. Hildebrand." Her voice was dead. "You have your victory for the moment, but I promise it will be hollow." Her father did not quite say "sticks and stones" again, but she knew he was thinking it. She spurned his aiding hand and stepped up into the back seat of the buggy by herself.

Phillip untied the mare's reins and climbed into the driver's seat. He hauled the left rein around roughly and smacked the mare with the right one. She fought against the pain of her bit before she straightened herself out and started off in a jarring canter that sent everyone back against their seats. Brutally Phillip hauled her back. Jenny reached into her reticule for a handkerchief but choked back her tears. *Hang onto the injustice, Jennifer Catherine*, she told herself. *Hang onto it and think yourself out of this situation. You're only doing this because you love Northtown. You know you also love Shane. Perhaps you can have both. Hang onto this thought and think yourself out of this predicament. Thinking is what you do best. You know you can work this out. Phillip is a self-indulgent, dissipated simpleton. You can outfox him and Father both, if you put your mind to it. They may have won the first round, but you will win the war.*

The train to River Bend left at 5:30. That gave them over two hours before departure. Her father rubbed his gold pocket watch and considered the time carefully.

"We've some time until the train leaves. Is there anywhere in this God-forsaken backwater where we can have dinner?"

"Only Mrs. Hammill's boardinghouse," Jenny responded.

"We'll stop there, then, especially since we need to return the buggy." Phillip, the eternal yes-man, nodded in agreement. Eventually they pulled up next to Josh Barnes' livery stable. Phillip led the mare back behind the building and turned her into the corral, leaving the buggy with the harness in a heap on the driver's seat. In the meantime, John Weston escorted Jenny down the board sidewalk toward Mrs. Hammill's. Fortunately, the door to the Royal Northwest office was closed. She had no idea what she would do if she encountered Shane, or for that matter, Paul.

Her father very properly opened the door for her and ushered her to a table. To her relief, the girl who waited on them was only a distant acquaintance and not Maddie or Flora Hammill herself. Jenny requested only tea, while her father ordered steak for both himself and Phillip.

"You're not eating, Jenny?" he asked.

"Do you really expect me to be able to?"

"Of course! You're going back to the place where you belong, after all." She deigned not to reply, fixing him instead with a glare that could curdle milk. He ignored it.

Phillip fell to his meal with a gusto that left her vaguely ill. She was sipping her tea when Paul came through the front door. She watched him assess the situation, then he made a beeline for her.

"Doctor Weston..." he began, but she interrupted him.

"I'm going back to New York, Corporal Weller," she said, touching his scarlet sleeve, a debutante's delicate gesture. Her failure to introduce Phillip and her father was a deliberate snub as evident as a lighthouse at midnight. "I'm glad for the chance to say goodbye to you and to thank you for all your gracious kindness toward me this summer."

"It's good that I caught you before you left, then. Could you please come back to the office for a moment? You filled out the death certificate for Mrs. Morris yesterday, but you forgot to sign the jurat on the back." There was no Mrs. Morris and certainly no death certificate, nor did they have jurats. But she played along.

"I'm so sorry, Corporal Weller. I'm still not used to Canadian paperwork. In the States the attending physician only signs in one place. There's no jurat. Father? Mr. Hildebrand? Will you please excuse me? I shan't be but a moment."

"Of course," her father said with a superior smile. *Magnanimous in victory, aren't you, you old bastard,* she thought sarcastically. She followed Paul into the office, and he immediately closed the door. Her control snapped. She flung herself into his arms, sobbing silently against the unforgiving wool of his Red Serge. His long arms gathered her against his chest.

"Jenny, Jenny, hush. Calm down and tell me what happened," he said soothingly. She gulped, got hold of herself by main force, and scrubbed her face with her handkerchief.

"Paul, they're making me go. Father always wanted me to marry Phillip. I can't stand the man. He makes my skin crawl. I've told him 'no' sixteen ways to Sunday, but he won't accept it. But unless I go back, his father is withdrawing his support from Northtown Surgical Clinic's research programs."

"Does Shane know about this?" More tears and a vigorous shake of the head.

"No. Neither does Uncle Richard. I'm sure you remember that he's in Cambridge to deliver a guest lecture at Harvard. Father and Phillip just arrived on the scene this morning with absolutely no warning, and I'm... Paul, I have to leave with them. I'll think my way out of this situation somehow, but I can't just out-and-out refuse. So much good comes out of

Northtown's research."

"But what of the good you do here? The lives you've saved? Jenny, you can't just up and leave Elk Gap. People here need you, too. And need I mention Shane? He's so in love with you that half the time he doesn't know whether he's afoot or on horseback."

"Please don't. You'll make me cry again, and Father will know something is fishy. Tell Shane…tell him somehow I'll be back, and as soon as I can I'll write to him and explain."

"He left early on rounds. He and your father spoke briefly. Your father told him you and Phillip Hildebrand were engaged and that Shane is beneath you. Your father said you and he had agreed you'd stay here for six months and then come home and marry Phillip. Shane believed it."

"Oh, no! That's so wrong! It's all lies, every last bit of it! I never made any such agreement, and Shane must know that." Then her defeat at her father's hands caught up with her and all the fight drained out like water in dry sand. "Well, then, let him believe it for the present. It's probably for the best. Somehow I'll get out of this mess, and I'll come back and make everything right. Tell him that for me, please?"

"I so hate to see you go. I haven't words. I'll tell him you'll come back. I'll also tell him your father was lying to him. Please take care of yourself, and come back to us soon."

"I will, Paul. I promise. Stay well and stay safe." She hugged him and pressed her cheek against his. It took some control to make her chin stop quivering. When she had herself in hand again he made a great show of very politely opening the door for her.

"Thank you very much. Doctor Weston," he said, his voice a shade louder than it needed to be in order to reach the two men at their table. "This fortunate coincidence has saved me a lot of work and worry. I'd have had to track you down, you know." She gave him a crooked half-smile.

"After all, they say the Mounties always get their man."

"Very true, Doctor Weston. Goodbye, then, and Godspeed."

"Goodbye, Corporal Weller. Take care." She returned to the table.

"What did Mrs. Morris die of?" her father asked when Jenny returned.

"Old age. A series of small strokes. She was 89. She just slept her life away at the end." He nodded mildly, a parody of Richard.

"A long, fine life, that. And an easy death when it came. So Canadian law is different?"

"Yes. I forgot to sign the part that says I swear under penalty of perjury that the information I entered on the certificate was the truth. It's really only important in cases of suspicious deaths, but here it's required on all death certificates." She was putting on the best impromptu performance of her life. In point of fact, Canadian death certificates were an almost word-for-word counterpart of American ones.

"Well, that's a useless fact you'll have no more need of."

"You have your pound of flesh. What more do you want?"

He ignored her rudeness as he had ignored all her arguments. "You were in there quite a while for just a signature."

"He had trouble finding the certificate. His filing system is somewhat informal, if you will." That was another fib. She knew that at Shane's insistence Paul and even Laurence could instantly put their fingers on any piece of paper in the whole office.

A moment later Paul closed the office door behind him and strode out without so much as a wave toward Jenny's party. He was going somewhere with long-legged determination, and since he was wearing his Navy Colt and carrying his Enfield, it was obviously no social call. Not long afterward, while John Weston enjoyed a leisurely cup of tea and Jenny sat numb with grief, she caught sight of Paul cantering Brandy eastward along Main Street.

****

Under the shadow of spreading trees and stirred by a breeze, the August air actually felt rather pleasant, as did the rhythm of Midnight's mile-eating gait. But Shane was beyond noticing anything. His life lay in shreds at his feet. *August curse,* he thought. *And this year it's showed me up for the fool I am. I never should have let myself come anywhere near Jenny. I knew all along she was as far above me as the Queen, but I never considered that associating with me could do her real harm. I'd cut my own arm off first.* His brown study broke up abruptly when three shots echoed through the woods around him. Reflexively he twitched Midnight's reins and the horse stopped. He drew his pistol and fired three answering rounds. Midnight's training was so thorough he did not even cock an ear at the racket. Then, in the silence that followed, Shane heard a familiar voice call his name.

"Paul!" he shouted back. He turned and cantered back the way he had come. Only a few moments later he had his partner in sight down a long, straight stretch of trail. He galloped toward Paul, and then both men pulled their mounts up hard.

"Paul, what in heaven's name is going on?" he asked.

"Come on. There's no time to waste. We need to beat the train to River Bend."

"Why?"

"Because I've talked to Jenny. Everything her father told you today was a pack of lies. She's not engaged to that fat popinjay. She told me she turned him down several times. You're the one she loves. Her father is forcing her to go back to New York with him under duress. You need to go after her or you're going to lose her."

However, his mind was still stuck back in the disastrous conversation in the Northwest Mounted office. "It's true that I'm part Iroquois."

"I surmise that most everyone in Elk Gap has known that from the beginning. It must have been an open secret. If it didn't matter before, it won't matter now."

"But if I'm really illegitimate…"

"Horseshit. I know what your birth certificate says. I've seen it in your personnel file. That's proof enough for anybody."

"I was born way out in a railroad camp, and my birth was never registered until I had to have a birth certificate to go to college. It says my parents were married only because I went to Angus and he falsified his medical records to say he had attended my mother

258

when…"

"There you have it!" Paul interrupted viciously. "Keep your bloody mouth shut and brazen it out! I've never known you to be afraid of anything or anybody. What's the matter with you now? Did you lose your balls somewhere? Listen, man, if you won't go after Jenny, I will, and I won't be nice about it, either!" He smacked Brandy's rump with the free end of his reins and booted her in the ribs. She leaped out into her leggy Irish Thoroughbred gallop. Shane watched after him for a moment. He knew Paul well enough to realize that his partner never said anything he did not mean, and on the rare occasion when he had his dander up he was a force to be reckoned with. He flicked Midnight's shoulder with his reins, and the gelding, with his sire's penchant for being first in every race, jumped at the chance to catch up.

The railroad tracks made a big detour to follow the Elk River, while the road itself ran straighter, giving them their only prayer of beating the train to River Bend. While they did not have to push their horses, they did not tarry, either. Midnight, trail-hardened, could have kept up his canter all day, and Brandy, just as tough as her breed came, stayed right up with him.

The train was just passing the edge of town as Shane and Paul pulled up at the station. Both horses were sweaty, and the heat plastered Shane's shirt nastily to his chest. As he and Paul dismounted, they could just see the train on its way in.

"I hope I eventually have cause to thank you for hauling me down here," Shane muttered sourly, giving his partner a hard stare. Paul, used to his superior officer's unnerving Scorpio gaze, merely shrugged.

"I can't stand the thought of that arrogant bastard getting away with it, lying to you and coercing Jenny. Just who in bloody hell does he think he is, anyway? Jesus Christ or His Father?" Shane knew all along that there had to be a limit to Paul's easygoing approach to life. He had just begun to see where it lay.

Chapter Fifteen

When the little spur train bumped and hissed to a jerky stop, John Weston was the first person off. Jenny declined the hand he held out, gathered her black skirt, and made her own way down the steps. Then she looked up and saw two very familiar figures in brilliant red tunics.

"Shane!" she exclaimed, her voice barely above a whisper. She detached herself from her father and Phillip and floated toward him.

He reached for the hand she held out. "Jenny..." he began, but he was summarily interrupted.

"I say, Inspector Adair, your presence here is most unwelcome!" Jenny's father began, making as if to come between them. However, Paul intervened.

"Doctor Weston, my partner has more right to be here than you do. Yes, I brought him here. I want you to account for the lies you told him," he began, only to be confronted by the older man, whose icy eyes blazed with fury.

"You, young man, are nothing but a common meddler! I strongly urge you to mind your own business!"

"Oh you do, now, do you?" Paul planted his fists on his hips, drew himself up to the top of his six feet three inches, and took a few steps toward John, who held his ground.

"This is a family matter. It is not police business."

"I'm the one who calls the shots here, Doctor Weston," Paul retorted, pointing at his own chest with his thumb as if to reinforce his words. "I say it *is* police business. This is my jurisdiction, and you are coming perilously close to disturbing the peace. May I remind you that you're aliens, here at His Majesty's sufferance. Heaven only knows what contraband you have with you. I'll have to check your luggage…"

"What did he tell you, Shane?" Jenny asked, diverting his attention from the escalating byplay between Paul and her father.

"That you are engaged to Phillip Hildebrand and you had a standing agreement to return to New York after six months in Canada. He said he had been in contact with you and you consented to go home with him."

"Oh, Shane, it's all lies! Not one iota of it is true! I have never been engaged to marry anyone."

"But then, why are you…"

"I have to go home with him. Please at least leave me my dignity, and trust me for now. I'll explain it to you when I can. Just rest assured that I am not engaged to Phillip Hildebrand, I am not going to marry him, and when I take care of the present situation I'll be back, I promise." She looked up at him, her pleading eyes filling with tears. She saw deep sadness in his face as he looked down at her.

He shook his head slowly, regretfully. "No, don't make any promises you can't keep. I respect you enough to let you go. Your father was right in one way. I'm not good enough to associate with you. Worse yet, I could harm your reputation. I know it hurts. It'll hurt us both for a while, but summer romances are meant to be got over. It's better that you're hurt a little by what's happened today than a lot by who and what I am."

"What on earth are you saying?" she asked, incredulous.

"That I'm not even dirt under your feet. I'm not fit to tie your shoe. Let it go at that, please. You just asked me to leave you your dignity. I'm willing to do that if you'll leave me mine." But it was not in her scientific mind to turn loose of a situation she did not understand.

"Not fit to tie my shoe?" she echoed. "You?"

With surprising venom he rounded on her. "All right, Miss New York Debutante with all your pretty manners and all your society pretensions, here's the ugly truth of it. I'm probably a bastard. My grandfather was a squaw man and so was my father. Men like that don't usually marry their women. They leave children behind and move on. I'm a half-breed. A Métis. Madame LaPorte is my grandmother and Thomas Wise Hand is my great-uncle. I grew up in that shotgun cabin in North Village where you operated on Jimmy Richardson. I'm even Iroquois enough that I went through the manhood ceremony when I was fourteen, and had warrior visions. After the episode with Bart Hankins I became eligible for the Warrior Society, and I was inducted last February. What do you think of me now?"

She realized that his towering anger was pure defense, and by now she knew him well enough to play to his vulnerabilities. She gave him her best limpid-eyed look. "Oh, Shane, what have I ever done to make you think I could be so shallow? I figured all that out when I first met you. It didn't matter then, and it doesn't matter now." She watched him deflate and seemingly shrink several inches, but then he recovered and took a breath as if to answer her.

Across the street, a liveried man had escorted Adrian Beaufort from the low building housing his warehouse and offices. The timber baron climbed into his ponderous touring car while his chauffeur went around to the front and gave the crank a heave. Shane continued, not noticing the automobile.

"Nevertheless, I'm saying goodbye, with my best wishes for your future. It's true that I'm a half-breed and my…" He was interrupted when the engine belched out a resounding backfire worthy of a ten-pound cannon. Brandy screamed, danced around, and kicked Midnight solidly in the chest. Midnight responded by pitching a tantrum of his own. He reared, pawing the air. Jenny ducked, and Shane moved automatically to shield her from the danger. He took a step toward her as the gelding's mad prancing snagged a hind hoof under the overhanging boards of the platform. Half falling, the horse lashed out hard, striking Shane's right temple with a lunging forehoof. Then he caught himself and tore off at a dead gallop, followed an instant later by the thoroughly panicked Brandy.

Jenny and Paul made simultaneous grabs as Shane, completely unconscious, crumpled like a dropped marionette. His head slumped against the front of her shirtwaist, leaving a wide trail of blood on the white lawn. Instantly Jenny, the girl in love, became Jennifer Catherine Weston, M.D. She slipped a hand behind his head, protecting his neck.

"Ease him down carefully," she said quietly. "This is way more than a bloody nose." With her free hand, she undid the top two buttons of his Red Serge and the shirt beneath it to ease his breathing. Her father came to his knees next to Paul, leaving Phillip standing dumbly. With gentle expertise she and her father log-rolled the unresponsive man onto his side so he would not choke on the blood pouring from his nose. Although he had a strong carotid pulse and he was breathing well, he was profoundly unconscious, had a profuse nosebleed, and there was blood in both ear canals. With ethereal gentleness, John Weston riffled through the dark hair at Shane's right temple. He of all people knew that he should not palpitate to diagnose a fractured skull. Midnight's hoof had left a mark well above and a little in front of Shane's ear.

"Probably a depressed fracture," Jenny's father said quietly, his tone grave. Jenny nodded, looking down at Shane. She was still holding his head. Her right hand was full of blood, and her white lawn shirt sleeve was stained halfway to her elbow. *Oh, Shane, don't let go. We'll make you well, and when this all blows over we'll be together again. I promise you. Just fight through this, please.*

Both Adrian Beaufort and his driver had sprinted across the street and were beside them, the older man red-faced and blustering.

"Doctor Weston!" he exclaimed. "Is he badly hurt? I've told this cretin a thousand times to watch for horses before he starts that infernal machine!" His remarks were directed to Jenny, but her father looked up, too.

"It's bad enough, sir. He has a fractured skull or worse, and he needs to be taken to the nearest hospital as quickly as we can get there. Get me a wagon. He has to lie completely motionless."

"Doctor Weston, who is that?" Adrian asked.

"That, Mr. Beaufort, is my father, Doctor John Charles Weston. He's chief neurosurgeon on the staff of Northtown Surgical Clinic in New York."

"You heard the doctor, idiot!" Adrian barked at his chauffeur. "Get a wagon! Get going!" His English was heavily Québécois, and he had a marvelously Gallic temper. His unfortunate attendant flapped off across the street like a scarecrow in a gale.

"I need something to cushion his head. Your coat, please, sir." John Weston's polite request came out a demand, accompanied by an outstretched hand. The large man pulled off his jacket and folded it precisely, slipping it beneath Shane's head at John's direction. Even after years of living in the world of high finance, Adrian Beaufort still had the broad, coarse hands of a lumberjack. While John's sensitive, knowing fingers adjusted Shane's head a minute fraction, Adrian turned to Jenny and Paul.

"I'm so terribly sorry. This is very unfortunate. Let me do anything I can."

"First things first, Mr. Beaufort. Accidents do happen, you know. Let's get him to the nearest hospital and see just how bad this is," John responded. At that moment, the hapless chauffeur rattled back with an empty freight wagon. Among the four men they lifted Shane in.

"To St. Luke's," Adrian commanded the teamster. "And take the smoothest way. This man is badly hurt. And you?" He turned to his chauffeur. "Go find those horses and bring them back, and I may let you keep your job!" His voice wound up into a roaring crescendo at the scrawny man, who tore off in the direction the horses had run. Paul boosted Jenny into the front seat of the wagon, where she sat ignored, trying to see what her father observed when he opened Shane's eyes. Paul climbed up next to her a moment later.

"It'll be all right," he whispered, touching her arm. She shook her head and looked down at her blood-stained blouse.

"Oh, Paul, the whole world is falling apart," she breathed.

"We'll put it back together. One way or another we'll make this right."

"Jenny, do you have admitting privileges at this…St. Luke's?" John asked, looking up at her. It was the first time he had addressed himself to his daughter.

"Yes, I do."

"Good. Your last act as a physician here will be to get this man admitted. He will need immediate surgery. And I want you to resign from the staff and sign yourself off any cases you may be currently attending. If you want me to treat him, you are going to have to stay well out of my way and do exactly as you are told. And no one else is to address you as 'Doctor' in my presence."

"Father, Mr. Beaufort could buy and sell the Westons and the Brisbanes ten times over. He can address me any way he wants to." Her voice was dull. It was another impotent shot, but she felt obligated to kick against the traces whenever she could, just to let her father know she had not given up.

They arrived at the hospital, where John heavy-handedly dished out orders right and left. He was as good as his word. She signed admission forms for Shane, did paperwork confirming her father as a consulting surgeon, then, accompanied by the Chief of Surgery, who incidentally was a close friend of Angus MacBride's, returned to the room where Shane was being prepared for surgery. His clothing had been removed and he lay on a cart, covered to his waist by a sheet. Her father was holding a stethoscope to his chest. He did not look at her but fixed his eyes on the doctor accompanying her.

"I'm glad you're here. He started with decerebrate posturing, then had a spectacular grand mal seizure," he said without preamble. "His pupils are only sluggishly reactive, and the right one is dilated. So you can see there's not a moment to lose."

"Father, this is Doctor Silas Dalton, Chief of Surgery," Jenny began.

"John Weston," her father said, moving the stethoscope to the apex of Shane's left lung. "We have a depressed fracture of the right temporal and possibly the sphenoid. I think there is bleeding around the brain, probably a subdural hematoma. If he isn't in surgery within the hour to evacuate that blood, we'll have a dead or permanently disabled patient on our hands."

"I've heard of your reputation, Doctor Weston. I've ordered the operating theater readied. We can move him there whenever you want."

"Good. I will require your best team, gloved and gowned. I want strict sterile procedures followed. Otherwise we'll finish with a fatal infection. Jenny, as much as I don't want you within a mile of this procedure, I need you to assist me. I know how you've been trained, so you're not quite the unknown quantity these other people are. Doctor Dalton, you too. Please get him into the operating theater right now."

"I've alerted my surgical team. They're getting ready as we speak."

Nurses materialized and took Shane toward the surgical theater. Jenny followed Doctor Dalton, and her father tagged behind.

For all River Bend's modest size, St. Luke's was a modern hospital. It had a scrub room outside the operating theater, and inside the entire room was tiled, walls and floor both. It even boasted adjustable electric lights, automatically delivered oxygen, and central suction.

With help, Jenny donned a sterile gown and scrubbed up next to her father, who largely ignored her. Then she turned to a nurse who wound gauze around her hair and tied a mask over her nose and mouth. The nurse glared at her with extreme disapproval. Jenny had been through that one before. She looked up into the woman's cold, blue eyes and thought, *If you wanted to become a doctor, you should have gone to medical school. Don't resent me because I had more courage than you did.*

Shane had been moved to the operating table. He did not even look like a living being to her. His face was waxy white, and a nurse was already shaving the side of his head.

"Don't bother to shave his entire head," John barked as soon as he entered the room. "Shave the operative site only. We haven't time for more. Turn him on his left side and sandbag his head so it won't move." The staff jumped to obey his orders. Inside the operating theater, Doctor John Charles Weston was God. Jenny moved up toward his right hand and saw with satisfaction that all the instruments he would require were already laid out.

John positioned himself above Shane's draped head and held out his hand. "Scalpel, please?" he asked. He was not one of those prima donnas who raged and stormed in the operating room. Instead, he became an icily polite gentleman. She passed him the instrument, not slapping it into his glove, but handing it to him firmly enough that he could grasp it without looking. "Thank you," he murmured. So the procedure began. Her entire world narrowed to the patient. He had ceased to be Shane. Instead he was a potentially devastating brain injury that she could help alleviate.

Jenny went into an alter reality. She watched her father make a big U-shaped incision that began behind the forehead and ended over the ear, reflected the scalp, removed a section of bone and incised the dura mater, then bared the essence of humanity: the brain. After a long, tense interval, he suctioned out a huge blood clot, then replaced the bone, carefully closed the incision, and bandaged Shane's head. He was the rare surgeon who did his own closures and his own bandages. And when Jenny went back through the scrub area and pulled the gauze off her hair, three hours had elapsed. Across the room, John Weston was also shedding gloves and his sterile gown.

"Father…" she began.

"The prognosis is grim, as I suppose you surmised. I don't think he'll make it." Her heart, which had died earlier in the day, could not sink any lower.

"Yes," she said, looking down at the green tile floor.

"But I thank you for your competent assistance. Now I expect you to resign your admission privileges and sign yourself off this case and every other case in this hospital."

"I can't," she responded. "When I signed the admission forms, the administration informed me that you are practicing under my privileges. If I sign myself off this case, I sign you off, too. If you don't want to follow up yourself, then fine. I'll resign and we can catch the next train out." She knew this was a bluff he would not call. He had committed himself to the care of his patient and would not abandon that commitment this side of Armageddon. She peeled off her gloves and dropped them into the scrub receptacle with its burden of soiled gowns, operative linens, and towels. One of the less resentful nurses moved up to remove her gown, but, remembering the blood on her blouse, she waved the woman away with a word of thanks. John considered her for a moment.

"Very well. Keep your privileges until this case is resolved, one way or the other. But as I said, his prognosis is extremely poor. I expect him to expire within the next forty-eight hours."

"Until then, I will wait in his room," she said quietly, daring him to forbid her.

"Jenny, you'll not…"

"I will wait in his room," she interrupted with the Weston firmness she had learned at her father's knee. She did not voice an *or else*. It was unnecessary.

"Very well, then. For the duration of his illness. But if by some miracle he does survive, the moment I judge him able to leave the hospital, I expect you to live up to your promise."

"I will. After all, you taught me to keep my word."

Chapter Sixteen

Her path to Shane's room included a side trip to the echoing, tile-floored lobby, where Paul was now waiting with Bob Shepherd. Both men rose when they saw her across the room.

"Please excuse my surgical gown," she began, before Paul interrupted her.

"Jenny? How...?" She shook her head, and the question died.

"Doctor Weston? How is he?" Superintendent Shepherd asked at the same time.

"He's still alive, but I won't sugarcoat it. He had a big blood clot under the outer membrane that covers the brain. The medical term is subdural hematoma. They are extremely dangerous because they put pressure on the brain. Since the resultant swelling has nowhere to go inside the skull, eventually that pressure can cause circulation to fail. Father was able to remove the clot, and it probably won't come back, but the prognosis is not good. Very few people survive an accident of that type."

"Oh, God," Paul whispered, his face going as pale as Shane's had been.

Bob looked crushed. "Well, then, I know Shane has no family, but is there anyone I should notify?" he asked.

"In point of fact, his grandmother lives near Elk

Gap. If...if the worst happens, I'll take him...the body...there for burial and tell her myself. But I think someone should telephone Angus MacBride. I'd like to be able to tell Uncle Richard, too, but he's away delivering a guest lecture. He's not due back until next week. By then we'll know one way or the other."

"Could I see him?" Bob asked.

"It wouldn't do any good. He's comatose. And if he...if this is...the end, Bob, I know he would want you to remember him as he was the last time you saw him, whole and well and happy. If he does manage to pull through, you and Paul will be the first ones I allow to visit him."

"If there's anything at all I can do..." Paul could not continue.

"No, Paul. Not really. Just please, if you will, pray for him. It really does help, you know. Oh, by the way, did Mr. Hildebrand leave after Father told him to go home?" A tic that could have been mistaken for half a smile tugged at the corners of Paul's mouth.

"Yes. I saw him off myself."

She had a picture of that. "I imagine you did, and in grand style."

"You could call it that. He wanted to argue with me. After I pressured him a bit, he let slip that he couldn't return without a firm marriage commitment from you, which brings to mind...ah...certain doubts about his financial solvency, perhaps? The word 'dowry' did come up in our conversation. However, in the end I persuaded him to leave, and on the way I gently informed him that he is *persona non grata* in my territory from now on. I went so far as to tell him that if he came back I'd be watching him like a hawk, and if he so much as said 'damn' or spat in the street he'd be under arrest so fast he wouldn't even see it happen."

"Thank you for that, Paul. And now I really must go. I'm going to sit with Shane. I'll let you know the moment there's any change."

"I'd appreciate that," Bob Shepherd said. "The telephone number at the constabulary is 422 and my home is 583. Do I need to write that down for you?"

"No. I'm good at remembering numbers. I won't forget."

"Marie and the girls are going to be devastated. Please keep in touch with us, won't you?"

"Don't worry. I will." She took her leave, her heart as inert as a chunk of granite in her chest.

Her father looked up from the far side of Shane's bed as she entered the room. To her surprise he was gloved, gowned, and masked as he had been in surgery.

"Swap out that contaminated gown, glove up, and put on a mask if you're coming in here," he warned her. "It was one hell of a bad prep. I don't want to expose him to any further risk of infection—not that it's probably going to matter much in the long run." Jenny nodded. A nurse helped her with a fresh gown and a mask. By John Weston's order, a box of gloves also stood on a chair. She took out a pair and put them on, even though they were much too large on her narrow hands. She went to Shane's side, leaned her elbows on the bed rail, and looked down at him for a long interval. He seemed to be clinging to life by the barest fingernail. *Whoever washed his face preoperatively did a hasty job,* she thought, noting the dried blood crusted around the rims of his nostrils. Silently she went to the sink, found a washcloth and dampened it with alcohol, and gently cleansed his face. Her father said nothing for a very long time.

"Just how close were you?" he asked, looking down at the unconscious man.

"Does it matter?" she responded icily.

"No. Probably not." She let the matter drop. *Oh, Shane, I wish I could tell everyone that I compromised myself with you, but I don't imagine Phillip would let that stand between him and the Weston money. He'd almost certainly marry me even if I were eight months gone with your child. Shane, please live. Please don't give up. I still have one big trump card up my sleeve, and I'll play it when the time is right. Please trust me, and fight to live. Please.* Then her unspoken plea turned into a desperate prayer.

Outside, night fell while Shane continued to lie comatose. To Jenny that was not unexpected, although she would have jumped up and shouted hallelujah if he had moved in the slightest. She did notice a bruise beginning to highlight his cheekbone, and, if anything, his heart action was growing weaker.

"I know," her father said, watching her count Shane's pulse. "He's going downhill quickly now. I don't think it'll be too long."

She gave him a dirty look and pointedly took the patient's hand. "I needn't remind you, of all people, not to talk in the presence of a patient. You were the one who stressed to me that comatose patients may be unconscious, but they're certainly not deaf. Shane, you can live. You can make it through this. Just, please, don't give up." She remembered how much he had made of the scent of her hand cream. She also knew that smell is the last sense to leave and the first to return. Hoping enough of her Honey Almond Cream would escape around her glove for him to sense it, she stroked his cheek with the back of her hand. "I'm here, Shane. I'm right next to you. I won't leave you. Just, please, try to wake up for me? Please, Shane?" He did not respond, nor did she really expect him to. Her father's expression was a mixture of pity and disdain.

"Well, Jen, I'm going to the cafeteria for supper. Will you accompany me?"

She shook her head. "No, thank you. I'll stay a while longer. I'm not hungry." Ignoring the nurse, she pulled up a straight chair and sat next to the bed, merely watching her patient breathe. The rise and fall of his chest was almost imperceptible.

She only napped that night, hoping for the change that did not happen. Instead, her father's prediction seemed to be coming true. No matter how hard she willed him to live, Shane was in a slow but steady decline. His blood pressure dropped and his heart, trying to compensate, beat faster but more weakly. The only positive sign was that his temperature seemed to be stable.

The next morning, the blood on her clothes necessitated a trip to the nearest dress shop, where she hastily purchased a black traveling outfit and wore it from the store, then left her other garments at a laundry. She was back within the hour, gowned and gloved, at Shane's bedside.

The afternoon train delivered Angus MacBride. She had wondered all along if Angus could be the slightest bit deaf, because he habitually spoke louder than necessary. But when he paused in the doorway, his voice came out a basso profundo whisper.

"Jenny, lass…" His voice broke, and had her father not been present she would have run into his embrace.

"Who is that?" John Weston asked.

"Doctor Angus MacBride from Elk Gap. He was Shane's mentor, and he's been mine. Angus, may I present my father, Doctor John Weston."

"Doctor," John acknowledged with a nod. "If you are going to come in here, use a gown, mask, and gloves, please. The patient had a hasty preoperative prep, and I'm a little concerned about the chances of infection."

"Understandable, Doctor Weston." Angus parked his cane by the door and complied without protest. It surprised her. The older man could be irascible. Then he took up his cane again and stumped over to stand next to her.

"He's about twenty hours postoperative for a subdural hematoma secondary to a fracture of the right temporal bone. At first I made it a depressed fracture, but when I got in surgically, I was fortunately wrong. However, he did have a big brain bleed, and I'm not ruling out contracoup injury to the left temporal lobe. As you can see by his chart, his condition is steadily worsening. I'm picking up a little pulmonary edema now. His heart just can't keep up. I was just considering raising the head of the bed to ease his breathing." John Weston's tone was detached and coldly clinical. Angus picked up the chart and read through it, his face expressionless. He replaced the chart, then fished beneath the surgical gown and took his new stethoscope from his coat pocket. It was identical to Jenny's. He had finally purchased one after she laughingly chided him for repeatedly borrowing hers.

"May I, Doctor Weston?" he asked.

"Be my guest," John responded with an airy gesture. Angus looked at him coldly. He listened carefully to Shane's lungs, swapped out the diaphragm head, and listened to his heart. Then he noticed Jenny was not carrying a stethoscope at all. He held his out to her.

"Lass? For all the times I appropriated yours."

"Thank you very much," she said with a shy half-smile. Defying her father, she repeated Angus's examination and nearly wished she had not. Her father had been right, in spades. John moved to the foot of the bed and patiently cranked up the frame until Shane was raised to something less than half sitting. The unconscious man did not react. Then Angus's faded blue eyes sought Jenny's.

"What a sorry mess this is," he said quietly.

"You talked to Paul?"

"Aye, I did. He explained everything." Angus glared at her father, who affected a mild detachment that made him look very much like Richard. Once again she marveled at the resemblance that ran no more than skin deep.

Driven by exhaustion, she spent part of the night on a sofa in the nurses' lounge. When she awoke in the early morning hours, she went back to Shane's room to find Angus in the chair John had vacated.

"Hello, lass. Your father went to rest a bit, too."

"How is he, then?"

"Aboot the same." His Scots burr always deepened with stress.

Automatically she drew on a gown and gloves, then came to the opposite side of the bed and leaned on the rail. After watching for a few moments, she lifted Shane's hand, counted his pulse, and merely held his limp hand for a long time.

"I love him so," she sighed. "I'd not tell anyone else this, but if he had asked me to marry him I intended to say yes, until Father came along and started all this ruckus. He's still adamant that I marry Phillip, even though Phillip let something slip to Paul that leads me to believe his father faces financial ruin unless he marries me."

"Paul explained the whole rotten mess. You have to stand up to him."

"I can't, at least not right now. If I do, it will bring down Northtown Surgical Clinic. Phillip's father, all questions of solvency aside, is the Chairman of the Board."

"Is it worth your life, then?"

"It will cost lives if it happens."

"Nae, lass. There may be a rousing grand catfight, but hospitals survive, and so do patients." At that moment their attention was wrenched back to Shane. His breath seemed to stop for a moment, then he caught up, gasping. Her heart seized with a pang, but to her relief, his breathing evened out.

"I don't like that apnea at all."

"Me either."

"Father is probably right. He said forty-eight hours." And as they watched, he quit breathing again. Jenny was expecting the onset of Cheyne-Stokes respiration, the so-called "death rattle" that signaled the shutdown of the brain, but once again Shane fought his way through it and started to breathe regularly again. She checked his pupils, and to her relief they were unchanged, if still uneven.

Eventually her father returned. This time, to her surprise, he entered the room without the gown he had ordered everyone else to don.

"How is the patient, then, Doctor MacBride?" he asked.

"You're not observing sterile procedures, Doctor Weston?"

"No. I don't think there's any more need. If he were going to catch something we'd have seen it by now. Instead…" As if Shane heard him, he went through another apneic spell. John checked him over. Then he draped his stethoscope around his neck and shook his head. The gesture said it all. He raised the head of the bed a fraction more and they settled in to wait.

"Jenny, I am going to order you and Doctor MacBride to go to the cafeteria and eat," John said, consulting his pocket watch. "It's already four o'clock. I don't think you've had a bite since the accident. You're not going to help my patient by making yourself sick. Oh, don't worry. He'll hold his own for the next few hours. Low tide here won't be until about midnight." It was on the tip of her tongue to refuse, but Angus stepped in.

"Please come with me, lass. He's right. I'm a tired, hungry old man, and I need the company."

"All right, Angus." She dragged herself to the doorway and peeled off her gown and gloves. Her father took in the black traveling outfit and gave her a disapproving look but, mindful of Angus's presence, said nothing.

"What did he mean by low tide?" Angus asked as

they walked down the antiseptic-smelling hallway.

"People like Shane, who are...who are declining slowly, almost always seem to pass away at low tide. If you've never lived around the ocean, you probably never had reason to make that connection. I've lived on the Atlantic coast all my life, and I've seen it time and again."

"Well, well. Learn something new every day, they say. And no, I've never lived near the sea. I'm strictly a Highlander." He opened the cafeteria door for her and stepped back to let her precede him.

"Angus, I'm actually sorry I didn't compromise myself with Shane and force us to elope. Then there wouldn't have been any question."

"I've always prided myself on being a broad-minded man, but that is a little too forward-thinking, even for me." He pulled out a chair and seated her at a small table. "But things will come right yet, you'll see."

Half a bowl of vegetable soup and two soda crackers later, she was back in Shane's room, counting down the hours as the afternoon grew long.

Evening came, though it was hard to believe that it arrived with the same rapidity as every other evening in her life. She noted there had been no change in Shane for several hours. Outside the night quieted, save for the usual city sounds: an occasional horse on the street, the cry of an insectivorous hawk, the yapping of a bored dog in the distance. Finally she grew tired of gazing out the window. She walked past her father, who sat primly with his knees crossed European fashion, reading an AMA journal. A glance over his shoulder turned up nothing interesting. She leaned against the bed rail and studied Shane's face. His complexion had become so pale that for the first time she noticed the merest track of an ancient scar parallel to the top of his left eyebrow. She found his right hand beneath the cover, counted his pulse, then simply held his hand.

"Oh, Shane, I wish you'd wake up," she whispered. "You've come this far. It's not like you to quit. I know you'll not stop fighting as long as there's any strength left in your body, but you have to win this battle soon, or you won't win it at all. Please, darling. Just a little more effort. Live, Shane. I know you can. I'm right beside you. I promise I won't desert you when you need me."

She entered the second night at his bedside, wondering if he would see another morning. He rested all too quietly, still teetering on the edge between life and death. It seemed that he struggled as Jacob was said to have wrestled with the angel, until he won by degrees. It was nothing dramatic, but as midnight came and went, his breathing and his heartbeat stabilized until even her father relented and allowed he had a chance.

She grabbed another few fitful hours of sleep, and in the early afternoon she was back in his room again. She walked up to his bedside and took his hand, and to her surprise, she felt return pressure on her fingers.

"Shane, did you do that on purpose?" she asked. "Do it again, Shane. Squeeze my hand."

His fingers tightened again. Angus looked at her with a question on his face.

"He did it, Angus," she whispered. "He did it!"

"He's obeying commands, then?" her father asked.

"Watch. Shane. Shane, squeeze my hand. Now, Shane. Squeeze my hand like you did before." They watched as his fingers contracted obediently.

"See if you can get him to open his eyes," John said. "He'll probably do it for you quicker than for either of us."

Chapter Seventeen

Shane was dreaming. He was in some sort of maelstrom where colors without names and languages not yet invented swirled around him. The hot, pebbled earth beneath his feet alone seemed real. He looked up to see the sky crawling with fire. A burning desert wind tore at his hair and seared his eyes. He rubbed them, and when he opened them, he stood in a barren, burned-over forest where the hot wind stirred clouds of dust and ash. He glimpsed his grandfather across a clearing, but when he tried to run after him, his legs were leaden. He drew breath to shout, and immediately his lungs were choked by burning dust. He fell to his knees, and then footsteps next to him made him look up. A doe stood on nearby rocks, regarding him thoughtfully. He reached toward her, and a voice speaking Iroquois told him to close his eyes.

"You will be well now, but do not follow me," the doe said, speaking in Jenny's voice. There was a touch against his forehead, and he opened his eyes again to see Jenny running away through the dusty fog, following his grandfather.

"Jenny! Come back!" he shouted as she disappeared into the mist.

The dream became physical, and by degrees he realized the voice he heard through the forest was real. Additionally, it was not leaving him alone.

"Shane, can you wake up for me, please? Shane, it's Jenny. Open your eyes for me? Come on. Wake up. I know you can do it. Open your eyes, Shane." Through growing awareness he heard her words and felt the hand that rubbed his shoulder. The effort of waking up was a physical struggle. He tried to speak, hearing his own slurred whisper echoing painfully through his brain.

"Shane, speak English, please. English or French, Shane. Nobody here speaks Iroquois." Oddly enough, it was having to choose among the layers of language in his mind that woke him completely. He opened his eyes just a crack, then just as quickly closed them again, squinting against the afternoon brightness in the room.

"That's good, Shane. Now do it again. Look at me, please?" The hand that caressed his naked shoulder smelled of the wonderfully familiar Honey Almond Cream. He could not deny her presence. In his fogged mind he was back in the North Village schoolhouse, where once she'd covered him against the cold and touched his shoulder in much the same way. *She needs me*, he thought. *No matter how tired I am, I have to help.*

"Jenny," he breathed.

"Open your eyes, Shane. Look at me." He forced his eyes open again. They would not exactly focus, so he saw her outlined in a blur of green light. She wore the black of deepest mourning, she had combed her hair back severely, and a look of concern puckered her forehead.

"Jenny? Who died?" He turned his head toward her, trying to bring his eyes into line, and was rewarded by a blaze of pain that started at his right temple.

"Nobody died, Shane." Her tone sounded puzzled. "How do you feel?" He could dredge up no answer for her. Instead he looked around, trying to fathom his unfamiliar surroundings. "You had an accident. Do you remember?"

"Accident? No. I…don't." His left hand wavered in the air, and Angus restrained it.

"Don't touch your head, lad. You've had a bad concussion." Shane looked toward him, realizing for the first time that the right side of his head hurt.

"Angus?"

"It's all right, Shane, lad. Everything's going to be fine now. Dinna' worry." As he looked up at Angus, his eyes escaped his control and closed of their own accord. It took some effort to force them open again. This time he noticed the man standing next to his friend.

"Richard? What are you doing here?"

"That's not Uncle Richard, Shane. That's my father, Doctor John Weston. How do you feel? Does your head ache?"

He looked toward Jenny, seeing her more clearly this time. "It's… Yes. What happened?" He reached back into his memory to dredge up the last image he could find, but it was too much effort, and he did not have the strength for it.

"A horse kicked you. Father had to operate. You're going to be all right. Now do something for me, please? Squeeze both my hands? She lifted his hands in hers and he tried his best to cooperate. "Good. Now move your toes." Obediently he moved his feet beneath the light cover. "Thank you, Shane. That was exactly what I was hoping for. Now, do you know what day it is?"

"Christmas." The word came from somewhere out

in the remote reaches of the ether.

"Well, not really. You were unconscious for a while. Do you know where you are?"

"In bed." He moved his legs fretfully. "My head…hurts."

"We'll give you something for the pain. You'll be all right, Shane. But I need to check one more thing before I quit bothering you. Tell me how many fingers I'm holding up." It took him a moment to make his eyes focus.

"Three."

"Good." Her palm moved to cover his right eye. "How many now?"

"Three again." Then she occluded his left.

"Now how many?"

"Two."

"Thank you. Sometimes when a person gets hit in the side of the head like you did, it can damage your eye. But you're all right. You'll get well, Shane. Just give it time."

"I'm thirsty," he whispered. John nodded to the nurse. She handed Jenny a half-full glass. She steadied his head and held the glass to his lips.

"Just a little at a time. We have to be sure it won't make you sick," she cautioned. Though the glass was far from full, he did not have the strength to finish it."

"Thank you," he breathed, exhausted.

"You're welcome. Don't worry about anything. Just let us help you, for a change." He managed to bring his hand up toward her. She took it in both hers.

"Just don't go."

"I'll be right here. I won't leave you. Now Father is going to give you an injection. It'll take your pain away, and you can sleep." His exhausted mind withdrew into Iroquois; her words made no sense at all to him. There was a slight sting, followed by a deep pressure in the muscles of his upper arm, and then he felt himself drawn down into a whirlpool that took his consciousness with it. The last thing of which he was aware was the dark, sweet scent that clung to Jenny's hand as she stroked his cheek.

The next few days were hellish. He was only semi-conscious, going confusedly from nightmare to nightmare, not knowing at any given time whether he was awake or dreaming, recognizing people only part of the time. The common denominator of all those days was pain. Even though he could not always distinguish the thin border between reality and his tortured phantasms, he knew when Jenny stood beside him, coaxing him to drink or merely holding his hand. There were days when he was incapable of a coherent thought, but gradually he sorted out the scrambled memories. They became clearer as the pain subsided and he no longer needed as much medication.

In the middle of one of the interminable nights, he woke by degrees from a troubled dream to find all about him dark and silent. The night felt friendly after the surrealistic corridors his mind had been wandering. He had been improving steadily, so the last few nights Jenny had begun leaving him in the care of one of the nurses. Since he did not want anyone to bother him, he lay feigning sleep as the steady tide of pain ebbed and flowed inside his head.

The tendrils of the last dream still enmeshed him, drawing him backward toward his childhood and the long, quiet nights in the sturdy North Village cabin. A pang of nostalgic loneliness pierced his chest when he thought of the peace and security he had known, lying in a pile of musk bear pelts by the banked fire, his arm slung loosely over the warm neck or flank of Lupi, the great white wolf hybrid that had been his constant companion. Laughingly Grandpère had given the dog his name: Lupi, short for Loup Garou, the French for werewolf. Shane had learned to walk clinging to Lupi's ruff while the dog slowly circuited the cabin, occasionally plying a wet tongue over whatever parts of Shane's anatomy he could reach.

Again the lonely ache washed through Shane. Grandpère had been the pole star of his early years, the one who had urged him onto his present path. It was Grandpère who had taught him the ways of the woods and wild creatures until he could track, shoot, hunt, and trap better than any of his full Iroquois cousins. Then Grandpère insisted he leave the mission school and go to school with the town children, and eventually walk the path of the white man. Grandpère, tall and hugely strong, a secure refuge for a small boy testing out the world. He always had a humorous anecdote or a word of encouragement or praise. Shane smiled as he remembered his grandfather laughing, his teeth strong and even as ivory piano keys.

Then the sadness gripped him again. Lupi had died just as Shane left North Village for the white school in Elk Gap, his shoulder torn by a rabid wolf. The wound was not serious, but the hydrophobia was. Shane had held the ancient, half-blind dog while Grandpère's muzzle-loading rifle spoke once. Lupi quivered only a moment before going still in Shane's arms, and they buried him in the soft, sweet-smelling forest duff.

Shane still detoured from the trail between North Village and Thomas Wise Hand's horse ranch to pause at the stone cairn over Lupi's final resting place.

Then Shane had gone all the way to Ottawa, not writing because there was no one to read. When he returned, wearing the proud Red Serge of a constable, Grandpère's opaque eyes could no longer see him. The old man's mind remained clear until the end, when a sudden stroke ended his life at the ancient age of ninety-seven. Shane, the Iroquois warrior, had not wept until years later.

Now, in the impersonal night-darkened hospital room, he felt tears tightening his throat again. He was as much Iroquois as white—Indian by early training and white by education. Why had he elected the complicated path of the white man? Why had he not stayed in the woods? The Iroquois trail offered peace and serenity, built around immutable unwritten laws and ironclad custom. Once one accepted the surrender of total discipline, the way offered peace. Grandpère, however, had not agreed. His words had held wisdom. *The way of the white man is upon us all. The railroad brought your father, after all, and the woods grow smaller every day. True, you have Indian blood and I do not, but eventually you will have to be white or you'll be swallowed up. You're too good for that, Shane. You're too talented and too intelligent. So go, with my blessing. Make an old voyageur proud of you, eh?*

So I went, he thought. *Five long, painful years away from the forest and the river. Five years among people who looked down on me. And for what? Ah, Grandpère, how I envy you the life you had. I hope you*

*have peace, and if your campfire is now among the
stars, you can look down and see me, you and Lupi ...*

The ache in his chest became an acute physical
pain. He stretched cautiously, trying to move only as a
sleeper would, but a sharp stitch in his side made him
cough and the pressure mushroomed into a blinding
headache as sharp as a lance. He curled onto his left
side—not the usual side he slept on—and touched the
bandage, trying vainly to stroke the pain away. Then he
heard the rustle of a long skirt and footsteps across the
floor. *Merde*, he thought. *The nurse knows I'm awake.*

Before he became aware of anything more than the
presence of another person, a familiar sweet, rich
fragrance washed over him. Jenny! But why was she
here at this hour of the night? A gentle hand supported
his neck and shoulder against another coughing spasm
that left him gasping in pain.

"Shane?" she asked quietly. He dared to open his
eyes and saw her standing beside him in the gloom. He
turned onto his back and forced himself to relax.

"Jenny, what are you doing here?" he asked.

"I couldn't sleep, so I relieved your nurse and came
in for a while. Is anything wrong?"

"No. I was just dreaming. I do that so much lately,
and it's always so strange."

"You will for a while. It's usual in head injuries.
Don't let it upset you."

"I was dreaming about my grandfather," he said
with a sigh.

"You should go back to sleep. It's the middle of the
night. If you're hurting, I can give you more
medication."

"Not right now, please. Just talk to me for a while.

If I go back to sleep right away the dream will just start all over again." Her fingers traveled over his forearm until they found his hand. She took it in both hers. He had become used to that over the past days.

"Don't play the stoic on me now, please. It's bad for you. If you're hurting, I can get you something to help."

"Why? It's just pain."

"Because head injuries only heal with sleep. If you don't sleep well, you'll just stay sick, and eventually you'll pick up some complication like pneumonia or a kidney infection that you won't have the strength to survive."

"Well, then, in a few minutes? I want to stay awake for a while."

"What were you dreaming that has you so upset?"

"Just about my grandfather."

"Tell me about him, then," she urged gently.

"Well...so much to tell." Another pause and another sigh. "My great-grandfather fled Paris during the Reign of Terror. His name wasn't LaPorte. That was just assumed after he came to Canada. The arm of the Revolution was very long. Even though they had gone clear out here, they dared not use their true identity. Grandpère, his youngest son by his second wife, was actually born here. He told me that after he was grown, his father told him their real family name was des Roches."

Jenny's breath came in sharply. "I remember that name from French history. He was a royal advisor. But all the texts say he and his family were executed."

"The ones that have it right say he disappeared and was presumed to have been executed. But I have the family Bible that says different. It goes back to the mid-1600s."

"You should show Uncle Richard. He'd be so excited."

"I should, at that. It just never occurred to me. I will as soon as everything settles down and I'm back home. What really happened was that Claude des Roches buried himself in the woods and raised four sons in the deep forest, as voyageurs. Grandpère was his youngest son. He never learned to read, but he knew the woods better than anyone I've known in my life. He lived by trading with the Indians and by running trap lines. He was ninety-seven when he died, well after I joined the Northwest Mounted. He taught me so much. There was nothing about the woods he didn't know." He stopped briefly, not knowing which part of their relationship had affected him the most.

"So you and he were close."

"Very. He was—incomparable. But I sometimes wonder if..." His sentence trailed into nothing as he sighed and shifted his shoulders restlessly.

"If what?"

"If it was wise of me to go to college. I might have been better off living in the woods the way he did. But he told me the old ways were fading fast and the woods were getting smaller every day."

"He was right, you know. And you're so intelligent and talented that not using it to help other people would be nothing short of a sin."

"That's very flattering, but..." Suddenly he composed himself and smiled slowly. "I can't say that. If I hadn't gone to school and become a police officer, chances are I'd never have met you—or if I had, I'd have been just another ignorant backwoodsman, and you'd never have given me a second thought. You'll stay a while longer?" he asked.

"Until you feel you want to sleep. Providing you tell me more about your grandfather. Do you look like him?"

"Oh, sort of, I think. My general build is like his. He was big and broad-shouldered, too. And I believe he's where I got curly hair. He wasn't especially dark, but I think the fair skin and light eyes must have come from my father. I was so young when the smallpox epidemic hit that I really don't have clear memories of my parents."

"Who had the graphic talent?"

"My grandfather. I have a lot of drawings he made. We used to draw together. After I was about eight I started helping him illustrate some of the folk tales. Some were French and some were Iroquois, and others were just yarns he made up that got wilder with each retelling. All in all, I had a good childhood. I didn't even realize we were poor. But then, poor is a relative thing. I had anything I really needed. I never went cold or hungry." Jenny looked down at him. He had finally opened the firmly closed door to his past for her, if only just a crack. It was bittersweet, coming as it did after her forced capitulation to her father. But she pigeonholed that thought for a while. She had a few days before she had to say goodbye to everything she had come to love since she came to Elk Gap. The future felt like a coming storm.

"Children do fine with basic needs and someone who loves them."

"I was lucky. I had my grandparents."

"Was it difficult for you to go to school in Elk Gap, then?"

"Oh, I'll say it was!" he said with a dry laugh. "I left the mission school as soon as my English was good enough to function, but for a long time I had quite an accent. It was part French and part Iroquois. There is no R sound in Iroquois, and the French one didn't help me at all. It was at least a year before I quit saying 'wabbit' and meanwhile I got in enough fights that the boys finally quit teasing me about it. Then to make it worse, when I got to the Conners' house I'd never slept in a bed or used tableware. Mavis had quite a time civilizing me."

"Mavis is quite fond of you, you know."

"Let's say Mavis would mother the whole world if she could, and she does have quite a proprietary interest in me. She cleaned me up enough times when I trailed home with a bloody nose. I think I spent half my life with a nosebleed, until I was about fourteen. Someone would call me a derogatory name, and I'd pile into them. And even though I usually came out the winner, I'd have a nosebleed."

"Oh, Shane!" Jenny laughed softly in spite of herself. "But a lot of boys get nosebleeds easily. They usually outgrow the tendency."

"I think I just outgrew the tendency to get into fistfights. I haven't had a nosebleed in years, but I haven't been in a fight, either. Unless you count a couple of hockey brawls in college, and one really good donnybrook the month after I came back to Elk Gap as a police officer, my life has been pretty quiet. When I was younger I got into some real dillies, though."

Jenny looked down at him in the gloom. While his

face was gaunt and showed his ordeal, Shane was behind the grey eyes again. The ordeal of the last days had refined her feelings, and she knew that she loved Shane nearly past bearing. As she held his hand in the dark hospital room, she thought back over the past months, from the first day he had come into her life.

"Do you remember anything about that Monday of your accident?" she asked at length, changing the subject.

"Some of it," he replied. "I remember telling you in somewhat uncouth terms that I have Iroquois blood and I don't know if my parents were ever formally married, but the rest of it, not really."

"Well, some of it's best not recalled."

"But where did the accident happen? There at the train station?"

"Yes. The horses pitched a ring-tailed hissy fit at Mr. Beaufort's touring car, and Midnight reared up and struck you in the head. You had a big blood clot on your brain. Father removed it and saved your life, but it took you two days to wake up. I still don't know where you found the strength. You nearly died."

"Jenny, I had no idea. I'm sorry for what I put you through."

"What else is a doctor for?" Even in the darkness she could see the embarrassment on his face.

"Certainly not that. Not you, anyway. Where's Midnight, then?"

"Mr. Beaufort has him. Midnight and Brandy both took off, and his chauffeur spent the better part of the afternoon rounding them up. He's in the Beauforts' stable until you can come after him. Rest assured he's receiving royal treatment."

"He is. Adrian Beaufort is good to his animals. In fact, he's as much of a soft heart when it comes to old pensioners as Richard is. He has teams as old as The Girls." Shane squinted, repressing a yawn.

"Are you sleepy? We've been talking a long time."

"I don't want to sleep. I'd rather be with you," he protested.

"It's time for medication. We'll talk tomorrow."

"You'll be here?"

"I will be," she said quietly, biting her tongue for the half-truth. Tomorrow, yes, but what about next week or the week after that? When would the sword fall? When her father decided it was time to return to New York, she would have no choice but to break Shane's heart. It was that or let an entire hospital and all its patients founder.

The nurse had left pain medication measured out on the table next to his bed. Jenny held out the pills and a glass of water. Obediently he swallowed them; she steadied the glass while he drank.

"Thank you," he breathed, letting her ease his head back to the pillows.

"You're welcome, Shane."

"I like it when you say my name," he murmured, his voice purposely low.

"Go to sleep. I can tell you're tired," she replied, stroking his ragged hair where it slopped over the gauze around his forehead.

"I really am tired now," he acquiesced, closing his eyes. Another night seemingly a century ago flashed through her mind. She had covered him with extra blankets against the cold in the North Village schoolhouse, and she had dared to stroke his hair then.

It was a bittersweet interlude now, after what had happened over the last week, but she bent over him, touching her lips between his eyebrows, then kissing him full on the mouth.

"Good night. Not another word, or I'll leave. Understand?"

With a contented smile he nodded, closing his eyes.

She watched him for a long time, her vision misted by tears she would not let herself shed. *Oh, Shane, the rug has long ago been pulled out from beneath us both,* she thought. *You just don't know it yet. I only wish one thing. If you'd ever declared yourself to me, if I'd known I could really depend on you, I'd have told Father to go chase himself. You have your reasons. I know that your mixed blood may be part of it. But it may be that deep down you just don't love me enough to want to be with me for the rest of our lives. If only I knew how you truly feel. If only you had told me. If only...*

Chapter Eighteen

Youth and strength stood Shane in good stead. He improved visibly every day, until within a week he could sit up in bed without dizziness or undue pain. He seemed in great spirits, but every hour that passed was one more bite out of Jenny. Then the thread that held her life together parted when her father announced he had train tickets for two days hence. It set Angus to muttering fresh curses, and the news brought Richard skittering to River Bend, up in arms. On the last day, with the minutes tearing out bits of her soul, she buried herself in Shane's room, trying not to act gloomy. He had been entertaining her with anecdotes of his early life. She told herself grimly that these vignettes would have to warm her heart for the immediate future, until she could find a way out of her situation and come back to Canada. She also tried to memorize his face. Finally he realized something was quite wrong.

"Jenny, you've been so quiet this evening. Is anything bothering you?" he asked.

"No, not really."

"Where have Richard and Angus and your father gone?"

"They're next door at Bimbo's, having dinner. I didn't feel like going with them."

"Heavens, I don't need a private nurse now. Go and get some supper."

"No," she sighed. "They're just about done now, anyway, and I'll have to leave soon."

"You act like you're worried about something."

"Actually there is something wrong, and I'm glad you didn't figure it out sooner. I have to leave Canada. I'm going back to New York with Father. Our train leaves at ten." He reached for her hand.

"You'll be back, though."

Slowly she shook her head and let the sword fall. "No, I won't. I'm going back to join the staff of Northtown Surgical Clinic. It's everything I always wanted to do, and it's the greatest opportunity in the world for me. I really don't have any other choice. This is all I've ever dreamed of since I was six years old and saw the miracles my father could work in people's lives."

"Jenny! No! I don't believe this!" The words were torn from him.

"Oh, yes. Believe it, Shane. You knew all along I was just visiting here and the day would come when I'd go home."

"But you let me think you cared for me…"

That was territory into which she did not want to venture. The ground was too shaky there. "Be that as it may, it's over. After all, no man really wants a woman with a career. No woman with a career should marry, either. There will come a time when she will have to put one or the other first, and her heart will be broken, perhaps his also. If you had to make the same choice, you know what yours would be."

"You have a medical practice here," he protested. "You're needed in a way you could never be needed in a big city like New York. Elk Gap needs you, Angus needs you, and I need you. Perhaps the men you're used to couldn't stand competition from your medical career, but I'm not most men. I wasn't raised like that. I could never pursue my own happiness at the expense of another person."

"I know our relationship has been special to you. It has been to me, too. But I need the experience I can only get at Northtown. It's a research hospital. The experimental procedure that saved your life was developed there, and now I can have a chance to be a part of all that."

"If you go to New York, as soon as Angus lets me out of this hospital, I'm coming after you," he vowed. She backed off, shaking her head.

"Don't, Shane. Don't even think of it. You'd receive a very nasty surprise. My life in New York isn't nearly what you think it is."

"I could always become one of New York's finest. But then, in a grand place like that, a half-breed shanty Irish cop wouldn't even be dirt under your feet." She steeled herself against the guilt.

"You told me how Ottawa made you feel. New York is twice as big. You'd die there. I'm sorry, but this is signed, sealed, and delivered, and there's nothing you can do about it." She gave him an intense look, hoping the conflict that raged inside her did not show.

"Why did you let me think you love me? Why have you been with me night and day for the last eleven days? Was it just to make sure I got well enough to survive? Jenny, it would have been more merciful to have turned your back on me and let nature take her course."

Her eyes brimmed dangerously with heartache and

anger, but her voice was low and controlled as she rounded on him.

"Shane Patrick Adair, don't you dare say anything like that again, ever! Don't you even dare think it! I could save ten thousand lives, but if I hadn't done everything I could to save yours, I could never have lived with myself. I'm sorry if it seems like I've pulled you out of the frying pan only to drop you into the fire. I didn't, really, and when the initial hurt wears off you'll understand that. You have your work, after all, and someday you'll find love. It's only in Victorian romances that people die of broken hearts. It's also only in fairy tales that people marry their true loves and live happily ever after."

"Please think this over. You're needed here."

"Needed, perhaps. But is just being needed here because I am a physician enough to build an entire life on? I have thought it over. I've thought it over and under and up and down and inside out and backward, and I keep coming to the same conclusion. I have to go to Northtown. I'll be needed there, too, and even though it would be nice to say I'd be coming back, I just don't know what will happen. In fact, right before the accident, I asked you to go away and leave me my dignity."

He looked down at his hands. His face was largely expressionless, but she read defeat written large in the set of his shoulders. "Then God be with you. But I won't let you go. I'll be in New York."

"I wish I could forbid you, but you're a free man. If you want to march off a cliff, that's up to you. Goodbye, then. I have to leave now. Thank you for being so kind to me over the summer. I have valued your friendship, and I will always remember you in my prayers." She turned away without looking at him; she would not have dared the merest glance. It would have ripped her resolve to shreds. She glided toward the door with regal detachment, as though she had a book balanced on her head and Aunt Eleanor critiquing her posture.

"Jenny," he called after her. "What happens if you decide you want love?" It was too little, too late, but his words still brought the tears. Out in the hallway she jammed a knuckle into her mouth to stifle the one sob that got away.

The little bistro was as authentic as they came, run by a real immigrant family from a nameless small town in the sunbaked south of Italy, where oregano, garlic, and olive oil were the staples of life. Heartsick in a way she had never believed possible, she slipped in. She spotted her father, Richard, and Angus at a table, and hung in the shadows where she could hear their conversation. She caught Angus in the middle of a sentence.

"...really going to make Jenny go back with you?" he asked.

"Jenny is going back to New York of her own free will, Doctor MacBride," John replied between bites of spinach-stuffed cannelloni. "Besides, I don't see that it's any of your business."

"It is indeed my business. After all, you're robbing me of the partner in my practice. She's an excellent physician, and she's been invaluable to me."

"Physician!" John exploded. "There's no woman in the world who's fit to be a practicing physician! Oh, she probably did well enough with runny noses and baby catching, but women can't handle real emergencies. Any type of bloody trauma and she'd probably faint dead away and give you two patients to treat instead of one."

"The first call she took in Elk Gap was a traumatic amputation, a boy who had his foot taken off by a leg-hold trap. Her procedure could have been in a textbook. She gave him a stump he could walk on."

"She was always good at embroidery," Weston said dryly.

"She kept her head at the scene of Shane's accident, didn't she?"

"I was there to tell her what to do. He was fortunate. Women's hearts rule their heads, and their biology runs the whole show. He's just lucky it wasn't the wrong time of the month."

Angus's cheeks flared scarlet, and his Scots burr rasped like a buzz saw. "Doctor Weston, I did not hear that last remark. If I had, I should be obligated to thrash you within an inch of your life. Jenny has been a consummate physician. She has an innate diagnostic sense, and she's always been right. She can put anyone at ease, from a frightened child to an old man with angina. I'm not going to elaborate, but I'd much rather have her share my practice than you, for all your self-promoted grand reputation."

Jenny's heart nearly stopped. She almost stepped out and halted the conversation, but her father's cool, condescending tone held her there in the shadow of a faux grapevine.

"You've been practicing in the bush too long, Doctor MacBride."

"What gives you the right to play God, Weston?

Did it give you satisfaction to flaunt your so-called brilliant skill out here among us unwashed heathens in the hinterlands and save a life just so you could turn around and ruin two? You're the one on whom the Hippocratic Oath is wasted, not Jenny," Angus retorted hotly.

John Weston looked up, his mild eyes deceptively echoing Richard's. His tone became pedantic and patronizing, as though he were talking to a very dense child. "Jenny is a woman. Women were created to get married and have babies. Jenny will be married soon, to a young man of impeccable family. One or two children, and she'll forget Elk Gap ever existed."

God, she thought, *how can you be so nasty?* At that moment Richard interjected himself into the argument.

"John, I can only agree with Angus. What you're doing is wrong. It's arbitrary, it's selfish, and it's cruel. Have you forgotten how Father objected to you and Catherine?" He paused to let it soak in. "Even though you hated him for opposing you, you're treating Jenny exactly as he treated you. If you make her leave on that train tonight, I never want to hear of or from you again."

John turned his gaze to Richard, masking his surprise like a poker player. It was an expression Jenny had seen before when someone turned the tables against her father. "The situation is not comparable at all, Richard," he said mildly. "Jenny is a woman."

Richard rose and laid his napkin next to his barely touched plate. "You have no idea how wrong you are, John. I hope you wake up before it's too late. Now I have nothing more to say to you. You are no longer my brother. If you will please excuse me, Angus?" After the polite formality he turned on his heel and strode away, but stopped at the doorway as Jenny stepped out of the shadows. Wishing she had interrupted the conversation before it got out of hand, she moved toward the table like one in a trance.

"Father, I believe your cab is here."

"Come here and sit down. I'm not through with my supper yet." She drifted toward him, nearly catatonic.

"Jen," Richard said softly. She turned to him.

"Goodbye, Uncle Richard."

"Can I do anything?" His voice was low and private.

"Take care of Fleur. If you don't want to ride her, give her to Shane."

"Aren't you going to want her with you someday?"

"No. I wouldn't take her to the city. I won't be riding anymore anyway." She stretched up to kiss his cheek. "I love you so. I'll write often, I promise. God bless."

"God bless you, too." He hugged her, and then she broke off and crossed the room. She had just started to sit down by her father when a uniformed nurse hurried up to Angus.

"Doctor MacBride, Inspector Adair tried to get out of bed and fainted. He's conscious now and doesn't appear to be in difficulty, but you should come immediately." He chucked his napkin down and lurched to his feet. For a moment his eyes met Jenny's, and he scooped her into an ursine embrace.

"God keep ye, lass." For a moment she buried her head against his broad shoulder.

"Oh, Angus," she breathed, muffling her face in his tweed jacket.

306

"Not tae worry, lassie. He and I will muddle through. 'Tis ye I worry aboot." He turned to her father, who merely glanced at them before diverting his attention to the remnants of his supper. Angus gathered his cane and squared his coat over his shoulders. "As for you, Doctor Weston, you're a cruel, heartless bastard. If there's any justice in heaven, I hope you're called to accounts for all the unhappiness you're causing this day." He stumped from the restaurant, and Richard followed.

A short time later, John Weston helped Jenny into the hired cab. She sat staring blankly ahead as he told the driver to start for the railroad station. The sluggish team pulled slowly into the street.

"Well, then, we'll be home soon," he began. "It's going to be nice, having you in the house again. Your room is as you left it. I did take the liberty of disposing of most of the clothes you left, except your ball gowns. Eleanor said your wardrobe was completely out of style, and since the Mission Board had a clothing drive, I shipped everything off to the less fortunate. You must let her take you shopping as soon as you get home. I also instructed Richard to send only your furs. You'll not need the books now, and as for the clothes, I'll not have my daughter looking like some backwoods farmer's wife. That brown checkered whatever-it-was is hideous, and I can't say much for what you're wearing right now. You shouldn't wear black. You're too thin, and your eyes are too dark. It's unflattering."

"Black is all I'll ever wear from this moment on. Let it be a reminder to you."

"Oh, you don't mean that. Of course you'll enjoy a new wardrobe. It goes without saying that cost is no object." She did not reply. Eventually he drew breath and spoke again. "I've given it a good deal of thought. We'll announce your engagement at the New Year's Ball. That's come to be a tradition in the family. How does it sound? Mr. Hildebrand has a brilliant future ahead of him. His father is thinking of a gubernatorial campaign. I was the first to endorse his candidacy. That young chap will follow in his father's footsteps, mark my words."

"I think the Hildebrands are bankrupt. Phillip let slip to Corporal Weller that he dared not go home without a firm commitment that I'd marry him and bring a substantial dowry with me."

"Oh, bosh. James is practically carrying Northtown's whole research program by himself."

"I believe the term is deficit spending. He is spending beyond his means and desperately needs the Weston money."

"You'd better have facts to back that allegation. I believe you're making it up. You're just trying to weasel out of keeping your word. But when you're married to Phillip you may be First Lady someday. What do you think of that?"

Her lethargy snapped. She turned hard eyes on her father, and at once they brimmed caustic tears of helpless hatred. "Why do you even bother to ask? Are you enjoying rubbing the salt in, then?"

"After a few babies, you'll think in an altogether different vein. You'll be doing what women were put on earth to do."

She rounded on him with surprising venom. "Father, you may force me to marry. You may even force me out of medicine. But there is no power on earth that can force me to have marital relations with a man I detest, or to bear his children. I will guarantee you this right now. I will never allow Phillip Hildebrand to consummate our marriage. I will force him to divorce me. It will be public and it will be messy, I guarantee."

"If you do not have a child within three years of your marriage, I will disinherit you."

"Didn't your own father threaten the same thing if you married Mother?"

"That's not in the least comparable, and you know it. I'm a man."

"Oh! I understand now! Bullying a daughter is permissible. Coercing a son is not. Fine. Disinherit me this moment! I welcome it! I can make my way in the world. And like Uncle Richard, once I am out of your household, I want no further contact with you, ever. From this moment, I have no father. You are nothing more to me than the neighborhood bully all grown up."

"You may feel that way now, but believe me, someday you'll thank…"

That was the last straw. She felt a rush of anger so strong that for an instant lightning flashed in her head and she was within a scant inch of lashing out physically. She heard her voice low and harsh, interrupting him in a way she had never dared before. "I'll tell you exactly when I'll thank you. I'll thank you when you and Phillip Hildebrand are both dead and I'm free!" She had heard the phrase *deafening silence*. Now it wrapped around them in the darkness of the hired cab.

"Jen?" he asked after a moment's pause. She was too angry to catch the slight hesitance that crept into his voice.

"Yes, Father?"

"You and Inspector Adair—do you love each other?"

"I'm not going to dignify that with an answer. You've lost no opportunity to let me know that you couldn't care a whit less what either of us feels toward the other."

"Just tell me, Jen." He suddenly sounded old and tired.

"Yes, we do. Why do you think he tried to follow me tonight? He knows you lied to him, and he also said that as soon as he's well he's coming to New York after me. You've not heard the last of him, and he's one man even you can't bully." John looked at her, his expression thoughtful and worried at once. She resumed staring blankly at the front of the cab. He reached up and knocked on the roof, summoning the driver.

The teamster slid his small hatch open and leaned over. "Yes, sir?" he asked.

"Pull over a moment, please. I need to check my valise. I think I may have forgotten something."

"Right away, sir." Jenny heard him call "whoa" to the horses, and the cab stopped along the right-hand verge of the unpaved street. She did not move.

"Jen?" he asked.

"Yes, Father?"

"I loved your mother more than my very soul. She was charming and gentle and lovely, and she was completely content to let me do all her thinking. You look so much like her that it's difficult for me to realize that you do think. And to boot, you think like a Weston." He broke off with a deep sigh. For a moment

310

she felt the merest glimmer of hope.

"How would you have felt if someone told you that you couldn't practice medicine? What would you have done if someone picked out a wife who made your flesh crawl and told you your feelings didn't matter? I meant what I said. Perhaps someday I will be grateful to you, but it will only come if you give up your heavy-handed interference in my life."

"Then you'll let Northtown go to the dogs."

"I'll live up to my end of the bargain. Tell the driver to go to the depot. But bear in mind that James Hildebrand is after your money. When you discover that he is indeed in dire financial straits, you'll know I've been right all along, and you'll have to live with the fact that you ruined your only child's life for nothing more than the satisfaction of your own stubborn, selfish pride."

"You'll not have to prove to me that you can keep a promise," he sighed. "in spite of what you may think now, my heart isn't made of granite. I've alienated you enough already. I don't want you to hate me for the rest of your life.

"You never knew your grandfather because we did not move to Parkfield until after his death. I thought I did not treat you as he treated me because I never made you address me as 'sir' or stand whenever you were in my presence. He did storm and fume and rage at me when I announced that I wanted to marry your mother. He objected most strongly to her Southern roots. We wed completely against his wishes, and he did disinherit me. I only shared in his estate because Mother, Richard, and Martha felt I had been treated unfairly, and they gave Parkfield to me. He also broke up your Aunt Martha's one true romance because he disapproved of the man's religion. Richard did not escape his wrath, either. He wanted at least one son to follow him into the military, and I had already chosen medicine. He berated Richard ceaselessly for choosing what he deemed to be a less than masculine career. And you know how your grandmother eventually came to feel about him, largely because of the callous way he treated his children. I confess I loathed him to his dying day, and yet I find myself behaving exactly as he did." He paused and sighed deeply again.

"You mean…" There was a sudden glimmer of light at the end of a very dark tunnel.

"Doctor MacBride says you've done sterling work while you've been sharing his practice, and I'll admit I felt no small pride when he said that. He's right. You're needed here, and if you choose to be a country doctor, then be the best. You can, you know. You're a Weston." He gave her a quirky, bittersweet half-smile.

"You're not making me go with you?" By way of reply he drew the train tickets from his pocket and eloquently tore them in half. "And what of Northtown?"

"Our Lord said let the dead bury the dead. Northtown can raise its own funds. There are enough rich widows who need charitable causes. Need I say that I am an eligible widower? I can appeal to them regardless of what James Hildebrand does. And if you and Inspector Adair decide you want to be married, I'll give you the grandest wedding New York ever saw."

"Even if his grandmother is a full-blooded Iroquois?"

"You're a lady of taste and breeding. I trust your

judgment." She did not believe her ears. She sat dumbfounded until he tapped on the roof of the cab. The driver leaned down again.

"Sir?"

"Go back to the hospital, please. I did indeed leave something important behind. You needn't hurry. I've missed tonight's train at any rate."

"Yes, sir," the teamster responded. He chirped to his horses, and the cab swung in an unhurried, deliberate half circle.

Jenny felt slow, relieved tears tracing their way down her cheeks. She decided to try to talk them away. "Shane is a wonderful man. He's sophisticated, kind, brave, honest, and gentle. He's also talented and intelligent. And his maternal great-grandfather was a person of some note. Remember your French history? Claude des Roches?"

"The name is familiar. Wasn't he some sort of royal advisor, supposed to have been executed in the Reign of Terror?"

"The truth is that he escaped to Canada. His youngest son by his much younger second wife was Shane's grandfather, who raised him after his parents and his older sister died in a smallpox epidemic." She had hoped she could distract herself from tears, but it did not work. They still fell, spotting the front of her traveling outfit.

"Jenny," her father said quietly, reaching toward her. She came into his embrace and sobbed against him for a moment. "Jenny, don't cry now. It'll spoil your complexion and make your nose red, and your young man is upset enough as it is, if you told him what I think you did. Go to him and make things right between you. I'll talk to him later, too, when everything has settled down." She dug into her reticule for a handkerchief, but her father produced one from his pocket and mopped her face as he had done countless times after childhood tumbles and bruised feelings. He pressed it into her hand. "There. Keep it. It's a lot more utilitarian than those lacy things you ladies carry."

"Thank you," she said hoarsely, gulping back fresh tears. She felt the surprising strength of her father's arms about her, and suddenly she was a little girl again, letting him keep the big, frightening world at bay. She cuddled against his chest and gave herself over to the clip-clop of the horses' hooves and the rocking of the cab.

At length he drew a heavy breath. "Jenny, I know I should never have opposed your entry into medical school. But there's more to it than the mere fact that you are a woman. Something deeper and much more personal. Do you remember your mother's little fainting spells?"

"Yes, but in her era ladies did that sort of thing."

She felt more than saw him shake his head slowly, sorrowfully. "No. She suffered from traumatic epilepsy after having been thrown from a runaway cart when she was four years old. Her seizures were neither severe nor frequent, and for the most part controllable with medication.

"Do you remember the day she died? She was standing on one of the garden benches picking roses, had a seizure, fell, and struck her head. She sustained an injury quite comparable to Inspector Adair's subdural hematoma. However, we knew much less about them then. We took her to Northtown. Stuart

Hoffman admitted her, and I scrubbed in on the surgery. I violated a primary precept of our profession in treating a member of my own family, but I was the only one with the requisite skill. And—God help me—we couldn't save her. She passed away four hours post surgery. It tore my heart out. I couldn't stand the thought that someday someone dear to you would die and you would be powerless to do anything about it. And, Jen, it almost happened." She was shocked at what she was hearing. She had never imagined her reserved and unemotional father would ever bare his heart to her in that fashion. Her arms tightened around him.

"Oh, Father, I'm so sorry! I never realized. No one ever said anything to me. But then it didn't happen again. You and I brought Shane through hell. It took both of us, and I'll be forever grateful to you."

"There's an old saying that all's well that ends well," he said comfortingly, echoing what Shane had told her not so long ago. He held her against the warmth of his chest, and for the moment she remained content to take shelter in his familiar strength.

It was dark by the time they reached the hospital. She did not wait demurely to be helped from the coach. Instead, she hiked up her skirt and jumped to the sidewalk, then flew up the stairs, once again the tomboy of her childhood.

She paused outside Shane's nearly closed door, gathered her composure, and nudged it open as quietly as she could. It was dim inside the room but not completely dark, and inside she saw a scene that would never fade from her memory. Angus was sitting at the far side of the bed, and Shane was staring up at the ceiling, ignoring whoever was trying to invade his private sphere of grief.

"Shane!" she exclaimed, her voice urgent but nonetheless soft. He looked around, and when he recognized her, an expression of disbelief came across his face but was quickly supplanted by a look of utter joy that all but lit the room.

"Jenny!" he exclaimed. She launched herself across the room and scooped him into her arms, and they clung to each other desperately. For the second time in an hour she found herself sobbing uncontrollably, her tears soaking into his butchered hair. Neither noticed when Angus left.

"What are you doing back here? Won't you miss your train?" His voice was muffled against her neck. She felt her bonnet dangling down her back. She impatiently loosed the ribbon and let it fall.

"I've missed it, and there won't ever be another unless we're on it together."

"Are you… You're not leaving?"

"No, I'm not. Things changed very quickly. It's a little more complex than I led you to believe, and I'll explain it later, but no, I'm not going to Northtown." She held him against her and felt his arms around her back. Then his hand touched her tear-wet cheek, traveled across it, and stroked her hair as though he had to touch her to believe she was real.

"Jenny, sweetheart, please don't cry. It's over now." His voice was strangely tight, and she felt his shoulders shaking. She took a deep, calming breath and felt her tears diminish, but when she looked at him his eyelashes and her shoulder were wet. Her emotions had turned giddy, putting her very close to laughter.

"Darling…" She pulled him into her arms again.

"Whoever said grown men don't cry certainly has a lot to learn," he muttered, letting her hold him.

"That's all right, sweetheart. Doctors do too, sometimes." He pulled her down and kissed her, and she tasted the salt of tears that could have belonged to either of them. Then she realized he was shaking with fatigue and the effects of adrenaline wearing away. She eased his shoulders back against his pillows and stroked the ragged hair away from his forehead.

"Jenny, what…"

"Hush. I'm not leaving, ever. Father and I worked everything out, even where you're concerned. He accepts you and my medical practice. He told me if I was going to be a country doctor, be the best."

"This is all too much for one day," he sighed. "My mind is running over." She took out her father's handkerchief and blotted his eyes, then her own.

"I know, I know. It's been too much for me, too." A stray tear escaped her left eye and she attacked it with the handkerchief. "I'm sorry. I must look an absolute fright."

He reached out and touched her left hand. "You've never looked more beautiful to me than you do right now, not even on the night of Adrian Beaufort's ball."

She paused with the handkerchief halfway back to her reticule. "I know you have a headache. I can tell by your eyes. This has been a difficult day. Let me give you something so you'll sleep."

"As long as you're a doctor again."

"I can find one. I'll be right back." She kissed his forehead. He leaned back, close to total exhaustion, but when she tried to leave, he reached for her hand and clung to it stubbornly.

"Jenny, this may not be the time or the place, but before you get away from me again, please marry me? I love you with everything that's in me. I have for a long time. If I'd only had the courage to ask you sooner, all this might never have happened. You'd have been able to tell your father you'd committed to me and you didn't need either Phillip Hildebrand or Northtown. I don't want to take a chance on anything coming between us again. Please say you'll be my wife?"

She turned back, giving him her full attention. "Of course I will. I love you, too, in a way I could never love any other man. You're right, you know. If you'd declared yourself to me sooner, I would have had more ammunition for the firefight I've been in for the last two weeks. But better late than never, as the saying goes." Her labile emotions swept her along like a whitewater river. She stifled the laughter that welled up inside her.

"What's so funny? I just asked you to marry me and you just accepted. That's the most monumental step in anyone's life."

"I was just thinking what I could possibly say to people when they asked me where we were when you proposed. I can't very well say 'in bed.'" Then the humor of the situation dawned on him, too, and his amused smile echoed hers.

"I promise I'll propose properly, on my knees, as soon as I'm able. But you know, I should play the love flute for you and leave a gift of meat at your door, and in accepting it you would accept me."

"I can do without the meat. And honestly, knowing your music ability, I wouldn't want you anywhere near a flute. You can commit murder just trying to sing."

"That's true, but since the flute only has five notes, there's really no way to do it wrong."

"I think you'd find a way. All right. Enough talking for a while. Let me go find Angus and get your medication so you can sleep." He nodded in acquiescence. She squeezed his hands, then disappeared.

She applied the handkerchief to her eyes one last time as she went to find Angus. The charge nurse on the floor directed her to the lobby, where she encountered Angus, Richard, and her father. Their conversation ceased too abruptly when she approached.

"Yes, Jenny?" Angus asked.

"I need to ask you to order medication for Shane. He's complaining of pain, and now that I'm no longer on the staff here..."

"I'll come, then," he interrupted her. "And you'll be back on the staff by morning. Not tae worry aboot that." He levered himself up with his cane. She did not look at her father or her uncle for the moment.

"I'll see that you're reinstated as soon as the director is here tomorrow," John Weston said. She had never seen him so subdued. "Is Inspector Adair all right?"

"I think he's just overtired. He's had too much excitement for one day. With a good night's sleep, he'll be fine."

"Good. I'll admit I was concerned when the nurse reported he had fainted."

"I don't think he hit his head," Angus replied. "His eyes look all right, but one canna tell in a situation like that. I'm just going to watch him closely for the next twenty-four hours or so. We'll be back shortly." Angus ushered Jenny ahead of him up the flight of stairs to Shane's room.

"If you don't mind, I'd like to check him again," he said.

"Since this afternoon, you're the physician of record on this case. I couldn't mind."

"What happened with your father? A miracle?"

"Just about. It's as close to a miracle as either of us will ever see."

The older man nodded. "It must have been, lass. I'm just glad everything will be all right." She sighed in agreement.

"Me too," she replied. "Me too." They climbed the last few steps in silence, and then she pushed Shane's door open. It was darker inside the room than it had been a few minutes before, but she could see he was lying in his favorite sleeping position, curled on his right side with his head inclined toward her and his right fist next to his face. She tiptoed up to him, trying to cushion the heels of her high shoes, but the care was wasted. He was asleep, his entire body relaxed and his breathing deep and regular.

"Well, it seems our intervention won't be necessary," Angus whispered. "I think the lad's exhausted. And I don't think he's the only one."

She looked down at Shane's sleeping form for some moments before she said softly, "He's not the only one, Angus. It's been too long for me, too."

"Let's just leave him be for now. You go back to the hotel and get a good night's sleep. I think I'd like to turn his case over to you and go back on the noon train tomorrow." He ushered her out and closed the door behind her.

"That was quick," her father remarked as they returned to the lobby.

"He was asleep when we got back to the room," Angus said, folding stiffly into a nearby chair. "I think we've all had a long day. I'll stay for a few hours, until I'm certain he won't wake up. The rest of you go to the hotel and get a good night's sleep yourselves. As I told Jenny, I'm going to leave this in her hands and go home tomorrow. I've left my practice too long."

"I'm about to leave mine a little longer," John Weston said, with a barely concealed yawn; "though I do have a *locum tenens* to take up the slack. Richard has convinced me to spend a week or two with him, at least until Inspector Adair is discharged and Jenny gets back. Admittedly I could use a vacation. I haven't seen Richard to speak of in two years, and I haven't taken a proper holiday since before Catherine's passing. Someone else can handle my cases while I'm away."

"I wish I could say the same. I expect I'll be besieged day after tomorrow."

"If you're under an avalanche, I'd be glad to assist you in any way I can," John volunteered.

"Oh, no!" the older man crowed. "You don't know what you've just volunteered for! And I'll certainly take you up on your offer. You can handle Jenny's part of the practice until she returns."

"Very well. I'd like to see where my daughter will be practicing."

"Has been practicing," Angus corrected. "She's been doing a stellar job, too."

John nodded in agreement. "After all, she is a Weston," he said with no small pride.

"I'm ready for bed," Richard interjected with a heartfelt yawn.

Jenny rose, shaking out the folds of her skirt. "I am, too. Good night, Angus. Don't stay up too late," she said.

"Nae, lass. I won't. I only want to make sure Shane stays asleep."

The next morning dawned cooler, the air thin with the first coming of fall. The four dawdled over breakfast, then showed up in Shane's room. Bathed and shaven, he had brightened considerably since the previous day and greeted everyone with a smile.

"Inspector Adair, may I have a private moment with you, then?" John asked. Richard, taking a big cue from his brother, ushered Jenny and Angus out of the room.

"I suppose you may, Doctor Weston, since there's really nowhere for me to go." Shane was full of suspicion. When the room was empty, John came to his bedside.

"Sir, I have wronged you deeply, and I tender my most humble apologies," he began, his voice an echo of the Old General's. "When I told you Jenny was betrothed to Phillip Hildebrand, I lied to you, deliberately and unconscionably. Jenny never gave her consent to any such betrothal. I tried to force her into it, in part by driving you away. She is not now, nor has she ever been, engaged to marry anyone. Yes, she agreed to come back to New York with Phillip and me, but she did so under duress. I have begged her forgiveness and I beg yours, too, if you can find it within you. Please accept my apology, for Jenny's sake if for no other reason. And I have another apology to make to you, too. I am sorry for impugning your family honor. No gentleman ever makes allegations like that unless he expects to be called out. It was beneath me, and I apologize."

Shane drew a deep, thoughtful breath. Then he raised his eyes and his level Scorpio gaze transfixed the other man like a spear that went in one side and came out the other. He meant it to leave no doubt as to his opinion of John Weston.

"Doctor Weston, you do not have to apologize to me. What did you do but call me a few names I've heard before?"

"Oh, but I do have to apologize to you. I did something very wrong, and both honor and conscience dictate that I make amends."

"Then I accept your apology in the spirit in which it was given, as you said, for Jenny's sake, because no matter what occurs between her and me I love her, and despite the conflicts you and she have had, I know she loves you. I'd hate to see her torn between us again."

"Thank you, sir. You are a gracious gentleman." John extended his hand, and Shane gripped it after a short pause that plainly expressed his reluctance.

"And as for, as you put it, impugning my family honor? In point of fact, I am what is commonly called Métis. I am one-fourth Iroquois. My maternal grandfather, a French voyageur, married an Iroquois woman. That sort of thing was very common in the old days. My mother, their daughter, may or may not have married an Irish railroad worker. She had two children by him. My parents and my sister subsequently died in a smallpox epidemic. I was the only survivor. I was born in a railroad camp near River Bend, and my birth was not immediately registered. I had no birth certificate until I was sixteen years old and needed one to go to college, so one was issued for me, *nunc pro tunc*. The government accepted the testimony of a physician who certified that he attended my mother, and they recorded my birth as legitimate."

"Then we must honor that. *De mortuis nil nisi bonum*, after all." John paused again. "And, Inspector Adair, if you and my daughter decide to take up the thread of your relationship where I so brutally parted it, you have my blessing."

"Thank you, sir." His tone was cold. Nevertheless, John smiled.

"My father was a Brigadier General under Grant during the Civil War. He was an old-order gentleman, a member of the Grand Army of the Republic, and a military officer to the end of his days. Of course he had his shortcomings, but he did teach me about making amends. He always said when honor demands an apology, make it sincerely and make it well."

"You certainly seem to have taken that lesson to heart," Shane allowed.

"Another valid piece of advice I received years ago regarding the lady in your life is that if you truly love her, never be too proud to crawl. I did, more than once, and I was never sorry. My wife Catherine—Jenny's mother—was a woman in a million. She was sweet and gentle and content to be a wife and a mother and let me make all the decisions. Jenny looks so like her that it's difficult for me to realize she thinks like I do."

"It surprised me when I learned she is a medical doctor, but I shouldn't have missed it. There were simply too many clues that she is a cut above the ordinary."

"Yes, truly. She may be many things, but never ordinary. Then, Inspector Adair, I will take my leave. I'm taking over Jenny's practice for the time being, so she can remain here with you until you're well enough to be discharged." He held out his hand to Shane again.

"Goodbye, then, Doctor Weston. And I should thank you for helping me."

"You're welcome. I'm only glad that my skill was adequate. Yours was a challenging case. And I certainly do not blame you for disliking me. I'll go a long way to go to prove myself to you. I intend to try to do so to the best of my ability. Not just for Jenny's sake, either. I owe it to you after my abominable behavior toward you both. Well, then, Inspector, good day, and take care of yourself." He took his leave, and Shane sat watching after him until Richard, Jenny, and Angus came back in.

"I just came to say goodbye to you for a while, Shane," Richard began. He glanced down at a leather-bound book in his hands. "I know you'll be bored now that you're starting to feel better. This might help." He handed over the volume. Shane took it and looked at the title. However, his thumb lay over the author's name across the bottom of the front cover.

"Hmm. *By the Grace of God.* I've heard so much about it. I've heard that even as a work of fiction it's quite historically accurate, and you know how I love history. I fully intended to read it, but I haven't been here in River Bend long enough to pick up a copy. Thank you so much, Richard. It's very thoughtful of you. I'll return it as soon as I've finished with it." He looked up at Richard and saw his wry smile.

"No need, Shane. I have several more where that came from. This copy is a gift. And rest assured that I have indeed read it thoroughly." Then Shane set the volume down on his lap and his eyes went wide. The gold-stamped lettering across the bottom of the cover read *Richard T. Weston, Ph.D.* His cheeks colored violently.

"Richard, you actually...wrote this?" His voice went up, breaking like a teenager's. With a cool smile worthy of a jade Buddha, Richard nodded slowly, spinning out the moment for all it was worth.

"It's the reason I came out here to the wilds of Ontario. In New York I couldn't even set foot outside my front door without being mobbed by autograph seekers." Shane opened the cover. On the flyleaf, in Richard's careful copperplate script, was the inscription, *To my good friend Shane Adair. Best wishes for a swift and complete recovery. Richard T. Weston.*

"Oh, my! Richard, you're actually famous! I'm so embarrassed I could die right here and now," he murmured. "This is the worst faux pas of my entire life."

"Well, if that's the biggest social blunder you've ever made, you're still in tall cotton. At least it was among friends. And now I think we should all just turn our backs while you take your foot out of your mouth."

"That will take me all afternoon and a crowbar," Shane responded with no small chagrin.

Jenny had a hand to her face, melodramatically stifling laughter. "Well, then, we'll give you your privacy," she said, unable to control her huge grin. "I'm going to walk them to the depot. I'll be back after the train leaves."

"You know where I'll be," he sighed. She moved as if to follow the three men out the door but turned and came back to his bedside. He set the book aside and reached toward her as she leaned over and touched her lips to his. He took her hands, and she had no choice but to sit next to him on the bed.

"Remember the night in Richard's kitchen? Every night for the next eighty years?" he said quietly, his breath brushing her cheek.

"You'll propose to me properly, then?"

"Need you ask?" he responded softly. "Eighty years?"

"Eighty years. I promise," she replied, and kissed him again to seal the vow.

A word about the author...

After a long and varied work life she began as an English teacher and ended as a computer support technician, Lael Neill retired to a new career: becoming a full-time author. She began writing somewhere around age eight, studied Creative Writing under (or rather, worshiped at the feet of) Dr. H. L. Anshutz at Central Washington University, and has finally fulfilled her lifelong dream. A transplant from the Pacific Northwest, she lives on two wooded acres in rural Central Texas with deer, bunnies, armadillos, hawks, the occasional skunk, and a resident roadrunner. In between stints of writing, she decompresses with volunteer work, knitting, and music.